UNSAFE

Lost in a world of cruelty...

On the day Karen Sharpe is promoted to Detective Sergeant, she loses control and attacks a prisoner she is interrogating. Karen is seemingly cleared, but the incident casts a long shadow. When the battered body of a young girl is discovered, Karen and trainee DC Marcus Roth are led to Mary Bradley, currently the carer for a helpless six-year-old boy, Andrew Farrar. As the truth of Mary Bradley's violent past emerges, the enquiry turns into a race against time before Andrew becomes another of her child victims. Meanwhile, Marcus discovers that when threatened, Karen has a tendency to ignore the rule book...

UNSAFE

UNSAFE

by

John Connor

Magna Large Print Books
Long Preston, North Yorkshire,
BD23 4ND, England.

British Library Cataloguing in Publication Data.

Connor, John
 Unsafe.

A catalogue record of this book is
available from the British Library

ISBN   978-0-7505-3050-7

First published in Great Britain in 2009 by Orion Books,
an imprint of The Orion Publishing Group

Copyright © John Connor 2009

Cover illustration © Jitka Saniova by arrangement with
Arcangel Images

Published in Large Print 2009 by arrangement with
Orion Publishing Group

Magna Large Print is an imprint of Library Magna Books Ltd.

Printed and bound in Great Britain by
T.J. (International) Ltd., Cornwall, PL28 8RW

To ANNA (for letting me sleep)

And THOMAS and SARA (for waking me up)

Many thanks to all of the following:

Phil Patterson, Yvette Goulden, Angela McMahon, Chris Gregg, Max McLean, John Parkinson, Chris Binns (and everyone else at HMET who was so helpful), Ray Dance, Claire Winship and Michael Timler.

WEST YORKSHIRE

8 SEPTEMBER 2007

Saturday Evening

1

Andrew Farrar was so frightened he began to pee himself. He felt it stinging as it came out, then running down his legs. He tried desperately to hold it in, but it was impossible. The screaming from the room above him was so loud that he couldn't even block it out by putting his hands over his ears. All he wanted to do was stand up and run away.

When Mary found out he had wet himself she would do the same as last time, which made him even more frightened. That had been three days ago. He had been watching television, downstairs, and had heard the same noises starting from the floors above him. For the first time he had realized what the noises meant. They had told him his mum had gone away, but now he knew that she was upstairs somewhere, shut into one of the forbidden rooms. The noises meant someone was hurting her. That had made him so scared he hadn't even noticed the wetness under his legs, soaking into the sofa. Normally, Mary wouldn't let him sit on the sofa unless it was covered with the heavy rubber sheet she kept on his bed. Not because he might pee on it, but because he was always dirty and the sofa was clean and expensive. But she had forgotten the sheet three days ago, so the pee had run straight into it.

For doing that she had pulled his trousers off so

15

roughly he had fallen backwards and cracked his head on the floor. Then she had held him there and dragged the rest of his clothes off, shouting and swearing at him. When he was naked she had started to hit him between his legs, slapping his willy so hard he had crossed his legs to try to stop her. But that only made her tell Martin to hold his legs apart. Martin was her son, and was meant to be his dad. His mum had told him to be good for Martin *because* Martin was his dad. But Martin had pushed his legs apart and just stood there, looking at him, while Mary slapped him on the willy. He had tried not to cry out loud, because that only made her more angry.

Now he had done it again. No matter how frightened he was he knew now when he was peeing because his willy still stung from the slapping. He didn't want her to do that again. But he couldn't stop peeing, because the noise made him feel like someone was pressing something sharp into his ears. The noise made *him* want to scream. And when he wanted to scream like that he always wet himself. He couldn't help it.

Katy could hear it as well. He had put his hands over her ears, but she had pushed them away and said, 'Mama.' He had to look after her. That was what his mum had told him to do, last time he had seen her.

He wanted to see his mum again, but they wouldn't let him. Yesterday he had got upset about that – the tears had started to run out of his eyes without warning. Then he had started shaking and howling, shouting out his mum's name at the top of his voice. They hadn't wanted that, Mary and

16

John. They said he was having a 'fit'. John had thrown something at him – a remote control for the TV – which bounced off his back. Then Mary had yanked him up the stairs and held him tightly from behind. She had pulled something across his mouth so that he felt as if he were suffocating. He couldn't cry any more then, so he had just lain on the floor and closed his eyes, shivering.

The stuff covering his mouth was thick, brown sticky tape. He found this out later, when Mary ripped it off. Before that, she had left it on through the whole night, so that he had woken up all the time panicking about it, struggling to breathe through his blocked nose. He had started to pull the tape off once, but it had stung too much. Besides, he was frightened she would hit him again if he took it off when she hadn't said he could. His lips still hurt from it now, as if the skin all around them had been burned. He knew what it was like to be burned because Mary had done that to him once as well, to teach him not to play with matches. But he didn't want to remember that. He was as frightened now as he had been then.

Though his mum had told him Martin was his dad (and though he couldn't remember any other dad), he knew from what they said all the time that Martin wasn't his real dad and Mary wasn't his real grandmother. They had stood him in front of the mirror in the bathroom and laughed about it, pointing to his skin – which was a dark colour (not like Katy's) – and calling him bad things. He couldn't remember the names they had used, but he knew they were horrible. He had started crying then as well. Martin had

17

slapped him across the face and told him to toughen up. Martin didn't hit him very much. A long time ago – when Mary had first told Martin to hit him – Martin had tried to stick up for him, saying things like, 'He doesn't know any better, it's not his fault' or, 'Let him cry, he's only five' (though he was six now, but maybe Martin had forgotten that). That was when his mum had still been here. Or when he was still allowed to see her. But Mary had told Martin to hit him and shut him up or she would. So Martin had also started hitting him. Now everyone in the house hit him, except Katy and Simon. Simon was always nice to him, but he didn't see Simon much. He had seen John and Mary hit Simon as well, though he was also their son and taller than both of them. Once, Simon had been crouched on the floor in a tight ball and John had kicked him really hard in the side and head, over and over again. Even Simon had started blubbing then, and Simon was a grown-up.

No one hit Katy. She was lucky, because she had beautiful, creamy-white skin and Martin really was her dad. But his mother had told him to protect Katy, to watch out for her. So he was doing it anyway, though it seemed to him she didn't need anyone to protect her, that it was the other way around.

He tried to play games with her, so she wouldn't listen to the screaming. They played the 'what noise does the pig make?' game, because Katy knew how to make pig noises (and dog noises, and cats and lions and horses and cows) and it made her giggle when she made the noises for

18

him. But when his mum was sobbing so much – and when he could hear the banging noise in between her sobs – it was too difficult. Sometimes their mum shouted out their names. That was the worst thing. Then they couldn't do anything but sit hugging each other, pushed up against the wall by the bed, waiting for it to stop. He felt bad that Katy could hear her mum shouting like that, and that he couldn't do anything to stop it.

They were in Katy's bedroom. Martin had put him in here when it had started. Usually they locked the door on him. But that was when Katy wasn't with him. They didn't lock Katy up. So if he wanted to he could get up and run out. But where would he run to? They had already warned him about running away – both Martin and Mary. If he ran away the police would *hunt* for him. If they found him they would either shoot him in the willy or tie him up and put him in a worse place than here. In the children's home, maybe. He had heard a lot about how bad the children's home was, how lucky he was to have a *real* home. 'Children in care are always hungry and cold,' Martin said. At least he had food here, and a bed with blankets.

A few weeks ago the social worker had visited and questioned Katy and him about how they felt, now that their mum had gone away. That was what the woman had told them – that their mum had 'gone away'. That was before he had heard his mum crying, so he had believed it. Probably it had been some kind of trick by the woman, to get them into the children's home, to take them away. But Mary and Martin had warned them both about the questions before the woman

19

came, so they had said nothing to the woman and she had gone away again, without them.

Katy was crying now, leaning against him, hugging him. He couldn't hear his mum any more, but Martin and Mary had started shouting at each other instead. The words were muffled, coming down through the floor. Maybe if he got up and told them Katy was crying they would stop. He stroked Katy's head – the way he had seen their mum do it – then whispered in her ear that he was going to go and tell them she was upset. 'Wait here,' he said to her. 'It will be OK. I promise.'

But she didn't want to wait anywhere without him. When he stood up she stood with him and held his hand tightly. She started shaking her head from side to side, still crying. 'OK, you can come with me,' he said. 'But you have to be quiet. Will you be quiet?'

She didn't want to do that, either. It was because she was only a baby. She didn't know what she wanted to do. He helped her get onto the bed and gave her the teddy bear his mum had given him a long time ago. That would work for a little bit. She cuddled it and he walked over to the door.

It took him a long time to summon the courage to open it. He had been warned about trying to open doors by himself. Just touching the handle made him shudder with fright. This time was different, though, because Katy was upset. But still it took him a long time to do it. When the handle creaked he had to stop and take a deep breath, and then start all over again. He felt very frightened, but determined, because he had said he would look after Katy.

By the time he had opened it they were quiet upstairs and he couldn't hear anything. He looked back at Katy, but she had rolled herself up in a corner of the bed, against the wall, making sobbing noises into the teddy bear's fur. He wondered who was in the room upstairs, and if there was anyone else in the other parts of the house. The house was very big, with four floors and many rooms. But he had only been able to hear Martin and Mary from the floor above him, where he wasn't allowed to go.

He took a last look back at Katy, then whispered to her that he wouldn't be long. She just kept bawling, so he closed the door and stood terrified on the other side of it, in the passageway with the low ceiling that ran from John and Mary's bedroom along to Martin's room, past Katy's. His own room was a smaller place, next to the cellar, downstairs.

The stairway leading up to the next floor looked dark. He walked quickly over to it, so petrified that he really wanted to cry now. He could smell the pee on his trousers as he started to climb up. He was sure they would smell it, too, but he was too excited to stop, because he had never been up here. And his mum was up here, so maybe he would be able to see her, even if only for a little while. He really hoped so. What would he tell her if he saw her? Maybe he would just hug her and press his face into her shoulder and cry.

At the top of the stairs he could barely see anything it was so dark. It must have been night outside, he thought. There was a crack of light coming from a door, but he couldn't see how many other doors there were. He could hear somebody whispering from behind the door. He crept towards it and listened. It was Martin, whispering something about 'finishing things', then Mary swearing about something, but quietly. He couldn't hear his mum at all.

From downstairs he heard Katy start to howl. He placed his hand against the door and felt it move slightly, the crack of light widening a little. He positioned his head so that his eye was near to the space between the door and the wall, then pushed the door again, so that he could see inside. At first he was so nervous he did it with his eyes closed. But then, when the door didn't make a noise, and when no one from inside said anything, he opened his eyes and looked.

2

It was already dark by the time Karen got home. The first thing she noticed as she stepped up to her front door was the absence of the CCTV camera on the wall above the porch – someone had finally removed it – then the smell of food. She could smell it even before she opened the door. Something with wine and garlic. She fitted her key, only to find the door wasn't actually closed. She pushed it open carefully – immediately wary – then stepped inside. She could hear music, quite loud, then the sounds of her daughter through in the kitchen, cooking. She checked the front room, listening also for anything unusual from upstairs. Nothing seemed amiss.

She shouted a greeting, took off her jacket and walked through to the dining room. The dining room opened straight onto the kitchen and Mairead was standing by the cooker, stirring something in a large casserole pan. The music – something modern that Karen didn't recognize – was turned up so loud that Mairead obviously hadn't heard her mother's shout. Karen watched her taste the food with a familiar sense of suppressed panic. No matter what life had thrown at her – and there had been enough – Mairead never seemed to learn. She was the same now as she had been five years ago. Relaxed, normal, switched off to the possibility of danger; despite everything, no caution at all. But maybe that was something to be proud of.

Something *had* changed during the last year, though. Mairead had grown up, it seemed, stopped being a girl, turned into a young woman. The change was subtle, almost imperceptible, but Karen was very aware of it. Her daughter was dressed now in close-fitting faded jeans, a washed-out green T-shirt displaying the words 'Kaiser Chiefs', rows of twisted, brightly coloured braided threads on her forearms (looking slightly hippy) and a silver anklet, just visible below the hem of the jeans. She had long, dark hair gathered into a ponytail that came down to the middle of her back. At a couple of inches over six foot she was slightly taller than Karen and strikingly attractive – to her mother, at least. None of that was new, but something had happened during the last year to alter her appearance. Mairead had a nineteen-year-old face – freckled, open, unguarded – but if you looked closely it was no longer the face of a child. Something had changed in the eyes. That and the way she held herself, especially if there were men around, shouted anything but child. That was the difference.

'The door was open,' Karen said, loud enough to be heard above a heavy bass beat.

Mairead started, almost dropping the spoon, then spun round. 'Mum! You could have given me a heart attack!'

Karen stepped over to the music system and turned it off. 'What's that?' she asked. 'Something Pete gave you?' DS Pete Bains was the man Karen had lived with, on and off, through most of Mairead's teenage years. He could hardly speak a civil word to Karen these days, but he still seemed to regard himself as a father figure to Mairead, and irritatingly, Mairead appeared keen to reciprocate. Worse than that, Karen suspected Mairead had secret hopes that she and Pete would try again.

'Pete?' Mairead frowned at her. 'No. Why?'

'Sounds like his stuff.'

'It's nothing like his stuff. Why did you switch it off?'

'So I could hear.' She stepped into the kitchen and glanced into the pan, then kissed Mairead quickly on the cheek. 'You cooking for us?'

'Yes. I warned you I was.' She grinned and glanced past Karen. 'Where's Mark?'

'He couldn't make it.' Karen caught a flash of something in Mairead's eyes. 'Mark' was Marcus Roth, a twenty-eight-year-old trainee investigator on her team. During the last five months Karen and he had got to know each other quite well, despite the age gap. Before Mairead had broken up for the long summer holiday Marcus had eaten at Karen's two or three times a month, usually on a Saturday night, and the practice had continued when Mairead had come home from university. Consequently she had met Marcus a couple of times. They had all got along well, but now Karen saw that there might be more to it than that, in Mairead's mind, at least. From what she knew of Marcus he was unlikely to be interested in someone her daughter's age.

'Sorry,' she said. 'Just me tonight. I can see you're disappointed.'

'I thought you said Mark was coming, too?'

'He was. But then he changed his mind.' She looked at her daughter, trying to read the expression. 'He might be attractive, Mairead, he might even be bright, but he's not reliable. And he's almost ten years older than you. He's not what you need, believe me.'

Mairead coloured slightly, then frowned and turned back to the pan. 'You know him that well?'

'I know he treats women like shit.'

'You're making a lot of assumptions, Mum. And forgetting I have a bloke already.'

'But you were cooking something special for Mark?'

Mairead shook her head. 'For whoever was at home. For me and you, I guess. And it's hardly special.'

Karen looked in the pan again. 'What is it? It looks and smells great.'

'Beef bourguignon.'

'Not what you usually cook for just me and you.'

Mairead put the spoon down, licked a finger carefully and picked up a glass of red wine. She leaned back against the counter and looked at her mother, a warning expression in her eyes. 'You going to be irritating tonight, Mum? Because if you are I'll go out.'

Karen held her hands up. 'OK. Enough. Who left the front door open?'

'Me, I suppose.' She took a sip from the wine.

'Anyone could have come in.'

'Hardly.'

'This isn't darkest Scotland, Mairead. You have to think about these things.'

'It's Ilkley, Mum. Don't be so paranoid.'

'Your memory is terrible. I have a lifetime of experience to make me paranoid about personal security. So do you.'

Mairead said nothing, just looked at her.

'They came for the cameras?' Karen asked, trying to get on to a comparatively neutral subject. The two other changes she had noticed in her daughter, since her starting university in Scotland, were that she drank more and seemed more sensitive to Karen's comments about her. Did that come with the sexuality? she wondered. In the latter respect, it was almost as if they had reverted to her early teens, when things between them had been very rough. Her daughter's reactions were extremely hard to predict these days. One day it might be funny to pull her leg about Marcus Roth, for example; the next she would take offense and eat out with friends. Karen had assumed the reverse would happen as she got older.

'Yes. They came about an hour ago,' Mairead replied. 'They took everything. The screens from upstairs as well. I hope that was OK. I wasn't sure what you wanted them to take.'

'I wanted them to take it all. I wanted them to take it all about eleven months ago.'

The cameras and security system alone ought to have kept Mairead from stupid errors like leaving doors open. Sixteen months ago Karen had spent nearly two months of her life wading through the finances and personal life of a middle-range thug called Gary Swales trying to assemble enough evidence to charge him with the murder of a drug dealer called Ben Smalley. There had been rock-solid informant information that Swales had ordered Smalley's execution, but that wasn't going in front of any jury. Getting hard evidence had proved more problematic. Swales was a rising star in the northern underworld and knew exactly how to cover his tracks. He came from a family of career criminals well versed in enforcing silence with brutality. Consequently, the enquiry had struggled with circumstantial evidence from the start. Though in the end Swales had been charged, Karen had always known the case would fail in court. The only surprise had been the particular way it had fouled up.

Whether Swales had killed Smalley, whether he was convicted or not, had meant little to Karen. Swales was a high-level target, and with men like that you always played the averages. There would never be a shortage of repeat chances. Besides, she was only one of a team of twenty investigating Smalley's death. It was work. That was it. She went home at night and forgot about it.

But Gary Swales had for some reason decided differently. Because in essence he was stupid, she assumed – good at some things, but with glaring blind spots in his intelligence and education. She was the face of the enquiry for him, the detective who sat across the table through six interviews. Half a brain ticking, he'd therefore put two and two together and got five – he'd decided there was something personal going on. So he'd paid someone to get her. Not to kill her – even Swales wasn't that reckless – but to frighten her. Someone was meant to knock her over. If they couldn't get her then her daughter would do instead. That was what she had been told.

For herself, she was used to threats, used to dealing with them. You didn't do the sorts of things she had as a young woman without acquiring a sixth sense about watching your back. She took routine precautions every day that her bosses would have written off as paranoid. If Swales sent somebody to try to knock her over she was confident she could deal with it. But with Mairead under threat the situation had run quickly out of hand. Karen couldn't handle that at all. Mairead had been sitting A levels at the time and Karen had done her best to insulate her from the facts, trying to protect her while never actually telling her of the danger. But that came at a cost to Karen's mental health. In the end it should have been predictable that she would snap.

Instead of pulling her from the enquiry, as

Karen had expected, the management had decided the risk was negligible because the information – from an unregistered and unreliable source – was 'clearly false' – a rumour put about by one of Swales's competitors. Karen had never believed that, though. She'd seen the truth in Swales's eyes every time she walked in to interview him. The information had thus precipitated three months of edgy, nervous hell for her. Once her A levels were completed Mairead had been warned and there had been very unwelcome restrictions on where she could go, who with and what time she had to get back. But Mairead had forgotten all that already, it seemed.

Physically, Swales looked like something from a late-eighties TV series - a get-rich-quick market trader from the Thatcher years - someone who might have started on a barrow in the East End and progressed to the trading floor by dint of sheer cockiness and greed. He was short and compact, with a jutting, aggressive chin and eyes that looked permanently angry. He had a powerful upper body, a head shaved short to hide the fact that he was very nearly bald on top, and was normally immaculately turned out in tailored suits and Jermyn Street shirts. He always looked better dressed than his lawyers. But there were extensive tattoos on his upper arms and chest that he had tried with only partial success to have removed since hitting the big time – probably less because they were a relic from his past than because they were distinctive and unique identifiers that were noted clearly on the PNC. Replace the smart clothing with a standard nylon shell-suit and Gary

Swales would slip unnoticed into the average prison population.

Not that he'd had much practice at that. For a forty-two-year-old middle-tier drugs dealer who had been growing his business for a good fifteen years he had a remarkably clean sheet. Two convictions as a teenager for violence, neither resulting in incarceration. The only time he'd spent inside had been on remand, and so far nothing serious had stuck.

In the earlier interviews he had spoken quite freely about himself, conveying a swaggering sense of personal immunity combined with a naked conceit on account of the position he had reached – which, on the surface, was that of a successful, legitimate businessman who had invested well. He even had the businesses to prove it. But the feral roots were never far from view. Karen had been left alone with him for five minutes at the close of the last interview and he had let his teeth show. His goading had been specific enough to convince her that the informant information was accurate. Swales had thought himself safe, no doubt – because she was a woman, because, as he thought it, the entire exchange was being recorded on camera. But Karen had known the cameras were down. She was alone with Swales only because her colleague had left to try to remedy the technical fault. Nothing was being recorded.

What Swales said happened next was that she had carried out a prolonged and vicious assault, striking him repeatedly with a heavy metal chair. Karen's version was simpler: she had defended herself from his aggression, hitting him once only. The only official certainty was that Swales had come out of it with a broken arm and Karen – on the day she had been promoted to DS – had been suspended.

Three months and two enquiries later, predictably Karen had been cleared – it was her word against that of Swales – but a judge had kicked out the case against Swales, partly citing Karen's attack as justification. To Swales this must have seemed like a result, a triumph, even – yet more proof of his invulnerability. He had waited a few weeks, then put it about – through the same unproven source – that the contract against Karen and Mairead was lifted. There was no longer a need to court that risk. But Karen had already spent nearly three months having to watch her back, worrying constantly about Mairead. As far as she was concerned the balance sheet was far from even.

'You in tonight?' she asked her daughter.

'I think so.' Mairead stepped forward and rested her head against Karen's shoulder. Karen took a breath, savouring the moment.

'I miss Julian,' Mairead said, after a moment. 'I wish I'd gone with him now.'

Julian was her bloke. That was how she referred to him at least. An American *boy* was how Karen thought of him. Mairead had hooked up with him within weeks of starting university, then brought him home very briefly – en route to London – during the Christmas break, and again at Easter. Karen had found him polite, attractive and attentive to Mairead, but naïve the way midwest Americans sometimes were.

31

'He'll be back soon enough,' Karen said. 'Only two weeks to go, is it?' Term started in early October, but Mairead was likely to return a week earlier. Julian was at his home in Ohio for the summer. Mairead had been invited but had declined. She wanted to go into acting once the degree was out of the way, and this summer she had been offered an internship at the West Yorkshire Playhouse.

'It's nice you're staying in,' Karen said. 'We can eat together, watch a movie maybe.'

Mairead sighed. 'Sounds OK.' She didn't seem convinced. 'You want a glass of wine?' She moved away and picked up the bottle. Karen thought she looked a little affected already. Half the bottle was gone, most of it into the food, Karen hoped. She didn't know what to do about the alcohol thing. It wasn't excessive – her daughter drank when she went out, or occasionally at home – but it was still a lot more than Karen drank. There was no point in even trying to stop it – Mairead could drink as much as she wanted when away, with no check on her save her own good sense. And then there were the drugs. There had been several hints about drugs.

'No, thanks,' Karen said. 'I'm on call tonight.'

The standard shift on HMET – West Yorkshire's new Homicide and Major Enquiries Team – was a regular nine-to-five, theoretically. But sometimes murders didn't happen during office hours, so the protocol between HMET and the local divisions dictated that divisional officers would normally deal with murder scenes notified outside daylight hours, handling all the initial actions until HMET took over, around seven in the morning. A senior investigating officer, appointed from within HMET, directed the divisional resources, and there was a single HMET team – one DS and four detectives – on call-out, to assist the SIO, the senior investigating officer The call-out roster was structured so that the duty circulated every seven weeks or so. Tonight was the first night on for her team. The SIO for the night was Alan White. If he pulled a suspicious death between now and 7 am, then Karen was expected to be there within half an hour, four detectives in tow, all sober.

'Is Marcus on call, too?' Mairead asked.

Karen nodded.

'Maybe that's why he couldn't come.'

Sunday

3

Marcus Roth got the call at 4.20 am., on his mobile. A woman from dispatch telling him about a body dumped somewhere off the M62, giving hurried directions. He'd been in bed less than four hours and had drunk too much during the preceding evening. He knew he would still be too intoxicated to drive, but there wasn't much he could do about that. It was a murder call-out. Only his second since starting on HMET.

He'd been a trainee investigator for only five months and a homicide call-out was the most exciting thing in his life, though it didn't pay to admit that to anyone. He was twenty-eight and had been in the police for just three years. He guessed most officers would regard it as an achievement to be placed on a dedicated murder squad so early in their careers, and maybe they were all secretly pleased with themselves on HMET – 100 per cent committed to every minute of it – but you couldn't tell that from working with them. The dominant approach in the office was one of studied indifference. That and constant griping about the workload. He tried to join in, but it was hard; every day he really was 100 per cent committed. Totally absorbed and lost in it.

In his kitchen – already flushed with excitement – he quickly drank strong coffee and stuffed himself with anything sweet he could find. His flat wasn't big and he could hear snoring from the girl in his bed, though he'd closed the door on her. They had met in a nightclub a week ago, then again last night. She was twenty–five, she said, but looked much younger and he was guessing her real age was eighteen, maybe nineteen. Tall, with shoulder-length hair so blonde it appeared bleached (it wasn't), she had the angular, feature-perfect face of a Nordic fashion model, with a thick Bradford accent. In the club, when he'd first danced with her the week before, she'd worn a short canvas skirt split at both sides as far as her hips, showing very long, smooth, muscular legs. But a few hours ago, without clothes and tightly wrapped around him, she had felt far too young for him, full of strange, slippery movements and childish noises, so keen to keep him close to her that he had begun to worry she might not quite realize what was happening. But she was no virgin, and he wasn't a priest, so he had pushed his worries elsewhere and got on with it. Afterwards she slept like a granny – flat out on her back, mouth wide open, drooling and snoring so loud he had to put in earplugs. The phone hadn't woken her.

She didn't know it yet, but he had a rule about sex: never do it twice with the same woman. The act itself generated bonds, no matter how much you tried to keep it the focus of attention, and the last thing he needed was a relationship round his neck – least of all with a teenager. Women in their early twenties had bodies that interested him, but they were a long way off having a personality worth the effort.

He made it to the M62 before 5 a.m., but after that progress slowed. The entire motorway was closed from junction 24, at Ainley Top, through to junction 23, in both directions. The westbound traffic was being diverted off at junction 24, down onto minor roads. At this point the motorway was already climbing into the Pennines, beginning the long ascent to Saddleworth. The land to the north was sloping fields and woodland, the beginning of the moor below Ripponden and Halifax; to the south were a few more fields, then the outer suburbs of Huddersfield – but mostly the landscape lying in the darkness beyond the motorway was open countryside.

The barrier at Ainley Top consisted of three traffic cars, lined up across the three lanes, ahead of the junction, then a series of cones and emergency barriers stretching back a mile in the direction of Leeds and gradually restricting the lanes to the single exit ramp. He used the hard shoulder to skip the two-mile tailback, shorter than it would have been on a weekday. Once off the motorway he counted fifteen marked vehicles, including four ambulances and two fire engines, plus a handful of unmarked cars, parked either on the ramp itself or back down at the filter roundabout and the roads leading onto it. The emergency lights were spinning a chaotic, flickering pattern of orange and blue over everything in sight. Above them, the motorway was lit as normal by huge floodlights, set at thirty-metre intervals. There was so much activity it would have been easy to imagine he was going to investigate a multi-vehicle pile-up.

He parked on the verge, under the overpass, then walked up to the motorway itself and checked in at an incident van, where he was told his DS was waiting for him at the scene. He got sterile overalls and a set of galoshes, then set off, keeping close to the Armco crash barrier, as instructed. It was a deceptively steep climb and he started to sweat immediately – good for his blood-alcohol level, not so good for anyone standing close to him. Past the barriers the motorway was almost completely clear – a wide, eerie stretch of brightly lit empty tarmac rising like an airport runway towards an area about a mile distant, where he could see more cars and lights clustered around the hard shoulder. To the east the sky was a soft pink at the horizon, bleeding into an indistinct grey. Within half an hour the sun would be up. Despite the continuous background noise from the traffic queuing to get off at the junction behind him, the empty sweep of road gave an impression of unreal silence. From the fields and trees beyond the embankment he could even hear birds singing, getting on with the dawn chorus the same as they had yesterday, or the day before, or any other day for the last ten thousand years. As if everything were normal.

It took him nearly fifteen minutes to walk the distance, plenty of time to imagine what was coming. At his last murder scene he had felt a dizzying disorientation as he had helped turn the body over, a sudden feeling of horrible, unwanted empathy for the dead man. After that he had walked around suffering a continuous, lurching nausea. It was probably going to be the same this time. The last body had been a man called Abdul Haq. He had been armed and was probably himself a killer. There was little in the death to inspire emotion, but Marcus had nevertheless felt awash with it. His thoughts had run deeper than the death of one man; the threat had felt more fundamental. As if the fact that people could do this to each other invalidated his entire upbringing and education.

The sensation had been incapacitating and embarrassing, afflicting him in front of the DS he had met only the day before and was keen to impress, and not only because she was his new boss. He had known a little about Karen Sharpe long before they were introduced, because nearly everyone had an opinion about her, usually critical. The rumours had been enough for him to dig around himself once he knew he was to be assigned to her.

From the internet and old news copy alone he had found out sufficient information to worry and intrigue him. It was difficult to work out whether she was, in career terms, a route to the top or a dead end. But even despite that, her publicly known past was unique enough to impress him. Whatever else could be said about her, she had certainly been there, seen it, done it. And she was old enough to have a personality worth the effort.

He guessed Karen was about ten years older than him, judging from her appearance. She wouldn't tell him her age. She had a daughter who was nineteen, so she had to be in her late thirties at least. In fact, he was meant to have a date with Mairead tonight. Because of his interest in Karen he had let a situation develop there that he should have nipped in the bud a few weeks back. Mairead was attractive, but she was nothing compared to her mother. Over the last five months his feelings for Karen had become a little out of control. Karen didn't know that. And she certainly didn't know what was going on with her daughter, but if he didn't put an end to it soon she was probably going to find out.

There was an articulated lorry on the hard shoulder, just beyond the actual scene, cab door open, two or three people gathered around it. Nearer to him were three cars parked up against the Armco, two of them marked police vehicles. The space between had been taped off by a series of concentric barriers ranging across the road, passing over the verge and up to the embankment, dividing the scene into four separate areas, for search purposes. There was a path marked through to the closest ring, in deep, uncut undergrowth. They had set up even more lighting there, using battery-powered tungsten lights on stands. Beneath the lights was a huddle of crouched people, perhaps six in all. That would be where the body was. Another ten figures were already on their knees at the far side of the second circle of barriers, forming a line that extended into the undergrowth, fingertip-searching with flashlights on their heads.

He took a deep breath and looked at it all, struggling to control his feelings. There were at least thirty people in the area, all wearing identical white, sterile suits, hoods up, faces difficult to see. But he knew which one was Karen immediately, because she was nearly always the tallest person in any group. She was at the centre, by the body. That meant he was probably going to have to look at it.

She walked over to meet him, green eyes on his, a strained expression on her face. 'It's a dead girl,' she said, keeping her voice low. 'Maybe about twenty years old.'

He nodded, his heart thumping.

'I want you to speak to the guy who found her,' she said. She moved a hand up and pushed a stray lock of black hair out of her eyes, back under the rim of the suit hood. It was a nervous gesture, one he had observed before. It meant she was stressed. Her face looked very pale. He had heard others call her a hard bitch and he knew enough about her to realize she was anything but a weak female, but to him she had always seemed less certain of herself. Her nose had been broken in the past and was off-line, imperfect. Maybe that contributed.

'You want to look at her first?' she asked. 'It's not nice.' She looked steadily into his eyes. 'You don't have to.'

He nodded again. 'I think I should,' he said. He kept his head down, trying to keep his breath off her, in case she picked up the alcohol.

'Part of your education,' she said, then smiled fleetingly, because that was part of a running joke between them – about her having things to teach him. 'The SIO is Alan White,' she said. 'He's over there. Keep away from him. He's as bad as you, but you still don't want your breath in his face.'

She turned away from him before he could reply.

He stood at the back of a rough semi-circle of five people – the SIC, his deputy, two pathologists and a police photographer and looked over their shoulders as they worked on the dead girl. She was on her back in the long grass, face up, eyes wide open, legs apart, arms splayed. She was limp and naked, her skin bone-white under the lamps.

He had heard it said so many times, before starting this job, that the dead no longer looked real, that you could tell just by looking at them that there was nothing there, no life, no animation, nothing to miss, nothing to lose. You couldn't feel anything for them, because there was nothing left to feel anything about. Whatever it was that had made them living, breathing and thinking was gone. You thought of it that way and got on with your job.

Maybe it would be like that for him, if he ever got to look at a long-dead body, something that was badly decomposed. But not so far. At first glance, the girl he was looking at seemed so alive that it took his breath away. Injuries aside, she was not very different from the girl he had left in his bed an hour ago. It seemed as if at any moment her eyes might move and focus on him, as if she would say something. He felt suddenly ashamed to be staring at her, undressed, helpless, every private detail visible. One of the pathologists was extracting a thermometer from her anus and examining it. It made him feel physically sick.

He let the bile rise in his throat and bring water to his eyes. He swallowed it back and kept looking. She was dead. He repeated that to himself. Whatever had happened to her, she could feel nothing now. He could see it was true, but it still didn't sink in. He had to force himself to notice the detail: the trickle of dried blood from one ear; the bruises over her face; the clotted mess at her left temple where something heavy had struck her; the hair shorn off roughly, as if hacked by a knife. One of her hands lay palm upwards, covered in defensive cuts. There were burns – some small enough to be cigarette-made, but others much larger – covering her breasts and neck, some even on her face. Deep-cut ligature marks were visible on her wrists and ankles, and many large bruises and swellings all over her torso and limbs – too many to take in. Injuries that had been inflicted deliberately, over time. She hadn't been hit by a truck or a car and knocked into the verge. She had been discarded here. And before that she had been tied up, beaten and burned. Where her mouth hung slack he could see broken and missing teeth.

Everything was misshapen now, distorted by the bruising, but he could still make out a small, once-delicate face, with thin lips, high cheek-bones, green eyes. She looked like a child – but too thin, like an anorexic. Maybe her killer had starved her. Marcus could still see the pain, etched into her convulsive death-grimace.

The question. The same question, always, buzzing insistently in his mind. How could somebody do this to another human being? His brain filled quickly with images of her alive, tied to a chair, gagged, cigarettes ground into her skin, screaming for help. A little girl, somebody's child. But no help came. Only whoever did this to her, again and again. Not a human being, like he was, or Karen, or anyone else standing there with her dead body, but something from another world, a world where this kind of thing was normal. A species of vermin, an aberration, a kind of malfunction in the human gene code. Someone who took pleasure in inflicting suffering. He could feel his muscles tensing in mounting, silent rage thinking about it. It was pure evil, the lingering stench of it here with them still, in the long grass.

4

Karen stood at the back of the lorry and started to tell Marcus what she wanted him to do with the driver. 'The uniform PC who is with him has already asked him how he found her,' she said. She spoke slowly, standing close to him and keeping her eyes on his, to make sure he was listening. He wasn't used to looking at dead girls. Moments ago she had stood just to the side of him as he looked at the body. He had started shaking, clearly angry and upset. There was more danger he would cry than be sick, she thought, but she didn't want him doing either. She was in a rush and needed him functional.

'Are you listening?' she asked.

'Yes.' He frowned.

He was almost her own height, with a thick

tangle of short, curly blond hair, startling light-blue eyes and strong bone structure. She thought he resembled an actor she had seen in some action film, but couldn't remember which film, or which actor. He had a fit, muscular body, kept in shape by regular sport, but he was no meat-loaf. She knew his personal history. He did well to fit in, standing around in his suit like any other CID trainee because behind the eyes he had a brain that worked. Most people she had managed could hardly rub two thoughts together.

'You can do what I'm asking you to do?' she asked.

'Of course. You want me to take him through it in more detail. I know what to do.'

'Even pissed?'

He looked away from her, embarrassed. 'I'm not pissed. I had a drink last night. That's all.'

'You stink of it. That means you're still process-ing it.'

At least he didn't deny it. She closed her mouth and paused, controlling her irritation. Now wasn't the time to speak to him about it. He was on the call-out roster five nights in every seven weeks. It was an easy enough thing to exercise a little restraint when he knew he might end up working. If her full team had turned up as they were meant to she would have sent him home as soon as she had smelled his breath. As it was she was still missing two detectives and Alan White smelled much the same, so probably he wouldn't notice anything. But that didn't alter the fact that Marcus had let her down.

'It's a murder scene, Marcus,' she said. 'It

doesn't get any more important. I need to know you're not going to miss anything.'

He took a breath. 'I'm sorry,' he said. 'It won't happen again. But I'm OK. I won't miss anything.'

She sighed. 'OK,' she said. 'The driver is called Graham Henley.' She looked along the side of the lorry, to where Henley was standing next to his open cab door, beside the uniform PC who had first dealt with him, and a civilian SOCO. 'He's the short guy with the belly and tattoos. He's keen to get away. Don't let him pressurize you, though. Be thorough.'

'What has he said already?'

'He was cruising at fifty in the slow lane when he saw what he thought was a body on the verge. He pulled over to the hard shoulder and stopped, then reversed to where we are now, got out and walked back to inspect. He assumed she was dead, didn't touch her, called nine-nine-nine on his mobile straight away. That's it. The PC has a note of it. It's fine if we assume he's innocent, but as you know – we don't do that on murders. You should assume he dumped her there. He needs to be asked detailed questions about himself, his life, where he was going, where he had come from, who he had seen there, alibi details for the last twenty-four hours, et cetera. Get enough detail to pin him to a definite story later, if it ever comes to arresting him – something he will have to explain to a jury, if he decides to change his account. When we've got a fuller set of facts then the SIO can decide whether to seize the truck for examination or let him go on his way. OK?'

He nodded. 'No problem.'

She still felt uneasy about letting him do it. 'I'll be with the SIO,' she said. 'Come and see us when you're done.'

Alan White was waiting for her in the back of one of the two marked cars that had driven up to the scene before they'd realized it was a murder and had a chance to seal it off. She got in the car and sat next to White.

'Do you think we can trust division to seize the CCTV material without a hitch?' he asked almost as soon as the door closed. He was a small man – at least four inches shorter than her, slightly built, so maybe only about her own weight – and about five years older. He had a neat face, with tidy, short black hair, slightly sallow skin and keen eyes. He always wore expensive tailored suits and looked sharp. Right now he was wearing an intense aftershave.

'I've already covered that,' she replied. He was referring to cameras covering the junctions either side of the scene. 'I sent DC Sanderson with them.'

'Good girl.' He smiled at her. 'I'm glad we're on this together, Karen. You know how I rate you.'

She gave him a look. '"Good girl"?' she asked. 'You think we can cut the sexist crap?'

He grimaced. 'OK. Let's not get touchy. What does the driver say?'

'I've sent Marcus to get the detail. He'll tell us when he's done.'

'DC Roth. He looked a bit sick back there.'

'He's young. He'll learn to hide it.'

'Like you and me?'

49

She raised her eyebrows, but White was smirking. She assumed he felt what she felt, which was virtually nothing. The dead girl wasn't family; she wasn't a friend. That was it. There was nothing personal in it for her, nothing to get excited about except the technical challenge of the job itself. One of the things she liked about Marcus was that he reminded her that more human responses were possible. If you were young enough.

'The lorry,' White said. 'What do you think we should do with it?'

'It's probably straight up. Let's see what Marcus gets out of the driver. Maybe keep the lorry, let the driver go.'

'I thought we'd keep both for a while. Just until we're sure she wasn't in the back at any point.'

She shrugged. He was right. 'What does SOCO say?'

'I'm still waiting.'

'And the pathologist?'

'Not much. Nothing on time of death yet. She wasn't killed there, though. She was dumped there dead, they think. She's maybe twenty years old. Multiple injuries – including burns, fag marks, et cetera – all the stuff we can see for ourselves. Probably the head wound did it. They're not sure right now. They're not sure about anything, as usual. He rubbed his eyes and yawned, looking suddenly tired. 'We can move her now, though, so they should get a full PM completed by midday, hopefully.'

'Nothing to ID her?'

'Nothing at all on her. And nothing so far from the searches. That's the priority.' He reached into a pocket and took out an expensive-looking, leather-bound black notebook and a fat Mont Blanc pen. 'Lets see what else I've got,' he said, opening the notebook. 'Tell me if you think I've missed anything.' He read from the list of initial actions and she listened carefully. There was little to contribute.

'I'm hoping to get a photo of her body put out via TV,' he said, halfway through. 'At least on the local channels. I'll cover it myself, but you could come with me – a female face and all that.'

'Is that wise?'

He smiled slightly. 'You think they'll recognize you from Swales?'

'Probably not.' Fifteen months ago there had been local press coverage of the incident resulting in Swales's arm being broken – all generated by Swales and his advisers – but she wasn't worried about that. There were things in her deeper past that made the Swales fiasco pale into insignificance. She wouldn't want a journalist dragging up any of that live on air. 'They could remember worse things,' she said.

White knew enough for her not to have to spell it out. He waved his hand dismissively, though. 'Ancient history,' he said. 'Local hacks have short memories.

'Not for shootings.'

He shrugged. 'You were commended by the chief constable. There's nothing to hide.'

5

I am trying to write down what has happened to me – what is happening to me – like Angela has told me to. She keeps going on at me about it – I have to write it all down, then read it out to her, as if it is somebody else's story, not mine. Because when I sit in there with her and she asks me to tell her things, my mouth just clams up and I can't say anything. I don't know why. Angela says I have seven A-grade GCSEs, so I should be able to talk about anything! But getting exams is different. Getting A-grade GCSEs was easy compared to trying to speak about these things.

Maybe it's because I feel so bad about it all, because I know how upsetting it will be once I start telling her. But I have to try to do something. They think that if I refuse to talk about it Andrew will get hurt. Angela told me that at our first meeting. But how would I hurt him? The idea is mad. It makes me want to cry just thinking about him getting hurt. It makes me want to tell her to mind her own business, but if I don't give her something she might think I've made no 'progress', as she calls it. Then they might try to take him off me. She seems like a friend, Angela – that's how she tries to come across. But at the end of the day she works for the same social workers who took Andrew away last year. I can't let them take him from me again. He's the only reason I'm still alive. He's my little baby, the only

52

thing I've got in the world. Except he's not so little now (in three months – I can't believe it – he will be three years old!), but still my little baby. He will always be my little baby. The most precious thing I've ever had.

So I have to write down something. I'll write it, then think about whether I can read it to her. Cross out what I don't want her to know. Today is the day to do it. Today it is one year, exactly, since it happened. I woke up in a terrible panic remembering that, remembering waking up on the hospital trolley, with the blurry vision and the masked faces and the drips and the buzzing noise. Then the choking when they pumped my stomach (though I told them I hadn't taken anything), the nausea and dizziness. The consultant told me that in three more hours it would have been too late, I would have been dead. I hadn't realized it took anywhere near that long to lose enough blood to kill you, otherwise I probably would have taken some pills as well. Because I meant it. I really meant to do it.

But Andrew saved me – my lovely little baby cried his eyes out for me, willing me to stay with him. Screamed and cried at the top of his voice, the neighbour said – the neighbour I never met, who never once offered help, a cup of tea, or even a kind word. Not once in the entire year I spent in that shit-hole in Chapeltown, though she must have been able to hear Andrew screaming each and every night, must have known I was only eighteen. But she called the police, at least. Not to help us, but so that she could get some sleep. She rescued us accidentally.

I don't know why I did it. Now I can't understand how I could have even thought about it, knowing what it would mean for Andrew. That is the worst of it. If I had died then he would have had to go and live

53

with them, with Beryl and Jack.

If I was going to tell you everything, Angela, I would start with the day Beryl found out that I was pregnant. I used to think that what I did with Ashok was wrong. Enough people told me afterwards that I was dirty and sinful – so I thought that everything that happened started then, with a teenage fumble in the back of his Imprezza that went too far. That was how I explained it to myself then, when I was young – but now I know there was nothing wrong with it at all. How could there be? Andrew wouldn't have been born if we hadn't had that fumble. So I wouldn't change a thing now – I'd do everything the same if I had the chance again. The problems didn't start with falling in love with a sweet little Asian boy – or even with him running off and leaving me pregnant and in tears – the problems started when they found out what had happened.

OK, I expected it would be hard. I expected that there would be screaming and shouting, that I would be slapped, locked in my room, marched off to see the priest for confession. I think I might even have thought they would insist on an abortion. But they are Christians, Catholics who go to mass every week and say prayers, who told me all my childhood to 'turn the other cheek', be humble, avoid pride and selfishness. And they are supposed to be people who love me. (Did they ever tell me they loved me? If they did I can't now remember.) But your parents are meant to love you. Like I love Andrew. What they did to me I cannot even imagine doing to Andrew (yet I tried to kill myself and leave him, I know…) Even the priest they brought round that night shouted at me. They should have been trying to keep me calm, not shout at me so much I might have had a miscarriage.

That was probably what they wanted. I was wrong about them wanting an abortion, of course. They couldn't tell me to get an abortion, not once they knew I hadn't been raped. The disgusting questions they asked that night! Forcing me to sit on the couch and answer the same things over and over again, her in tears, him screaming at the top of his voice, trying all the time to find out who 'he' was, if he had raped me, or forced me in 'some other way' with drugs or threats. They wanted me to say I'd been raped by him – they would have been happier if I had been raped! – because they are Catholics and that's what Catholics are like. Abortion isn't allowed unless you're raped, they told me. The priest said 'not even then' in his thick, stupid Irish accent. But I wasn't raped and my lover was an Asian, which couldn't have been worse for them.

I told them Andrew's dad was Asian after about four hours of it. I had to tell them something. But I didn't give Ashok's name. I lied and told them it was someone called Mohammed Khan, a Muslim, not a Hindu, so they couldn't go into Harehills looking for Ash (though by then he was down in London, running from it – I didn't find that out for another two weeks). In the end their only option was to force me to put the baby up for adoption, after he was born. They thought they could legally force me to do it – because I was only sixteen. It took them a month to find out that the choice was legally mine, and then the pressure really started. But I stuck to my decision. I wouldn't agree to any of it. I didn't want him adopted. You would have been proud of me, Angela. I loved him even then, you see, before he even came out, before I even knew whether he was a boy or a girl. I could feel

55

him moving in my tummy every night. I spoke to him when he was in there, told him I loved him and would care for him. I promised him. How could I give birth to him, then just abandon him to Social Services? How can any mum do that?

God, how I hate that woman now. I've started calling her Beryl, instead of Mum, or Mother, because you said that would be a good way to distance myself from her, to make it hurt less inside. Same with him. Jack. Not Dad, or Daddy. Jack and fucking Beryl. I dream that one day Beryl will miss us so much that she will turn up on my doorstep with that long horse-face of hers (so perfect for nagging, griping and complaining about everything) and she will beg me to let her see her beautiful grandchild, and I will take a deep breath and just close the door right in her face.

Too late. Because she kicked me out. Kicked me out to get on with 'my own life' when I was already four months pregnant and only sixteen years old. What mother does that to her child? I'm asking you, Angela – how could she do that to me? Because of the shame? In the year 2001! Shame about what? It's not as if they had any appearances worth keeping up. They live in a cheap little three-bedroom semi in a grotty, boring suburb of Leeds. And what is Leeds? Hardly the centre of the universe. A trashy, working-class northern town. So their daughter got pregnant by a Paki when she was sixteen. So what? Did they have a better life to offer me? What did they have to be ashamed about?

I can still hardly believe it. I haven't seen her since. They forced me out knowing that I knew nothing about anything, knowing I was to live in a damp, barely furnished shit-hole on the worst estate in Leeds. They told the entire family I had left of my own free will, that

I was a 'stranger' to them. No one would speak to me, not even by phone. Not even my aunt Jackie in Harehills, who I saw every week up to then. Beryl and Jack got to her first and warned her. They wanted me to be an outcast, cut off from everything I knew. They thought that would bring me back to them quickly – repentant, contrite, willing to dump the baby I was carrying into some shitty care home the moment he was born. But I couldn't do that, Angela. I couldn't do it.

I didn't even know they were racist until it happened. Or, if I did, I hadn't thought anything about it. I must have heard them saying things when I was growing up, but it hadn't made me racist. I thought Ashok was beautiful. He was beautiful. There have been times since then that I have wanted him so desperately, wanted that thing he gave me – for such a short time – that feeling of being wanted by someone who was really into me. He told me I was beautiful every day I met him. He used to stroke me and touch me in ways that I never experienced before – and I'm not talking just about sex. He used to just sit there beside me, in the car – when we were out by the airport watching the planes take off – and gently stroke the back of my neck. And I used to lean my head on his shoulder and everything felt OK. Everything. That was all it was. He made me feel like everything was good about me, everything was safe. If I looked at him I would catch him looking at me like he loved me, like he really loved me. He didn't say it. That was too embarrassing. But he felt it. I could see in his eyes that he felt it. And I said it to him. I told him all the time that I loved him, that I wanted to be with him. I would even have married him, I think. It was the happiest I've been.

6

The slots for the lunch-time TV and radio interviews clashed, so Alan White sent Karen by herself to do an interview with one of the local radio stations, while he went off to a local TV station. She managed to leave the M62 by 9 am., stop in at Dudley Hill to help organize her team, rush home and change clothes in order to get to Leeds just before midday. She was punctual, but they still kept her waiting in reception for nearly an hour.

She used the time to think about how she was going to share taskings between her team members. First briefing was scheduled for 2 p.m., but Alan White had already told her how he was going to split the cake. He intended to divide the six available teams into two groupings – two teams under himself – including Karen's – and four under Ricky Spencer, the deputy SIO. Spencer's teams were to man the phone lines, initiate national missing persons enquiries, complete the CCTV examination and attempt to trace the estimated one thousand vehicles caught on camera from the M62, and also try to ID the victim via a search for her medical records. Karen's team were tasked with local MISPER – missing person – reports, media and public appeals, disseminating the photo White was obtaining of the victim, locally and nationally, and enquiries with Social

Services departments and local charities. DS Bill Naylor was to be tasked with digging out local intelligence and co-ordinating the job of milking the county's informants for information.

White had a hunch – that was what he actually called it – that the victim was local and had come through the care system. Kids out of care lacked close family connections, were isolated. Close family usually meant the relatives were standing in a police station long before the body was found. That hadn't happened. Ricky Spencer, on the other hand, thought she was more likely to be a prostitute, but also local. Karen had no idea why they would assume she was from anywhere near West Yorkshire. 'I can tell from looking at her,' White had said, in reply to her objections. 'She's a Leeds girl. It's written all over her face.'

At nearly p.m. a tall, skinny youth in his early twenties appeared to take her upstairs. He was dressed as if he were about to go surfing and had a vague, disinterested manner. He turned out to be the producer of the show she was to appear on. Upstairs he sat her on a chair directly outside one of two studios and then returned to a semi-circular desk set up with numerous computer screens. From his position he could see straight into the studios through curving glass partitions.

A man called Roger Hungerford was to interview her. She had never heard of him or his show before. She had been told the show was the lunch-time news slot. The format was to alternate songs with news items and features, usually pieces with a local angle. Every hour Hungerford summarized the national news, with a slot for more serious local items following that, but the bulk of the programme seemed to consist of him talking. As she sat outside the studio the show was being piped into a monitor directly above her head, so she had time to listen to him, while watching him in action through the studio partition.

Five minutes of it confirmed why she never listened to local radio, either in her car or home. Hungerford's tone, like that of any other local presenter, was a kind of canned, perpetual cheerfulness. He slipped effortlessly from serious news items to home-grown musings on anything and everything. His thoughts were meant to be funny, she assumed. She also assumed that he was some kind of celebrity in his own right – otherwise why would anyone be even vaguely interested in his opinions? – but that didn't make him any easier to listen to. He was only doing his job, of course, and perhaps she should have felt admiration that he was managing it so well, but it still felt wrong to hand over the details of a brutalized young girl to this kind of trivialization.

Just after one o'clock the youth took her into the studio itself and introduced her to Roger. He was seated at a large circular desk with a bank of switches and monitors in the middle. He didn't stand up to greet her, but slipped off his earphones and extended a hand across a monitor. He didn't smile. On air they were playing a twenty-year-old pop hit. The producer had already explained to her that the play list for the show was selected at random by computer.

'Sit down, Officer,' Hungerford said. 'I hope we can help you.' He had what she thought of as a posh Yorkshire accent. He sounded like he was from Yorkshire, but not any particular part of it.

She sat at the desk, in front of three microphones. The producer explained to her that she would be interviewed for about fifteen minutes. He told her not to lean into the microphones. He pointed to a single green light on the wall. When it was illuminated they were live and everything she said would be picked up. He left her with Roger.

'We've got about a minute,' Hungerford said. 'Then I'll do the intros.'

'You want me to talk for fifteen minutes?' she asked, worried. 'It won't take anywhere near that long.'

'I thought we'd make it personal,' Hungerford said. 'That way more people might listen.'

'Personal? In what way?'

'Talk a little about yourself and your job. Tell us how you feel about the case. That sort of thing. Fifteen minutes isn't long. There are two songs to fit into that time.' He sat back and looked at her. He was about her age, maybe a little older, with a heavily lined, weatherbeaten face, skin dark with the kind of tan you got from spending a lot of time outdoors. On a yacht, maybe. Off the air, she noticed, he didn't smile much.

'They gave me some of your background,' he said. He fiddled with a single sheet of paper lying on the desk. 'It's riveting stuff. Very interesting.' He sounded like he meant it.

'What stuff are we talking about?' she asked.

He held up the sheet and read from it. 'Commended in nineteen ninety-eight for the rescue of

61

a kidnapped eight-year-old.' He looked at her. 'I remember that. I even think I might have covered it at the time. There were some casualties, weren't there?'

'That was a long time ago,' she said. 'Is that all it says?'

'About that? Yes. But I remember the detail,' he said. 'It was a bit unusual. You shot three men, I think. Is that right?'

She shrugged, still quite calm. 'That's right. But I don't want to talk about it, as you can guess.'

'Not even in broad terms? It would help get the message across, I think.'

'Would it? I think we should just concentrate on getting out an appeal to ID this poor dead girl.'

Poor dead girl That was how White had told her to say it.

Hungerford shrugged. 'Maybe. But people like a bit of personal interest. It makes them sit up and listen.' He was still looking at the sheet of paper. 'Karen Sharpe,' he said, as if trying to bring something to mind. The song was finishing. 'Weren't you also suspended and investigated, about five years back, in connection with another shooting?'

'Once again, it's not something I would want to discuss on air–'

'That would make a great angle.' Was he listening to her? 'You are investigating a murder. But you've been on the other side of the fence. You know what it's like to be accused of murder. I like it.' She was bothered now. She opened her mouth to make it clear to him that he was not to go there, but he was already doing something on the console in front of him. Then he started speaking again, at once, at the same volume, so at first she thought he was speaking to her still: 'Seven past the hour. More news on the half-hour.' He moved another switch and the remains of the song faded out. She glanced up. The green light was on. They were live. 'You're listening to Roger Hungerford...' He made a few comments about the weather, then looked over to her. 'Right now, something important. I have with me DS Karen Sharpe, from West Yorkshire Police. Good afternoon, Karen.' He winked at her.

She took a deep breath, still frowning hard, still trying to get the message across to him. 'Good afternoon, Roger.' Automatically she leaned into the mike. 'Thanks for bringing me in.'

'Anything we can do to help. That's why we're here. DS Sharpe is working a major enquiry in West Yorkshire. You've been hearing about the effects of it all morning. Traffic chaos on the M62.' He said it like it was the trailer for a movie. 'Is that situation any better, Karen?'

'I believe it is clearing. We re-opened the road at nine. It's Sunday, so the effects weren't as bad as they might have been.'

'And what can you tell us about the reasons for these problems?'

She tried to put her worries to one side, but he had thrown her. She started speaking about the body, umming and ahing, clearly nervous. She stopped, cleared her throat and started again. She gave the description they were using and managed to make the appeal, using the words White had advised. 'This poor girl has been brutally attacked and murdered,' she said, her voice as near to dead-pan as she could get it. 'We urgently need to identify who she is. The description isn't a lot to go on, but I would appeal to anyone who might have a suspicion as to who this is to contact the incident-room without delay.' She gave the incident room number.

'A terrible, terrible case,' Hungerford said. 'Let me give you that incident-room number again.' He read it from the sheet of paper, then looked at her, as if she were supposed to say something else. 'Let's hope we get a response,' he said, then added, 'These cases must affect you deeply, Karen.'

'Of course,' she said. 'These are quite difficult cases to work.' Especially if they drag you from your bed in the middle of the night. 'But all homicides are difficult.'

'How do you manage to maintain a professional level of involvement? It must be very upsetting.'

It was sliding into the personal. He hadn't caught the warning at all. Or he was ignoring her.

'You concentrate on the task, Roger,' she said. 'Like we all do.' She gave him her best thunderous look. She even raised a finger and wagged it at him. He smiled, then looked puzzled, as if unsure what she meant.

'You're no stranger to drama, of course,' he continued, tone unchanged. 'You've been in situations of extreme danger yourself, I know...'

She shook her head vigorously. Waved both hands. He was looking right at her. His expression didn't change at all.

'Maybe you could tell us a little about that,' he said. 'Going back about five or six years, for instance. There was–'

She stood up quickly and reached across to him. He was in mid-sentence when she got her hand on the controls. He must have thought she was going for the sheet of paper and didn't move at all. His eyes widened in surprise as her fingers hit every button and slider she could see. The panel was a long, wide bank of switches, like a mixing desk. She had no idea which switch would cut the sound from the studio, so she tried to throw every single one. It was a panicky, desperate gesture, but short of thumping him, she didn't know what else to do.

His reactions weren't too fast. He pushed hack from the desk, then began to gesticulate frantically through the glass screen behind her. He didn't try to stop her. From the corner of her eye she saw the green light flick off. She took a deep breath and backed off. He stood up behind the desk, staring at her as if she were mad. The silence was deafening. She sat down again, feeling flush with embarrassment. Behind her the door opened and the producer came in.

'What's happening, Roger? What's up?' He sounded admirably calm.

'Are we off air?' she asked.

'This mad bitch just cut the feed,' Roger said. 'Did you cover the gap?'

'I started the next song. There was a three-second break. No more.

'Fucking hell.'

Disaster. A three-second radio silence. She

65

watched him swallow, the colour rising rapidly to his face. 'You were moving into areas we agreed to avoid,' she said. 'I suggest we start again and repeat the appeal. I suggest we stick to chat.'

'You must have a fucking screw loose.'

'I'm the kind of woman who shoots people. Remember? You think I'm like you? You think I work by *your* rules?'

'Maybe we could discuss this outside the studio,' the producer suggested. He sounded less sure now.

'You saw my warnings,' she continued, staring at Hungerford. 'You knew what you were doing.'

'She's off her rocker.'

'A screw loose. Exactly. But if I say keep off my past, I mean it,' she said.

7

First briefing finally kicked off at 3 p.m. By then Marcus had spent nearly five hours working on missing persons reports, back at the HMET West office in Dudley Hill. There was a national data-base for MISPERs, and a force co-ordinator at Wakefield, but the rule was that they didn't notify either until after thirty-six hours. So to cover the most recent missing persons – on any force – you had to contact individual forces and divisions, and request information on anything that might roughly match the description of your body, then initiate the follow-up actions for those that did.

On each division in West Yorkshire alone there might be between ten and fifteen MISPER reports each day. Nearly all concerned children, and mostly children in care. Simple enquiries with the national database would yield results for those missing longer than thirty-six hours. But someone else had been given that task.

The new reports were handled much the same across the entire country. The local divisions filled in a log (a paper log in West Yorkshire, though other forces had computer versions) and decided how to action the report. It wasn't practical or possible to assume that fifty people a day, across the county, had been kidnapped or murdered (whatever the Association of Chief Police Officers and the Homicide Manual might suggest), so usually the assumption was that they had run away or the report was an error – which was normally the way it turned out. The local division decided when to change that assumption and initiate a major enquiry. The timing of that depended on the precise information available, the age of the MISPER and other variables. Sometimes it took a long time to track down all the possible relatives or friends with whom a MISPER might be staying. Crossing the thirty-six-hour boundary didn't mean you became a major enquiry, just that your details went national.

There were 110 open MISPERs in West Yorkshire that morning, all from the preceding thirty-six hours. Marcus worked through them with a detective called Gerry Owen, a miserable, untidy and seriously overweight man nearing retirement, who said very little about anything and about whom Marcus had learned virtually nothing, despite working with him for the last five months. They sat alongside each other in the incident room, along with everyone else working the enquiry, some on MISPER queries, about the same number again on other lines. They called each division in turn and spoke to the operations inspector, or whoever he nominated to deal with them. Then they went through each and every log, by phone, looking for a possible match to the description of their girl.

The incident room was a modern, uninteresting, functional space. There were three such rooms in HMET West all identically equipped, with adjoining rooms set up for the terminals dedicated to the Home Office Large Major Enquiry computer system – HOLMES. From the outset, every action had to be logged on HOLMES and cross-referenced by a team of indexers; then HOLMES itself could begin to generate possible follow-up actions. But that didn't really kick in until the second day or so – until then they were all working flat out to clear a list of initial actions drawn up manually by the enquiry management.

The deputy SIO had thought their body might be a MISPER he knew of called Melanie Simpson and the description was very similar – but Melanie Simpson was located alive and well before 9 am. By 10 am, they had worked out that there were thirty-one other possible matches, but of those fifteen had already been located an hour later, leaving sixteen open reports by midday. These all concerned teenage girls in care and didn't look promising. Though, to be absolutely safe, they were working on the assumption that their dead girl could be aged between fourteen and twenty-five, the pathologist had already said she was probably between twenty and twenty-four – too old still to be in care. Nevertheless, they made sure that the divisions concerned were working the sixteen possibles as a matter of urgency, reporting back to them regularly.

They broke at midday to eat sandwiches that Ricky Spencer had shipped in, then kept going, shifting onto still open major enquiries into missing girls, and looking back over a ten-year period, in case she had been kidnapped long ago. The national database hadn't been backdated. Owen and he covered West Yorkshire. Other detectives dealt with neighbouring forces, gradually moving further away from home. In all, prior to first briefing, there were twenty full detectives and five trainee investigators in the room, eight of whom were working on bottoming the current information on missing people. The work was mainly done by phone. There was no small talk.

By 3 p.m. – when they filed into the meeting room next door for first briefing – they knew it was unlikely their girl was a current missing person in West Yorkshire or any of the surrounding counties. As far as open major enquiries went, it seemed there were only eight outstanding missing girls from the last fifteen years in the entire north of England, and none matched the description. The national database had also come up with a straight negative in response to their particulars.

Karen was already in the meeting room as

Marcus took a seat near the front, next to DC John Sanderson (a better option than sitting next to Owen, whose thighs and belly took up space enough for two men Marcus's size). She was at the front desk, talking to Ricky Spencer. Spencer looked annoyed about something, but that didn't mean much. Marcus knew that Karen and the SIO had covered three radio appeals and one TV interview that morning, because the staff tasked with answering the phone response were also seated in the incident room and he could overhear what was being said, but he hadn't seen or heard any of the appeals.

Behind Karen, pinned to the wall, was an A3 blow-up of the dead girl's face – the image they were intending to use for identification enquiries with the media and general public. He felt nauseous looking at it. They had done their best to make her look alive – because it wasn't effective to hand out shocking images – but they had only succeeded in making something more horrific. Someone had applied make-up over the most obvious contusions, and closed her mouth to hide the broken teeth. But the skin looked slack, the face puffy and grey. Now she really did look like a corpse, he thought. Were they going to be asked to show people that image? Beneath the image was a one-line description, the one he had been using all morning: *Caucasian female, 20-24 years old, 5 feet 3 inches, very thin, with a pale complexion, dark-brown hair and green eyes.* To that they had now added a further line, presumably as a result of the post-mortem findings: *Old scarring to left wrist indicating possible suicide attempt in past.*

It wasn't very precise, taken together, but it still said too much, he thought. Did she have pale skin when alive? Was she thin like that when people last saw her? Did the scarring really mean she had tried to kill herself?

Alan White walked into the room with someone else and Karen moved away from Ricky Spencer and sat down on the chair next to Marcus. There was so little room that her thigh and arm were pressed tightly against his own. He smiled at her, not moving his leg. She had changed clothes since they had left the scene that morning, which meant she had been home, he assumed. Now she was wearing a long, dark skirt and matching jacket, with flat, black leather shoes. Bare legs, though not much of them visible. A pale-blue shirt beneath the jacket. Her hair was pulled back into a long, black ponytail. As usual, no jewellery and no perfume – though he was close enough to pick up the warmth from her body – but something was different. Was it the first time he had seen her in a skirt?

'How you doing, Marcus?' she asked softly, leaning towards him. 'You recovered yet?'

He opened his mouth a little and exhaled gently, right into her face. 'You tell me.'

'Thanks,' she said. She looked down at his leg and frowned. 'Not much room in here, is there?'

'You look good in the skirt,' he said. 'That your media-interview gear?'

She shifted position slightly, as if uncomfortable in it. 'I hate it,' she said, wrinkling her nose, but he could see she had coloured ever so slightly.

At the front Alan White took off his jacket,

hung it neatly on the back of his chair, cleared his throat and began to speak. The murmur of voices subsided at once.

'Welcome to exile,' he said. He smiled mysteriously. No one said anything. No one understood. He stood up. 'Exile. E-X-I-L-E. That's the name they've assigned to this enquiry, at random, as per usual.' At his side Ricky Spencer sat poker-faced. 'It's a Cat. B, with six teams for the moment. We've managed to get everyone in, I think.' He looked around the room. It was full – which meant over thirty-five detectives – and already stuffy, hot and airless. Outside it was full summer – more like mid-July than September – and the air conditioning didn't work, despite the building being relatively new and purpose-built. White asked someone at the back to open a few windows, then looked at his watch. 'I won't waste time. This room is unpleasant to spend too long in. You know already what it's all about, I assume. It's not like the old days – you're all dedicated murder detectives now. You know what you're doing.' He smirked, as if to suggest he couldn't believe that. 'The next twenty-four hours are crucial. In that time we have to get an ID on the body. That's the priority. Remember that. I'll start with how she was found.'

He began to talk them through the chronology, most of which Marcus already knew because he'd been at the scene. The truck driver Marcus had interviewed had only just been released, having been held voluntarily prior to that. SOCO had finally decided that it was extremely unlikely the body had ever been inside his lorry, though a

72

definite decision on that awaited proper forensic results from samples taken from inside the truck, which had meanwhile been impounded.

SOCO had also reported that it was 'highly likely' the victim had been brought to the verge via the motorway, in a vehicle of some sort. They had possible tyre impressions from the edge of the verge, but weren't giving a clear opinion on the type of vehicle yet. A large amount of CCTV evidence had been seized and analysis had already begun, yielding a preliminary list of more than a thousand vehicles that had passed the site within a few hours of her being found.

'That brings me to the pathologists and the post-mortem,' White said. 'Time of death is a rough guesstimate as usual, but they're placing it between three and nine hours prior to discovery, which would mean very roughly between six and midnight yesterday. She was certainly already dead when she was placed at the scene. There is almost no blood at the scene itself.' He paused and opened a large, bound policy log on the desk in front of him. 'This is what they say about injuries.' He looked up. 'We're dealing with a young woman – probably twenty to twenty-four, they tell me now, looking at femur measurements and such-like. She has died as a result of a head injury causing a brain haemorrhage. The profile of the haemorrhage makes it likely that she was sick from it for quite some time, maybe weeks, rather than days.' He reached a hand up and touched his own head, to the left side, just behind the temple. 'Struck with a heavy, blunt object, just here.' He turned his head so they could see. 'The object may have a distinctive crush pattern and we're getting another expert to look at that.' He turned a page. 'There were many other injuries. Mr Slater – the consultant pathologist – enumerated over seventy-eight separate injuries, fifty-one of which were serious. He said it's the worst case he's seen in his career.' He paused to see whether anyone would react. Slater was renowned for saying that the injuries were the worst he'd seen, but no one laughed. 'Ricky has put together a briefing sheet detailing them,' he continued. 'With a diagram. Where are they, Ricky?'

Spencer pointed to an A4 pile at the end of the desk. 'Pick one up as you leave,' he suggested.

'I'll summarize what it all means,'White started again. 'This young woman was tortured before she died and she endured that torture for a long period. The oldest injuries are perhaps four weeks old. At some point she was bound tightly – hands and feet, probably with electrical cord – though not recently. So maybe that happened near to when she was taken, assuming she *was* taken. She was burned with a variety of objects, ranging from cigarettes to heated metal bars, we think. A large burn on her buttocks suggests prolonged contact with a very hot domestic iron. It's a clear shape, a very deep burn. Someone must have held it there for several minutes. She was cut – superficially – with bladed instruments – mainly across her wrists, thighs and the soles of her feet. And she was beaten. Severely beaten with two or three blunt objects, one of them wood. She has extensive bruising to her breasts and buttocks, to her genitalia and her back. Her arms show many defensive-type injuries. The bruises are in various stages of development, the most recent being from close in time to when she died, the oldest going back several weeks. That means it's possible she was held somewhere for at least a few weeks. That means she may have disappeared some time ago. We have to keep the field of enquiry wide open.' He cleared his throat. 'She has internal injuries to her liver, kidneys, bladder and spleen, consistent with the external trauma, but there is no evidence of sexual contact or abuse, no evidence of penile or digital penetration of vagina or anus, no seminal fluid. So, at this stage, no sexual motive to help us. That makes this a bit unusual, I think. What else?' He looked down at Spencer. He was a little red in the face now. The atmosphere in the room had changed as he spoke. The silence was tense now.

'Hair shorn off,' Spencer suggested.

'Yes. Her hair has been hacked off, as if it were done to shame her.'

'And fingerprints negative,' Spencer added.

'No match from her prints,' White said. He looked at his notes again. 'Two other things of great significance. Firstly, she has given birth before, at least once. So it's likely she has had a child or children at some point. Where are they? Are they alive? Are they in danger? Are they with relatives? If they are, then why has nobody reported her missing? So far all work on MISPER reports has drawn a blank. Two, she has old scarring injuries which might not have been inflicted by someone else. It is possible that she

75

has both self-harmed – by slashing herself along the arm – and attempted suicide by cutting her left wrist quite badly. These details may be important in trying to ID her. If she tried to kill herself there will probably be a medical record of treatment somewhere. Similarly her dental set-up – there is evidence of recent filling work in some teeth – certainly within the last two years. Several teeth broken or knocked out, too – I forgot that.' He looked at Spencer again. 'You want to talk about forensics, Ricky?'

Spencer nodded, then stood up as White sat down. He was a taller man than White. Marcus guessed he would be more or less Karen's age, which meant his career had got snagged some-where for him still to be a DI, because he was certainly ambitious enough to have wanted more. Maybe that had made him a little bitter. His mouth had a perpetual sneer. Marcus didn't like him. Most of life was a question of pretence, of knowing who you needed to be in any given situation. Karen would call it arse-licking, but that was to ignore the fact that *all* of life was like that, every little human transaction, from buying groceries to falling in love: pick the mask and wear it. Marcus prided himself on being good at that, but Spencer made it challenging because he acted as if he were treating you as competition, when that shouldn't have been the case between a DI and a mere TI. He didn't smile much, hardly ever cracked a joke.

'There's a welter of outstanding forensics,' Spencer said. 'We have blood from the body and from the scene, some of it not hers.' That led to a little ripple of excitement in the room. 'We will get DNA from it, we think, but the results are at least forty-eight hours away. We can't sit back and wait. We have fibres from both body and scene, but they won't be any use unless we get a suspect quickly. Most matching fibres will be shed from the suspect's clothing within the next forty-eight hours. We have scrapings from under her nails, material from her hair as well. There are no obvious signs that she was a drug user, but we still await full toxicology results. Her stomach was empty, by the way – so no recent meals to go on. It's possible she has been deliberately starved. She's seriously underweight for a woman of that height and age. We also have potential soil and pollen traces from her hair, which may or may not help with where she has been before ending up in West Yorkshire. Probably not, they say – unless it's somewhere far-flung and unusual.' He looked up, thinking. 'I suppose it's possible she was brought across the Channel in a lorry from Turkey, in which case we might get to know about it from the pollen. I'm not sure. Results from that will take even longer to come back. Ethnically, she is said to fit a "European profile", which means she could be from anywhere from here to Russia. No help there, then.'

He looked at his own policy log. 'You've heard about the man who found her – Henley – we think he's legit. But we have all the usual samples from him. Seems unlikely he's involved as he says he hasn't touched her. He'd be more likely to say he bent down and gave her mouth-to-mouth if he had done something. That way he'd cover the

DNA angle.' He took a breath. 'A more minute search of the verge is going on as we speak, covering a larger area – it's possible the murder weapon was abandoned in the verges, at a different spot.' He stopped, turning pages, double-checking. 'That's it, I think. Fairly positive, all in all.' He sat down and White stood again.

'So what do we do now, before the forensics come back?' he asked, then turned to a whiteboard and started to write. 'I've got four different lines in mind. I'll divide the teams accordingly.'

8

They held Karen back in the meeting room when it was over, just White, Spencer and herself. She guessed the radio station had made some kind of complaint about her. Spencer stood up as Ian Miller – the last DS out – closed the door behind him. He went over to the door and made sure it was shut.

'Is this about Hungerford?' Karen asked White.

'Hungerford?'

'That prick at the local radio.'

'What about him?' Spencer asked. He walked back to the desk.

'We had a little dispute. I assumed he complained.'

White shook his head, looked over at Spencer.

'Was that the interruption in transmission?' Spencer asked. 'I heard the appeal. I was wondering what happened.'

'He wanted to talk about things that were irrelevant,' Karen said. She nodded at White, as if to say, *I warned you.*

'So what did you do?' Spencer asked. 'Hit him?'

He laughed. Karen tutted. She had worked with Ricky Spencer in the past. Their relationship had often been uneasy. 'I don't do that kind of thing, Ricky,' she said. 'You know me.'

'I would have thought there was always that danger with you, Karen,' he said. 'What happened – you turn over a new leaf?' He laughed again. No humour in it, though.

'I don't know anything about Hungerford,' White said. 'This is about the injury.'

She frowned.

'The cause of death,' White explained. 'I said it might be a distinctive injury in the briefing. But I didn't give the whole picture.' He looked at Spencer again, as if wondering whether to go on.

Spencer nodded, then spoke himself. 'In fact, the pathologist said quite a lot about the characteristics of the head wound. It's distinctive. The skull has been broken in a pattern. Slater thinks he's seen the pattern before. He's consulting another expert, in London, but meanwhile...' He reached down to his rigid black briefcase and extracted something. 'He thinks we should be looking for one of these.' He slid a telescopic baton from its leather holder and tapped it sharply against the desk, then flicked his wrist down to open it up. Retracted, the weapon was less than six inches long, but it opened up to nearly three feet, a slim, rigid metal rod with a compact, heavily weighted nodule at the end.

'An Asp,' Karen said. She didn't have one, but she knew how they worked. They were standard issue on the Force.

'An Asp,' White said. He took the implement from Spencer and fingered the nodule. 'This bit here leaves a distinctive crush pattern,' he said. 'At least, that's what we're being told.'

'Different from a hammer?' she asked.

White shrugged. 'So Slater says. Maybe he's wrong. You know what he's like for guesswork.'

'It's the combination of slim stem and heavy, rounded end,' Spencer said. 'If it strikes certain flat surfaces at a specific angle, so that both the end and the stem come into contact, it can leave a pattern of distinctive fissures around the crushing injury which Slater says he has seen before. It wouldn't show on a leg, or an arm, but it might on a skull, where the bones are close to the surface and relatively flat. He thinks our victim has two injuries with this pattern. One near to the temple – which caused the fatal bleed – and another to the back of her head. He also thinks – though this is less certain – that some of the bruising patterns on her thighs and back might be attributable to this kind of weapon.'

'We'll know for certain whether there's any-thing in it from the London expert,' White said. 'That will take a couple of days. Meanwhile, we need to run with what Slater is telling us.'

'And the secrecy?' Karen asked, though she knew the answer already.

White pulled a face. Spencer answered. 'Just to be careful,' he said. 'I don't know who has access to these weapons apart from police, but it's possible – just possible – that we're looking at an injury caused by a police weapon.'

They sat in silence for a moment, thinking about that.

'What do you want me to do, then?' she asked.

'Run a few discreet enquiries,' Spencer said.

'How discreet?'

'Just you,' White said. 'Maybe one other, if there's anyone on your team you think you can absolutely trust to keep a lid on it.'

She thought for a moment.

'Is there?' Spencer asked.

Could she trust Marcus? He had let her down this morning, but he was a white sheet compared to the other three. 'I'll consider it,' she replied. 'You want me to try tracing missing batons from this Force?'

'See how available they are to the public first,' Spencer said.

'Then go as wide as you need to,' White chipped in. 'But keep it quiet. We don't want to tip anybody off.'

'Or be accused of that.' Spencer smiled ironically. 'We don't want the press getting it at all, in fact.'

9

6 September 2004

Something fantastic has happened to me. I feel as if my whole life is about to change – all the shit I've suffered over the last three years. I met a guy at college and he seems really interested, in a serious way. I have to write it down, even though the sessions have stopped with Angela now, and nobody is forcing me to write anything any more. But I've got used to scribbling to myself, so I have to write about this – there's no one else I can tell, and I'm so excited about it. I have my legs and fingers crossed that nothing will happen to mess this one up, like with Ash.

I'm almost too frightened to even write his name, in case it's bad luck. But that's silly. Why should it be bad luck to think about him, to think about what might happen? I feel like just lying back and dreaming about him all day! He has been so kind to me. If I was talking like Beryl – or the priest – I would say, 'As one door closes, another opens.' The priest would say it was Jesus, watching out for me. Or my guardian angel. Ha!

His name is Martin Bradley and he's my age – twenty – but his birthday is in November, so he's really almost twenty-one and a year older than me. He seems very old, very sensible, but with a strange sense of humour, so sometimes I can't work out when he's joking and when he isn't. I don't mean he's stuffy or boring. I just mean he's mature – he's seen things and done things and knows what life is like. Not like that little boy I was with two months ago – Ruben – who almost fell through the floor when I told him about Andrew, and didn't even call me again afterwards. I wouldn't have wanted Ruben to meet Andrew, anyway. Same with that guy Robbie, the month before. They were both nice – attractive, fit guys with a lot going for them (Robbie said he had a trial for the Man United youth squad) – but they were too young to be serious with. They were fun, and that was that. Truth is, I couldn't even talk to them for very long without getting bored. And anyway, talking wasn't what they wanted to do.

Martin isn't like that. He's talented – an artist, or at least that's what he wants to be. I've seen some of the things he's drawn and they are fantastic, the best pictures I've ever seen. He did a painting of the front of the college and it looked just like a photo. Then he does other stuff which looks like the things Andrew does, but I suppose they must mean something, because they let him on the foundation course and, anyway, I've seen his normal stuff, so he really can draw when he wants to. He knows he can't do it to earn money – he's already trained as a car mechanic – but it's what he does to be himself, he says, at least while he can't find work in a garage.

I met him at college, because I used to see him hanging around during break periods by himself, and finally I felt so sorry for him that I went over and spoke to him. I didn't need to, because college has been one of the best things to ever happen to me, and I've three or four really good friends from there, so I'm almost never by myself. I could have just stood there with Jenny and Sue, laughing at him (wondering about him, too, I bet, because Sue told me a few months ago that she thought he 'had it' – she likes guys with long hair and Martin has long, wavy brown hair, down to his shoulders).

I'm so glad now that Angela forced me to enrol, though I should have stuck to my guns and tried for the French course, instead of science foundation (which Angela thought I'd be so good at, but which is too much of a struggle and makes me feel thick). The languages students all get to do a trip to their foreign countries once a year, which is what I would really want – something really exciting like that. We don't get to do anything interesting. It's not that I hate Shipley and want to escape or anything. This flat they gave me is brilliant. It's the first place I've lived with Andrew that I haven't been able to hear the neighbours all the time. And it's only a five-minute walk to the canal and the Five Locks and the Glen, which Andrew loves. We really have an OK life here, compared to the shit we went through in Chapeltown, or even Keighley. If they didn't deal smack down by the bins it would be perfect. So I don't want to sound ungrateful, but I've always wanted to see other places, further away. I don't want to be stuck in this country all my life, like Beryl and Jack. Jack thinks it's something to be proud of that he has never been outside England all his sad, stupid life. That's how small-minded bigots are made. I want Andrew to know a bit more of the world, so he doesn't grow up like that.

Martin doesn't get on so well at college, I think. I'm not sure it's his thing. I'm more forward than he is. You have to be a bit pushy to meet people there, and he's not. He's more shy than pushy. He seems happy

84

to stand around, with no one to talk to. When I went over to him and asked him for a light he looked too shocked to speak. I asked him if he came here often, which was a joke, obviously, but he didn't get it. He was a bit more relaxed next time I spoke to him, though. That was when he told about the trouble he'd had with his parents, and why he was going back to college at the age of twenty. So we have something big in common. We both hate our parents.

He wasn't kicked out, like I was. He still lives with them, but they sound as bad as Beryl and Jack. They forced him to leave school when he was sixteen, to get a job in a garage. They don't know he's going to college. If they found out he was doing the art foundation instead of looking for a job they'd kill him. That's what he said, though he's nearly twenty-one now, so he can't have meant that. He can do what he likes really, like I did. I told him that, but he got upset about it. He talks about his parents as if they are disgusting, but he doesn't like me joining in. I can understand that – even after I knew Beryl was a cow I didn't used to like it if someone else said it to me.

Martin ran away twice, he says, but they sent relatives to find him. I think they might have hit him when they found him, because he shivers a bit when he talks about it, like he's afraid. It's a big family, everyone poking around in everyone else's business. Martin's on the council waiting list for a flat – they don't know that, either.

It's not a flashy love thing, looking at each other like stupid teenagers, because we're both too old for that – we've both seen too much of it and how it ends. But he told me yesterday that he cares for me seriously, and that meant more to me than anything any of the *others said, because he's slow to say things like that, so he must have meant it. I wouldn't want it to be an infatuation. It would be too hard with a three-year-old in tow. OK, Andrew goes to nursery now, so there's more time to sit around and dream, but it's still hectic compared to most teenagers' lives. I think what we feel about each other is something that will last a bit longer, and that's why I'm excited about it, but in a different way. We haven't even been to bed yet. We've kissed and cuddled – and me being me I always want to go further – but he says we should take our time, make sure it 'means something'. I think he might be a virgin, though I wouldn't dare tell anyone that, because Sue and Jenny would laugh if they thought he was still a virgin, living with his mum at nearly twenty-one years old, when there's nothing to laugh about at all. That's his choice and there's nothing wrong with it. Though sometimes I think it might not be his choice and he might have a problem instead. Sometimes when we're kissing and we get a bit carried away I touch him there and he pulls back really quickly, as if it hurts him or something. As if it gives him an electric shock! The first time it happened I was really stupid and insensitive and laughed out loud – because it was so surprising. He got very angry about me laughing. He can look a bit frightening when he gets angry, but all men are like that. And it didn't last long. I didn't dare ask him about it after that, though, so I don't know what's going on, but I don't like to think it's a problem, what Angela would call an 'issue'. He'll get round to these things in his own time, I think, which is fine. It's not the most important thing.*

I told him about Andrew straight away, and I knew

at once that he wasn't bothered about it. It didn't put him off at all. I waited until we'd met a couple of times, outside college, before I let him meet Andrew – because you have to be sure. But it was all fine – they got on really well. OK, Andrew cried a bit when Martin snatched him off me too roughly once, but Martin's still the first guy I've met who hasn't thought that Andrew was some kind of dead weight round my neck.

10

Marcus had wanted to work the night. Not because it would have given him a good excuse to cancel Mairead, but because it summed up why he wanted to work homicide enquiries at all: they were cases where the results were important enough to make working through the night necessary. A young woman had been tortured and beaten to death. It didn't fit to knock off at five, go home and eat, watch TV and get an early night – as if his job were no more significant than any other nine-to-five. But that was what his team had been told to do.

His mind was working overtime anyway. All the way home he couldn't stop thinking about the girl, couldn't get the image of her body to fade away. He met Mairead as planned – at a restaurant in Leeds – partly to try to get his brain to focus on other things, but then spent most of the meal talking about the case. Or rather talking about why he might feel so badly about these things generally, since he didn't want to go into too much detail about the facts. He hardly touched the food. He got so animated talking about how people could deliberately burn and mutilate each other that he actually started shaking. He forgot entirely his resolution to keep his boss's daughter at a distance.

It wasn't good. It gave Mairead the excuse to sit staring at him as if he were the only man on the planet who still cared when people got hurt. Maybe that was her image of him – part of why she was so interested in someone nine years older than her. The sensitive, protective figure. The father figure, of course. When he started to shake it gave her the chance to reach across, take his hand and whisper reassuring things. 'I haven't met any other police officers who get upset because they brood about the last hours of a murder victim – including my mum,' she said, as if it were a point in his favour instead of something clearly dysfunctional.

But he appreciated the contact. It was what he needed. The day had left him feeling like a frightened child. He craved warmth, affection – sensations that would crowd out the horror. It had been the same the night after his first murder call-out, but he hadn't known Mairead then.

He had met her a little over two months ago. She was on the long summer holiday from university – English lit at St Andrews – and was staying with her mother in Ilkley. Around the end of May he had fallen into a routine of going round to Karen's most Saturday nights for dinner.

Mairead had eaten with them a couple of times in early June. They had hit it off in a way he imagined would have created tension with her mum, since it was so obviously based on them being much younger than her, but Karen had instead encouraged them, it seemed. Since then things had drifted effortlessly into more complicated arrangements. They had met at least five times without Karen knowing about it.

He drove her daughter back to his flat feeling confused. He would have liked to have felt balanced enough to insist on dropping Mairead back at Karen's place, but he definitely didn't want to be alone, and Mairead was keen to see him – so why fight it? She was good company; she listened well, responded with empathy. Most nineteen-year-olds he knew weren't like that. It didn't feel like he was sitting there with a child. And his responses to her, as on every other occasion he had met her, took him a little by surprise. He hoped it wasn't just that she reminded him of her mother.

She had Karen's green eyes, a similar facial structure, dark hair and height (she was a little shorter than him, which would make her about the same as Karen). She had her mother's build, too except that Mairead was so young she really did look boyish; tall, slim, small breasts, but with broad shoulders and the kind of subtle muscle definition he would have assumed came from a gym, if he hadn't known she went rock climbing every weekend.

What she wanted to do after uni was act, and she had already got a couple of one-line parts in a soap they filmed in Manchester. He hadn't seen the episodes, but was sure she looked good on screen. She carried herself to her full height, walked and moved with a presence most teenagers lacked, and had exactly the shape he habitually went for in younger women. She was easily more attractive than Karen, if looks alone were what counted, but by itself appearance had never produced that spark for him. Usually it made him want to go no further than sex.

With Mairead he had resisted that so far. Partly because he worked with her mother (would prefer to sleep with her mother, in fact), but also because he really did get something out of being with her. He didn't get the impression – as he had the night before (at least before the snoring started) – that he was scribbling obscenities across something pristine and perfect, a *tabula rasa*. Mairead could *almost* keep up with him. It had limited mileage, because at the end of the day, no matter what she had seen and done, she was still only a teenager. But it made him feel slightly more normal than usual to be sitting in a restaurant with someone younger. The women he usually ended up taking for dinner were nearly always considerably older than him.

In his flat he poured them glasses of wine, checked the time (he was due on at eight the next morning and didn't want to stink of booze again), then kicked off his shoes and settled back on his sofa, head propped on a cushion. He lay the entire length of the sofa, so she couldn't come and sit next to him. It was a futile delaying gesture, a nod to his resolutions. It wouldn't last long – she was

90

only there at all because he *wanted* her to be near to him. She sat on the chair by the TV.

'Maybe I took a wrong turn,' he said, still feeling agitated. 'Maybe I should have gone into something else instead.' He looked over at her. 'You never wanted to follow your mum into the police?'

She pulled a face, as if the thought were merely risible, then realized that might insult him. 'I've had enough of that already,' she said. Her voice wavered – she was probably a little drunk, he realized; she had put away three large glasses of wine with the meal. 'You wouldn't believe some of the things that happened to me because of Mum.' She stopped, censoring herself.

'You don't give much away about yourself,' he said. 'But I'd like to hear more.' *More about your mother* would have been more accurate. 'You don't seem like other nineteen-year-olds I've met.'

'I'm not,' she replied quietly. 'Maybe one day I'll tell you why. When I can trust you with it.'

'You can trust me now.'

'I can trust you as far as I can throw you,' she said. 'But maybe I like it that way.' She stood up and walked over to his CD collection, took out some CDs and inspected them.

They had been back to his flat before and she knew her way around. On both previous occasions she had slept in his bed and he had slept where he was now, but it had been hard to keep things that way. On both occasions she had wanted him in the bed with her, and had made that very clear. She usually wasn't slow to say what she meant. The last visit they had had a long discussion about it all and still ended on the

91

couch with neither of them wearing much. The memories of that flicked through his mind. She had been beautiful to touch. But no more than any other young body. Skin like the girl last night, for example. Smooth, taut – no wrinkles or flab. Or like the dead girl might have had, before the beating and the incipient decomposition. Images of her slotted into his brain and he rolled slightly on the couch, feeling queasy. He took a gulp of wine.

She turned back from the rack empty-handed. She had joked that the stuff he listened to – mainly music from the nineties, when he had been her age – was old men's music.'

'You didn't follow your father into the police, did you?' she asked.

'My father was a social worker,' he said. 'He's retired. Haven't I told you that already?'

'I don't think so. Maybe you see too many women to remember what you've told each of them.' She smiled as she said it, but didn't look amused. So far he had been honest with her about his sex life. She had been more evasive about her own, though he knew she had a boyfriend at uni she was supposedly 'committed' to.

'What about *your* dad?' he asked. Watching the way she moved, he already regretted taking up the whole couch. There was an implicit sexuality to her movements that was completely absent in her mum. It made him want her closer. 'Your name comes from him, right?' he asked. Her name was Mairead Martin, not Mairead Sharpe.

'My dad?' she said, as if thinking carefully what to say. 'He isn't a social worker. And, yes, his

92

name is James Martin.'

'He's still alive?' Karen had never mentioned him.

She nodded.

'But separated from your mum?'

She frowned. 'You could say that.'

'Does he live here, in Leeds?'

'He lives in Northern Ireland.'

'He's Irish?'

She laughed strangely. 'That's what he would say. He's British. I said *Northern* Ireland.'

'Are you from there? Were you born there?' She had no Irish accent.

'No.'

'You don't want to talk about it?'

'Not really.'

He shrugged, pretending to be uninterested. 'OK.'

She sat down again. 'So why *are* you in the police, Mark? Mum says you're bright enough not to be a fascist thug.'

He laughed at that. 'Does she? I'm not sure she's right. Maybe I once was. But your brain is like a muscle. Parts of it die if you don't use it.'

'She says you were a *child prodigy*, that you're wasted in anything requiring submission to authority.' She had a sly look as she repeated the expression, as if she were taunting him.

'You talk about me a lot with your mum, then?' Was she inventing it? If not, what did it mean – that Karen approved or disapproved? 'I hope you don't tell her the things we get up to. I'd have to stop seeing you if she knew.'

'We don't get up to anything. So there's noth-

93

ing to tell. *Yet.*' She looked provocatively at him, wine glass in front of her face.

'Not yet – no,' he said. He watched her drink slowly from the glass, eyes still on him. 'But it might be difficult to keep it like that.'

'Might it?'

'For me. Maybe not for you.' He shrugged. He knew that wasn't true. But all the same, maybe he shouldn't assume she was going to stay the night. Maybe she would change her mind, get up and leave him alone. He didn't want that.

'Is it true, then?' she asked, sliding her eyes away. 'Were you a prodigy?'

'I went to university early. That's all.' He tried to sound casual about it, but it was where all his problems – such as they were – had begun.

'What age? Where?'

'You interrogating me?' If he was going to talk about himself he really did want her closer. He moved his legs on the sofa, making room for her. 'Sit down here and I'll talk to you about it.'

'I thought we'd decided not to go there again.'

'I'm only asking you to sit next to me.'

'Are you?' She stood up, moved over and sat down, placing a hand on his thigh. He relaxed a little. She was wearing a light dress with a dark abstract pattern in purple and blue. It came down to just below her knees. She had sandals on her feet and a delicate silver anklet on the left ankle. She had removed a light, very long cotton cardigan when they arrived and the dress beneath was so thin he could see the outline of her underwear. She wasn't wearing a bra. He could feel her skin pressing against his legs, see her nipples pressing against the dress.

'I just want you to be nice to me,' he said. 'I'm feeling fragile.'

It was so pathetic she might have laughed – if she had been older she would have. But she was too young for emotional cynicism. She stood up and moved past his head, then shifted him down the couch a little, so she could sit behind him, with his head resting on her thigh, almost in her lap. This was how it started last time, he remembered, with her taking the initiative like this. She placed her hand on his head and stroked it gently. He looked up at her but she flushed when his eyes met hers, like a guilty schoolgirl, he thought – suddenly too aware of the physical proximity. Or maybe it was the age difference. 'Talk to me,' she said, maybe to cover her embarrassment. 'Relax.'

'I went to Oxford,' he said. 'But I started when I was fourteen.'

'You went to Oxford at fourteen? You must have been a real goggle-head.'

'Maybe.' Childish ridicule. He was used to it.

'I didn't mean it to sound bad. I meant you *really* must have been a child prodigy. How incredible!'

He looked carefully at her. Was she serious? 'Sounds impressive, but it's not,' he said. 'It fucked me up.'

'You're not fucked up.'

'You don't know how fucked up I am.'

'In what way?'

He took another breath. 'In all sorts of ways,' he said. *Like I want to fuck your mum more than you, for example*. 'I was the victim of a little social experiment, you see.' He started telling her about it, concentrating. He had to concentrate. When he spoke about it, it was like his breath kept catching in his throat, so that he had to make a conscious effort to breathe normally. It had always been like that, yet when he told people the story they never quite seemed to get it. Mostly he had the impression they thought he must have been looking to *invent* childhood problems.

'When I was seven the head teacher at school *decided* I was a child prodigy. No one had noticed anything before that. At least, that's the way my parents still tell it. I don't remember any of this. The head met my parents and offered them a little experiment. They could start me in a class four years above my own age group, to see how I got on. My mother was against it, but my father was all for it. They argued about it and he won.' He stopped and sipped from his wine, feeling the resentment twisting inside. He was distant enough from it now to know that his father had done nothing really wrong, certainly nothing malicious. He was given the opportunity to advance his kid and so took it. But that didn't stop the lingering resentment – directed at both of them. His father was behind it, but his mother hadn't stopped it. With an adult perspective he could just about forgive her that now – he knew enough about the relationship between them to guess how difficult it would have been to resist his father, once he was set on the plan. But through most of his adult years he had hated them both for it, and still held it against his father in many ways, no matter how much he now understood the reasoning.

'It worked?' she prompted him.

'If you judge these things by exam success, yes, it worked. I sat GCSEs at twelve and A levels at fourteen. I got a place at Oxford to study pure mathematics.'

'Fucking hell. Pure maths at fourteen!'

He caught her eyes and saw the admiration, amazement even, yet it didn't seem either admirable or amazing to him. 'Don't be so impressed. My brain just happened to work that way. At the same time I was breathing in theorems and proofs I could hardly write my name. I couldn't do what you're doing – write essays on things – *still* couldn't.'

'Those things are easy.'

'Depends on your brain. They're not so easy for me. And anyway, pure maths is utterly useless once you've finished uni. It teaches you nothing about anything.'

'I think it's incredible, Mark.' She leaned forward and pecked his forehead, her voice betraying uncertainty. She could see him breathing too fast, he thought, though he was working carefully to conceal it. She was observant, like her mum.

'It's not incredible at all,' he said. 'It should have been ignored. There are more important things to do for your kids. The effect on me was...' He paused, groping for the word. 'It was *devastating*. And I didn't even realize that until much later.'

'Devastating?'

She wasn't getting it. He had told the same

story to her mother. Karen had got it at once, of course.

'Imagine it. From the age of seven you are mixing exclusively with kids four years older than you. Imagine it carefully. Can you remember how much older the kids just one year above you seemed when you were at school?' Only last year, he thought, so she should remember. She didn't reply, though. She was concentrating on his face, looking for cues. 'It was like I was mixing only with adults, through all my childhood,' he said. 'When I went to uni it was worse. I stayed with an uncle who lived in Cowley, so I had only weekly contact with my mother – sometimes less – and all the people I was with were adults. I mean, they really were adults. They were free to do whatever they wanted – drink, smoke, fuck, live in their own places, earn money, spend it, travel, whatever – but I was legally still a kid. I couldn't join in anything they were doing, yet that was all I was able to do, all I had been pro-grammed to do for the last eight years. I couldn't mix with kids my own age any more. I couldn't even talk to them. They seemed like babies. They *were*, by comparison. So I was caught in between. The net effect of their little experiment was to make me an outcast from my own age group – a kid who didn't fit in anywhere. The only friend I had was my uncle. It was totally fucking miser-able. I can't even begin to explain to you how miserable and depressed I was throughout my teens. I will never forgive them for it.' His voice rose as he told her, the hostility seeping into it. 'Do you understand what I'm saying?' he asked,

98

twisting back and looking up at her. 'Do you see what I mean?'

She nodded too vigorously. 'It sounds awful, Mark,' she said. 'I feel bad for you.' She was frowning intensely. But she was already an actress at heart, so maybe it meant nothing.

He sat up. 'I'm sorry,' he said. 'I didn't mean to get angry.'

'I can see why you're angry.'

'I doubt you can. Nobody ever understands it. They think I must be mad – to start out so *gifted*,' he tried not to spit the word, 'and yet to resent it so much.'

'Did you get on with your uncle?'

'He was fantastic. He didn't believe my father should have done it. He was like my real father. At least, that's how I thought of it. But then he died.'

'While you were living with him?'

He nodded. 'He died in my last year at Oxford, just before finals. Of course, that didn't stop me sitting them.' He waved a hand, contemptuous of himself. 'I had to get used to friends dying on me. He was just the first. Everyone I get close to dies young.' He heard his voice crack with unwanted emotion. 'If you are so fucked up that you can only form friendships with people much older than yourself then it's a kind of occupational hazard that they begin to die on you.' He stood up and shook his head, trying to clear it. 'Maybe I shouldn't be telling you all this.'

'Why not?'

Because you're just a kid, he thought. 'It's not good for me to talk about it. It's not what I need tonight. It makes me sound a bit mad.'

She stood up, looking confused. 'Sorry. I don't think you're mad. I only asked because I'm interested in you. Do you want me to leave?'

He tried to keep his eyes calm. 'No. Don't leave. I don't want you to leave.' He stepped closer to her. She was too young, but she knew how to soothe him. He would have to fuck her to get there, no doubt – because that was what the young thought you had to do – but afterwards she would lie there and stroke his head, and it would be worth it for that alone. That was the *real* story of his life, maybe, the only lasting consequence of the experiment, that all he was looking for, all of the time, was simple affection. Weaned too soon.

'You want me to stay like before?' she asked. 'With me in there and you in here?' She looked like she might actually refuse, if that's all that was on offer.

He tried to look doubtful. 'I don't know. What do you want?' They were standing very close to each other now, hands at their sides, like idiots. She was so like her mother it was irresistible.

'I want to sleep *with* you, Mark,' she said. 'You know that.' She stepped forward and put her arms around him, very gently. It almost felt like she did it with love, so that for a moment he feared he might start crying, it was so tender, so touching. But he didn't. Now would be the time to tell her about his rule, he thought, instead. But he had already done that, ages ago. It hadn't changed a thing.

Monday

11

'You've been checking up on me,' Karen said. She kept her voice low and slow, didn't move her hand from where it was resting on Michael Surani's bare chest, didn't shift her position in the bed at all. She tried to make it sound casual. Her cheeks were still flushed from what he had just done to her, so that wasn't too difficult. Surani was on his side, his legs entangled with her own, his head resting on an elbow so that his eyes were no more than ten inches from hers.

They were in an enormous bed, which was just about the only piece of furniture in a very large room. The covers were long since abandoned on the parquet floor – the ambient temperature was air-conditioned to a pleasant twenty-one degrees – yet Karen was so hot she could feel the skin on her chest, shoulders, upper arms and neck burning. She was slippery with perspiration. One of his hands was still moving between her legs, absent-mindedly almost, so that she had to try to ignore it to concentrate. The sensations were keeping her off-guard, with only half a mind on what he was saying. Was that the point? For a moment – when he had moved his knee between her legs – she had thought he was going to start on her again, while they were both still slightly breathless, but then the questions had started. Just gentle enquiries at first, as if he were interested in her and wanted to know more – and surely that was true, except it very quickly became clear he already knew things she had worked most of her life to keep secret, things you couldn't get from asking someone to trawl through newspaper clippings.

'Of course I've been checking upon you,' he said. 'I care about you, Karen. I want to know more.' He had a seductive voice – unusually deep, with crisp, clear, public-school vowels and a tendency to crack in the lower registers, as if he had a permanent cold, but without the stuffiness. It wasn't the voice he had been born with. He had told her it was the result of a botched childhood operation to remove polyps from his vocal chords.

'So if you wanted to know more why didn't you just ask me?' she said. Her voice caught a little as his fingers slid inside her, his thumb doing something else entirely at the same time. He knew how to get her going. She had to resist the urge to stop him.

'I *am* asking you. I'm asking you now,' he said. 'And anyway, are you saying you haven't checked up on *me?*'

She held back a gasp as he moved and did something with his other hand. 'I'm a police officer,' she said. 'I was paid to check up on you. You were a witness in a murder case.'

'You're sure you're not still being paid?' He smiled, then before she could answer, he leaned forward and started to kiss her. She opened her mouth and closed her eyes. He was so good at it she was panting slightly now. How many times had they been like this? Only six or seven times, in just over a month, yet it was as if he had been sleeping with her for a year. He had been a keen, active little explorer in the time available to them, made sure he knew exactly what made her buzz. He was good at coming up with variations, too – nothing dramatic, so far – but something different each time, getting progressively more deviant. She had been happy to lie back and enjoy it, give him the feeling he was leading, but no doubt he would change that when the time was right as well.

'And you actually killed three people? Shot them?' He broke away to ask, but only a few inches. He sounded as if he might be asking about something admirable. It gave her an excuse to frown, shift weight, move away from him a little more.

'I don't like to be reminded of that,' she said. She had to take a deep breath to be able to say it clearly.

He stopped moving his fingers. 'I'm sorry. Of course not. How insensitive of me.'

But he had changed the subject.

That he knew about the shooting incident from ten years ago didn't bother her. It had been all over the newspapers. It was public knowledge. Her own investigation for murder in 2001 was more sensitive. But the questions that alarmed her hadn't been about that, either. What he had started asking her about had been Northern Ireland. That was infinitely worse. She hadn't even told him she had grown up there, but he had made a comment about Jim Martin – Mairead's father – and that wasn't something he could read about anywhere other than her personnel file.

105

'Where did you find out about that?' she asked. His fingers were still inside her. He moved his upper torso closer, pushing tightly against her. He was shorter than her, but much thicker set. He had a chest like a barrel, packed with muscle, with an upper-arm strength sufficient to crush her. At least, that's how it felt. She had been inside three of his properties now. There was a gym in each and every one. The place near Sherburn was kept by a full-time personal trainer. Surani got to use him about once a month, but he made sure he worked out in one of the gyms for at least an hour a day, each and every day. If you met him on a professional basis he was like every other top-drawer businessman – impeccably dressed, scrupulously polite, but beneath it full of prowling, animal energy. Category-A crooks were exactly the same, and it was almost certain Michael Surani was a bit of both. But so far she had never felt afraid of him. Once things had become personal between them his ability to relax and focus had surprised her.

She slid a hand between them and found that he was rock hard. He groaned, stretching against her and moving to kiss again. She moved her head away. 'Where did you find out about that?' she asked again. She pretended she was playing a game: *Tell me or I go no further.*

He grinned, picking it up. She moved her hand gently, encouraging him. He stopped grinning, closed his eyes. 'About you shooting three men?' he asked.

'No. Who told you I was from Northern Ireland? Who told you about Jim Martin?' It was all she could do to make it sound relaxed. Whatever was happening between her legs was irrelevant compared to him knowing that.

'Does it bother you I know?' His eyes were still closed.

'It bothers me not knowing how you know.' Again, she tried to sound light-hearted, but it was too much – something slipped through the mask, into her tone. He caught it at once, opening his eyes. 'You're serious? You're bothered?'

She sighed, then took her hand away. She rolled further onto her back, so their legs separated and his fingers slid out. The way to play it is always as close to the truth as possible, she thought. Assume he knows everything, then use that. Men of less means than Michael Surani had managed to buy access to her past, so why shouldn't he have? What she needed to do was get him to trust her so much he would start talking about himself without her prompting it. That wasn't the entire reason she was here – not any longer – but that was *meant* to be the entire reason. That was how it had started. She could give him bits of her past to encourage that. Assuming he already knew it all already, there was nothing lost.

So far she had spent nearly five weeks just letting him play with her. It had been exciting, easy, stimulating, and something was definitely developing between them that went beyond the sex. That was how she wanted it. It was the only sure way to hook him. If conflicts developed she would deal with them. It wouldn't be the first time. Meanwhile, since she had been moved off Sledgehammer – the enquiry in which he was potentially a suspect – she hadn't asked him a single sensitive question about himself. She had certainly gone nowhere near his brother in Pakistan.

Surani was British, born and educated in the UK. He had grown up in London and his father had spent most of his life there, but the family came originally from what was now north-west Pakistan – Surani was a Pathan name. She had first come across him because a man called Abdul Haq had been shot outside the very property they were in now. As far as they had been able to determine, a competitor from Pakistan had probably put a contract on Surani, sending Haq to do the dirty work. But Haq had screwed up somehow. Instead of shooting Surani he had himself ended up dead.

They had been unsure what the competition was about, because they didn't know just how dirty Surani's money was. All they knew for certain was that there was a lot of it. One transport company he owned had been recently sold for a fat £1.3 million. Karen had spent the best part of six months digging into his funding, finances and business network, with no clear conclusion. Maybe bulk heroin importation was behind it, maybe not. Suspicion and informant information were different from evidence.

The Sledgehammer enquiry had treated Surani as a victim, of sorts – on the face of it he was a wealthy, productive member of society – while at the same time quietly devoting considerable resources into examining whether he had killed Haq. At the time Surani had employed a pro-

108

fessional bodyguard called David Ostler, a former Special Services man who was no stranger to killing. The suspicion had been that Ostler might have shot Haq, on Surani's orders. But the enquiry had got nowhere with that, or any other line, and after four months it had been scaled back and Karen and her team moved on to other jobs, officially ending her involvement with him.

Until Francis Doyle had become interested. Doyle was the present front-end of Karen's lingering involvement with 'Intelligence and Security' – as Doyle liked to put it. The connection had been long and fraught, spanning some twenty-five years of chaotic, intermittent taskings, and commencing with her induction – as a student in Belfast in the early eighties – into a military-intelligence cell that no one now admitted had ever existed. Contact with her former handlers had been infrequent since then, but addictively intense. The security services were not interested in Surani himself – whether or not he had ordered Haq's killing meant nothing at that level – but in his brother, still living in Pakistan, who ranked very high on someone's intelligence wish-list. Karen hadn't been given more information than that. What Doyle wanted – what would count as success – was for her to get Surani so relaxed that *he* started talking about his brother, without her even having to let on she knew he had one. It might be a long game to play, but it was what Doyle had asked her to do. That she happened to be so strongly attracted to Surani was a gift.

'I don't care that you know I killed three men who were sexually abusing a little girl on the

Thorpe Edge Estate,' she said. 'I'm not proud of what happened. But I didn't do anything wrong. They were armed; they were killers. There weren't any choices to be made at the time.' She rolled sideways and sat on the edge of the bed. She had to act as if the memories disturbed her. That was how normal people would be, if they had shot and killed men. 'That you know about Jim is different, though,' she said. 'That makes me frightened Michael. Nobody knows about that.' She looked back at him. 'So how *do* you know?'

He sat up, frowning. 'I'm sorry, Karen. I didn't think you would take it like this. I have money, as you know.' He shrugged, as if to apologize for the fact. 'I didn't sit on the Internet and read about you. I paid someone to find out. He gave me a report. It was all very professional.'

As if she were a prospective employee. Application for the post of cleaner, perhaps.

'Who?'

'Who did I pay? David, of course. David Ostler. He won't have done it himself, I'm sure. He will have contracted it to an agency. It will have been discreet.'

David Ostler. The bodyguard they suspected of killing Abdul Haq. She stood up, genuinely agitated, no need to act it at all. On the floor she found her clothes. She started to dress.

'What are you doing, Karen? You're not going?' He sounded ever so slightly panicky.

'I don't know,' she said. 'I feel cold.'

'So come back to bed.'

She glanced back at him. He was still frowning. He looked so fucking attractive, so fucking innocent, all the time, whatever the allegation. As if ordering Ostler to kill someone couldn't even enter his mind.

She paced over to the window. They were in a house at the edge of the moorland above Sutton-in-Craven, surrounded by fields and woods on three sides. The building was new, a modern design he had drawn up himself, he said. In total, he spent about a month in the place each year. Most of the time he was in London, or Pakistan. The bedroom they were in now took up an entire floor roughly the same area as her whole house, double en-suite bathroom, jacuzzi, sauna and steam-room not included.

'I thought Ostler was no longer with you?' she said. She turned to watch him.

He coloured, suddenly embarrassed. 'I'm sorry,' he said. 'This was about two months ago. Maybe more.'

'You got somebody to investigate me over two months ago?' She was surprised, though she shouldn't have been. Their relationship hadn't even started then. 'Did you do that for everyone on the squad – everyone who dealt with you?'

'Of course not. Just for you.' He looked away, still embarrassed. He wasn't hard any longer. His hand ran through his hair, nervously. He was her own age, but his hair was still dark. If he dyed it – and she suspected he did – it was done very well. 'I liked you long before any of this began between us,' he said.

And that's what you do when you like someone, she thought. She leaned on the windowsill and looked out across the lawn to the gates and the lane beyond. A light late-summer evening, conditions not very different from the night Haq had been shot, right there, beside the gateposts, the forensics clearly indicating he had been shot where he fell. Yet they had failed to locate a single witness. No one had heard the shot; no one had even seen the body until halfway through the morning after. The turn-off to the gates was deeply recessed, the road quiet and exclusive, but even so, she could see the odd car driving past on the lane right now. All it would take was a glance towards the gates. Instead, by the time they had found Haq, there was no real way of disproving Surani's account. There were security cameras on the gates and all over the gardens. They should have recorded the event. She knew that Surani's present bodyguard – a man called Dean Summers – was somewhere in the bowels of the house right now, watching the screens. Maybe he had even watched them fucking. There were no obvious cameras in the room, but that meant nothing.

Surani and Ostler had been in London on the night Haq was shot, he said. The cameras – which were set to record twenty-four hours a day, even when the house was empty – had been malfunctioning. It was proveable that Surani *was* in London, but as for Ostler, that had come down to Surani providing him with an alibi. Maybe it was true. Maybe it wasn't. Without the CCTV footage they couldn't say. Either way she didn't like the idea that Ostler had been sticking his nose into her past.

'Can you find out where he got the information?' she asked. 'It's important.'

'I can. Of course.'

'Thank you. Was there anything else he told you that I should know about?'

Surani shrugged. 'I can't remember all of it. The stuff about you killing people stood out. That and the fact that Martin – a convicted IRA terrorist – was the father of your child, Mairead. There was some speculation about what you might have done in Northern Ireland for that to happen.'

'And what was the conclusion?' Her voice shook as she spoke. She didn't like it at all.

'Does it matter? Why don't you tell me about it yourself? Then we'll have the truth.' She looked at him and he tried smiling at her. 'Come back to bed, Karen. We all have pasts. It's nothing to be worried about.' She resisted the urge to ask him about his own, though it was a perfect cue.

We all have pasts. She'd heard it before from other men forced to face up to what she had done. Was it really possible that Michael Surani already knew all of that? She expected men to walk out on her if they found out the full story. Maybe not Surani, though. He didn't even look remotely concerned. All that was getting to him was that she'd stopped the sex just when he was warming up again.

'I wasn't trying to hurt you,' he said.

'Maybe I will tell you about it,' she said. 'One day. When I can trust you.'

He nodded. 'Of course. I understand.'

'Do you have the file here?'

'No. It's in London. I could get it tomorrow, probably, if I ring now.' He slid off the bed and began to search the pile of clothing on the floor, looking for his mobile. 'Gary Swales,' he said, as he was going through the pockets of his clothes. He said it as if it had only just occurred to him. 'That was another thing. There was something about you breaking his jaw, a year ago.'

Arm, not jaw – and the injury was a hairline fracture that hadn't even required a cast – but that was also something you could find out from reading newspapers. It needn't have bothered her, but something in his tone prompted her. 'You know Swales?'

He paused, mobile in hand, then sat back on the bed. 'You want me to call for the file?'

'Yes, but later will do. Do you know Swales?'

He hesitated, considering the question. 'I've done business with him.'

'A lot of business?'

'Enough. I know him quite well.'

'Swales is an upper-tier heroin dealer. What kind of business do you do with him?'

He shrugged, as if the information were news to him, but not of any consequence. 'I don't know anything about that,' he said. 'Obviously.' He stared at her, face expressionless.

'But you knew he was charged with murder last year?' She sounded like a police officer now.

'Of course. It was in the newspapers. He wasn't convicted.' He patted the bed beside him. 'Come back over here, Karen. Don't stand so far away, as if you hate me.'

Was that the impression she was giving him? She exhaled heavily, forcing her muscles to relax a little. She was very tense again. 'Of course I don't hate you,' she said. She gave him a weak smile.

'I'll be gone tomorrow for four weeks,' he said. To Pakistan. He had told her already. 'This is the last time we'll be together for a while. Let's not be like this.'

She nodded, smiled again, a bit brighter this time. It was an effort. 'You're right. I wish you weren't going.' She started to walk back towards him. 'But the Swales thing touches a button. Is he a friend of yours?'

'Not a friend, no. Like I said, I've done business with him. *Did* you break his jaw? If you did he's never mentioned it to me.'

Over drinks in the bar of some golf club, no doubt. It sounded too close for comfort. Ostler with her personal file; Swales and Surani chatting about her. It made her spine prickle. 'It was his arm, not his jaw,' she said. 'Swales was a murder suspect. Things became a bit personal between us. He put a contract on me.'

Surani raised his eyebrows, surprised. 'You sure about that?'

'Fairly sure,' she said. 'Why?'

'It seems a bit careless,' Surani said.

'And Swales isn't careless?'

'I wouldn't know. But you said he was upper tier. I assumed he would know better than to go for the police. That isn't what I would do – were I upper tier.' He smiled wryly.

You would get into bed with them, she thought. Keep them happy, ply them for information.

'What kind of contract was it?' He asked the question as if he were talking about something

115

legal, not something that had terrified her for three months of her life.

'What they call a breaker,' she said. She sat down near to him. He moved a hand across the distance between them, inviting her to take it. She didn't. 'That means someone was meant to damage me,' she said. 'The information was that if they couldn't get to me then my daughter would do as a replacement. There was a plan to run her over. That was what bothered me.'

He looked genuinely appalled by that. He had a son himself, though never spoke about him. She only knew he had one from the background information they had given her. It hadn't come up through the enquiry at all.

'So you handled it by breaking his arm?' he asked, as if that were a rational option.

She shook her head. 'Depends who you believe. Swales said I put him against the wall and swung a chair at him. I said he lashed out at me and I defended myself.'

'And what really happened?'

She smiled at him, then took his hand. 'There were no witnesses and the CCTV camera covering the interview room was malfunctioning. So it was my word against his. Who would you believe?'

'You, of course.'

She nodded, then let him pull her towards him a little. When she was close enough he leaned forward and kissed her cheek. 'You're still angry with me,' he said. She didn't reply, so he kissed her again. She tried to thaw, enough to encourage him. He moved so that he was seated alongside her, touching her.

'The case was kicked out by a judge called Morgan,' she said. 'The evidence was too weak anyway, but that doesn't matter. I think the judge believed Swales. The malfunctioning CCTV bothered him.'

He shrugged. 'These things do happen. In real life.'

No trace of irony.

12

28 February 2005

I am so confused. I don't know what to do. I feel like just sitting here and crying, all the time. Everyone is being nice to me here, yet I feel like a prisoner. I even said that to Mary, a few days ago. It took a lot of courage to say it because I can recall all too well what she was like last year. Last year I think she would have hit me if I'd said something like that. I mean actually hit me. She has a terrible, explosive temper. I've seen her hit poor Simon, and he's almost twice her height. Once she picked up a pan off the cooker – full of food – and threw it at him. He had burns all over his face. She is so horrible to him it's hard to believe he's her son. I think he should move out, or report her to the police. Someone should do something to stop it. Martin says it's his arm. His mother can't stand the fact that she made something imperfect, that Simon came out of her, like that. Everything else in

117

her life is so neat and controlled. She has an obsession with cleanliness and keeping things tidy. She's much worse than Beryl ever was. Simon has a 'withered arm', as they used to call it. It's not perfect enough for her. Poor Simon. I think he is very unhappy. I wouldn't be like that to a child of mine. If this baby, when it is born, should come out with a problem like that – God forbid! – then I really don't think it would make any difference at all to me. Children are children. They all need to be loved and cared for. They didn't ask to be born.

I was sitting in the bathroom when I said it – when I told her how I felt. Sitting on the floor crying. Andrew was in the room they've made for the new baby, upstairs. They tolerate him being in there at the moment, but I can see they hate it. They hate Andrew, hate that he is here with us. And the worst thing is that I can see some of that rubbing off on Martin. He used to treat Andrew as if he were his son, but now I'm pregnant with his 'own' child he's different. He's started to behave like they do. Not as much, but I can see it starting. He's impatient with Andrew, shouts at him. He even said something about him being 'half-caste' the other day, and started asking me questions about who the 'real' father was and whether he wasn't interested in seeing his son. It sounded too much like his mother. He used to come back from visits to her last year – when we were all living in Shipley together – and report to me that his mum had said exactly those kinds of things. Because she didn't want him with me then, of course. She didn't want him with me full stop, but it made it worse that he was 'pretending' to be father to some 'half-caste monkey' – those were her words. Has Martin forgotten all that? We should

118

never have come here. We were happy in Shipley; everything was working out. Why did me being pregnant mean he had to go running back to his mum for help? I don't understand it.

She said it must be something hormonal when I told her I felt like a prisoner. 'It's your hormones, love,' she said. 'You can't think straight. It's a bit like being mad. But we'll watch out for you. Don't worry. You're family now, sort of. We look after our own here.' Then she told me about when she was five months pregnant with Martin – everything seemed weird, she said – because all she could concentrate on was the baby in her tummy. She loved him so much, even before he 'popped out'. I can see that, of course – because she dotes on Martin like he's still a five-year-old. It's as if the sun shines out of his arse. Why do I write it like that? It's not supposed to be a bad thing.

But surely it is bad? I can't understand why he puts up with it. She tells him exactly what to do, where to go, what to eat. And she smothers him. Literally. It makes me sick to watch. He's twenty-one years old, for Christ's sake! He's meant to be a grown man. He's the father of my unborn child. Yet she forces him to sit on her knee and cuddle her! At first, when we had just moved in here, he was embarrassed about it. But everything is changing. Now he just gives in. Now it's like it's normal – like he thinks that's what normal mothers do.

But she's not normal. She's no more normal than my own mother. She might even be worse. Until the beginning of December, when he told them I was pregnant, she wouldn't even speak to me. Refused to meet me. I was taking her little boy away from her. That was my impression. Martin even said that.

119

Back then he was sufficiently distant from her to be able to see things clearly. Now it's like he hasn't got a mind of his own. He's stopped painting altogether, quit college. He's meant to be looking for a job as a mechanic. His father is meant to be finding him one. But I don't think she wants that to happen. I think she wants him unemployed, so he just has to sit around here all day, keeping her company. It makes me feel ill to think about it. He's not like the person I met last year.

Everything changed overnight, once he told them I was pregnant. She wanted to meet me immediately, said she would be 'delighted' to help me, pleased to call me her 'daughter'. I shudder at the thought. It took me long enough to get rid of my real mother. I don't need another freak ruining my life. But that's what is happening. I didn't even want to get married. But she insisted, which means Martin insisted, too. It had to be 'legal', now that I was carrying 'her grandchild'. It had to be done properly. Which meant a grotty little register-office ceremony where they – Mary and John – were the only witnesses. They didn't even want Andrew there, but I insisted on that. Martin just goes along with everything she suggests, as if he doesn't have any opinions at all. When we first spoke about getting married, when I first found out I was pregnant – back in October last year – he said he didn't believe in marriage. For that matter, he wasn't even that keen on keeping the baby until he found out how pleased she was. I didn't give a shit how pleased she was. She was still the same bitch as far as I was concerned, but I could see Martin loving it. He hates her – or at least, he did last year – but he needs her. I don't understand it at all. It's so childish. He couldn't stand it when he had no contact with her, even though he could sit there and slag her off for hours. He knows what she's like. He knows it's bad for him, yet he brought us to live here with her! Half of that wasn't his fault, of course. They contacted the council themselves and said we could live here. I'm still angry about that. The council says it had nothing to do with the decision to move us back to Keighley, but would that have happened if they hadn't known that I had somewhere else to go?

This house is huge. I don't know how they got to live here. She doesn't do anything and John works in a garage, as a labourer. He couldn't earn enough to buy a place like this. He can hardly speak, he's so stupid. This place is what I imagine posh people would live in – doctors or lawyers. But the Bradleys are estate scum, the sort of people my mother wouldn't let me play with when I was little. None of that matters to the council, though. So we ended up here. The alternative was to go back to the estate in Keighley, and I couldn't do that. Not like this. The lifts never worked and I'm exhausted all the time.

Martin promised me it wouldn't be bad, that things had changed between them, that she was a different woman now. And for a couple of weeks it was OK. They were nice as nice to me. They still are nice as nice, on the surface. But it feels wrong, as if they are all putting on some kind of act. Not Simon, of course. And not Martin, I suppose. I guess Martin still loves me, though we don't even get to sleep in the same bed now. 'You can't do that thing any more,' she said, first day we were here, as she showed me to my room, right next door to hers. I could tell she was appalled at the idea that I would be sleeping with her Martin. Now she had an excuse to stop it. 'You might damage my little Katy,' she said. 'I know what Martin's like. He's like a rabbit at times. We women have to protect each other.' God, it makes my flesh crawl to hear her say these things. How would she know what Martin was like? And anyway, he isn't like that at all. He's so slow about sex I'm surprised I got pregnant at all. Maybe he's like a rabbit with her. God, what a sick, awful thought. Maybe it is my hormones...

She's convinced the baby is a little girl and insists on calling her Katy, though I hate the name and think it's bad luck to call it by a girl's name when we have no idea whether it's a girl or a boy. But what do my opinions matter? Sometimes I feel so frustrated about it I think I would actually be better off going back to Beryl and Jack. But it's too late for that.

'You're not a prisoner,' she tells me. 'You can leave anytime.' But I can't even get to the bathroom down the hall without her appearing and asking me what I'm doing. She's knocking on the fucking door again now, asking me if I want a drink, so I'll have to stop writing this. She doesn't know I'm writing anything. I have to keep the book hidden under the bed...

Wednesday

13

'The appointment is for midday,' Marcus protested.

'Midday is when I eat,' Gerry Owen replied, unconcerned. They were in the McDonald's car park in Headingley. Owen was on the point of getting out of the car.

'You can't wait half an hour?'

'I eat at midday. No exceptions.'

'So why didn't you say that when I booked the time?'

'You should know by now.' Owen pushed himself with difficulty out of the car, slammed the door, then leaned back in through the open window. 'You can do it yourself, Sherlock. Pick me up in half an hour. It'll be good practice for you.'

Marcus watched him shuffling across the car park, thighs audibly rubbing through his suit, and felt his usual disgust. It wasn't that Owen was so fat, or even that he was so lazy; it was the attitude that bothered him. At midday Owen had to eat. It didn't matter what they were doing, or how important it was, Owen worked the way he wanted to work, to his own timetable. He had to stop at regular intervals to stuff his face with more sugar and fat, and nothing could get in the way of that. Certainly not a dead body.

But then Owen's attitude wasn't particularly unusual. As the days passed without development,

125

Marcus was beginning to wonder whether he was the only person on the squad who actually cared about identifying the dead girl. It was already over eighty hours since the body had been found and they had nothing. The victim had even been given a name around the incident room, as if there were no hope at all of discovering her real one. Earlier in the week a DC called Patrick Rushton had made a casual, if bizarre, comment about the body resembling his daughter Emma. Despite his protests the name had stuck. So now they were looking to identify 'little Emma', or 'Pat Rushton's kid'. The joke – if that's what it was – was a species of playground cruelty such as Marcus had long hoped to have left behind.

Owen and he were meant to meet a therapist called Angela Miller at midday. She had already explained that she could only give them a few minutes of her time. Owen's attitude to that had been predictable enough– 'She'll give us as much time as we need, when we need it' – but Marcus was more worried. There was no obligation for her to speak to them at all. No obligation for anyone to speak to them. For that reason he tried always to be punctual and polite when dealing with the general public. It was more effective than being abrasive, and their enquiries were meant to be urgent. But Owen had a lot more service than him, so usually Owen led the interviews, leaving Marcus to watch with growing frustration as one potential witness after another got irritated and hostile. Owen couldn't help it, it seemed. He radiated resentment, especially when dealing with professionals.

Miller's workplace was a converted Victorian terrace no more than a five-minute drive from McDonald's. Marcus got there in time, running up the stairs from the street so fast he was out of breath as he arrived. An elderly female receptionist showed him to a tiny waiting room and explained that Miss Miller was running late. He would have to wait. Owen would have liked that.

He sat on one of three hard-backed chairs and flicked through a pile of trade magazines from some kind of professional therapists association. The waiting room was so small he thought it might've been a converted cupboard. There were no decorations at all on the walls. Presumably you were meant to focus on the upcoming session.

His mobile rang and he checked the number. Mairead. He let the phone ring, then listened to the voice message. It was the fourth time she'd tried him that morning. Yesterday evening he had sent her a short text telling her it would be better if they didn't see each other for a while. She sounded a little desperate now. He felt bad about that, but it wasn't his fault and there was nothing he could do to help. He had given her ample warning. Besides, she had made it clear many times that she had a thing going with an American student at uni who she had no intention of leaving, whatever happened between Marcus and herself. She was meant to be in love with the American. Marcus had been relying on that to provide some measure of protection for both of them.

He guessed she was feeling more confused than hurt at this stage. That was how it normally went.

Women *expected* to be abandoned after sleeping with guys who paid them no attention in bed and were obviously only there for their own sexual pleasure. But Marcus had never been like that, had never been able to be like that. For him, sexual contact was *always* emotional contact. Most often women went away feeling too strongly for him, thinking him a kind, keen, attentive partner. Nearly always they wanted more of it. He knew because they told him that afterwards, apparently surprised that it should he so. But it was true. Two nights ago he had given a part of himself to Mairead and she had given a part of herself back. The act had been tender and gentle, a far cry from the kind of poke in the dark she might have been used to at uni, even from the guy she was meant to love. That made it doubly important that he should stick to his rule, of course, but it also made it harder for Mairead to understand. He was considering sending her another text, to explain things, when the door opposite him opened and Angela Miller appeared.

She was a short, neatly dressed woman in her mid-forties. She had a friendly, round, attractive face, though she was a little on the large side for his taste. She wore thick-framed spectacles and her hair in a bun. She looked homely, he thought. Like a mother. Maybe that was the idea.

'DC Owen?' she asked. Behind her he could see an empty room. No client on the point of leaving. 'DC Roth,' he said. He smiled his polite smile and shook the hand held out to him. She had a firm grip, dry skin.

'Why is it you need to see me? You know I have

client confidentiality rules?'

'Of course. I wouldn't ask you to breach them. I was given your name by Beth Sumner, from Leeds Social Services. I actually wanted to speak to a woman called Patricia Fern, who works over there, but she's on leave at the moment and we can't get her.'

'Patricia, yes. Most of my referrals from Harehills come through her. Who is it about?' She led him into a larger, lighter room, with two large double windows. It didn't look like a consulting room, and was in stark contrast to the waiting room. There were three or four comfortable sofas, one of them piled high with cuddly toys, including a very large teddy bear. The walls were hung with big, bright pictures of wildflowers, or prints of Klimt paintings. There was the obligatory portrait of Freud over a small desk in the corner (the Viennese connection providing the link to Klimt?) and, beside that, a huge print of a section of *The Beethoven Frieze*, the part showing the beast in amongst the naked maidens. He knew it well because he had seen the original many times in Vienna.

Throughout his teenage years he had spent almost every summer with an aunt in Vienna and had strong memories from those months. The aunt had been his father's sister, but nothing like his father. A relatively wealthy, cosmopolitan European Jewess. She had introduced him to many things: Vienna itself; a kind of secular but passionate sense of his Jewish roots, through art, culture, history; the German language (through his father he had grown up bilingual, but until

Vienna hadn't really *lived* in German); even his first experiences with sex and women, in the form of a family friend ten years his senior. The summers in Vienna had been rich and full of experience, very different from the desiccated statistical formulae which were by then his steady diet at home. Vienna was the city he *should* have grown up in, he thought. He felt it so strongly he had once believed that he must have lived there in a past life. Teenage thoughts.

All that had ended with the death of the aunt, in her late forties. Just another parental replacement who had died on him. He must have stared at the Klimt too long, thinking about it all, because Angela Miller had to repeat her question. 'Who is it about?'

'I'm afraid we don't know,' he said. She was offering him a seat on one of the sofas. Maybe he should ask her about people dying on him, he thought. For that matter, it seemed suddenly surprising that he had never had any therapy in his life, of any sort. He surely needed it.

'Just move the box of tissues,' she said.

He sat down beside the tissues, imagining the streams of suicidal clients who had sat there before him, dipping into the box for comfort. Did Angela hug them when it got too bad? he wondered. Was that part of the trick? She had the physique to give a good hug. 'It's a murder enquiry,' he said. 'The victim is unidentified, but scarring on the left wrist suggests she may have attempted suicide in the past. So we're trying agencies that might have dealt with young girls with that kind of history. I was told that Patricia

Fern contracted that kind of work to you.'

'Yes. I do that kind of work. Mainly with young mothers who are suicide risks. Usually through post-natal-depression issues.'

'Our victim had given birth before, so it's possible she was referred from Social Services to yourself. Would that kind of thing happen?'

She sat down on another sofa, opposite him. From behind the glasses he thought she might be watching his mannerisms quite carefully. Maybe she was trained that way. She moved without haste, as if she had all the time in the world for him. 'Yes,' she said, after a pause. 'If she was a young mother and tried to kill herself, and if she was living in Harehills at the time, then she might come to me through Patricia. But I deal with many attempt suicides, not just those coming through Patricia or from Harehills. Is there a connection to Harehills?'

'Not that I know of. I'm going round all the people who might have dealt with that kind of case, across the area.'

'I see. Is this the case I've heard of on the radio?'

'Probably.' He took out the photo and held it face down on his knee. He'd been given strict instructions about showing it to people. At the beginning of the week Alan White had tried to get a variety of TV stations to broadcast the image, without success. The BBC had led the way, flatly refusing to screen an image of a dead girl. That had severely hampered the usefulness of the TV coverage they had achieved. (They had even gone national on Monday evening, but, again, without the image.) Without the photo the description

131

was very limited, making the TV coverage about as useful as radio time. As a consequence, there hadn't been the anticipated flood of calls from the general public, so now they were working on getting the photo round to a broad range of healthcare organizations – Social Services, drugs and prostitute charities, local council-housing departments but they had been given instructions from on high about showing the image without warning. Miller was a professional, so she could be expected to be a little harder than some others, perhaps. He saw her looking at the back of the photo. She was frowning.

'I have a photo of the victim,' he said. She held her hand out at once to take it. 'But I'm afraid it's a photo of her after she was killed,' he said. She moved her hand back and bit her lip. 'It's not very nice,' he added. 'You don't have to look at it. I don't want to distress you.' That was the warning.

'I won't know if she's one of mine if I don't look.'

'So there's no one who has recently missed appointments and fits the description?'

'What's the description?'

'You'll have heard it on the radio.' He gave her it again.

'It's not much to go on,' she said. 'But no, I don't think I know anyone who has missed appointments recently who fits that description. Show me the photo. Is it very bad?'

He handed it across. 'No. Not too bad. Depends what you're used to. We tried to cover the worst injuries.'

He watched her turn it over and look. He had

already been through this four times today, fifteen times yesterday, with a variety of health-care workers. No one had even paused to consider the image for more than a second. That was the reaction he had got used to. But Miller held on to it. He felt his heart quicken. He saw her frown deepen, then her hand go to her mouth, momentarily. She took a breath and glanced at him. He could see she was shocked. But perhaps that was just because the girl was so obviously dead. She looked back at the photo, then held it slightly further away from her, still staring at it.

'God! I think it might be Becky Farrar,' she said, at last. She didn't sound sure, though.

'Becky Farrar?' He took out his notebook and pen to write it down. But her eyes were still fixed on the image.

'I think it is,' she said. There was a trace of something else in her voice now. 'I think it's Becky Farrar.' She stood up suddenly and walked to a small filing cabinet by the little desk. She pulled a drawer out and extracted a file in a blue jacket. When she turned back to him he saw that she was shaking. Her face looked very white. He stood up, a little excited now. Maybe this *was* it.

'This is her file,' she said. 'I stopped seeing her a long time ago. She had tried to kill herself in April two thousand and three. It happened in Chapeltown, not Harehills. She's a single mum. She had one kid while she was seeing me, and I heard that she had another one afterwards. I only have the file still because I used her case history for an article I wrote last year.'

'Are you sure it's her?'

She held on to the file and looked at the image again. Her face crinkled slightly and he thought she might he about to cry. 'Poor Becky,' she said. 'What happened to her?'

He took the photo from her. His heart was pounding now. 'Are you sure?' he asked again.

'I think so. It's hard with the photo being like that, but I think so. She was a lovely, sad little girl. Very pretty. Very intelligent. Very articulate. Rebecca Farrar. Her parents kicked her out because she got pregnant by an Asian boy. He ran off and left her, and she insisted on keeping the baby. Andrew, he was called. It was a courageous decision. We managed to arrange decent enough housing for her, in the end. In Shipley, I think. I have the address in here. I also have the details about the suicide attempt. She was treated at Leeds RGI...'

He could hardly believe what he was hearing now. He took his mobile out. 'Would you look at the body itself?' he asked. 'Would you identify it?'

She looked frightened at that. 'If I had to,' she said. 'Yes.'

'Would you do that now? Urgently?'

14

The house was a squat, ugly block, put together with huge slabs of Yorkshire stone, the windows so deeply drawn they looked like fortifications. There was a basement, topped by two floors, then a more recent conversion in the loft. The chimney stack was long disused, though the walls were still black with soot from the days when mill smog had cloaked the entire valley. The roof was slated with storm-tiles, many of which were broken. One gable-end had subsided and was bulging outward, riven by thin cracks the second-floor joists had been reinforced long ago with iron supports, held together with heavy S-braces.

Even on a sunny, cloudless day like this the place looked forbidding. The date over the massive door lintel said '1786', the sign on the granite gatepost 'Lower Wyke Manor'. The clump of solitary yew trees growing near the front wall looked dense enough to have been planted when the place was built. Karen guessed it must have been a farmhouse, originally. There were two large, derelict outbuildings in close proximity and a broken dry-stone wall enclosing a yard on three sides. A dirty white van was parked in the yard, ex-BT. She could still see the logo under the paint job. The nearest neighbours were about a hundred yards away, across muddy fields.

She sat in the car, at the end of the rutted lane leading round to the back of the place, and waited for Ricky Spencer to give the radio signal to go in. DC John Sanderson sat next to her; in the back seat were two uniformed officers, borrowed from Halifax Division, one with a hand-held battering ram. When the time came they were to go in via the rear exit. Spencer was going in the front with ten other detectives. Right now they were assembling out of sight of the house, in the car park of a pub at a junction half

135

a mile back towards Halifax, off the road leading to Chain Bar junction on the M62. From here to where they had found the body was a five-minute drive.

'You know the place already?' Sanderson asked her.

Next to Marcus, Sanderson was the member of her team she most rated. He was in his mid-thirties and still keen. He didn't have much imagination, but he knew how to be thorough, which was almost as useful. She was thinking seriously about bringing him in on her enquiries around the murder weapon, the Asp. To date, she had done everything herself with that line, though the results could be summarized on half a sheet of A4. West Yorkshire issued retractable batons according to operational needs and there was meant to be a system for recording and matching serial numbers to warrant numbers. There were strict rules about reporting lost or stolen batons, but neither the recording system nor the reporting rules were well observed. So far as she could make out, about eighteen batons had gone astray over the last three years. She was still working on trying to match them to individual officers, but hadn't even started on other Forces yet. On Saturday Ricky Spencer had downgraded the urgency of the action because Slater – the pathologist – had apparently changed his mind about the injury pattern. Now he wasn't so sure it meant anything. He still wanted the opinion of the London expert, but Spencer meanwhile didn't want Karen prioritizing the Asp idea.

'I've never been here before,' she said to Sanderson. 'But I know the place on paper.'

Two hours ago, when Ricky Spencer had got the DNA result from the blood found in their victim's hair, she had hardly been able to believe her luck. The match was to a forty-five-year-old man named John Bradley. He was low level, with form for everything from assault to theft, three short stretches in prison, but not for anything serious. Up until now, in himself, he was merely a nuisance nominal. But he was married to a woman called Mary Bradley. The house they were looking at was owned by her, according to the Land Registry, but Karen knew better. Gary Swales had put up the money for the place six years ago. Mary Bradley was his younger sister.

'We looked at confiscating it when we did the Swales enquiry,' she told Sanderson. 'Gary Swales paid for this place with a suitcase of cash.' Her mobile started to ring and she took it from her pocket.

'A gift to his sister?' Sanderson said. 'That's nice.'

'A nice way of cleaning a hundred grand,' she said.

Swales had bought the place cheap and almost derelict. He had paid others to renovate it, again with cash. By the looks of the outside, they were still working on it. There was a JCB in the front garden of the place, mounds of earth, piles of flagstones waiting to be laid.

She answered her phone. It was Marcus, at Bradford Morgue. Earlier he had found a witness who might be able to ID their victim.

'We're still waiting to go in,' Marcus said. 'But I saw the hospital records on the way over.'

'Without an order?'

'I spoke nicely to them; they let me look. But they wouldn't let me copy them. It looks good, though. The scarring would match the suicide injuries. She was admitted in April two thousand and three. The blood group matches, the age also. She's called Rebecca Farrar, if it's her.'

'Rebecca Farrar.' She made a mental note. It rang no bells. 'Does she have parents?'

'Haven't got there yet. Thought I should get a positive ID from Angela Miller first.' He sounded excited. With good reason, if he really had managed to identify her. 'You gone in yet?' he asked.

'Still waiting for the green light.'

'You sure you shouldn't back off?'

He sounded genuinely worried for her. She ignored it. 'Ring me when you have something,' she said, then cut the line.

Ricky Spencer had already given her the chance to 'back off', inviting her to move squads because he guessed she might not want to stir up the Swales grudge and risk all that grief again. He should have known better. She had been waiting sixteen months to get the chance to stir things up. Swales had put a contract on her. That an enquiry had found otherwise meant nothing. Karen knew the truth.

Placing a contract on a serving police officer should have had major consequences. Only someone as stupid as Swales would have had the cheek. There should have been a major enquiry, witness protection for the informant who had tipped them off, the full works. The entire Force should have hounded Swales without mercy until he was safely tucked away in Armley. Not because the contract was on her, particularly, but because that was the only way to protect your personnel – by hitting back hard. Instead – obsessing about the broken-arm incident – West Yorkshire Police had set up an enquiry into *her*. Given the circumstances, the result of that could only have been a forgone conclusion, yet they had still suspended her, still followed the formal rules to the letter.

'You do know this place is on the domestic violence index?' Sanderson said.

She turned slightly in her seat and looked at him. 'What's that got to do with anything?'

He shrugged, reluctant to go on. He knew how strongly she felt about Swales.

'You worried I'm going to do something I might regret, John?'

He shrugged again. 'It's John Bradley's DNA we have on the victim,' he said. 'Not his wife. That's all I'm saying. His wife is down as a *victim* of domestic violence, a victim of *him*. It's John Bradley we're going in to arrest.'

'I know that.' She glanced back at the two uniform PCs. They'd been selected for size and looked uncomfortable squashed into the back of a Focus. The day was too hot to be wearing flak jackets. Too hot to be wearing SOCO suits and galoshes, too, which all the detectives cleared for entry – herself and Sanderson included – had been asked to wear. It was the best they could do to avoid contaminating the scene in advance of the real SOCO teams arriving, once the place was secure. 'Not long now, boys,' she said. One of them smirked at her.

'I've seen the call-out log,' she said, turning to Sanderson again. 'Mary Swales has called division twice claiming that Bradley whacked her. But both times she refused to give a statement against him. First time she didn't even want him arresting. So she's not that much of a victim. I'd say she could handle Bradley if it came to it. I know her. She's a tough little bitch.'

Sanderson sighed. He didn't try to argue.

'Besides,' Karen said. 'You think Gary Swales would put up with someone thumping his little sister? I don't think so. Gary Swales is the fucking lunatic who puts contracts on serving police officers. Yet Bradley whacks his sister and gets away with it? My guess is the only reason Bradley can still walk is because Mary Swales wants it that way.

The radio crackled with static. She picked it up and waited.

'You in place, Karen?' Ricky Spencer, ignoring all the protocols.

She pressed the button. 'Waiting for you, Ricky.' She didn't bother with the call-sign they'd given her. The intelligence on John Bradley was that he was low risk. They weren't expecting a fight. He was an unemployed waster. Probably he was still in bed.

'OK. We're going in now,' Spencer said. 'See you inside. You copy that?'

'Affirm. Green to go. Good luck.' She turned back and looked at the heavies. 'That's us, boys.'

They climbed the dry-stone wall and walked at a leisurely pace across the weed-strewn yard. Sanderson checked the van and outhouses as he passed them. By the time they reached the rear porch they could hear loud banging from the other side – Spencer's men kicking the door in. There was one rear entrance – a huge arched door made from wooden planks the size of railway sleepers. Karen knew the moment she saw it that they wouldn't be able to force it with the little hand ram. She tried to see through the rear windows as the two uniforms tried. They swung eight times but nothing gave. There were thick net curtains over the windows so she couldn't see anything inside. She could hear shouting, though, then a sound like children crying.

They'd moved to act so quickly on the DNA hit they had no idea who might be in the place, aside from John and Mary Bradley. The most up-to-date information on the property came from her own research during the Swales enquiry, some eighteen months ago. That showed John and Mary Bradley occupying Lower Wyke Manor with their son, Simon, thought to be in his mid-twenties. They hadn't been able to get a response from Social Services before setting up the raid, but the domestic violence index entries – from just under a year ago – confirmed that position. No kids, no particular markers for danger, no special circumstances. But she could definitely hear children crying now. She felt a momentary panic because of the lack of detailed current knowledge. If Bradley really was their killer then there might be unexpected complications if there were children within. They might even be their victim's missing kids. She thought about asking the uniforms to put one of the windows in, then tried to get Spencer on the radio instead. He answered almost at once.

'We're stuck,' she said. 'The rear door won't give. I can hear kids crying. Repeat – I can hear distressed children. You want us in through the windows?'

There was a pause, then heavy static interference. She repeated the last part of the message. Then Spencer spoke. 'Negative, Karen. All sweet here. We'll let you in. Wait a moment. OK?'

She waited. The shouting died down, but the children were still making noise. She thought the sound was coming from the first floor. After a few seconds she heard bolts being pulled on the other side of the rear door.

'I think it's our lot,' she said to the heavies. 'But get ready, just in case.' They stood back a bit, dropped the ram to the ground. The door opened and a white-suited DS Bill Naylor smiled at them.

Inside, the place already looked like the set from a sci-fi movie. Two detectives in identical hooded, squeaky-white zoot-suits were poking their noses in the cupboards and drawers in a tidy, modern fitted kitchen. In the next room John Bradley was lying face down on an outrageous red shag-pile carpet, another zoot-suit astride him. At least, she assumed it was Bradley. If it was he seemed calm enough. Wearing nothing but a pair of blue boxer shorts, he had a lean, muscular body, with tattoos on his arms and shoulders, and untidy short brown hair. He looked like a convict already. He wasn't speaking, shouting or struggling – a model prisoner. The man above him was a very large detective named Armstrong. He was in the process of cuffing Bradley's hands behind his back. Ricky Spencer – also in white overalls – was squatting on the floor beside Bradley's head, talking quietly to him. He glanced up at Karen and winked.

They were in the dining room, she guessed. There was a long table – a large hardwood production that looked polished and costly – a couple of oak dressers with antique plates and such-like, various pictures on the walls. Carpet aside, there was nothing trashy (but then for all Karen knew, bright-red shag-pile was all the rage right now), nothing that matched Bradley's tattoos. The paintings were even modern-art originals of some sort. The wallpaper was subtle and looked new. The place was tidy and expensively furnished, contrasting sharply with the overgrown yard and borders outside, the scrappy BT van. Only the tasteless carpet brought to mind the woman Karen remembered screaming into her face over a year ago, in the foyer of Leeds Crown Court. That had been at a preliminary hearing for Gary Swales. He had been in custody and the sister had been part of the support committee. As Karen had walked towards the court entrance she had stepped out and screamed at her like a cheap little estate tart, her face purple with rage. Karen couldn't even recall the words now. Someone else from the Swales camp had pulled Mary away and Karen had walked on without responding. That was at the height of the contract scare, when she was trying to keep a low profile.

She had expected the home of the woman who had shrieked at her to look a little less neat. She walked away from John Bradley into the next room. It was a very spacious living room, with huge widescreen TV, plush white suede sofas and similarly restrained decor. Everything looked pristine, like a show-home. The carpet pile was a normal length. She wondered whether Swales had paid to have the place done out by interior decorators. That would be another way to wash cash. She was reluctant to believe Mary Swales could be responsible for the tasteful ambience. The place looked like a normal middle-class home, and Mary Swales could never be middle class. There was another detective on hands and knees at a low cupboard, but otherwise the room was empty. A door led through to a hallway and the open front door, now hanging off its hinges.

She could still hear a child crying upstairs. She followed the sound to a staircase with inlaid wood panelling (they would have to strip all that out, she hoped) and walked up to the next floor. Four or five doors opened off a long passageway. The ceiling was much lower here, the spatial impression more suffocating. Maybe people had been shorter in 1786. She pushed open two doors and looked into empty rooms – one clearly that of a young child, one a bathroom – before finding the room she wanted.

Within the master bedroom Mary Bradley was seated on the edge of a king-size bed, balancing with difficulty as she tried to hug two small children to her. One of them was a pretty little girl, a toddler. She was the one crying. The other was an older boy – perhaps six or seven, with very dark skin and unmistakeably mixed-race features. His face was wet, as if he'd been upset, but he was quiet now. He was trying to push himself away from Mary Bradley.

Mary looked up as she came in. There was a moment before Karen saw the recognition flicker in her eyes, but no reaction other than that. She was a short woman with a round, ruddy face, tight, curly black hair and eyes that looked perpetually unfocused, as if she needed glasses. Karen knew she was in her mid-forties and that she'd had two kids. Her body looked full, but not flabby. Her neck was so short and thick it looked as though her head grew straight out of her hunched, heavy shoulders. She had the body of a woman used to physical work. The same physique as her brother, in fact. They were both short and ugly.

She was dressed in black trousers and a matching black short-sleeved shirt, with jewellery on her wrists and neck – matching strings of pearls. Another gift from Gary, perhaps. The room was thick with the scent of the perfume she was wearing. It smelled like toilet spray. She was stroking the head of the little girl, muttering soothing noises into her ear. She was the picture of maternal concern, but Karen knew the children weren't hers. A detective called Dave Joss was sitting on the bed beside her, trying to ask her questions. Karen watched them for a moment, listening to the questions; then she stepped back

145

out and quickly checked the other rooms on the floor. A detective coming from a stairway leading to the floor above told her there was 'another' upstairs and 'that was it.' Under the entry plan she had responsibility for ensuring the place was secure and safe enough to call in the forensic teams.

She went up. In a room with a steeply sloping ceiling she found an officer sitting on a folded sofa-bed, next to a very tall young man. If he stood she estimated he would reach nearly seven feet, though there was no chance of that in this room. The ceiling was so low he was almost folded over himself. He was extremely thin, strung out, as if the growth had taken him by surprise (which given his mother's physique, might well have been so) – all angles, elbows and knees poking through the pyjamas he was wearing. His complexion was very poor, the face red with acne. He held one arm strangely, across his body, as if protecting it. As she came in he looked at her with troubled, dark eyes. He moved slightly and she saw that the arm he was protecting was too short. It looked like the arm of a six-year-old. A birth defect.

'Simon Bradley,' the detective sitting next to him said. 'Simon is John and Mary's son. He's a bit disturbed by what's going on. He wants to go downstairs, but I've told him he can't just yet.' He spoke gently, as if he were speaking about a small child. She assumed he knew something about Simon's mental state that she didn't. Simon Bradley looked to be on the point of tears.

'You just stay here, Simon,' Karen said. 'We

146

won't be long. Nothing bad is happening. Your mum is downstairs with the kids.' He didn't look as if he had heard her.

She looked through two other rooms on the same floor. One – the smallest room – had no sky-light and no furniture at all. That made it unusual. There was a detergent smell in the air. She bent down and touched the carpet. It was damp. It had been washed recently with a commercial product. The walls looked freshly painted also. She touched the paint; it wasn't sticky, but it was very clean. She backed out and spoke into the radio, calling for Ricky Spencer. 'I think we're clear, Ricky,' she said, when he answered. 'We should get everybody out now and call in SOCO. There's an empty room up here that looks recently cleaned. I noticed the same in a bathroom on the first floor.'

'OK. Will do. Thanks.'

She heard him calling out from downstairs, telling everyone to leave asap. She made her way back down to the master bedroom. The detective there was helping Mary Bradley to her feet. Karen heard her say, 'Be careful with him. He's a terrible, violent man.' Talking about her husband, presumably. Already covering her tracks, painting the victim picture.

'Who are the kids?' Karen asked, looking at the detective.

'Children of Mary's son, Martin,' he said.

'Where's their mum? She looked at Mary as she asked the question.

'Mary says she left them, weeks ago. Social Services are aware, she says. I've already requested they attend.'

Karen nodded approval, then bent down by the little boy. He looked scared, dishevelled, dirty. His sister looked clean and prettily dressed. 'What's your name?' she asked him. He stared at her, but didn't answer.

'His name is Andrew,' the detective said.

'What's your mum called, Andrew?'

Again he didn't reply and the detective spoke for him. 'Rebecca Bradley,' he said. 'Married to Martin. Martin works at a garage in Keighley. He's not here.'

Karen looked at the boy, smiled at him. The first name was a match to the woman Marcus had identified – Rebecca Farrar. Would the little boy know what his mother was called before she was married? She doubted it. She stood up and looked at Mary. She was staring at her, but there was no hostility in her expression. She was playing the part well.

'Hello, Mary,' Karen said. 'DS Sharpe. We've met before.'

Mary seemed to think about it, then shook her head. 'Really? I don't recall.'

'No?' Karen put her hand on the head of the boy, stroked his hair gently. He didn't pull away. Mary had an arm over his shoulder. 'What's his mother's maiden name?' Karen asked. She watched Mary trying to work that one out, trying to decide whether to lie or not. 'Farrar?' Karen prompted, when she didn't reply. She saw a shadow of panic flit across Mary's face. She recognized the name. No doubt about it.

'Could be,' Mary said, tight-lipped. 'I don't recall.'

Karen felt her heart quicken. It was as good as a yes. 'You're a liar, Mary,' she said.

Mary frowned, as if the antagonism puzzled her. 'We're trying to forget her,' she said, her voice rising. 'She left them weeks ago. We don't talk about her in front of the kids. She ran away and left them. I'm their mother now.'

Karen laughed grimly, then looked into the eyes of the boy. She saw nothing but fear and uncertainty. She looked back at Mary. 'I've got you,' she whispered. 'I've fucking got you.'

15

18 June 2006
11a Shap House, Bradford

It's starting again. For weeks she has left us alone, but today she came back and scared the life out of me. I'm so frightened of her. I'm just sitting here with all the doors locked waiting for Martin to come home. We're in the back bedroom – me, Katy and Andrew. They're playing on the floor. Katy seems OK but I don't think she would hurt Katy – that's not what she wants. And Katy is only fourteen months old. But Andrew was very frightened, I think. If it hadn't been for Andrew she might have got away with it. Then I wouldn't have had a clue what was happening.

We can't go on like this. Martin has to say something to her. It has to stop. I thought I would go mad before Katy was born – the woman was so suffocat-

ing! I think she's totally mad. I thought it then, before she had ever done something like this. But now I know it.

I never thought I would think that Katy being premature might have been a godsend, but it was. If we hadn't had to stay in the hospital for so long we would never have got out of that place. Martin didn't have the strength. I don't think he would even have told me about getting an offer on this place from the council, not if we had still been shut up in that hell-hole with her. The hospital let him see things better, I think. We had such a shock, with Katy almost dying and all. It brought us closer, despite everything she said and did to pull us apart. I'm convinced she wants us apart. Not just that, she wants Katy. It's mad, but it's true. She wants my baby. She wants to steal her from me, to have her as her own. Martin won't even let me suggest it, but what else can explain what she has done today? When I tell him about today he will have to see what is going on. The woman would have me dead if she could. Both me and Andrew. She hates Andrew, just like she hates Simon. He's not pure enough for her; his skin is too dirty. She made that clear when we were living there. I will never forget the day I found her trying to force him into that bathtub. The water was so hot he was shrieking with pain, fighting against her. Martin said she made a mistake, but I could see that she knew. She knew exactly what she was doing. She was trying to scald him. I really believe she is capable of it.

We were so lucky to get out of there. I don't know what is wrong with Martin that he let it go on for so long. The council had offered him another place before this, in March last year, when we were all still cooped

150

up in Lower Wyke. But he didn't even tell me. He only told me that dreadful night in the hospital, when we had the showdown, when I finally told him he had to choose between his mad fucking mother and his family.

Choice Night, I call it. Time for Martin to finally grow up. Until today I thought it was the turning point. He made the right choice, but it was close. I can still see him hunched up on the end of the bed, hugging his new baby and blubbing away because he was so petrified that he was finally going to have to confront his mother. And in the end it didn't even happen. We came from the hospital to here and we didn't even hear from her for two months. It was bliss. I even think Martin liked it, at first. But then he started thinking about it. I bet she planned it all along. Sit and wait. Let Martin stew. Let Martin come running back to her.

And that's just what happened. He started going round there without telling me. To see his brother, he told me later. But he hates Simon as much as his mother does. Still, I could have put up with it if she hadn't started coming round here. Or even if she hadn't done the things she did when she was here. In the end it was so obvious she used to say the things in front of me. Running me down the whole time, telling Martin I was poisoning his child with junk food, not washing Katy enough, not breastfeeding her for longer, not giving her enough attention (because I was always playing with 'that dirty Paki'). The list was endless. I'm surprised she didn't offer to breastfeed her herself she's so crazy.

I didn't dare let her touch Katy at first – her eyes were so mad when she looked at her. I thought she would crush her or something. She wanted to hold her

151

so badly, and cuddle her and coo and push her face into hers. It was disgusting to watch. She wanted to do all the things to Katy that she did to Martin. Then we had that blazing row about it all and I really thought she was going to attack me. But she just walked out and the visits stopped. Instead, she tried to get Martin to take Katy to Lower Wyke, without me. He wanted us all to go, every Sunday, like we would be some kind of normal family. But I wouldn't let Katy out of my sight and I didn't ever want to see that cow again. I'd had enough. That was six months ago. I thought it was over. I thought she'd finally given up on it. I know Martin was still going round there, but they're his family. If he wants to see them I can't stop him. But I don't have to put up with them. I know she will have been slagging me off every time he visited, accusing me of all sorts of shit, but he never reported any of it so that's fine. Let him go, I thought. As long as it keeps her out of our lives.

But today I was doing the ironing in this room. It was mid-morning and I had the radio on. That's probably why I didn't hear anything. Katy was in the living room, but she was asleep. She always sleeps through till one now. Andrew was playing in his room. I didn't hear a thing. My God! It makes me shiver with fright when I think about it. Next thing I know Andrew comes through – God bless him – and tells me Katy has gone. I thought he was joking, but he looked really worried. I told him where she was, but he insisted she wasn't there. So I go through and look at the rocker chair – where I left her sleeping – and all I see is this big empty space. I will never forget how my heart jumped. The front door was wide open so I ran out onto the outside landing immediately, thinking –

152

as was true – that somebody had come in and snatched her, but wondering how that would be possible, given the door was shut and locked. There was no one there so I ran down the stairwell and immediately I could see her walking across the street, Katy in her arms. I shrieked at her from the balcony, thinking it would stop her. She started to run!

I came down the stairs so fast I'm surprised I didn't break my neck. She had to put Katy down to get into her car, so I went as fast as I could, knowing I'd left Andrew by himself upstairs, in the flat. I caught up with them when Katy was still sitting on the ground. I was shouting at the top of my voice. I saw red. I've never felt so angry in my whole life. I lashed out then, slapped her across the face as hard as I could. I hit her so hard her nose started to bleed. I don't know where I got the courage or the strength. She's such a hard, aggressive bitch. I thought she would start on me then. I wouldn't even be surprised if she walked around with a knife. But she just rubbed her hand across her face, where I'd hit her, wiped away the blood and stared at me. 'Is that any way to behave in front of your child?' she asked. 'You don't deserve to have her.' I picked up Katy and started to run back home then, quickly, really terrified of what she might do. But she just stood there staring at me.

She's mad, completely fucking mad. She was still standing there when I got back up to the first-floor balcony. Just standing by the car looking up at us. I wish I had grabbed the keys off her now. How did she get keys to this place? Martin must have had a set cut for her. That stupid little fucker. She came into the house and stole my child. She actually did what she has always wanted to do. I should report her to the

153

police, but they'd think I was mad. She'd say it was some kind of mistake. And she's Katy's grandmother. Maybe they would even say she has a right to see her. That would be worse. That's the sort of thing she says to Martin – that she's going to get a lawyer and go to court for access rights. It's such a nightmare. I don't know how we will end it. We will have to move. Move and not tell her where we are. But he wouldn't do that. He would go along with it at first. Like he already has. But in the end he will always go back to her, tail between his legs, her pathetic little son. It's not his fault. She has made him that way, deliberately. She didn't want him to grow up. Now he has she wants his daughter as some kind of replacement. It's evil. If Martin won't do something about it then I will leave him. I'll take the kids and go. I've done it before and I can do it again.

Thursday

16

The ID from Angela Miller was positive. Their victim was Rebecca Farrar, married to Martin Bradley in January 2005. Marcus had tried to locate her parents for a second ID, but they had moved from the address Leeds Social Services had for them, so he had taken Martin Bradley to the morgue instead. Martin had arrived home from his day job to find Lower Wyke Manor taped off and crawling with white-suited forensic teams. John Sanderson had given him the news that his wife was dead, then reported back to Karen that his reaction seemed genuine enough, though nothing excessive. No tears or shaking. But then, according to both Martin and Mary Bradley, Rebecca Farrar had left them all some three weeks before. So why cry for her?

Karen had already made clear to Ricky Spencer that she didn't believe their account about Rebecca running away and wanted to arrest them all – Mary, Martin and Simon – not just John. But Ricky wasn't having that. Unless something came back from the forensic examination of Lower Wyke Manor – suggesting Rebecca had been killed there, for example – then the present evidence was against John Bradley alone. Neither of the two vehicles kept at the Bradley house – John's van and Martin's car – appeared on the CCTV material from the M62 they had been painstakingly analyzing, so at the moment the *only* evidence was the blood trace linking John Bradley to Rebecca. It would be two days before they had full forensic results from the house. Meanwhile, they had moved John Bradley to the cells at Trafalgar House and left him to stew overnight.

Karen started the day by arguing with Ricky again. The first interview with John Bradley was scheduled for eleven o'clock. They had a dedicated team to do interviews, so Karen had expected she would spend most of the day following up on the ID evidence. But when she got in she found out that Chris Gregg, who ran HMET, had already pulled four teams from the squad – including the interview team. There had been three suspicious deaths in the last twenty-four hours on HMET East's patch and he needed the personnel there. A DNA hit from blood in the victim's hair meant that John Bradley was going to be charged unless he had a copper-bottomed explanation for the trace.

For Karen the DNA was just the beginning – she didn't want the case wrapped up with a charge against John; she wanted to focus on his wife – but for Chris Gregg the pressure was off. Consequently, Alan White was allocated to one of the new Leeds-based enquiries, which in effect left Ricky Spencer running Exile with only two teams. He gave the interviews to Karen's team. She liked that, but she was less keen about Ricky deciding to do the first interview with her. Ricky's interpretation of the disclosure rules were bound to be more restrictive than her own.

They argued about it on the phone, while Karen was still at Dudley Hill and Ricky was on his way to Trafalgar House. There was a legal obligation to disclose to Bradley's solicitor, before any interview, the nature of the evidence against his client. But Karen didn't want to mention the DNA. She wanted to surprise Bradley with it, *after* they had got his story. Ricky said they had to tell him about it in advance. In the end they compromised and agreed to tell the solicitor only that there was forensic evidence linking his client to the victim's body, without specifying what.

Ricky also told her that the report from the London weapons expert was in. Mr Slater had taken a guess and got it wrong, it seemed. There was nothing so distinctive about the injury pattern, nothing to suggest an Asp, or any other identifiable weapon, had caused the injury. So that was the end of that line.

She set the rest of her team on to following up the identification issues. The last contact Social Services had with Rebecca Farrar was in early 2005, when she had been moved out of emergency accommodation in Shipley and had gone to live in Lower Wyke Manor with her parents-in-law. That file needed to be obtained and examined, along with all traceable medical records, including from the suicide attempt in April 2003. Now that they were the records of a deceased victim, court orders wouldn't be necessary, so things would move quicker.

From the files they ought to be able to locate her parents and friends, assuming she had any.

(They hadn't come forward to report her missing and Martin Bradley had thus far been unable to volunteer any names.) Perhaps they could also find the father of the first child. (Martin had said Rebecca refused to name him.) Mary Bradley had made it very clear that only the smaller child – Katy – was a Bradley. Karen had tried to use that – plus her own suspicions – to convince Social Services that both children should be taken into protective care, but that had got nowhere. At the moment there was nothing to disprove the Bradleys' story that Rebecca had run away. The suggestion was that she had started a relationship with a man from the Roskiss Estate, in Shipley, where she had lived when she had first met Martin Bradley in 2004. Martin had said his name was Dave, but that was it. DS Bill Naylor's team had the unenviable task of trying to locate Dave. The flat at Shap House, in Tyersal – where Martin had told them Rebecca and he had lived between 2005 and earlier this year, when they had moved in with his parents – had already been located and sealed awaiting a forensic search. Bill Naylor's team would cover that too.

It was nine-thirty by the time she got to Bradford South HQ. Ricky drank a coffee with her; then they found an empty room and planned how they were going to run the interview. Ricky had a fixed approach. He wrote down the order of questions so they could stick to it. It was all pretty obvious and logical. Not how she would have done it at all. She looked at his interview plan without reading it, then kept her mouth shut. She had to think her way into John Bradley's shoes.

Bradley looked nervous and tired when they brought him into the interview room. He was wearing a standard set of custody overalls, all his clothes having been seized for analysis. He asked if he could smoke straight away, before they even got the video running. Ricky ignored him and spoke to his solicitor instead, a thin, bespectacled man in a heavy pinstriped suit, early fifties, carefully combed grey hair. He listened as Ricky explained that everything would be videotaped and recorded digitally. Ricky showed him the location of the camera, then started it. Bradley again asked for a cigarette and was again ignored.

Karen watched the solicitor closely. He said nothing to either of them, but he looked as if he might know what he was doing. He was private, not state-funded, sent up from London – Geoffrey Lane from Shelley & Lane. The name rang bells. She wondered if Gary Swales was paying for him. When Ricky had done the disclosure with him he had said virtually nothing.

They all sat down – Karen and Ricky on one side of the fixed table, Bradley and Lane on the other. Ricky did the introductions and the caution, then explained to Bradley that there was no smoking anywhere in the police station, but he could have other refreshments if he liked. He had only to ask. Bradley started to bite his nails instead. There wasn't much left to bite away. He had big hands, with a fighter's lumpy knuckles and fingertips stained yellow by nicotine, all the nails bitten down and cracked. The solicitor put his briefcase on the table, opened it and took out

161

a notepad and pen. They had given him as long as he wanted with Bradley, after the disclosure, which had turned out to be less than five minutes. She assumed they had a plan.

Ricky started asking background questions, about Bradley, his lifestyle, his family, where he lived. Bradley answered with a subdued voice, glancing frequently at Lane as if to get permission. He spoke with a Bradford accent and a low voice. Lane didn't look at him, didn't say anything, didn't stop him, so the plan wasn't to keep silent, at any rate.

He was a bricklayer, by trade, he claimed, though hadn't worked in a while due to a back injury. He was married with two sons. They lived with him. He was Bradford born and bred. He went to school in East Bowling, left at sixteen, had been married to Mary Swales for fifteen years…

It went on like that for nearly half an hour, Ricky doing all the asking, Karen listening, crossing the items off the list and making a note of what was said. Ricky was sitting in rolled-up shirtsleeves and she could both see and smell the damp patches spreading under his arms. The solicitor was sweating a little, too, the moisture glistening at his temples, where the hair was thinning, but the room was hot and he hadn't taken off his thick jacket. He looked calm, as if there were no danger of anything unexpected coming up. Only very occasionally he wrote something down on his legal pad. Karen began to wonder about him.

'Tell me about Rebecca Farrar,' Ricky said finally.

'She's married to my son Martin.' Bradley

sounded miserable about it.

Ricky explained that Rebecca's body had been found on the verge of the M62 four days ago and that she had been murdered. Bradley nodded, not looking at him. He already knew she was dead, if only because they had revealed that when they arrested him for murder, and also as part of the disclosure. All the same, he didn't look particularly bothered.

'When did you last see Rebecca?'

'Over three weeks ago.'

'Go on.'

'Go on what?'

'Tell me how you saw her last, under what circumstances.'

'She lived with us. Martin and she shared a room. Katy and Andrew had their own rooms.

For the tape, Ricky explained who Andrew and Katy were. 'How long had she lived with you?' he then asked.

Bradley shrugged. 'Too long.'

'Meaning?'

'A day would have been too long.'

Ricky waited, but Bradley didn't continue, so he asked the obvious follow-up: 'You didn't like her?'

'She was trouble, high-maintenance. But I didn't kill her, if that's where you're going.' He looked at the solicitor again. Unsure whether he should have said even that? Karen caught the glance and watched Bradley closely as he looked away. He was nervous and tired – who wouldn't be? – but there was something else in his eyes, too. Could he be frightened of something? The solicitor paused from writing and looked at

Ricky. It was as if Bradley wasn't there for him.

'So how long had she lived with you?' Ricky asked.

'She left three or four weeks ago. So about a month.'

'That's all?'

'That was too long, like I said.'

Ricky took out an electronic organizer and looked at a calendar. 'Would that have been in mid-July?' he asked. 'Did she move in with you in mid-July? Is that what you're saying?'

'Sounds about right.'

'Where did she move from?'

Karen sighed. Bradley was scared of something, but they weren't going to find out what like this. She put the pen down on the table and sat back. Ricky didn't look at her, but the solicitor did. Did he recognize her? Not from the interviews with Swales, but from one of the bail hearings, maybe? She started making notes again, but now tried to focus on the body language between Bradley and Lane. The name was definitely familiar – Geoffrey Lane. Where had she come across him?

The questions continued at a monotonous pace. Bradley was either telling the truth or he had the story well rehearsed. Only his voice failed him. The more he spoke, the more it began to waver. After twenty minutes it was so cracked it sounded like he was shaking as he spoke. If they had come at it sideways they might have tripped him, somehow, but Ricky kept it all in a straight line, chronological. She imagined even Bradley would be able to predict at least two questions ahead.

After an hour and a half, at Bradley's request,

they took a refreshment break. Bradley went back to his cell; his solicitor went with him. Karen and Ricky stayed in the interview room. She read through her notes and they tried to flag up anything that might require more detailed questions. There wasn't anything, yet Ricky looked mildly pleased with himself, as if he had made some progress. She could see no progress at all.

As Bradley had told it, Rebecca Farrar had first lived at Lower Wyke Manor in early 2005, around the time she married Martin. She had moved out after giving birth to Katy later on that year. They hadn't got on well, Bradley said. Not just him. No one in the family liked her because she created arguments out of nothing. He thought she was mentally unstable. At various times he had caught her trying to harm herself, both in 2005 and more recently. She had slash marks on her arms that he had seen. She liked to sit there pressing the point of sharp objects into her skin. He had seen her do it repeatedly, until she bled. Once he had seen her stubbing a cigarette out on her own skin. Spencer had tried to hone in on that, as Rebecca's body had twenty-seven burns that were consistent with a cigarette having been used on her. But Bradley had only seen it happen once, he said: 'Once was enough. It was freaky. Like she didn't even feel the pain.' He looked genuinely disgusted by the memory, but Karen knew self-harmers did it precisely to be able to feel the pain.

He talked freely about her character faults. She was a terrible mother. Dirty and untidy. She didn't wash the kids enough. His wife had to do it all for her. She wanted to be fetched and carried after, like she was some kind of princess. His wife was a star with her, patient, kind. Mary wanted her to be happy for Martin's sake. He didn't know what Martin saw in her or why he had married her. He was glad when they moved out after Katy's birth.

They went to live in council accommodation – Martin, Rebecca, Katy and Andrew. But the trouble wasn't over. She tried to split the family from there, tried to stop Martin coming to visit. That led to arguments, of course, sometimes bad ones. People might have heard them. (Might as well cover that base, Karen thought.) They argued when they visited each other. There was no physical violence, though sometimes Rebecca threw things at them. The flat was a pit whenever Mary and he visited. Rebecca didn't clean it. She thought cleaning was beneath her. Either that or she was too busy lying in bed.

He thought she was an alcoholic. Martin had told him the doctors said she was depressive, clinically sick. But he thought she was just a drunk. He thought she might have been taking drugs as well. He couldn't be sure. (Ricky didn't correct him, but the toxicology results showed no elevated substance levels in her body – whether alcohol or drugs.)

He knew she had tried to kill herself in the past and thought she might have tried again. He had the nerve to ask if they were sure it was murder. Martin had told him she had cut her own wrists in the past. If someone was capable of that they were capable of anything, he thought. She had moved back in with them in mid-July because

166

she was going crazy and couldn't look after the kids. Martin had told him that. They – Mary and he – hadn't wanted them to come back, but Martin had begged and they had given in. They shouldn't have. A month later she abandoned them all. She ran off with someone she knew from before, they heard. He was called Dave something. That's all he knew. They hadn't heard from her since. He didn't wish death on her, but he wasn't bothered she was dead.

'Even though she's the mother of your grand-children?' Ricky had asked.

'Grandchild,' he had corrected. 'Katy is my grandchild. The older one is nothing to do with us.'

'Though you have custody of him?'

'That's Mary...' he had started, then glanced sideways at the solicitor. 'She's nice like that,' he said.

17

The beginning of the second session was worse. Ricky tried to get back to the arguments with Rebecca, obviously trying for a motive, but instead playing straight into Bradley's hands.

'She was out of control during that last week,' Bradley said. 'Once I had to stop her from burn-ing herself with a clothes iron. She was that mad.'

'Be specific. When was this?'

'During that last week she was there, in August

sometime. I don't know when. A Friday. A Saturday. I'm not sure. She was getting worse every day.'

'*Did* she burn herself with the iron?'

'Not that I saw. I grabbed it off her and she lashed out at me. That was it.'

'She hit you?'

He put his hand up to his nose. Karen thought the hand was trembling. 'Nothing bad,' he said. 'She was strong, but she was little.'

'She hit you, though? Is that what you are claiming?'

'I'm not *claiming* anything. You asked me so I told you. That's what happened. I was there. She bust my nose. It wasn't the first time.'

Karen couldn't help smiling. She saw the solicitor notice, but he didn't react. This was their attempt to explain the DNA trace, then. Which meant Bradley had already known it was blood they had from him, blood that he had to account for. That didn't mean he was lying, of course. Not necessarily. They would have to go back to the lab and ask for some kind of dating estimate for the source. She didn't know how large the trace found in Rebecca's hair had been. It was possible they couldn't date it accurately, in which case Bradley's explanation might work.

'She back-handed me,' he continued. 'She was violent, very quick to lash out. She's hit Mary in the past, too.'

'Did your nose actually bleed?'

'A bit,' Bradley said. He touched his nose again, as if remembering. The hand was definitely shaking, and not from the memory of a

168

bloody nose, if that were true.

'Was there much blood?'

'I don't know.' He shrugged, all innocent. He was playing it well. 'It was just a normal nose-bleed. It didn't matter. I've had worse.'

Ricky had to stop to think about that for a while. Karen looked at him, waiting. She could see which way his thoughts were going. Running through the dating possibilities, as she had, then thinking that Bradley had probably given them a workable explanation for why his blood should be in her hair. Without an incriminating DNA trace they probably didn't even have enough to hold him. She cleared her throat and spoke quietly: 'How long was her hair?'

Everybody except Lane looked surprised she had spoken. Bradley stared at her without speaking. She had to repeat the question. Still he didn't answer. Probably *he* was trying to work out if his blood could still be in her hair from several weeks ago, or if the lab could accurately date it. Or maybe not. Maybe that wasn't the point here.

Karen tried again. 'Did she have long hair?'

'When?'

'When she attacked you.'

He frowned, then bit his lip, clearly uneasy. He looked at the solicitor. He suspected some kind of trick. He didn't know what to say, didn't know what the question meant. The solicitor took off his spectacles and began to polish them with a little cloth, very deliberately.

'Her hair was short,' Bradley said finally. He looked as if he was guessing the answer.

'How short?'

Again he looked to Lane for a cue; again he got nothing. 'Cropped and untidy,' he said. 'She hacked it off herself one day.'

'With what?'

Beside her she heard Ricky move in his seat. They had agreed he would ask the questions.

'I don't know. One day I came in and she had cut it all off.'

'You weren't there at the time?'

'No.'

'So your wife might have done it for her, then?'

'No.'

'As a nice gesture, I mean. A woman's thing. Help Rebecca cut her hair.'

'No.'

'How do you know?'

'She told me Rebecca had done it. She saw her do it.'

Karen nodded. 'So she was in at the time, then?'

Bradley stared at her, then looked at the solicitor.

'Why are you looking at Mr Lane?' Karen asked him.

'He's my solicitor.'

'He can't answer for you, though.'

'I don't want him to.'

'No need to anyway. You've already told us your wife saw Rebecca cut her hair.' She made an elaborate note of it, on the pad.

'This has nothing to do with my wife,' Bradley said. He sounded panicky about it.

'No?' She looked up again and smiled at him. 'Where were you Saturday evening? Saturday just gone, five days ago.'

'I was...' He stopped. The solicitor had moved suddenly, twisting his chair to look at Bradley. Bradley paused as if waiting for instructions from him, but Lane was merely staring at him, glasses still off.

This is the point, Karen thought. And this is why Lane is here. 'Yes?' she prompted. She glanced at Ricky, but he was focused on Bradley. He was letting her run with it now.

'I was at home,' Bradley said.

'From when to when?'

'All night. All day and all night.'

'With Mary?'

'No.' He answered that one very quickly.

Karen watched Lane put his glasses back on and nod slightly.

'No? Where was Mary?'

'What has Mary got to do with this?'

Ricky moved his chair again, trying to get her attention. Maybe he wanted to ask the same question.

'I'm just taking alibi details,' she explained. 'Where was Mary?'

'Not with me. No one was with me.'

'Where was Mary, then?'

Lane cleared his throat, politely.

Karen looked at him. 'Do you want to say something, Mr Lane?'

'Yes. Thank you. I just wondered, Officer, if you were taking alibi details for my client, why you would want details about where his wife was when he is clearly telling you she *cannot* provide him with an alibi, because she wasn't there?'

'Do you represent Mary?'

He frowned at that, as if she had been cheeky. 'No. Of course not. Mary Bradley has not been detained–'

'So stop worrying about her. You're here to look out for Mr Bradley's legal rights. Isn't that right?'

'Of course. But–'

'Or is it?'

'I beg your pardon?' His face began to turn red.

'Are you really here to look out for John Bradley?' she asked. She remembered where she had seen him now. Beside her, Ricky made a grunting noise, then cleared his throat.

'Are you suggesting something, Officer?' Lane asked, voice full of righteous offence.

'I don't think DS Sharpe is trying to say–' Ricky started.

'I'm just clarifying,' she said. 'It may be you have been retained by the whole family. That could lead to a conflict if we arrest other family members.'

'I think I would be the best judge of possible conflicts, Officer–'

'You seem very nervous, John,' Karen cut in, looking away from the solicitor. 'Are you really sure you want to tell us that on the night this girl was murdered you were at home alone, with no one to vouch for your whereabouts?'

Bradley looked at Lane again. Lane frowned at him, a big, deep frown.

'It's not much of an alibi,' Karen said.

'I don't need an alibi. I didn't kill her.'

'Maybe you didn't,' Karen said. 'But you want to make sure you tell us the truth about where you were when she died. Just in case somebody else wants you to take the blame for it. So I'll ask

172

you again – where were you on Saturday night?'

'Excuse me. Please, Officer. I have to interrupt.' Lane again, a low, insistent, pedantic voice. 'You made a comment about somebody else wanting my client to take the blame. I think you will have to explain that.'

Beside her she could feel that Ricky was really bothered now. Probably he wanted to break right now, stop it all, shout at her. Nothing she was saying was on his list. But he didn't dare do anything because it would look bad on the recording.

'I think your client looks very nervous,' she said. 'Maybe he has been told by someone that he has to say this.'

'Told by someone? By whom?'

She shrugged. 'I'm guessing. John looks uneasy and nervous. Like he's taking a fall and doesn't want to.'

'Taking a fall?' He spoke as if the phrase were gutter slang of uncertain meaning. 'You have evidence to suggest this?'

'None at all, Mr Lane. Can I just ask you, though – have we met before?'

'Not that I am aware of.'

'Really? You didn't represent Gary Swales at a bail hearing about fifteen months ago?'

'Karen...' Ricky, speaking softly, to warn her.

She put a hand up to stop him. 'Did you?'

'What relevance does that question have?' Lane sighed.

'So you did?'

He shrugged. 'I may have. I have many clients. I can't remember all hearings.'

'Have you spoken recently to Gary Swales?'

173

'Karen.' Ricky again, but louder this time.

Lane only smiled, though. 'You must know, Officer,' he said, 'that I have a duty of client confidentiality. So even if I had spoken to the person you've named, I would not have to–'

'Last chance, John,' she said, interrupting and looking at Bradley again, point made. 'Do yourself a big, big favour. Tell the truth. Where were you Saturday night?'

'Officer, I object to that kind of pressure being used to–'

'I was at home.'

'All by yourself?'

'Yes.'

'Where was Martin?'

'Out.'

'Do you know where?'

'No. Ask him.'

'Once again, Officer, I must ask–'

'Where was Simon?'

'Out.'

'Where?'

'I don't know. Ask him.'

'The kids must have been in. Were they with you, Katy and Andrew?'

'They were out. Everyone was out.'

'What about Rebecca? Was she with you?'

'No.'

'Where was she?'

'Gone. Buggered off. I already said.'

'Did you see her at all during Saturday?'

'No. She was gone already. She left weeks before.'

'Did you see her the day she left?'

'I don't remember. Maybe. It was weeks ago. We were out. We came back home and she was gone. She didn't even leave a note.'

'And you definitely didn't see her on Saturday?'

'In the house?'

'Anywhere?'

'Nowhere. I saw her nowhere.'

'Did you see Mary?'

'When?'

'Saturday. At any time during the day, Saturday just gone.'

'I already said–'

'Was she in the house?'

'I already told you. She was out.'

'My client has made this absolutely clear, Officer. I don't think–'

'Did you see her leave?'

'Please, Officer. Please. This is becoming ridiculous.'

'Did you wake up with her?'

'I didn't see her. She wasn't there.'

'You didn't wake up with her, even? You *are* married to her, right?'

'I didn't wake up with her. I didn't go to sleep with her. I can't make it any clearer. I don't know when she left. I don't know where she was. I was in the house all day by myself. I was alone.' He almost shouted it. 'Martin, Mary, Simon, Katy and Andrew were out. All of them. They were out together. On Saturday I was the only one in. That's all I've got to say.' He sat back suddenly, a kind of grim resignation to his expression. He didn't look at Lane now. He'd said what he'd been told to say and that was that. Karen was sure of it.

175

Lane nodded slowly, then wrote something down. He was still very red in the face. Karen looked at Ricky. His eyes met hers and he glanced up at the camera. His lips were set firmly together.

'That's very clear, I think,' Lane said slowly. He looked at Ricky. 'Can you tell us where this unfortunate woman was murdered, Officer?'

Ricky moved his chair back. 'Maybe we could have a short break at this point.'

He didn't shout at her, because he had learned not to do that in the past. Instead he stood very close to her, right behind the chair she was sitting on, and spoke very quietly: 'What did that achieve, Karen? What did you get out of that?'

She turned in the chair so that her face was far too close to his. She shrugged. 'Not much. But we were never going to get much–'

'We had agreed a way to do this–'

'I'm sorry, Ricky, but he's being set up for it. He's been told exactly what to say. Probably by Lane.'

He moved back a pace and ran a hand through his hair. He looked like he wanted to shout at her. 'You sound mad, Karen. You realize that?'

'Listen to what I'm saying. Bradley was nervous when he came in and it got worse. He kept looking at Lane, frightened of him. You must have noticed. We should seek authority to exclude Lane and start again. If we do it quickly we might crack him. He might give us the truth. As it is we might as well have Gary Swales sitting in there with us.'

'Gary Swales?' Ricky shook his head, slowly, eyes still on her. 'Now why did I think it was all going to come back to Gary Swales?'

'Lane represents Swales. He didn't personally do the prelim where he got off, but he did some of the early bail apps. I'm almost sure of it. That's why Bradley is frightened of Lane. That's what's going on here. He's been told to say there was no one in the house with him. He wasn't giving us an alibi for himself. He was giving us an alibi for Mary Swales. I saw it in his eyes. He was terrified. I'm sorry, Ricky, but in a couple of days we are going to be told by forensics that Rebecca was murdered at Lower Wyke Manor. When that happens he'll change his story. He'll say he lost his temper and hit her by accident. She died and he panicked and dumped the body. No one else knew what happened because no one else was in. He knows he's going to be charged; he knows he's going to go down for it. With an early plea to manslaughter he'll be out in three years, he hopes. But he didn't do it. We're going for the wrong person if we go for him. It's his wife we should be looking at.'

18

At four-thirty, while Ricky was still on the phone arguing with Alan White about Bradley, she got a call from Bradford Social Services, a woman called Jean Fitzroy. She was responding to an earlier enquiry from John Sanderson, as to whether they had any information on Lower Wyke Manor. They did. Fitzroy had visited Mary Bradley towards the end of August. A doctor who had treated Katy had alerted them that the girl's mother had abandoned Katy with her grandmother. Karen asked her if she could drive up to Dudley Hill to give a statement, then went through to the incident room for de-brief at 5 p.m.

White wasn't there, but had clearly instructed Ricky to hold Bradley until the forensics from the house were completed. The SOCO searches had apparently recovered many traces from the building, including blood, especially in the empty top room, the first-floor bathroom and the kitchen. They were waiting for DNA comparisons before doing a full report, but if the blood was Rebecca's then it was at least possible the house was the murder scene. Ricky looked directly at her as he passed on this news, then smiled a little, acknowledging that Alan White, at least, thought her predictions could prove correct. The news brought a murmur of interest to the room. 'It's not certain,' Ricky cautioned. 'Let's wait for the full report.'

'Will we be arresting the others if the house is the murder scene?' It was someone from Bill Naylor's team who asked the question. 'And if so, will we get more manpower? Two teams is too small for a multi-hander.'

'We'll re-interview John Bradley first,' Ricky said. 'See what he has to say about it. He has no alibi for Saturday evening, so it should be interesting.'

That also brought a murmur of interest, so he started to give them a full update on what Bradley had said in the course of the day. Karen left halfway through it, when security paged her

178

that Jean Fitzroy was at the front gate and waiting for her.

Fitzroy was a slim, young black woman, no older than her late twenties. She was dressed in a neatly pressed olive-green suit. The skirt reached almost to her ankles and she wore a white shirt beneath the matching cotton jacket. There were large frills at the collar of the shirt, which was open to show a necklace of very large wooden beads. She wore a brightly coloured headscarf round her head, enclosing all of her hair. She greeted Karen in a foreign language, so that Karen had to ask her to speak again. *'Assalam alekam,'* she repeated. The Muslim greeting. Karen shook her hand and smiled politely.

On the way to one of the interview rooms she explained to Karen that she had just returned from a two-week holiday and had been intending to action the Bradley file immediately. It sounded like she felt guilty about something. Karen made her a tea, then sat with her as she leafed through a thin file, telling Karen what they knew.

'Mary Bradley brought Katy to the surgery of Dr Whitfield, in Hipperholme, on the tenth of August,' she said. 'Katy had a fever, but it wasn't anything serious. The doctor noted that Katy was an adequately nourished and healthy child, aside from the viral infection that he diagnosed.'

'But he still sent notification to yourselves? Why?'

'Mary Bradley told him that she was Katy's paternal grandmother. She said the child's mother had run off some two weeks before.'

'Two weeks before. You're sure?'

'That's what he told us. Is it important?'

'Not sure.' The timing would mean that Rebecca had left the Bradley home in late July. John Bradley had told them she left in mid-August, roughly. It was a discrepancy. Discrepancies were always useful. DS Naylor would be doing some work on the Shap House address, which was still officially let to Martin and still, apparently, contained some of the family's belongings. Naylor's team would try to find out when the neighbours understood Martin and Rebecca to have disappeared, information which might cast more light on whether John or Mary Bradley were lying about when Rebecca moved in with them.

'Is it normal to report such things to your-selves?' Karen asked.

Fitzroy shrugged. 'He must have been worried about some aspect of it. I can see why. I was also worried when I visited them.'

'When was that?'

Fitzroy turned a page, looking a little embarrassed. 'About two weeks later,' she said. 'At the end of August. It wasn't high priority. That's what you have to understand.'

'Of course.' She tried to sound like she understood.

'I attended by appointment on the twenty-eighth of August,' Fitzroy continued. 'I saw Mary, Katy and Andrew. I interviewed them together and separately.'

'How did you get the appointment?'

'I rang in advance.'

'They were OK about you visiting?'

She shrugged again. 'Seemed that way. Katy and Andrew wouldn't say much to me and I noted that they were probably disturbed about their mother leaving. They were reticent. But I was a stranger. It's not necessarily unusual.' She frowned, as if wondering now whether other conclusions might have been possible. 'Mary was very forthcoming. I found her to be energetic, caring and concerned. Those are the words I've written down.' She looked up. 'In fact, that wasn't my complete impression of her.'

She seemed to require a prompt to disclose more. 'What was, then?' Karen asked.

Fitzroy looked out of the window, considering what to say. Karen waited.

'It all felt a bit excessive,' she said eventually.

'Excessive?'

'Yes. It's hard to describe. Sorry.'

'Excessive in what way?'

'It was hard to put my finger on it then. I'm still not sure. She wanted to hug the little girl all the time. She kept going on and on about how beautiful she was.' She shook her head. 'Maybe I'm wrong to think anything of it. I didn't note any of this. It was just a hunch, really. But it felt like there was too much love there. For a grandmother, anyway. It was as if Katy were her own child. I don't know how to characterize it.' She pondered it again. 'Something about the situation was wrong. It all seemed a bit desperate, that's all.'

'What about the little boy? Was it the same for him? Did she shower him with kisses?'

'No. She hardly spoke to him. That was strange, too. It clashed with her treatment of the little girl.

181

And, of course, the boy is mixed-race. The girl is white.' She smiled a tight, humourless smile, as if she had implied a conclusion too obvious to state. 'I think that's why I decided to follow it up.'

She went on to explain that Mary had told her Rebecca had run off with someone called Dave, from the Roskiss Estate. She had decided to try to locate Dave – as a means to finding the children's mother – before writing off the file. That was the limited extent of her unease about the situation.

'Did you manage to find him?' Karen asked.

Fitzroy coloured. 'It wasn't urgent,' she said. 'Not on the information I had. I put the file in my desk and went off on leave, I'm afraid. You know how it is. We have to break sometime. And there were more urgent cases in the queue. I was about to start on it today when I had the call from your-selves. The children haven't been harmed, have they?'

'Not so far. They're still with their grandmother, though.' Fitzroy had already been told their mother was dead. 'Social Services did an assess-ment on them when we raided the house,' Karen said. 'That was your department, I assume.'

'I expect so. I haven't seen a report, though.'

'Do you think they had access to your file when they did it?'

'Probably not. I didn't have time to put the details on the system. Like I said, it was low priority. There was no evidence of a threat.'

'Just your hunch about Mary?'

'Yes. And a hunch isn't evidence. Maybe I shouldn't have told you at all.'

'I'm glad you did. Whoever did the assessment decided to leave the kids with Mary. Would seeing your file have made a difference, do you think?'

'I doubt it. My notes say nothing cautionary. I'm telling you things I didn't write down.'

'Of course. I understand. Does she have any mental-health history?'

'Mary? Not that we know of. But we wouldn't necessarily know.'

'What do you think about her?'

Fitzroy thought for a while about it, staring out of the window again. 'I think she might have some issues,' she said, in the end. 'She was polite enough to me, though. Nothing overt.'

'Aside from racism, I meant.' It had to be a given that someone like Mary Swales was racist.

Fitzroy sighed, then shook her head. 'I don't know,' she said. 'Like I said, she may have issues. But I wouldn't like to guess what they are.'

Karen had forgotten her front-door keys that morning, so she got the spare back-door key from her neighbour and let herself in, not expecting Mairead to be home yet. The internship at the West Yorkshire Playhouse involved mainly backstage work, but Mairead had to be there for rehearsals, which began in the afternoons. Karen had got used to her coming home well after midnight when there was a show on. She was surprised therefore, as she stepped into the kitchen, to hear Mairead talking from somewhere within the house. She opened her mouth to shout a greeting, but something about Mairead's voice stopped her. Instead, she gently closed the door, stepped into the kitchen and listened.

Mairead was upset. That was what she had noticed. She was talking to someone on the phone, and her voice was clearly emotional. From the volume Karen assumed she was in the back room, next door to the kitchen. She started to walk through, feeling bad about listening in (though she had heard no distinct words), then heard Mairead say 'Mark'. Before she could get any further Mairead raised her voice a little. Now she could hear everything clearly. 'He's a DC,' Mairead said. 'My mum works with him. I think he fancies her. I think he's dumped me because he wants to shag my fucking mother.' Karen froze.

The conversation went on. 'He's got a thing about older women. He told me himself. I shouldn't have gone near him. I got what I deserve. He might even have fucked her already. I don't know. Maybe it was a little game for him. Shagging mother and daughter at the same time. He probably wanted us both in bed together.' There was a pause, while the other person spoke, some monosyllabic replies, then, 'I don't know, Prem. I'm totally miserable about it. I can't even sleep. I don't know how I let this happen.'

Karen stepped back to the kitchen door, opened it gently, then closed it with a bang. She called out, keeping her voice as normal as possible: 'Mairead? You in?'

She walked into the kitchen and put her bag down, thinking furiously about what she had heard. Mairead appeared almost at once, walking from the dining room.

'Hey, Mum. You sneaking in the back?' Mairead

184

looked miserable, her eyes red, as if she'd been crying.

'I forgot my keys.' Karen tried to think ordinary thoughts, as if she had heard nothing. 'You OK, darling? You look upset.'

'I'm fine,' Mairead replied, too quickly. She looked as if she might be about to walk over and hug Karen. It sometimes happened these days. Not as often as a year ago, but sometimes. But then she turned quickly and walked away, towards the stairs.

'You home early?' Karen called after her. But she was already on her way up to her room and didn't reply.

Karen walked into the dining room, where she had been. She touched the landline handset. It was still warm from Mairead's hand. She had been speaking to Prem, her best friend from childhood, who was in Australia on a year out. Karen thought that she should at least be grateful Mairead hadn't used the mobile to call her. Karen paid the mobile bill, too.

She leaned on the windowsill. Her head was spinning with thoughts. The conversation couldn't have been clearer. Mairead had slept with Marcus and he had dumped her. If she hadn't overheard it she would probably never have found out. Not from either of them.

In the months before Mairead left for university their relationship had probably been the closest ever. It had seemed as if, for the first time in her life, Mairead trusted her, was prepared to confide in her. They had sat down and talked through her teenage problems, reacted to each other like there

185

had always been that natural mother/daughter thing going on.

But there hadn't. For much of Mairead's teens – and even from before that – the relationship had been fraught, bordering outright dysfunctional. Given their history that wasn't surprising. What was unusual was that it had settled into something precious just as Mairead was about to leave home. But maybe that too was no coincidence. Karen was all too aware that she had no one but herself to blame for how things were with her daughter. For a whole variety of reasons she had – she was convinced – completely failed Mairead until very recently indeed. And the differences now were all too little and too late. She was lucky Mairead came home to visit her at all. Could she blame her for wanting some distance? That shouldn't be confused with hostility, perhaps. The fifteen-year-old had been openly hostile, more resentful than rebellious. Most of the time she had acted as if she detested her mother. They hadn't quite got back there yet.

But they would, if she wasn't very, very careful. She had to tread carefully. She looked up to the ceiling, towards the room where Mairead would be. She wished dearly she could speak to her about it. Mairead was upset and needed comforting. But how could she go up and do anything now? She had only found out there was a problem by listening in on her daughter's private call. It was typically despicable. There was no way she could give away the fact that she knew what was wrong. Which meant there wasn't much she could do at all.

She deserved what she got. She stood up and walked through to the kitchen, thinking that everyone got exactly what they deserved in life. It was that simple. She sat down on a chair by the window and stared at the garden and Rombald's Moor beyond. Mairead was her daughter. She could hold nothing against her. But Marcus? She took a breath, then wondered if they had done it here, in her house. Maybe even in her bed. Marcus liked her, she had thought. Obviously he had told Mairead it was more than that. Would he have deliberately brought her here, to sleep with her daughter in her own bed, behind her back? Was *that* what was going on?

She shook her head, to clear the thought. It was an absurd, inappropriate parental reaction. What did it matter where he had slept with Mairead? Or even that he had done it at all? Mairead was old enough. She could be trusted to be careful, with contraception, with disease risk. Karen herself had introduced them, so fair enough. Maybe she had even thought Mairead would be interested in Marcus. She could understand that. Marcus was attractive. If he weren't so young she might be interested herself.

The thought made her shudder. Maybe Mairead was right. Maybe he *had* been working his way towards something more exotic, involving both of them. Or at least thinking those things, in his head, while he was with her. How well did she *really* know him? She stood up and paced. Inside, she could feel herself seething with anger. Whatever they had done, it didn't matter. The detail was unimportant. What mattered was that *he* had done it without telling her. That was the offence. It was a betrayal. She couldn't just let it go.

19

2 August 2007

I am writing this down now, though I can barely move my arm without it hurting so much it makes me want to scream. I am writing this because I am terrified. More terrified than I have ever been. I am frightened something more will happen. I am frightened they will come for us and find us and something terrible will happen to me. If that happens then I want whoever might find and read this to know what has happened, so that they will know who was behind all this, because my greatest fear is that if they kill me they will try to get custody of Katy. That is what she has always wanted. That is what this is all about. I do not know what they will do with poor Andrew. My poor little babies. I have to write it down…

I had to stop because it hurts so much. I can't see out of my left eye; my right eye is closing up. I need some hospital treatment, but they won't risk it. Martin and Gary, his uncle. Her brother. They say we have to sort it between ourselves, within the family. But they are not even my family. I just want out of this. I want to take my children and run from them all. They are freaks, evil, weird. There is something wrong with all of them. How do I know that Gary will be any different? We came here in the early hours of the morning because Martin did not know who else he could turn to. He is too frightened to go to the police. Besides, it's his mother and father, so he cannot, he says. We sat crying on each other, as he told me what we were going to do. He is too weak. He cannot protect me from them. I know that now. I think my left wrist is broken, maybe some ribs as well. I can hardly breathe. When I move I have a shooting pain that it so strong it makes my legs give way. It comes from somewhere near my stomach. Gary says it will be my ribs, that they will heal and be OK. He says if I'm not OK by tomorrow evening then he will get a doctor in. I don't know why we need to wait until then. I have almost passed out twice now with the pain.

I think Gary is serious about helping us. I hope so. He has just been in and spoken very quietly and gently to me, asking me what Mary did, what John did. He seemed shocked. I could see he was angry about it. Martin says he is head of the family. I don't know what that means. He says his sister will listen to him. I have never met him before, but Martin says he was close to him when he was little. I am writing this in his house, somewhere in Thornton. He doesn't have kids or a wife, though he's about the same age as his sister, I think. I cannot even think about her without wanting to cry now. I should have known this would happen. I should have run while I had the chance. I hope it's not too late now. I hope Gary can speak to them and sort this out. I have to stop, again. It's too much pain.

I need to sleep. I need to curl up in a ball and sleep. I

need to be in hospital. They have given me painkillers, but they don't work. Katy is asleep now, thank God. Andrew is just sitting here watching me. Poor Andrew. He doesn't know what is happening, but he's old enough to be afraid. I stroke his head and try to soothe him, but I can't write this and hug him. And I need to write this, to protect him from them. I think I will write it and try to leave it somewhere, when I get the chance. What else can I do? It feels already as if I cannot do anything that I want. What I wanted was to go to the police, to go to hospital. But Martin stopped me. And now we are here. Will Gary really not tell them I am here? Oh God help me. Please help me, if you are out there, if you exist... Or if not me, then help my kids. Please help my little kids. I need to sleep. I need to pass out. But I have to write, quickly now, because my strength is running out and my eye is closing up. I keep sobbing all the time. I can't help it. I'm so afraid.

True Account of What Happened.
They came yesterday, in the afternoon. John and Mary. There was no warning, because we hadn't seen her for weeks. Then suddenly they are at the door telling us 'enough is enough' and we have to go with them now, go with them to Wyke to live. Go with them to Wyke to live. That was what they said. It was like a nightmare. I couldn't even understand what was going on. She was accusing us of harming the kids, of keeping little Katy a prisoner, of hurting her, of bringing her up in a slum. I didn't know what she was talking about. She was raving like she was mad. I told Martin to tell them to leave; then I went to the phone to try to call the police, but he got hold of me straight away, from behind – John, I mean, her husband,

Martin's dad. He held me with both arms around my chest, crushing me. I tried to scream and he covered my mouth. I was kicking my legs at him, desperate. I couldn't breathe. I felt my ribs cracking. Then I just slumped and passed out. That must have been what happened, because I can't remember anything else. It can't have been for long, but the next thing I remember is that they already had Katy and Andrew in the car and were trying to walk me to it as well. John and Martin, that is. Martin was helping him. Why? Why would he help him do that? He says he was terrified. He says that now. Maybe it is true. But he still should not have helped them. I was staggering and sick, trying to stand. I looked for the neighbours and tried to shout out again, but John whispered in my ear that he would kill Andrew if I didn't behave and come with them. That's what he said and I believed him. He said he would kill my little baby Andrew. I think he is capable of it. He said he would put him in the bathtub and hold his head under the water. 'His dirty little Paki head...'

They had come in his van. They put me in the back and John sat in there with me and the kids and Martin. Martin was just hanging his head and star-ing at the floor, like he was a six-year-old and had been told off, like the whole time with me – marrying me, living with me, loving me – had been some naughty episode and he had finally been caught and brought back home. He is sick. Sick in the head. I know that now... They took us to Lower Wyke, to that house. When we got in they tried to take Katy away from me and I had to fight them... But they took her away anyway, though I wailed and screamed about

191

it. They took my little baby away… John held me on the floor so she could do it. He had his foot on my face, on my head. He was pushing his boot into my eyes, then stamping on me. Then she came back and she was screaming at me, telling me all the things they would do to me unless I 'gave them custody' of Katy. They hit me so many times I lost count. They hit me in the face, body, arms, back, legs. She was just kicking and kicking me, while he held me on the ground. I must have passed out again. My memory is patchy after that. I can't remember everything that happened. Everything is blurred and fuzzy. He held me up against the wall at one point and head-butted me. I think he broke my nose. I can't breathe out of it and there is blood all over. She was just standing there watching. Telling him what to do. I don't know where Martin or the kids were. I could hear Andrew crying. I tried not to cry out so as not to frighten him. But I was so terrified I wet myself. When I started shouting they tied my arms behind my back and pushed a rag into my mouth. I could hardly breathe through my nose, so I thought I would die. They locked me in a room in the cellar of the house. They dragged me down the steps so my head banged off them. I thought they were going to kill me. Then I could hear them arguing with Martin upstairs. It went on and on. I couldn't hear the kids. I tried to shout out, for help, but if I shouted I passed out because I couldn't breathe with the thing in my mouth and my nose all crushed. I must have fainted again, or slept. I don't know. The shouting must have stopped. I can't remember. Martin came and let me out. He surprised me that he had it in him. They had hit him as well. He had bruises on his face. He told me they had got drunk and collapsed. We got out of the place as quickly as we could, through a back window. We took the keys for the van and drove it here. I was hugging and hugging the kids. I thought I would never see them again. I am sobbing and sobbing now. I can't believe any of this has happened. I can't believe it.

Friday

20

The address in Mirfield backed on to the Calder and Hebble Canal, with the front entrance opening onto a tiny yard that had been turned into a garden full of potted plants. The place would have been called a cottage in an estate agent's advert, though to Marcus it was a one-floor terrace. He guessed it would have two small rooms downstairs and a bedroom in the converted loft space. Nothing fancy – cheap housing for canal workers when it was built, but probably a little small even for two people these days. He wondered if the close proximity of a stretch of near-stagnant water would boost or deflate the price. There was no path leading from the low stone wall to the door, so he had to walk through a narrow snicket and onto the towpath of the canal itself to find the rear entrance.

He pressed a buzzer and then looked back at the view. The canal was in the shadow of the willow trees on the far bank at this time of day. The water looked like dirty motor oil. He shook himself to suppress a shiver. Behind the willows a scrap of field with a couple of scraggy horses grazing amongst nettles and broken fences backed on to the railway embankment carrying the line between Huddersfield and Leeds. To his right was an industrial enclosure of low sheds and chimneys.

No one answered, but the potted plants in the front yard looked well cared for. He checked the address in his notebook. This would be the twenty-first 'B.' or 'J.' Farrar he had visited in the last two days. The information he had on Rebecca Farrar's parents – from both Angela Miller and Leeds Social Services – gave her father as Jack and her mother as Beryl, but in the last five years they had moved from the two sets of addresses he had traced, before vanishing without trace, leaving him forced to work online, from the electoral register, telephone records and utility-company data, some of which only listed occupants by initials and surname. This one came from a telephone directory and was listed only as 'B. Farrar'. He had repeatedly tried telephoning without success.

He pushed the buzzer again. This time he heard movement from behind the door. He wrinkled his nose, an odour of sewerage bothering him. Was it the canal? He turned and looked at it again, reluctantly. He didn't like water, especially still water. He didn't even like looking at it. It hadn't always been so, but at the age of twenty-three he had spent nearly two years with a deep-sea trawler fleet fishing out of Alaska. Between the ages of seventeen, after he had graduated from Oxford, and twenty-five, when he had joined the police, he had 'dropped off the map', as his father put it. He had been expected to walk into a sensible job, or do a Masters – at any rate capitalize on his great good fortune in starting adult life so overqualified and young – but instead found that nothing a pure maths degree equipped you to do (which was precious little) was even vaguely appealing. So he became an adolescent instead, to make up for having missed the first opportunity. The rebellion (it was *that* childish) found focus in the need to avoid anything involving theory and mathematics. He sought a series of jobs that were carefully chosen to bitterly disappoint and alarm his parents.

He had sailed (as they euphemistically put it) four times with the Alaskan company, on one or another type of vessel, without mishap – without in fact, seeing very much of the sea at all. Mostly he had been below decks, gutting at first, then operating a section that froze the catch. The only things he had learned were how to adapt to the constant motion and a very rough mix of Filipino and Spanish, but then he hadn't taken it on in order to learn anything.

Deep-sea trawlers weren't the comfort-free zones they were made out to be. Generally, he'd found them to be about as stable as a cross-Channel ferry, providing the conditions weren't overdramatic. They had the level of facilities you could expect on an oil rig. He knew because he'd done both cross-Channel ferries and oil rigs for a little while, too.

Spending months on end in the bowels of a trawler wasn't what had changed his view about deep water. But coming ashore in Anchorage at the end of his last tour, he had been in the middle of one of the short metal ramps linking ship to shore when faulty support pins had buckled and sheared, sending himself and another seamen on a twenty-feet drop into ice-cold, very deep water.

Experiences like that got into you at a level below rational thought. He could still swim now, if he wanted to, but not without his body panicking about it.

The water itself hadn't been the issue. He had managed to get enough clothes off before the boat moved to guarantee that he could have probably stayed alive until they got a line to him. He was a strong swimmer, back then. But the boat *had* moved, and his only option then had been to dive beneath the waterline to avoid being crushed against the concrete jetty. He could remember with absolute clarity the feeling he had then, submerged between the hull of a 1500-ton trawler service vessel and the jetty, desperately waiting for a crack of light to show above him so that he could surface and take in air.

He had started to swim at once, of course, heading underwater down the line of the boat, trying to make it past the prow. It had been nearly midnight, and the water was so black and lightless that he had at first to gauge whether he was up or down by the feeling in his ears. There had been no time to think about the muck he was swimming through, no time to ponder the terror of it, no time, even, to register the extreme temperature change, closing around him like a vice. Everything had been practical – the boat was moving against the jetty, blocking his access to air, so he could either surface and risk having his head crushed or keep down and try to swim the forty feet that would bring him clear.

He made it, but not conscious, and his last moments of awareness, before the water rushed into his lungs, stamped him with a profound, instinctive fear of deep water. The terror had been physical, completely bypassing his brain. He had clawed his way upwards hoping to be clear, hanging on to his breath. But something in his body – the primitive, overriding need for air – had taken over before he got there, short-circuiting his power to decide. There were no half-measures when it came to the reflexes, it seemed. When his mouth opened it had been to suck with all his might, filling his lungs with water in one huge breath.

After that he could recall nothing. He had woken up in hospital. They had pulled him out and given him CPR. He had spewed the water from his lungs and begun to breathe after nearly three minutes unconscious, they told him. But he couldn't remember it. The other guy had died and it had taken them fifteen days to recover his body.

The door in front of him opened.

'Yes?'

He was looking at a woman of about average height, probably in her early sixties, with average-length, dark-brown hair, average weight and average clothing. Her face had a pained appearance, with deep lines running from the edges of the nose past the sides of the mouth, drawing her lips down and making her look miserable, like face-paint on a clown. The eyes were dull, grey-green, regarding him not so much with worry as irritation. There was a large wooden cross hanging round her neck, along with a set of rosary beads. Marcus had only ever seen nuns wearing a cross that large.

'Sorry to disturb you,' he said. 'I'm DC Roth, from the police.' He held up his ID for her to look at. She squinted at it.

'I need my glasses,' she said. 'I can't see it.' She spoke with a Leeds accent.

'Are you Mrs B. Farrar?'

'Yes?' She looked at him again. 'I'm Beryl Farrar. What's wrong?'

Right name. 'Can I come in, Mrs Farrar? I need to speak to you.'

She sighed and stood aside. He stepped past her, straight into her living room. She was only the second Beryl Farrar he had found since he had started this line of enquiry. He had been convinced, because of the name match, that the first had been Becky Farrar's mother, but had been wrong. Beryl wasn't so common a name (unlike Farrar), but he knew now there were at least two Beryl Farrars in the area, so this also might not be the one he was looking for.

The room was tiny, with a very low ceiling braced by two huge beams of dark, splitting wood. There were two armchairs and many photos over the wide stone fireplace (bricked in and occupied by a gas fire). He walked casually over and looked at the pictures: Beryl with assorted people – a man appeared several times, but he could see no one who resembled Becky, at first glance – and a variety of priests, including, if he wasn't mistaken, the Pope. Above the photos was a large crucifix. There were other religious items on the walls and mixed in with the photos – pictures of the Virgin Mary, mostly, but also a black-and-white photo of a monk holding his hands up to show blood running from stigmata. He looked around, listening. There was no sign that anyone else was in the place. Beryl Farrar came towards him wearing thick-framed glasses and asked again to see his ID. She really did resemble a nun, he thought. He showed her.

'Please sit down, Mrs Farrar,' he said, when she was satisfied he was indeed police. He had gone through this rigmarole each and every time he had checked a name, just in case the person was the dead girl's mother and he was about to pass on bad news. He hadn't been trained to pass on news of a close family death, at least not since his induction course, and that had been a joke. Normally HMET used dedicated family liaison officers to do the job, but with the enquiry down to two teams Karen had told him to do it alone, on the basis that he wasn't actually being asked to notify next of kin, just to find next of kin. That morning they had had a little argument about the tasking. He had tried to insist that someone more experienced should be working with him, but she was dismissive. She was in some kind of mood with him, he thought. He couldn't work out why and hadn't had the chance to ask her. It felt as if she'd given him this line of enquiry – boring and repetitive, with the constant possibility of having to deal with parental grief that he wasn't trained to deal with – because she was angry with him. She hadn't said a civil word to him all morning, yet with everyone else she seemed normal enough.

'You can sit down, too, young man,' Beryl Farrar said. She sat on one of the chairs and frowned at him, waiting for it.

He took the chair next to her.

'Is it bad news?' she asked. 'Is it Jeannie?'

'Jeannie?'

'My sister.'

'No. That's not it. And I don't know whether it's bad news. Not yet.' How should he approach it? It didn't look like this Beryl Farrar would break down on him, if Becky was her child. But why should she? The information from Angela Miller and Social Services had it that this woman – if it were her – had kicked Becky out to fend for herself when she had become pregnant with Andrew. Did that go with the rosary beads and cross? he wondered. Maybe she'd changed since then.

'Do you have a daughter, Mrs Farrar?' he asked.

The frown deepened, but she didn't reply. In the end he had to ask the question again. 'A daughter called Rebecca?' he prompted.

She took a gulp of air. 'I *had* a daughter called Rebecca,' she said stiffly. 'But that was a long time ago. We have no contact now.'

He felt a twinge of relief. Best to double-check, though. He took out the photo. 'I'm on a murder enquiry,' he said. 'A young girl called Rebecca Farrar has been killed.' They had released the name yesterday. It had gone into the newspapers and out on local radio. Maybe she didn't keep up with the news. He saw her eyes struggling with the information, but she didn't react. It was hard to tell what she was feeling. 'I have a photo of the victim,' he said. 'Perhaps I should show you it. First thing we need to do is make absolutely sure we are talking about the same Rebecca Farrar. I don't want to alarm you unnecessarily. Farrar is a common name. The photo was taken after death, though. It would be better if you had a photo of your Rebecca that you could show me. Do you have a photo of her?'

'*My* Rebecca?' She said it with a sneer, then shook her head. 'I have no photos of *my* Rebecca.'

'None at all?'

'None at all. She left us. Many years ago. Walked out. Ran away. She made a choice about it.' She looked down at the floor. 'She chose to live without us. I've got used to thinking she doesn't exist.'

'We still need to check we're talking about the same person,' he said, insistent. 'Will you look at the photo, please?' He wasn't sure it was the right thing to do, but couldn't think of another way that would hurt less.

'I'm not sure I'd recognize her,' she said, chopping the words out. 'I haven't seen her for many years.'

If the records were correct, it was just over six years ago. Not that long. 'Just try, please,' he said. 'It might not be your daughter at all.'

He leaned towards her and gave her the photo. He watched her look at it, her lips twisting even further down. The hand holding the image began to tremble. 'It could be,' she said. 'It could be her.' Her voice sounded hard, but the edge was forced. He could see her trying to control her breathing.

'Do you recognize her?' he asked gently.

She swallowed, then opened her lips and gasped slightly. She was still looking at the photo.

Her face was turning crimson, filling with blood as if she were angry. One hand went compulsively to the cross at the end of the set of rosary beads. The fingers gripped it hard.

'Yes,' she said, finally. 'Yes. I think it's her.' She moved her other hand aggressively, throwing the photo back at him. It landed on his leg, then dropped on the floor. He bent over and picked it up. When he looked at her again, she was sitting as straight as a pole, head turned away from him, breathing quickly. He couldn't see her face. She might have been muttering something softly. Maybe a prayer.

'I'm very sorry,' he said.

'Don't be. She was nothing to me.' She hissed the words, like she was trying to control herself.

'I'm sure that's not true,' he said delicately. He could see it wasn't true.

'She walked out on us,' she repeated loudly. 'She made her choices. There was nothing we could do to stop her.' It wasn't how Rebecca had told the story to Angela Miller. He kept his mouth shut. It hardly mattered now who was to blame.

'You don't know what it's like,' she said, voice packed with bitterness. Her hand released the cross and moved up to her mouth. She held it there. He thought she might be biting it, but couldn't see. 'Unless you have kids you don't know.' He wondered how she would guess he didn't have kids. 'They break your heart. You do everything for them and they break your heart. Nothing is ever good enough.' Her shoulders heaved up and she let out a strangled sob. 'She killed her father. He died seven months ago of cancer.' She turned suddenly and stared at him. Her eyes were fierce now, filled with tears, rimmed red, her lips quivering. She looked like she was about to start shouting at him. 'We had to sell everything,' she said. 'The house. Everything. This hole,' she waved an arm around the room, 'is rented. It's all I can afford.'

He nodded sympathetically. That explained why she had been so hard to trace.

'We had to spend everything to try to keep him alive,' she continued. 'To get private treatment. The NHS was useless. Utterly useless. They said the drug he needed wasn't approved, so wouldn't pay for it. He paid his national insurance all his life and they wouldn't pay to save him. This was just seven months ago. We paid ourselves. But it was too late then. Now he's dead and there's only me...' She sobbed again, louder this time, then looked away from him, as if embarrassed about it. 'She might have saved his life if she had come to see him. He was in hospital for eighteen months. All he wanted was to see his Becky again. But she couldn't do it. She couldn't bloody do it, could she?'

'Did she know he was sick?' he asked carefully.

She shrugged. 'She would have known if she had visited. She never visited. She hated us.' She started to cry, softly, her shoulders shaking. He wondered what he should do. The sobs were getting longer, louder. He thought she might completely break down on him. He stood up. Maybe he should call an ambulance. Was that a stupid idea?

'Is there anyone you want me to call?' he asked, standing over her. She was starting to make a muffled wailing noise, both hands jammed in her mouth. 'Anyone who could be with you?'

'There's no one...' She stuttered the words, nose dribbling, mouth hanging open, eyes streaming. 'There's no one left but me. She was my only child. My only child ... my poor little Becky...'

Sunday

21

On Sunday Marcus usually went to his mother's for Sunday dinner. He thought of it like that – as going to see his mother – but his father was there as well, of course. They were all there – father, mother and Oscar, his twin brother. The event was a family production that had taken place as long as he could remember. He had escaped it for about ten years – the three at Oxford and the seven afterwards, when he had refused to speak to his father even if he was in the area. Contact with his mother had been more problematic, too, for a while – though he'd never had the wish to cut her off completely, as he had with his dad.

The thaw in their relations had brought the event back into his life. In fact, given he hardly ever phoned them, 'being in contact' more or less *meant* going for Sunday dinner. 'At least we all still get together once a week,' his mother would say repeatedly, implying once was too little (to his ears, at least). The criticism, if that was really what it was, could only be directed at Marcus, since Oscar still lived with them.

'Dinner' in this case meant they ate at around 3 p.m. Almost invariably it was roast beef. Occasionally, she varied it with lamb or chicken, but never with pork. It was a little joke gone wrong that they never ate pork because one side of the family was Jewish. His father, of course, was atheist and, according to his own account of it, neither of his children could be Jewish because that distinction passed by the mother's side only. Throughout his life, it seemed to Marcus, his father had gone out of his way to deny his Jewish roots. But the prohibition on pork was something ingrained in him. There was often some carefully restrained needling about it, over the dining table, comments between his mother and father that suggested they had argued about it long before the kids were around.

Normally, Marcus tried to get there for about 1 p.m., which meant he had to waste the better part of three hours in his dad's presence. That was how it felt, food aside. (The food was always very good.) Contact with his mother would have been less of a duty if he could have got her by herself. But with his dad and Oscar around everything was always poisoned.

He had his jacket on and was about to leave when the door intercom for the apartment buzzed. He walked over to the CCTV screen and looked at Karen.

'It's me,' she said. 'Your boss.'

'I was just coming out,' he said into the mic. 'You got something for me?' Hopefully something that would mean he didn't have to go to Horsforth for lunch.

'It's a social visit,' she replied, not looking at the camera. 'I can come back another time if you're leaving.' She was carrying something.

'I can always spare time for you,' he said. He released the catch to let her up and took off his jacket.

'I brought some bagels,' she said, once she had shut his open door behind her. She must have used the stairs instead of the lift, because she was out of breath. Marcus had the loft apartment in a five-storey block. 'I thought we could do breakfast,' she said.

He smiled (the bagel thing was a joke, no doubt) and looked at his watch. 'Breakfast? I was about to go to Horsforth for lunch.' Strange she had come right now, since she knew he went there every Sunday.

'Well, maybe I'll eat them,' she said. 'You can have a coffee with me, though. Right?'

'Sure.' He looked hard at her. Her attitude was different from yesterday. It was like she was bringing him a peace offering. But he still didn't know what he'd done wrong. She was dressed in a skirt again, something with dark colours and a very light fabric. He thought he recognized it, though he was sure he had only ever seen her in a skirt that week, at work, and it hadn't been this one.

'You took my advice,' he said.

'About what?'

'About wearing skirts more often.'

She grinned. 'You like it? I'd do a twirl for you, but I don't know how.'

'No need. I can see you perfectly as you are.' She was standing right in front of one of the open skylights, the sunlight flooding in behind her.

'What do you think?' She held her arms up, inviting him to look.

Was she flirting with him? There was more than the usual eye contact.

'You look great,' he said. The skirt was long –

almost down to her ankles – but with the sun coming through the fabric it was thin enough for the view to be intimate – he could see straight through it, see the exact shape of her. She had good legs, long but not too thin. He let his eyes linger awhile. She didn't seem to mind. Did she know what he was looking at? He felt oddly disturbed.

'It's not a skirt,' she said. 'It's a dress.' She lifted the light-green sweater slightly, for him to see. Then he realized what was wrong. It was Mairead's dress, the one she had been wearing last time he had seen her. He brought his eyes up from it and met hers, looking directly at him, a little smile playing around the edge of her mouth. Did she know he had seen Mairead in it? Was that what this was about?

'Dress or skirt – it still looks good on you,' he said.

He went into the kitchen to make coffee, thinking about it. When he came back with two mugs she was sitting on his sofa, her legs pulled up beneath her, shoes kicked off She looked very relaxed. He put the coffee next to the bagels, on the glass coffee table, then sat down opposite her.

'Actually I lied,' she said.

'About what?'

'About this being purely social. I have a job for you, too.'

He nodded. 'I thought so. If it's something that will get me out of lunch then I'll be grateful.'

'I'm afraid not,' she said. 'But it is something that requires me to trust you. She reached forward and picked up the coffee mugs. 'Do you think I can trust you, Marcus?' She took a sip,

214

burned herself and put it down.

'You know you can trust me,' he said, interested now in the task, whatever it was going to be, but also wondering about her tone. 'We're friends, Karen,' he added. 'It's not just a work thing between us.'

'Does that make a difference?'

He frowned. 'It does to me.'

'It does to me, too,' she said. 'In this world only friends and family matter. Full stop.'

He'd heard it before. 'That's not how I see it,' he replied. 'But if you're asking whether you can trust me with some kind of sensitive tasking then I'm sure you already know you can.'

She looked away from him and seemed to think about it. Then she nodded. 'Yes,' she said. 'Maybe I can trust you with work things.'

Again her tone was off. Had Mairead said something to her? He kept quiet and waited for her to go on. If there was something she wanted to say about Mairead then she could say it and he would deal with it. His conscience was more or less clear on that. But he wasn't going to prompt her. Mairead was the one who had wanted to keep things secret from her mother. And Mairead was an adult, independent of her mother. Maybe Karen had to learn that. Karen had introduced them and encouraged them to spend time together. He couldn't see any real problem with it. Maybe it was something else.

'So what is it?' he asked, when she didn't speak again.

She sighed and looked at him. 'It's about the injury,' she said. 'The head wound that killed little Becky.' Her way of speaking about the case had changed over the last few days. Previously it had been a job for her. Now she had something that made it personal – a connection to the Swales thing. That seemed to infect everything she did with it. She was more enthusiastic; in briefings she radiated a sense of urgency. The victim had become 'little Becky', as if she'd known her. Her focus was getting 'Becky's poor children' away from Mary Swales. (She never referred to her as Mary Bradley.) She already believed there was a conspiracy to prevent that (centring on Social Services, who weren't sympathetic to the idea the kids were in danger).

'What about it?' he asked her.

'Information about it was held back from the briefings,' she said. 'Sensitive information.'

He waited.

'What I am about to tell you – what I am about to ask you to do – must be between us only. You understand?'

'Of course.'

'I'm giving you this because you're the only one I feel I can trust on my team. I was instructed – by the SIO – to limit knowledge of this. But there are things that need doing and I can't do them all by myself. So I'm going to ask you to help me.'

'OK. Shoot. What do you want me to do?' Whatever it was, he was up for it.

'There is evidence to suggest that the fatal injury was caused by a very specific instrument,' she said. 'There is a crush pattern which has been examined by experts. Our pathologist says that he has seen the type of injury before. He

216

thinks it comes from an Asp.'

'An Asp? You mean a collapsible baton?'

'Exactly.'

'A police weapon?'

She shrugged. 'Is it? I'm not sure about that – I'm not sure we're the only people who use them, I mean – but you can see why, at the moment, we need to keep this low key. So far my enquiries have been limited to trying to trace lost batons on our own Force – on the assumption we are dealing with a missing police weapon.'

'Instead of one currently used by one of our officers, you mean?'

'Of course. I'm looking at that as well, though.'

He sat back, thinking about it. He couldn't see how the culprit being a serving police officer would fit with any of the other evidence they had. The standard kind of link that sprang to mind was 'prostitute', but they had no evidence that Becky had been one. So how would she have established a relationship with a serving police officer without them finding out about it? It didn't work. If it were his call he would charge John Bradley rather than go down that line.

'One of the things I need to do,' she said, 'is find out just how readily available these things are to non-police, to the public. I want you to do that for me.'

'OK. No problem.' He considered it. 'How?'

She shrugged. 'I don't know. Try to get one, perhaps. On the net. Find out if you *can* get them. Find out if there are any safeguards. They're meant to be illegal, after all.'

'I can do that. That's easily done.'

'Good. But keep it to yourself, like I said.' She looked around. 'Do it from here. Don't use a machine at work. If you can get one then maybe get it sent here instead of to work. You get the idea? This really has to be confidential for now.'

'No problem. I'll get onto it immediately.'

He thought he must sound irritatingly keen, but really all he wanted was to avoid his parents. She smiled knowingly at him. 'It can wait until tonight, I think,' she said. 'I don't want to get between a child and his parents.'

He was late, in the end, which meant there were three unanswered messages on his mobile from his father and everyone was already sitting around the table when he arrived. But he did manage to order an Asp. A collapsible, telescopic baton was an offensive weapon, per se, as the lawyers called it, which meant it was illegal to trade in them in the UK. So he had to stray as far afield as France to get one. Special delivery within two working days was the promise, anywhere in Europe. Price 270 euros, charged to his Mastercard. He would claim that back, he guessed, once the line was out in the open.

'You're very late,' his dad said, opening the door. They lived in the same four-bedroom detached house he had grown up in – a mid-war property in a street full of semis, which for some reason had escaped connection to the rest – just. 'Technically detached', his dad called it, since the distance to the nearest neighbour, on one side, was all of eighteen inches. But the gardens – to front and back – were a decent size, and the hedges and trees were all mature and high, offering privacy to the lawns at the expense of light. His dad had been complaining about the trees all his life because of that, threatening to cut them down. At his mother's insistence they were still there.

'We've already started to serve,' his dad told him, as if it were really too late to come at all.

'Work,' Marcus explained, stepping in. 'I'm on a murder squad, remember? People don't stop killing each other for lunch.'

'That was your excuse last week.'

'And it's the same case this week. Enquiries like this take longer than a week. You know that.'

His dad grunted and followed him through. These days his dad was permanently in a mood, it seemed. Or had it always been like that? He even wore the tattered cardigan – an obligatory emblem of the grumpy-old-man brigade. Sometimes he was so uncommunicative Marcus thought he might be depressed, properly clinically depressed. He had asked his mum about it once, but she had been typically dismissive: 'You know your dad. He's an irritable sod. Always has been.'

By contrast his mother got up to greet him warmly. He hugged her, feeling the same strange mix of unidentifiable emotions he had felt all his life when she had hugged or kissed him. Or since his teens, at least. Another reason he should have had some therapy in Vienna.

'We thought you weren't going to make it,' she said. 'I assumed something must have come up at work.'

'Something did.'

'Well, I'm glad you got away. You know you

219

don't have to come, Marcus. If ever you can't make it you only have to ring, you know.'

'I know. I'm sorry, Mum. I should have called to warn you.' He looked over to his twin brother, already forking food into his face. 'Hello, Oscar. I can see you're OK, so I won't ask.'

Oscar said nothing in reply, didn't look up.

'Oscar's very hungry,' his mum explained, and then, to Oscar, 'Say hello to your brother, Oscar.'

'We've been waiting for you,' his dad chipped in, resuming his seat beside the joint (which it was always his job to carve). 'That's why Ossie's so hungry.'

'Don't call him Ossie,' his mother said automatically. His dad was always dreaming up new nicknames for Oscar, none of which his mother liked. 'His name's Oscar.'

'You think I don't know that?' His dad picked up the carving knife and looked for a moment as if he wanted to slash something with it. 'He's my son. I'll call him what I like.'

Marcus sighed and sat down. 'Glad to see nothing has changed here,' he said. It was his opinion that his mum and his dad should have separated years ago. Neither of them liked each other, and that was clear in just about every transaction between them.

'I like meat,' Oscar said, looking at his father now. 'I like meat very much.'

'Good, Oscar. Good,' his mother said. 'Eat plenty of it. It keeps you fit and healthy.'

Was Oscar the reason they were still together? Marcus had passed his entire life without being able to look his brother in the eye. They were

220

non-identical twins, but Marcus had 'slipped out' a full ten minutes ahead of Oscar, and that gap had made all the difference. Marcus had developed into the child prodigy, his brother into an imbecile (as his father had once so memorably and unkindly put it). The official (and medical) explanation was that the umbilical cord had become wrapped round Oscar's little body and twisted on itself, cutting off the blood supply in the cord for a vital three or four minutes. Almost exactly the same time period Marcus had been unconscious when he fell from the boat in Alaska. He had survived that without impairment, but for the tiny, fragile Oscar, it had been enough to damage his brain beyond repair. His subsequent development had been slow and painful, and had stalled at a mental age somewhere between two and fourteen. It was difficult to be more precise about it than that, because some things he did were almost adult, but mostly it was like dealing with an eight-year-old. Sometimes he was very childish indeed, like a toddler.

'You had a good week, Oscar?' Marcus asked, as his mother brought him a plate.

'It was OK.'

'You do anything new?'

'Played Sim City.'

That wasn't new. He'd been doing it for years. Sim City was some kind of computer game.

'Does he play well?' Marcus asked his dad. 'Is he good at it?' Hadn't they had the same conversation last time he was here?

'He can't play it properly,' his dad said, not looking up from the carving. 'You know how it is.

221

He plays it like a kiddie. What can you expect when his brain doesn't work properly? But he does OK, I suppose. It keeps him amused.'

Marcus took a breath. His mum was in the kitchen or there would have been a row, no doubt. She would never have spoken about Oscar like that in front of him, maybe not at all.

'I'm sure you do great,' Marcus said to Oscar, feeling a need to mitigate his father's criticism. But Oscar was head down again, tucking into his mash. Maybe he hadn't even heard.

When she returned, Marcus let his mother heap his plate with food, then waited while his father gave him meat. His mum and dad cooked the meal together, every Sunday, arguing about it all the time.

'Looks fantastic,' Marcus said, when his plate was in front of him.

'You say that every week,' his dad said. 'You're like a stuck record.'

Marcus picked up his knife and fork, biting his tongue to keep quiet.

'The carrots are hard,' Oscar said.

Marcus forked one and bit into it. Unusually, the carrot was overcooked, soft and tasteless. No doubt his fault for being late. 'You mean they're soft?' he asked Oscar. Opposite him his mother sat down.

'They're fine,' she said. 'Just eat up, Oscar. There's a good boy.' She reached over and patted him gently on the arm. It looked absurd to Marcus – still, after all these years of watching it. Oscar was a grown man – twenty-eight years old. He even had a sex life of sorts. His dad had complained many times about him furtively masturbating in his room. Yet here he was being treated like a child. The image didn't match the actions or the words. Marcus was looking at a man not very different from himself – well built, strong, tall. And not too bad-looking. Yet sometimes, when he got his 'mad half-hours', his parents walked him around the house holding his hand to stop him running into things.

It all seemed tragic, horrible, too painful to be near. Had someone told them once that he was to blame for it? He had sucked out all the brains and intelligence, all the nutrients that made such things even. He had condemned his brother to this limbo while they were still hugged up against each other, in the womb of the woman opposite him. Or slipped out early, leaving his brother without air. He knew what it was like to be without air. Maybe his dad had told him all this. He couldn't remember anyone blaming him, but it would have to be his dad. His mother was just nice. All the time, just nice and motherly. Only his dad had resentment enough to say such things.

It was all nonsense, of course. Oscar hadn't gone without air. He wasn't even breathing then, when it had happened. He had gone without *blood*. What could Marcus have had to do with that?

'I'm learning to ride my bike,' Oscar said. He'd been learning for years.

'Good,' Marcus said. 'It's fun. You'll like it.' He ate a bit of meat. It was tasty, done the working-class English way – cooked so much it was dropping to pieces.

I'm not to blame, he thought. Except that he

had pushed himself out before Oscar, selfish as ever. And those few minutes had made the difference, hadn't they? If Oscar had come first then everything would have been reversed.

He thought about that as he thought about it every time he came here. For a moment it seemed desirable. To be enveloped in his mother's love all his life, protected by her, with no worries about the future or the past, nothing to achieve, nothing to strive for. All Oscar had to do was sit back and enjoy it. Or play games all day. But they'd taken that away from him at the age of fourteen. Sent him away. Hands full with the disabled child, they couldn't wait to get rid of him.

22

'You've been lying to Mary, Andrew. I know that.'

Andrew shook his head, trying not to look at the man. But the man was gripping his face with one hand, stopping him from turning his head. He could feel the man's fingers pushing into his jaw.

'You know what will happen to you if you lie to *me* like that?'

Andrew tried to shake his head, but couldn't.

'If you lie to me I'll do something to you that you won't forget in a hurry. Do you want to know what I'll do to you?'

Andrew didn't want to know. He tried to tell the man he was hurting him, but he couldn't open his mouth. He wanted to scream and cry he was so frightened of the man, but the hand on his jaw was so big it was impossible to do anything.

When he had first got here the man had been nice to him. Andrew had already met him before they came here, and heard Mary talking about him. Sometimes the man had visited them at Mary's house, before all this had started, before his mum had vanished. He didn't remember the man being nice to him in the past, but when they had got here tonight the first thing the man had done was crouch down beside him and smile. Then he had reached out a big hand – the same hand now gripping his face – and ruffled his hair. 'Hey, Andrew,' he had said. 'I'm your uncle Gary. Remember me?' Andrew had said he did, though he hadn't known the man was his uncle, only that he was Mary's brother. 'You'll be OK here,' Gary had said then. 'Don't you worry about anything.'

They had been stuck outside for a while because he had been too frightened to walk in and had refused to move. He had expected them to force him. He expected Mary to shout at him and punch him until he had to move. But she didn't. She went inside with Martin and Katy, and sent this man out instead. Andrew hadn't wanted to go in, because he thought that if he let them close the door on him he would never get out again. That was the feeling he had. When he looked at the place from the outside he thought Mary was trying to trick him, driving him here in the middle of the night – the place was a children's home and they had brought him here to punish him for lying to them. It looked huge enough to be a children's home, and black enough, with very tall walls, many windows and a massive chimney at one end. It looked more like a factory than a house. He had seen old factories on the way to school, and imagined that the children's home – where children were freezing and hungry all the time – must be like a factory.

Earlier, it had been dark when they had left Mary's house – Mary, Martin, Katy and himself. They hadn't told him why they were leaving but he guessed at first it was something to do with the police coming, and his mother disappearing. The police had taken John away and he hadn't come back yet. Andrew was happy about that, and hoped he wouldn't ever come back, but he didn't tell anyone that.

No one spoke about John now, at least not in front of Katy and him. Since he had gone Mary and Martin had done a lot of whispering to each other and sometimes he could see Mary staring at him with that look on her face that meant she was angry with him, but since the police came she hadn't hit him, hadn't even shouted at him. Mostly Martin had looked after him. Since the police came things had been different.

Then tonight they had woken him up and told him to get dressed, without saying what was happening. They had put him in the car – in the back with Mary and Katy – but hadn't told him where they were going. As they were leaving Martin had told him he believed him and had stopped asking the questions. But Mary still said he was lying. Mary always knew when he was lying. She spoke to him as he was getting into the car, calling him a liar again. Then he thought that they were going away because of that, somehow – because he was a liar.

He didn't know why he had lied to them, but now that he had started he had to keep it up. Before the police came Mary had stood him in a corner and kicked and slapped him every time he gave the wrong answer. But he hadn't given in. He had cried and cried and curled up in a ball on the floor, but he hadn't told her the truth. He knew that if he told her the truth she would really hurt him, because then he would have admitted the lie. To lie to her was the worst thing he could do – she had told him that many, many times.

He wished now that when she had first asked him what he had seen that night he had just told her the truth straight away. But he had been scared of the way she asked – not shouting at him, or threatening, like normal, but with a smile, as if she were being nice to him. He had guessed that there could be a wrong answer and a right answer and hadn't known which was which, so he had just stood there shaking his head. That wasn't meant to mean that he had seen nothing through the door, just that he didn't know what to say. But she had taken it the wrong way. He knew now he had to stick to the lie no matter what happened, because if he changed his story everything would be worse.

But now everything was getting worse anyway. The room Gary had put him in was big, with three or four chairs and a TV. The TV was a widescreen TV, like the one they had at home, in Mary's house. At first Gary had turned the sound up very high; then Gary, Mary and Martin had all gone away. He didn't know where they had put Katy. He thought they had all gone into the next room, which he had seen – before they shut the door on him – was the kitchen. Despite the sound from the TV he had been able to hear that they were arguing about something. Martin and Mary were shouting. Only Gary spoke very quietly.

Then the door had opened and Gary had walked in, smiling at him. He had sat down next to him, here on the sofa, and asked him questions about the TV programme. Andrew had tried to answer, though he hadn't been watching it very closely. After a little bit Gary had switched the TV off and turned to face him. 'Now we have to be serious,' he said. Andrew had nodded, though he hadn't known what he meant. 'I'm being nice to you, aren't I?' Gary asked him. Andrew had nodded again. 'That's because I like you, Andrew. But I will stop liking you very quickly if you tell me lies. You know you have to tell me the truth, yes?'

'Yes.'

That was when Gary said he had been lying to Mary. That was when he had reached over and grabbed his face. Now Andrew knew Gary wasn't going to be nice to him and he was frightened all over again. Now he wished he had turned round and run away when they had left him outside, by the car.

'I'm not like Mary,' Gary said. 'I'm not nice like her. If you lie to me you will never forget what I will do to you. Think about what I could do to you. Think about it now.'

He didn't want to think about it.

'I could cut your eyes out, with a knife. Or cut your tongue off.'

Andrew started to shiver. There were tears coming out of his eyes again, but Gary didn't stop.

'Or I could take you up to the bathroom and fill a bath with boiling water, then push your head under and hold it there. I can do this to you and nobody would stop me. There's nobody who cares about you. Nobody to stop me. Do you understand what I'm saying?'

There was a sobbing noise coming out of his throat, but he still couldn't open his mouth or move his head.

Gary let go of his face. Andrew sat still, eyes down, not daring to move. Behind Gary he could hear someone else moving in the room. He hoped it was Martin. Maybe Martin would do something to stop Gary. Or Simon. Where was Simon?

'Listen carefully to what I ask you,' Gary told him. 'Look at me when you answer.'

He nodded, still shaking and sobbing.

'Mary tells me that you disobeyed her a few weeks ago and crept up to the top floor of the house. Do you remember doing that?'

He nodded.

Gary grabbed his face and tilted it up again, so that he had to look at him. 'Look at me and answer properly. Do not just nod. Do you remember that?'

'Yes.'

Gary let go again. 'Did you see anything when you did that?'

He shook his head quickly, then remembered

229

and looked up just long enough to say 'no'.

'You saw nothing?'

'No.'

'Did you push open the door to the room where Martin was?'

'No.' He forced himself to keep his eyes on Gary's face when he answered, though he felt terrified now and was sure he was going to wet himself.

'Are you lying to me?'

He shook his head from side to side. 'No. No.'

'Did you see your mother up there?'

His mother. The thing he had seen was horrible. He didn't want to remember it. Was it his mother? Mary had asked him again and again about it. But she hadn't said anything about his mum. He didn't want to think about her, not up there, in that room. He didn't want to talk about it. He didn't want the pictures to come into his head again. It was easy to lie. He *had* to lie to stop seeing the pictures. 'I didn't see anything,' he said.

'You're lying to me.' Gary spoke louder, but didn't shout.

'I'm not. It's the truth.'

'Look at me when you speak. Did you see your mother?'

'No. I didn't see anything. I was outside the door–'

'Look into my eyes when you answer!'

'I *am* looking into your eyes.' He was trying to, as best he could. But his eyes wouldn't stay on Gary's eyes. They kept moving away.

'Don't be cheeky. Look at me!'

'I'm trying–'

'You're lying. I can see it in your eyes. You're lying.'

He started to deny it, but suddenly Gary was gripping him under the jaw, fingers round his neck. 'You little Paki shit. I told you what would happen...' Gary's face was right in front of him, the eyes staring into his head. Andrew felt his fingers digging into his skin. He couldn't breathe. He started to choke.

He heard Mary shouting something; then Gary let go and he fell backwards on the sofa, coughing and spluttering. His throat was burning like it was on fire. He could see Mary standing behind Gary, pulling at his arm. 'No marks!' she shouted. 'I told you. No marks. The first thing they'll do is check for fucking marks.'

Monday

23

Karen watched John Bradley as Ricky Spencer went through the details of the preliminary forensic tests from Lower Wyke Manor, just back that morning. Ricky had given her strict instructions not to depart from the interview plan, but this time she was sure there would be little point in her saying anything at all. Everything was panning out as predicted. She toyed with the pen and pad on the table in front of her, resisting the urge to doodle, feeling sure she could write out the gist of Bradley's answers right now, before he even opened his mouth.

Geoffrey Lane was on hand as before – looking slightly worn after his prolonged sojourn in Bradford – to make sure John Bradley did precisely as he was told. Karen didn't bother arguing with Ricky about his presence, though enquiries since the last round of interviews had confirmed that Shelley & Lane had indeed represented Gary Swales at one point during last year's sad saga of errors. Despite her predictions, Ricky was too excited by the forensics to contemplate anything that might put a damper on proceedings. He was having difficulty keeping his voice to a normal pace and tone. Lane sat impassively, taking few notes. He had already been given a summary during the disclosure session, and as always if Ricky did the plan, there weren't going to be any surprises. Lane had probably sussed that already.

'I'll just recap,' Ricky said. 'The forensic tests show that Rebecca Farrar very recently suffered a traumatic injury in your house, John. She lost a lot of blood, most of it in the kitchen. But there are other traces apparent at various parts of the stairway, in the first-floor bathroom and – again, in large trace quantities – in the small, window-less garret room on the top floor, next door to Simon's bedroom. I reiterate – this is definitely Rebecca's blood we are talking about. That has been confirmed through DNA analysis, the results of which we only received a few hours ago. She was hurt in your house, John. That's what it shows. And the lab report is telling us this didn't happen years or months ago. This hap-pened recently. "Within a period of days" is what it says. They are also telling us that the blood has been cleaned up. "Extensive" efforts to remove traces. We gave the report to your representative earlier. You've had time to consider it. Someone hurt Rebecca, possibly causing a fatal injury; then somebody tried to clean up the blood, all recently, all in your house. You have to account for that, John. Now is your chance.'

Ricky stopped speaking and they waited. Bradley had his head down, not looking at any of them. It was true that he had to account for the forensics, Karen thought, but only because if he didn't suspicion would fall on everyone living in the house. That was what Lane was here to prevent. If Lane weren't in the equation – if it were a normal, honest defence solicitor giving Bradley advice – then the best thing to do would be to ride it out in silence, or just deny knowledge of the blood and clean-up exercise. Because the fact that there were so many other suspects could work to protect John Bradley – to protect all of them, in fact. The prosecution had to prove which person or persons did the act. They couldn't just charge everyone in the house and say to the jury, 'The likelihood is she was killed here and therefore one of these four had to have killed her.' It didn't work like that. They had to be able to prove beyond reasonable doubt precisely who it was. Despite the forensics they didn't, as yet, have enough evidence to do that. Because it could have been any of them. And even if they could prove that all of them had known about – or taken part in – the mopping up, that still didn't get them far enough to charge any of them with murder.

In fact, as far as Karen could see, they couldn't actually show that Rebecca had died in the house at all. If Bradley had a free hand then he could invent some variation of the self-harming story to account for the blood. The timing wasn't that precise as to cause him real difficulties. He could even have got his story straight with the others. But he didn't have a free hand. Because Gary Swales wouldn't want his sister under suspicion. Karen was sure of it.

'Did you hear me, John?' Ricky asked. 'Do you need me to go over the new evidence again?'

Bradley shook his head, then spoke, still looking down. 'I didn't mean to hurt her,' he said. 'I was only trying to help her.'

Karen saw Rick, let out a slow, controlled breath, the relief evident. 'You tried to help who?'

he asked.

'Rebecca. She came to pick up her stuff.'

'Rebecca Farrar came to Lower Wyke Manor to pick up her stuff?'

'Yes.'

'When was this?'

Bradley shrugged. 'Last Saturday. The Saturday you asked me about. The day before you found her body.'

'Saturday nine days ago?'

'I suppose so.'

'That's Saturday the eighth of September.'

'If you say so.'

'She came to Lower Wyke Manor?'

'Yes.'

'How did that happen?'

'She rang me to arrange it.'

'When?'

'I don't remember. A few days before, maybe.'

'On which phone?'

He shook his head, still face down. They had seized his mobile and were in the process of trying to obtain usage details on that and the home phone. 'I don't remember,' he said.

'She phoned you to pick up her stuff. Which stuff are we talking about?'

'A black bin bag of clothes. That was it. We cleared the rest out when she ran away. We took it to the dump.'

'Which dump?'

'The incinerator. They'll have burned it all by now.'

'Go on, then. Tell me about it.'

'I said she could come round on the Saturday.

238

I told the others to leave.'

'The others?'

'The family. Mary, Martin, Simon, Katy.'

'Not Andrew?'

'Him as well.'

'Where did they go?'

'I already told you. I don't know. Maybe a relative. I just wanted them out. I didn't want any friction.'

'Go on. Tell us what happened. We'll come back to the detail later.'

'She came round. I gave her the bag of stuff. She wanted to check that was all, though. So I let her in. I went upstairs and waited in the bedroom. Tried to keep out of her way. I knew there'd be trouble. But after half an hour she was still there, so I went to find out what was happening. She was in the kitchen, sitting on the floor, crying. She was cutting her arms with a kitchen knife. I couldn't fucking believe it.'

He stopped. Ricky waited. Lane didn't bat an eyelid. Karen started to note the details, with pointers for follow-up questions.

'There was blood all over,' Bradley continued. 'I tried to get the knife off her. She was mad. She was doing it all the time – trying to harm herself – I told you about it before. She was already covered in scabs and sores and stuff when she turned up at the door. Hair all shaved off like a lunatic. Now she's sitting there trying to do herself with a nine-inch blade. What was I meant to do?' He paused, as if someone might answer. But nobody spoke. 'I went to take it off her,' he said. 'That was all it took. She was on her feet like a fucking cat, having a go at me. She wouldn't let me have it. She was lashing out all over, with a kitchen knife. I thought she was going to kill herself. Or me. When I got close to her she smacked me in the face. More than once. Bust my nose. That must be how my blood was on her. In the end I had to hit her. Just the once. Clouted her across the face. Not hard. Not really. I was just trying to calm her down. I dunno what happened. She must have slipped or something. She sort of fell over sideways onto the floor. I bent down and took the knife off her and she was lying there with her eyes open, breathing heavily. I told her to stop mucking about. I put the knife away and started to clear up. She had all the clothes out of the bin bag, strewn across the floor. And blood all over. Her arms were covered in blood. There was blood all over the house. She'd been walking around with her arms cut to ribbons while I'd been sitting in the bedroom waiting. I went to get a mop and pail from the cellar and when I got back she was still lying there, eyes open. I had a look at her and realized something was wrong. She wasn't breathing.' He stopped, took a deep breath. 'I panicked, I suppose. I should have just called the police – you lot – and the ambulance. But she was dead. I think she was dead. I tried to get her breathing again, doing mouth-to-mouth. It was disgusting. She was dead already. I shouldn't have touched her, but I just panicked.'

He seemed to have come to a halt. Karen looked up at him. It might be all rubbish but it had kept her busy, head down. So many questions they needed to put if they were going to pick holes in it.

'What did you do when you panicked?' Ricky asked.

'Put her in the van and dumped her. Came back and cleaned up.' He spoke matter-of-factly, without any emotion. He wasn't a particularly good liar, Karen thought. 'It was stupid, I know. But I wasn't thinking straight. I thought you lot would say I'd killed her if I called you. Which is what happened anyway. But I didn't mean to hurt her. She was just going crazy. I had to do something. She must have hit her head when she fell. That wasn't down to me. It was an accident. That's all.' He brought his head up and looked at Lane, who gave him a very slight nod. 'That's all,' he repeated. End of story. Karen wondered if there was any truth in it at all.

Ricky took a moment to consider it. He was almost smiling. 'OK, John. I'm glad you've told us all that,' he said. 'We need to go into it in detail now. We need to ask you questions about each bit...'

Bradley was shaking his head already. 'That's all,' he said again. 'That's all I'm telling you. You lot are out to fuck me over. All I did was try to help the girl.'

'That may be,' Ricky said. 'But we still have to go over it in more detail.'

'That's all. You heard me. I've said enough.' He looked at Lane, who shrugged. 'I don't have to say anything else.'

'It might he better for you if you–'

'I think my client is right,' Lane interrupted. 'He still has a right to silence. He can exercise that whenever he chooses.'

'It's a bit late now, Mr Lane.'

No. That's not true. My client has been honest. And he can choose to say nothing further whenever he wishes. That's the law, Officer. You know that.'

Karen sat back, enjoying the charade. Ricky was looking a little desperate now.

'Perhaps at this point I should speak to my client in private,' Lane said.

24

It was just after one-thirty as Karen turned into the long cobbled street that led steeply uphill to Gary Swales's new place in Thornton. Sixteen months ago he had been living in relatively cheap housing in Halifax. The house had been only three or four years old – a modern Barratt-type development – with neighbours too close for comfort. The place had been upmarket for Halifax, but it was already way below even Swales's supposedly legitimate means.

Swales was an irritating mix of rash and cautious. He had been stupid enough to target investigating officers (though given the result she would have to think now that maybe that wasn't so obviously off the wall), but cautious enough to have carefully and intelligently layered almost ten years of drugs money into ordinary, working businesses. By the time they had started on him the original source of his funds was well and truly buried. That made it difficult to get asset-seizing orders, or even to get access to the hill accounts. Swales was usually just one investor in the firms he managed, sometimes not even the main investor. Mostly, the life he led looked legal.

People could have very short memories – if money was involved to help the process. These days not many cared to remember the days when Swales had been a mere runner for a minor crack dealer named Phil Brown. Karen hadn't been in West Yorkshire then, but even eleven years ago, when Swales had been working for someone Karen *had* looked at – a middle-range dealer called Mark Coates – he had still been a relatively small fish in the pond. Then Coates had gone down for eighteen years and Swales had 'inherited' the business. Or so they thought.

As if to rub their noses in it, just under a year ago he had bought and moved to the place she was going to now – something on a much grander scale than the Barratt home. At the end of a fairly normal terraced street 'the Swales complex' (as they had taken to calling it) was set back from the road a good distance, making it much more private. From afar it looked like an old factory, constructed from solid slabs of Yorkshire stone. As with Lower Wyke Manor, Swales had spent a lot of money completely renovating the premises, but in this case also treating the stone to remove the smog stains. There was little in his life that hadn't benefited from a good scrubbing.

There was a long, block-shaped central building, four floors high, with a tall, round furnace chimney rising at one end, then other smaller buildings partly enclosing a cobbled courtyard. Most people would guess it had been a mill of some sort, but Karen knew the place was the old workhouse. Before Swales had bought it up you could still read the crumbling letters chiselled into the gatepost masonry: 'Thornton Workhouse for Indigent Children.' All Karen knew about workhouses came from watching Charles Dickens adaptations at Christmas. From which she imagined the place had witnessed a fair amount of misery a couple of hundred years ago. But gutted, redesigned and spruced up, with the surrounding yards landscaped and carefully tended, it looked like an attractive, spacious property for the area's top slicers. Not something a police officer would ever be able to afford, not even at ACPO level. Swales, she knew, had taken out loans to pay for it. His funds were so carefully integrated into legitimate fronts that these days he probably found it genuinely hard to get his hands on raw cash.

She parked the car and covered the last two hundred yards on foot, turning left at the street before the crest of the hill. The houses leading up to Swales's place were all built along the same lines as the workhouse, but were much less grand. The street that led around to the rear of the hill comprised ordinary working-class, back-to-back terraces. She took a snicket at the end of it (smelling of stale urine and littered with empty beer cans) and walked through some long-neglected, overgrown fields until she came to a high hawthorn hedge.

There she crouched down, uncapped the field glasses she'd brought from the car and scanned the view beyond the hedge. She now had a clear view of the main building as well as part of the half-enclosed yard and the rear gates. Between the hedge and the house was a low wall, topped with shards of broken glass. She knew Swales had security cameras installed – and found them quite quickly – but guessed he wouldn't have gone as far as employing someone to monitor them 24/7. He might be in the same golf club as Michael Surani, but he was still a long way short of Surani's wealth and lifestyle. Or class.

There were two cars in the yard, one of them Swales's Merc, the other a red Polo she didn't recognize. She swept the windows looking for signs of movement, specifically for signs of Swales's sister. That was why she was here.

John Bradley had stuck to his decision to say nothing more for an hour and a half, while they put to him a whole series of obvious follow-up questions. Ricky even let Karen join in. But Bradley had his instructions and wasn't going to move. So what they were left with was a clever confession, of sorts, and a mass of loose ends and unexplained inconsistencies. The gaps hadn't bothered Ricky. He was riding high – to his mind the case was all but closed. By the time the interview was over he had already decided to put the file up to the lawyers to authorize a charge and cut the enquiry back to one team – her own – with immediate effect.

He knew Bradley had to be lying, of course. There was even evidence to prove he was lying – at least about parts of the account. The medical evidence, for instance, strongly suggested that the fatal head injury had been caused well before the time of death – a matter of days rather than minutes. And it was impossible Bradley had taken Rebecca's body to the M62 in his van because they had already scoured that for blood traces and found nothing. The van definitely did not appear on any of the relevant CCTV footage. The idea that Rebecca had covered her own body with injuries, then been accidentally killed by John Bradley was simply comical.

But more than that he had to be lying because there was no *reason* for him to have killed Rebecca Farrar, because he had no good motive. What could constitute a good motive for tying up a young girl and systematically torturing her, before eventually delivering a blow so powerful that it killed her? This wasn't a gangland killing, so the idea had not been to extract information, or strike revenge, or set an ugly example of group discipline. And it wasn't a sex case: she hadn't been put through all that for male pleasure. So what was left?

The few words Mary Swales had spoken to Karen about Rebecca and her children had betrayed the tip of something twisted, she thought. There had been no sympathy for Rebecca. Mary hadn't cared that she was dead, or what had happened to her. That wasn't within the normal range of female responses to such a situation. Add to that the image of Mary desperately hugging one of the victim's children, as if the little girl were now her own – an image that even a social worker had found uncomfortable – and you could get the start of a different theory.

A car registered to Mary Swales was on their list of outstanding vehicles caught on the CCTV footage. A grey Nissan SUV had passed the place where Rebecca's body was found during the early hours of that morning. Mary had been asked about it, of course, and had come up with a simple explanation – the car had been registered to her for insurance purposes, but was in fact her husband's. As far as she was aware he had sold it on, some months before. That had been enough for the enquiry to assume that John Bradley had used the missing vehicle – the Nissan – to dump Rebecca's body. That he was now saying he used his van was a puzzle for Ricky Spencer, but nothing bigger than that. Ricky had a confession, and as far as that went he was old school through and through. He wasn't going to push the boat out to lean on anyone else, because even if John Bradley was lying, there was no doubt that he had taken some part in the killing. Her blood was in his house and in his hair. For Ricky the questions and gaps were details around the edges. For Karen they pointed fingers elsewhere.

She had to argue the case for pulling in the others for a good twenty minutes. Ricky finally gave the go-ahead only to humour her, she thought. Or to get her off his back. But by then it was already too late. When they got to Lower Wyke Manor there was no sign of Mary, Martin, Simon or the children. The indications were that they'd cleared out in a hurry. She sent Marcus and Gerry Owen to Martin Bradley's work premises in Keighley, then came to Swales's place alone, guessing Mary might have run to her brother for protection.

Marcus had called her ten minutes ago to confirm they had found Martin, who on arrest denied he knew where his mother was, but confirmed he had spent the last night at his uncle's place. He had used his one personal phone call to contact Gary Swales, who was reportedly on his way to Trafalgar House, so if Gary Swales was still at home Karen could expect that to change soon. Marcus had asked whether she wanted assistance, but she had told him to get a search warrant for Swales's place instead. If she could spot Mary Swales now she wouldn't wait for the technicalities, but it was as well to have them covered.

She had been watching for less than fifteen minutes when Gary Swales came into view at one of the doors to a side building. He was wearing a suit, open-neck shirt, no tie. He paused in the doorway, talking to someone within. She thought he looked harassed and in a rush, anxious to get away from whoever was holding him back. She adjusted the focus on the binoculars and saw that whoever it was had an arm on his and was literally holding him back. As far as she knew Swales was unmarried and lived alone, with no current girlfriend. She saw him prise the arm away and walk towards the Merc. From behind the door Mary Swales stepped into view. Bingo.

Gary got in the Merc and exited with a squeal of rubber through the rear gates, so keen to get out that he forgot to close the gates behind him. Karen waited for a few minutes, then walked to the end of the field, onto the lane Swales had used to drive away, and then down to the entrance. There was a camera on the driveway, so if anyone was bothering to watch she would be in full view. She guessed Mary Swales would have other things on her mind.

Once she was in the courtyard she stood by the door Swales had emerged from and listened. She could hear nothing. The building was a low, one-storey annexe to the main dwelling. She tried the door and it opened. She pushed it back and stepped inside, paused, listening again, again hearing nothing. She was standing in a small passageway leading to a stairway. Two doors came off in front of her. She placed the binoculars on the floor at her feet. It wouldn't hurt to look around, she thought, see what was new in Gary's life.

She started with the nearest door but immediately found herself looking at the sleeping form of one of the Farrar children – the younger, the little girl. She was flat out on her back in a cot, breathing peacefully. In a quick glance Karen noted a table and chair, as well as two or three plastic boxes of toys. There was rubber crash matting on the floor. For a room the child could only have been in a few nights, in the house of someone who had no kids, it looked quite cosy. On the chair was a baby intercom unit with a single green light showing. She wondered how sensitive it could be. Through the flooring, or the walls, from another part of the building, she thought she could hear, or feel, movement – footsteps, or a door opening.

She held her breath and closed the door very carefully, then moved on to the next room. This time the door was locked, with the key in the lock. She turned it slowly, but it still made a loud enough noise to be picked up if there was another intercom within. There wasn't. Instead she opened the door on to the elder of the Farrar children – the boy. He was sitting against the wall in a bare, completely unfurnished room, wide awake, staring straight at her, eyes big with fright. The contrast couldn't have been more alarming. Martin Bradley's natural child was set up in a room with toys, a cot, comfort and warmth. His stepchild was in here, frightened and alone.

Karen felt something shift inside her. She had been focusing quite coldly on the possible threats to Rebecca's children, more because she was keen to get Mary Swales than because she cared about the children, but here was the reality of it. She could see it in the child's eyes, in the way he was sitting. He was frightened because a stranger had come in on him – yes – but there was more to it than that.

'Andrew?' she said to him, stepping forward. 'Are you OK?' She could feel her pulse quickening a little. The child looked miserable, isolated, on the point of tears. His face was dirty, streaked with grime around the nose and eyes. Probably he had been crying to himself for hours, shut up in here, without attention or contact with anyone else. He was six years old and locked into a room by himself, with nothing to amuse him. What was it – some kind of punishment?

She felt the thing that had moved inside her twist up in sudden anger. Her own childhood had been littered with such punishments, all at the hands of her mother. She pushed the feeling back, then tried hard to smile again. She took another step towards him. She had spent nearly five years on the Child Protection Team. She knew infant desperation when she saw it. It was something that lurked in the back of everything they did. If the abuse was bad enough, prolonged and severe enough, then they never got rid of it. Even when you got them smiling you could still see it there, behind the laughter. Kids started out with a fundamental trust in adults. They lay on the floor as helpless babies and couldn't function any other way. They *had* to trust you. They didn't expect their parents to lean down and stub cigarettes out on them. But once that started all the assumptions got knocked out of place. They quickly grew a carapace of fear. Then you could see the constant wariness in everything they did. It wasn't a mere belief they grew but something more fundamental, below belief. Other people became things that hurt you, and that lesson became hard-wired into their personality. It stopped them being able to form relationships in later life; it made them into partially socialized teenagers who inflicted the same treatment on those around them. It was all they knew.

'It's OK, Andrew,' she said to him, quietly. He looked like he was about to start screaming. But now she could hear footsteps on the stairs behind her. Someone *had* heard something. Whoever it was, they were already in the passageway, moving quickly. She kept her eyes on Andrew, then stepped back towards the doorway. 'I'm police,' she said to Andrew, but loud enough to be heard by whoever was approaching. 'There's no need to be afraid...' It was all she had time to say before Mary Swales came into view, moving so fast she had to slow suddenly as she entered the room.

Karen had her in the corner of her eye and was turning to face her when she saw her arm swing out. She flinched, and ducked, but too late. Something heavy struck her across the side of the head. The blow was hard and unexpected enough to surprise her, hard enough to bring a flash of pain to her eyes, but not powerful enough to take her legs away. She yelled and stepped sideways, bumping into the wall. To her left she heard Andrew start wailing, then Mary's high-pitched voice, shouting above him, 'Fucking thieving burglar!'

She felt another blow, glancing off the back of her shoulder, then recovered her balance and shouted at the top of her voice, 'I'm police. Cut it out, you idiot. I'm police.'

'Liar! Fucking liar!'

Swales was swinging again. Karen crouched beneath the blow, turning to look at her. Swales was closing fast on her, determined to get a good shot in. Was it a poker she was holding? Karen waited until she pulled her arm back to strike again, then quickly covered the space between them. She tried to get a leg behind Swales, to trip her, but Swales was quicker than she thought. She saw it coming and lunged at Karen, arms flailing. The weapon dropped to the ground with a clatter. Karen felt nails rake her face.

It was messy, desperate, undignified. Fights always were if there wasn't a serious weapon involved. She didn't feel threatened by Swales, didn't even feel much of an adrenalin response kicking in. But as Swales's nails stung her skin she thought enough was enough. She didn't want the woman to mark her. Ducking again, she balanced herself, then brought an elbow up into Swales's chin. She heard a grunt of pain, felt the head jerk back, but Swales didn't slow much. She was going for her hair now, trying to get a handful of it, to make a real cat-fight out of it. Karen let her fill her hands, then slipped a leg behind her and put all her weight against the short, compact body, catching an arm as Swales toppled backwards, still hanging on to a clump of her hair with one hand.

It worked, partially. Swales ended up on her side with Karen holding her right arm and hand in a more or less authorized restraining grip, twisting it straight up and backwards to keep her pinned to the floor. But the hand she was holding was still tangled in her hair and her scalp was smarting, bringing tears to her eyes and keeping her bent over double to stop Swales wrenching the hair out at the roots. She shut her eyes and twisted back on Swales's hand. Swales started to shriek, but still didn't let go.

'If you don't let go of my hair,' Karen said, gritting her teeth, 'I'll break your wrist.' She applied more pressure.

Swales let go.

Karen straightened up, still locking the arm, then looked for the boy. He was sitting exactly where he had been when she had first come in, knees hugged up against his chest, shivering uncontrollably. He'd stopped screaming. 'It's OK,

Andrew,' she said, out of breath now. 'I won't hurt you. I'm a police officer. OK?' He stared at her, then looked down at Mary, writhing on the floor, still in pain. 'I said I'm police,' Karen repeated, raising her voice. 'Do you understand what that means?'

He looked back at her, then wrinkled up his face and began to whimper. Karen changed her grip on Swales's arm, holding it clamped against her body. She managed to get her mobile phone out of her back pocket. She hit the fast dial for the CAD room, gave her details and requested urgent assistance.

'You're under arrest for murder and for assaulting a police officer,' she said, once she'd got her phone out of the way. 'You understand me, Mary?' She restrained an urge to kick the woman.

25

'I don't know who she spoke to,' Martin Bradley said. 'I don't know if she phoned. I wasn't told how it happened. I was told that she was coming to the house to pick up her stuff. That's it.' He spoke quietly, his gaze mostly on the table in front of him, but every now and then he would look up and make brief eye contact with DC John Sanderson. He hadn't looked at Marcus since being brought into the room. Marcus thought he made just enough eye contact, at just the right moments, to make it difficult – from body language alone –

254

to decide whether he was lying. His clothes had all been seized, as was routine, and he was clearly uncomfortable in the yellow custody overalls. He kept moving as if the suit was sticking to him under his arms, or too tight across the chest. That made him seem more nervous. But nerves didn't necessarily mean he was lying. Surely he had to be nervous whatever his involvement? He had been arrested on suspicion of his wife's murder.

'Who told you that?' Sanderson asked. 'Who told you Rebecca was coming?'

'My dad. John Bradley. He wanted everyone out of the house when she arrived. He didn't want trouble. That's what he said.'

'What kind of trouble?'

Martin shrugged. 'I don't know. That's what he said.'

'Did you know what he meant?'

'I'm not sure. I suppose he didn't want any arguments.'

'So he told everyone to move out of the house?'

'Yes. We all had to leave.'

If he was lying – and so far Marcus was almost sure that he was – then he was doing it well, striking just the right note. He had already built them a picture of a family living in constant fear of a violent father figure, but he had managed to do it while appearing reluctant to say too much against John Bradley. For that matter, he had even resisted the kind of wholesale character assassination John Bradley had indulged in about Rebecca. Martin seemed unwilling to criticize Rebecca at all. That was also a nice approach – nice for building sympathy from the jury. Suggest very delicately that

Rebecca could be difficult – that was as far as he'd gone – but without openly attacking her.

'Wouldn't there have been easier ways to return Rebecca's property to her than to shift an entire family out?' Sanderson suggested. 'Take her goods to her, perhaps?'

'Maybe. But I did what I was told to do.'

'Are you frightened of your father?'

Martin shrugged again. 'He wanted to deal with it that way. That was OK, I guess.'

'And you didn't want to see your wife yourself?'

He shook his head.

'You're shaking your head. Does that mean no?'

'I didn't want to see her. No. It was over between us.'

'But she was the mother of your children?'

'My child. Katy.'

'You're Andrew's father, too, aren't you? Legally, I mean?'

'Am I? I don't know. I'm not his natural father.'

'We know that. But you've played the role of father figure in his life for some time.'

'Of course. I've tried to.'

'My client has been in loco parentis,' his solicitor said, interrupting. 'He accepts that. And he's been a caring, careful, diligent father. But I'm not sure that affects the legal position. What's your point, DC Sanderson?'

Marcus watched Sanderson react to the interruption. The solicitor was called Geoffrey Lane. He had been sent by a 'bent' London firm. That was how Karen had already explained it to Marcus. Lane had represented John Bradley, at first, had been in an interview with him that very morning. But now he had dropped him. There was a conflict of interest, he claimed. He couldn't represent both Martin and his dad. Karen had warned them this would happen. Yet John Sanderson was still incredibly careful with Lane, Marcus thought. Presumably he didn't want to appear antagonistic on the video recording. The onset of video recording had made everyone over-careful, Marcus thought. He wanted to tell the solicitor to shut up and let his client answer the questions. But his role here was limited. He was note-taker, in effect, too junior to be allowed to ask questions. As Ricky Spencer had made clear, he was lucky to have been allowed in at all.

'So when did you leave the house?' Sanderson asked. He had been thrown by the interruption. He had been about to try to get at why Martin didn't see his wife himself. That was a good line, rich in possibilities. But Lane had made him forget it now. Marcus had already noted with disappointment that John Bradley's confession was ineluctably pushing Sanderson into using this interview more as a tool for getting corroboration against John Bradley than unearthing his son's role in the killing.

'We left the day before,' Martin answered. It was what his father had already told them. Somehow, despite John Bradley being in custody, they had managed to get a story together.

'We went to an aunt's place. Mavis Rimmer. She lives in Hipperholme. You can check with her, I guess.'

'Who went with you?'

'All of us went. Me, my mum and the kids.'

257

'The kids? You mean Katy and Andrew?'

'Yes.'

'So what about Simon?'

'Simon as well.'

'Right. And how long did you stay?'

'Until the next day. We came back early evening.'

'I see.' Sanderson paused to turn a page of his preparatory notes. 'I'll come back to that in a moment. But for now can you tell me what you saw when you came back to the house?'

'What I saw?'

'Yes. Did you see Rebecca, for example?'

'No. She'd already left.'

'Had she? How did you know that?'

'That's what I was told. By my dad.'

'So your dad was in when you got back. Can you be very specific about the time you returned?'

'No. It was early evening. I can't remember the exact time. There was no need to notice the exact time. I didn't think anything was wrong.'

'What was your dad doing when you got back?'

'We didn't know.'

'How do you mean?'

'He was upstairs. He told us not to come up. He shouted down the stairs to us, telling us not to come up.'

'Did you do that? Did you do as he told you?'

'At first. Then I think my mum went up to ask how it had gone. With Rebecca, I mean. I heard them arguing so I went up, too. After I'd got the kids to bed.' He brushed a strand of hair away from the side of his face. He had long, dark-brown hair, wavy as it got past his shoulders. When they had first arrested him, at the garage

258

where he worked, he had it tied back in a ponytail that fell to below his shoulder blades. Marcus thought he had quite delicate features – feminine, even: a small nose and chin; wide, blue eyes with long lashes. He could see how he might appear attractive, in a sensitive way, but he wondered how hard life was at the garage. The society of car mechanics was a very male affair, no doubt. Martin didn't look as if he would naturally fit into it. Even his hands were graceful – long fingers and precise movements. They didn't look as though they would be much good at wrenching loose stuck bolts. But then Martin had been working on reception when they arrived, so maybe he didn't actually get his hands dirty. Certainly, they weren't dirty today. Not a trace of oil or engine grease. The garage was owned by Gary Swales, of course, his concerned uncle.

'You heard your mum and dad arguing. Arguing in what way?' Sanderson asked.

'It sounded like an argument. I wasn't sure.' He shifted in the seat, apparently embarrassed. 'They can argue very badly, sometimes shouting...'

'Violence? Was there ever violence between them?'

'You know there was. You've been called to the house before.'

'Were they both violent?'

'My mum's not violent. No.'

'Was your dad being violent on this occasion?'

'I thought he might be. Or I thought it might get there. That's why I went up.'

'To do what?'

Good question, Marcus thought. Martin

wouldn't be capable of handling his father. They were so different they were like different species. The father was built for violence. Not so the son. The son had been spoilt by his mum, perhaps. Was that the key to him?

'To stop him, maybe,' Martin said. 'I don't know really.'

'Have you had to stop him before?'

He shook his head. 'I haven't been there when it was bad.'

'But on this occasion you went up. What did you see?'

A long pause. Martin averted his gaze and stared at the floor.

'Can you tell us what you saw?'

Still no reply.

'It's important you tell us, Martin.'

'I don't know whether I should.' He looked at the solicitor for help.

'Do you need to ask your solicitor in private?'

'That's all right. I can advise my client now,' Lane said. He turned to Martin. 'You should tell these officers the whole truth, Martin. You must do that.'

Marcus felt something like admiration for them. It was a well-worked double act. Sanderson wasn't a match for it.

'I saw blood stains,' Martin said, almost too quiet to be heard.

'Can you repeat that a bit louder, please?' Sanderson asked.

'I saw some blood stains along the walls of the stairs. My dad was cleaning it up. He said he'd had a nosebleed.'

260

'So you asked him about it?'

'Yes. We both did. My mum and me. He had cleaned out one of the top rooms and washed the walls. We didn't know why.'

'Did you ask him why?'

'Yes. I told you that.'

'And what did he say?'

'I told you. He said he had a nosebleed.'

'How much blood was there?'

'A lot. Quite a lot.'

'More than a nosebleed would make?'

'Maybe.'

'Did you say that to him?'

'No. He was in a mood. He'd been drinking, I think. I didn't want him getting aggressive. We were trying to calm him.'

'Did you ask him about it after that night? Perhaps when he was calmer. The next day, for example?'

'I don't think so. I don't remember.'

'You sure about that?'

'I might have asked him. But if I did he will have said the same.'

'Were you happy with that?'

'Happy?'

'Did you accept his explanation?'

'It wasn't up to me to accept or reject it. That's what he said. That's all.'

'But you knew something had gone on?'

'Something. Yes. But I didn't know what.'

'And didn't ask?'

'I did ask. Yes. He said he'd had a nosebleed.'

'But that was ridiculous, wasn't it? That couldn't explain the blood. I told you earlier about the forensic evidence suggesting that large quantities of blood had been–'

'I didn't see large quantities.'

'Because your dad had cleaned it?'

'I don't know. I can only tell you what I saw. Or what he told me. That's what I've done. I've told you the truth.' He looked confused by it. 'He's my dad. You understand that?'

Sanderson looked at him for a while. 'Yes. I understand that,' he said. 'Would you give evidence about what you've just told us? Even though he's your dad?'

Martin looked at Lane, who spoke quickly. 'If that is being suggested, Officer, then we should not be in a formal interview with my client under arrest. You know that. We should be taking a statement from him instead.'

'Yes. Of course.' For a moment Sanderson looked at a loss for words. He flicked through the sheets of paper in front of him, then glanced at his watch. 'We've been going over an hour,' he said. 'I think now would be a good time for a break. When we come back then we can go over all you've already said in more detail. Then we can decide what to do. Is that OK, Martin?'

Martin nodded.

'All right, then,' Sanderson said. He turned to Marcus. 'Do you have anything to add?'

Marcus was surprised. But not too surprised to let the opportunity slip. He had kept his mouth shut, as instructed. But Sanderson was giving him permission now, whether he intended to or not.

'Just a couple of things,' he said quickly. 'Firstly, Martin, I would like to ask you about your relationship with Becky.'

'What about it?'

'Did you love her?'

'Love her?'

'Yes. Did you love her?'

Martin looked troubled by that, as if he didn't know what the word meant. 'When?' he asked.

'At any time?'

'I'm not sure.'

'You had a child with her?'

'Yes.'

'Was that intentional?'

'What do you mean?'

'Did you both want to have a child? Was the child planned?'

'Yes. We tried for a child. We wanted one.' He coloured bright red.

'So you must have felt something for Becky?'

'I did. Yes. I did feel something.'

'Just not love?'

'I'm not sure what you mean by that.'

'Aren't you? I'm just using the ordinary English word. Nothing complicated. I love my mother, for example.' But not my father, he thought. '*You* love your mother, too, right?'

'Yes. Of course.'

'Do you love her a lot?'

He looked puzzled by that. 'A lot? I love her like you're meant to. Like any normal person.'

'Of course. So you know what I mean by love, then.'

'It's not the same, What I felt for Becky isn't what I feel feel for my mum. They're two different things.'

263

'I realize that. You had sexual relations with Becky. Not with your mum, So you were closer to Becky, in fact. Is that not right?'

The words 'sexual relations' made him almost flinch.

'I... We did... Yes ... we did ... *that*. We did what you said. Does that make me *closer*? I'm not sure.'

'You're not sure? Sorry. I was making assumptions. I shouldn't do that. You think it's possible that you might love your mum more than you loved Becky? Is that what you mean?'

'Well ... yes...' Beside him, his solicitor started to stir. They were both unsure where the line was leading, but they both sensed danger. 'I've known my mum all my life. I only knew Becky for a few years.'

'And it's a close family.'

He didn't reply.

'Would you agree it's a close family?'

'In a way. It's a normal family.'

'You're close to your mum and your dad?'

'More my mum.'

'Your mum has probably protected you from your dad, right? When you were growing up?'

'Protected me? Sometimes. Maybe.'

'Because your dad has a temper?'

'Yes.'

'Used his hand on you? Hit you?'

He shrugged. 'Yes. I suppose so.'

'But not your mum?'

'No. Never. My mum would never hit me.'

'Did your mum like Becky?'

He opened his mouth to reply, caught himself, then closed his mouth again.

'Did your mum get on well with her?'

'I think so. Like I said, Becky could be difficult sometimes.'

'You think it might have been a bit difficult for Becky, living with you and your mum? Maybe that was why she could be "difficult". I mean, you were a very close family unit, before Becky even arrived, right?'

A frown, but no reply.

'Do you think Becky could have felt isolated living at Lower Wyke Manor? You were closer to your mum than to her, after all.'

'I don't know.' He was flustered. 'I don't know what she felt.'

'You didn't ask her? You weren't even *that* close to her?'

'I was close to her. I didn't say I wasn't close to her.'

'Neither did I. I just said you were closer to your mum. Which you agreed with. You loved your mum but you didn't love Becky. That's what you said.'

He sat in silence, looking at the table. But he didn't deny it.

'Did you not even love her in the beginning, when you first met her?'

'That's all foolish stuff. Stupid infatuation.'

'You don't believe in love like that, then?'

'It's not love when you want to ... you know ... when you want to...'

Marcus waited.

'When you want to have ... sexual relations. That's just a teenage thing.'

'It's what made your daughter.'

265

'That was later.'

'When you felt even less for Becky? Is that what you mean?'

'I don't know. You're confusing me now...'

'What's this got to do with anything?' Lane spoke, finally.

'It's quite important,' Marcus replied. 'You know that, Mr Lane.' He shifted his eyes to Lane's and stared impassively at him. 'It's important to establish what your client felt for Becky because someone – maybe more than one person – murdered her. And that's what your client was arrested for. On suspicion of doing just that.' He paused momentarily, then turned back to Martin again. 'This would explain why you don't seem at all bothered about Becky's death, Martin. Because you didn't really care for her, did you?'

'I didn't want her to die.'

'Are you bothered that she died?' If he was he hadn't said so. It was an obvious omission, the main reason Marcus thought he must be lying.

'Of course I am.'

'Did you cry when, you found out?'

'No... I mean ... no. But I was upset. I didn't want her to die, but she had left us. She walked out on us all. She left her kids.'

'Did you care that she walked out?'

'Of course I did.'

'Why?'

'She abandoned the children.'

'Not you? She didn't abandon you? That isn't what you felt?'

'I was more concerned about the kids. But yes ... she abandoned me as well.'

'Did you cry about that?'

'No. I had too much to do. I had two kids to support, to care for.'

'And you didn't love her anyway.'

Martin stared at him. 'Maybe I did love her. How do you define that?'

'Did you *like* her?'

Another frown, deeper this time.

'We're talking about your wife, yes? Did you like your wife?'

'I know who we're talking about. I'm trying to think...'

'You have to think about whether you liked her?'

'Yes. I've already told you how difficult she could be. Sometimes it was very hard.'

'Would you have considered divorcing her?'

Martin mumbled something.

'I didn't catch that,' John Sanderson said. 'Can you say it again, please?'

'Maybe,' Martin said. 'Maybe.'

'I see. So you really weren't getting on well at all?' Marcus asked.

'When?'

'When she left you. That's what you say happened, so let's run with that. When she left you, you weren't getting on with her at all, right?'

'No. We weren't getting on. Obviously.' His face was turning red again.

'Could that be why she left?'

'I don't know. I really don't know.' His shoulders twitched. He sniffed hard.

'She was miserable because she was living with a man who didn't love or like her, because that man loved his mother more, because...' He paused.

267

Martin's lip was trembling, his eyes moist. 'I don't know,' he mattered. 'Poor Becky. Poor, poor Becky. I don't know.'

'Did you ever see poor Becky harm herself?'

He shook his head. It was an instant response, while the emotions were distracting him, perhaps. Marcus saw Lane frown deeply and look over at Martin. But the tears were running out of Martin now – he wasn't looking at anyone.

'You never saw her burn herself or anything like that?'

'No. No. Nothing.'

'And you would know if she did do that, obviously. You slept with her after all. You saw her naked.'

'My client is upset,' Lane said. 'You've upset him with this line of questioning. It's too intrusive.'

'Murder is intrusive,' Marcus said, not even looking at him. 'You did sleep with her, didn't you, Martin?'

Martin nodded.

'You're nodding. You slept with her but you never saw any marks that she herself made on her body?'

'No. I saw...' He stopped and looked up, remembering, perhaps, that allowing the injuries to be inflicted by his father, and not Becky, might have implications for more than John Bradley. Because the injuries, as he knew, were caused over a period of several weeks. 'I don't know,' he said. He glanced at Lane.

'I think we should break,' Lane said. 'We can't continue with Martin in tears. It's oppressive.'

Marcus opened his mouth to argue with that,

but John Sanderson was there first. 'Of course. We can break if that's what you want, Mr Lane. That was the plan anyway.'

Marcus closed his mouth. That was it, then. The chance was gone. If they paused then Lane would speak to his client, and Martin would get himself in order. But there was nothing he could do about it. Sanderson was in charge. He took a breath, then smiled. 'Of course, Martin,' he said. 'You obviously need time to consider your replies.'

26

Before Social Services arrived Mary sat on a chair in her brother's kitchen and kept up a steady torrent of verbal abuse for twenty minutes, only pausing to try to console the smaller child – Katy – when she became too upset by it all. The arrival of two uniformed officers had served to end the physical struggle, but that was it. They moved Mary and the children to the kitchen to await Social Services and almost immediately the abuse began. The presence of two other police officers didn't seem to deter her.

Nor did the presence of children, not even Katy, whom she clearly cared about, even if it was in some dysfunctional way. Karen didn't dare move the kids away from her until the social workers arrived, so the kids were privy to the whole thing. Swales sat with the little girl on her knee, stroking her hair and shouting at Karen.

The boy sat on a chair opposite her. If the girl started to cry, Karen noted, then Swales was quick to provide both physical and verbal reassurance. By contrast, the boy was hardly looked at. He would have been left to shiver in silence, had not one of the PCs knelt down beside him and tried to distract him by showing him items of kit from his belt.

Karen didn't like the kids being distressed, but the priority was to get them – or at least the boy – away from Swales, so she wanted Swales still to be in full swing when the social workers arrived, so they could see the reality of it. She sat next to the boy and smiled at Mary, waiting for her to take a breath, then asking, with monotonous persistence, 'What was Andrew doing locked in a bare, unfurnished room, Mary? Can you answer that question, please?'

There was never an answer, never even an acknowledgement that she had heard the question. Just the same run of insults and accusations. 'You're a fucking dyke bitch. You hear me. I know what you fucking are. You're a dyke. Get these fuckers out of the room,' nodding at the two uniformed men, 'then we'll see how strong you are. I'll break your fucking neck. You're persecuting us. You're trying to ruin our lives. You tried to kill me in there. The kids are witnesses. You smelly fucking cunt. You're a bitch and a cunt. You know you are. You'll pay for this. It won't always be like this. You listening to me? One day you'll be out by yourself, without your big gay friends, your puff brigade. You'll never know what fucking hit you. You don't fuck with us. You don't fuck with a

Swales. You tried to fuck over Gary before. He'll have you. I want a phone call now. I want him to know you're here, to know what you've done. You're fucking frightened of him, aren't you? That's why you won't let me call him. Where's Martin? He's Katy's father. He should be here. The poor kid shouldn't have to see things like this. You're damaging her. She can't stop crying. Martin should be here. I should have a phone call. I'm entitled to a phone call. Give me my fucking phone call. You've broken my arm. You broke Gary's arm; now you've done mine. I want medical attention and a lawyer. That was an unprovoked attack on me. The kids saw it. When Gary finds out what you've done he'll rape your fucking cunt. You ugly fucking twat. You're filth. Filth. I can smell you from here. You're polluting my brother's house. You have family. I know you have. You have children. You should think about that. The world's not a safe place. Anything could happen to a cunt like you. Your kids will never see the end of the year. I bet they're ugly little runts. Ugly little runts with a dyke bitch for a mother...'

If they weren't crying, both children listened in a cowed silence. If they had seen her like this before then they hadn't got used to it. Karen thought they were both old enough to understand what was being said, to understand the tension, the pure hatred seeping out of Swales, and be frightened by it. Karen tried her best to reassure the little boy by putting an arm round him, but he pulled away from her as if she had hit him, which was exactly what Mary then accused her of doing. One of the PCs put a drink of water in front of him, but Swales told him not to touch it.

Then the social workers arrived. The change was instant, almost too extreme to believe. As soon as she heard them coming through from the front of the building Mary shut up, looked down at the table in front of her, pulled the little girl to her and took a deep breath. By the time the social workers were in the kitchen she was silently sobbing, tears dripping onto the surface in front of her, a perfect picture of passive docility, a victim. Karen caught the eye of one of the PCs posted at the door and saw him grin, but she was less complacent. Getting the kids away from her meant persuading the social workers that she might be a threat to them.

The lead social worker was called Toby Hughes. She guessed he was about twenty years younger then her. Probably too young to have kids of his own. She'd met him before, but couldn't recall the case. He was wearing jeans, a T-shirt and a zip-up black fleece, training shoes, and stud earrings in both ears. He looked relaxed as he came in, not fazed by the situation, and seemed competent enough throughout the preliminaries. He had a good manner with Andrew; better, in fact, than his female colleague.

He left her – first name Shola – speaking to the kids, then went with Karen through to what she guessed was Swales's dining room – an enormous, expensively designed room with a high ceiling, very little furniture or decoration, clean white walls – and sat at a long gleaming metal dining table while Karen explained the position.

'I came here looking to arrest Mary on suspicion of murder,' she said. 'She attacked me as soon as I came in.' She pointed to the livid lines running down the side of her face. Swales had only just failed to break the skin. She indicated her possible head injury as well, then told him how Swales had gone for her in front of the children, despite her announcing clearly that she was police. She then went on to tell him who the children were, what had happened to their mother, who the suspects were, that their father was already in custody and how she had found Andrew locked alone in an empty room.

Hughes listened in silence, carefully taking notes. She could force him to remove the kids, of course, but only for as long as it took to get them back to temporary accommodation, after which it would be up to Hughes to determine what was best for them. Better to get him on side from the beginning. Given that placing them in care was always a last-ditch option, she anticipated Hughes would try to find a relative to place them with while Mary was in custody. To prevent that she spent some time briefing him about the Swales family before she was interrupted by his assistant opening the door and asking to speak to him, in private.

Karen went back to the kitchen and watched Mary weeping silently. Had Mary been in on things last year? she wondered. Had Gary told her that he'd put out a contract to damage Mairead? It seemed unlikely. Moments ago Mary had happily cursed her children – in the plural – and wished them dead, so she couldn't know that

273

much about her. Or had she merely forgotten that Karen only had one child? She had no doubt Mary wouldn't object to such a thing. To knock over someone's innocent child.

Karen ran a hand through her hair and tried to relax. She couldn't think about those months without feeling a panic in her gut. Last year the fear had crippled her mentally, ruining her ordinary composure and sending her into a spiral of insomnia and mental instability. She didn't want to risk all that again. But she didn't want to leave the score unsettled, either. She *couldn't* just leave it. A lesson was owed. The need to retaliate in kind was so deeply ingrained in her it left a residue like scar tissue, deep within her brain, something she felt every day she did nothing about it. Was it possible Gary Swales would react to pressure on his sister by trying something similar? If he did she knew she would deal with it very differently this time, more directly. And Mairead would be a long way away, in Scotland.

'Can I have a word?' The PC at the door interrupted her thoughts.

She stood and they moved out of earshot of Mary. He told her quickly what Mary had said to Hughes's assistant, Shola – the long and short of it being an accusation against Karen of brutality combined with tearful contrition that she had made the mistake of misidentifying Karen as an intruder. 'She said she was only trying to protect the kids,' he whispered. 'She wants Hughes to phone her brother so he can come and look after the kids, keep them here. I think the young girl was taken in by it all.'

He was right. When Karen went back into the dining room Hughes and the girl – she *was* a 'girl', Karen thought, perhaps no older than twenty, tall, very pale, with a habit of avoiding eye contact when you spoke to her, as if she were embarrassed – looked up as if they had been caught whispering about her.

'Shola says the brother isn't under arrest,' Hughes said to her. 'And this is his place, so the priority would be to trace him and get him to take the kids, we think.'

Karen sighed, sat down opposite Hughes and looked up at Shola, who was standing behind the chair next to Hughes. Karen smiled at her. Shola looked away. 'That's right, Shola,' she said. 'Gary Hughes isn't under arrest. But he is at Trafalgar House, I believe, trying to assist the children's father.' She turned to Hughes again. 'I already told you that,' she said. 'It's possible Gary, Martin and Mary are all involved in this murder. The investigation is ongoing. I wouldn't be happy having the kids placed with Gary.' She said the words calmly, as if she were merely passing on a professional opinion, not something that mattered to her. 'Anyway, I doubt Gary can get here in time. We need to get moving on this, get Mary down to Trafalgar House. It's a murder enquiry, remember? We need to keep the sense of urgency in mind.'

'If Gary can't come back then he might be able to nominate a relative who can,' Hughes said.

'Someone the kids have never met? Another Swales? Have you looked closely at Andrew Farrar? He has that look in his eyes. You know what I mean. Something is seriously wrong. We can't just abandon him.'

Hughes frowned. 'We need to ask Gary Swales. Care is a last option. You know that. You might have all sorts of suspicions, but there's no evidence right now.'

Karen's turn to frown. 'Maybe. But care might be the *safest* option, in this particular case.' She turned to Shola. 'Did you ask Mary why Andrew was locked into a room alone?'

Shola glanced at her. 'Not yet. No. I haven't had the chance yet.' She spoke with a public-school accent.

'I would have thought that was a priority,' Karen said.

'Mary Swales has made serious allegations against you,' Shola replied, almost blurting out the words. 'She says she heard an intruder and came to find you already in the house. She says you–'

Karen waved a hand, silencing her. 'I can guess,' she said. 'But there's a procedure to deal with all that. We're talking about the children now.'

'We have to decide who is telling the truth,' Shola said, now clearly radiating antipathy, though Karen couldn't guess why. 'Then we can decide where the children would best be placed.'

'That's OK, Shola,' Hughes said to her. He looked uncomfortable. Shola's tone betrayed too much emotion. 'I think DS Sharpe knows the procedures.'

'I was learning the procedures while you were in nappies,' Karen muttered, not looking at either of them in particular. It was true of both, no doubt.

'That was a long time ago,' Shola said. 'Things change.'

'Shola. Please.'

'You have a problem, Shola?' Karen asked her. 'A problem with me?'

Shola looked at her properly for the first time. 'I have a problem with brutality,' she said. 'I have a problem with police officers bending the rules.'

'Aren't we on the same side here?' Karen asked, looking at Hughes again, appealing to him. She didn't want to get into an argument with a trainee social worker.

Hughes nodded. 'Of course. We're all here to think about the kids. I suggest we try to find a neutral relative – one you don't object to. Then we can progress things. A relative is always better than care.'

Not always, she thought, but she kept her mouth shut. She couldn't imagine a child would be safe with anyone by the name of Swales, but it was as good as she was going to get. She had to get Mary down to Trafalgar House and interview her. If she could prise something useful out of that then Mary wouldn't be in a position to care for kids for a very long time.

27

At Trafalgar House Marcus gave her a rundown of Martin's interview comments. Nothing surprising there. Not even the fact that Lane had been his solicitor. Marcus had been present when Gary Swales had called Lane on behalf of his nephew. Lane had dropped John Bradley immediately. She considered going in to Ricky Spencer and trying to get Lane excluded from the interview with Mary, but the point of that was past now. He had already achieved what he wanted. John had 'confessed' and placed his wife and family away from the scene.

She decided to take Marcus into the interview with her. He knew in detail what Martin had already said, so he would be useful. Before they started she showed him her notebook, into which she had carefully written the gist of Mary's 'reply' to caution, on arrest.

'I'm showing you so you can watch a professional liar in action,' she said. 'Watch and learn.' He looked puzzled by the comment.

Mary sat at one side of the table with Lane; she and Marcus sat at the other. Mary looked subdued as they began the preliminaries, bleary-eyed, red-faced and deflated. Like someone who had been through hell and then stayed up all night crying about it. Her clothing had been seized and she sat in custody overalls, the dirty-yellow variety. She had the slouch and demeanour of a defeated, disorientated and confused woman. Karen found it hard to keep her expression blank as she looked at her. Mary couldn't meet her eyes now, or wouldn't. Karen wondered if direct eye contact might be too risky for her; it might force her to slip into herself. That would be a disaster for her. Mary knew the cameras were watching, recording every gesture and word. She knew that if she screwed up this would be a performance for the jury.

Lane looked exactly the same as the last time she had seen him. Karen didn't bother giving her opinions as to his role. She had let Marcus go in with him beforehand to do the disclosure. She wanted as little to do with him as possible. Even sitting near to him made her feel dirty.

'So tell me all about it, Mary,' she said, once they'd got through the formalities. She sat back and placed her pen on the table in front of her. She expected Mary to pretend confusion, but instead she started talking straight away.

'I'm so sorry about earlier, Officer,' she said. She looked at the table as she spoke. 'I'm so, so sorry.' Her voice was shaky, but loud enough to be heard.

Karen waited for more.

'I didn't know you were police, you see. I heard a noise through the baby intercom and I knew there was an intruder. I rushed down. The poker was the first thing I could get my hands on. I could hear Katy screaming. I was terrified for her. I'm so sorry. I don't know what was in my head. I thought you were an intruder, or...' she paused, '...or even John – I thought it might have been John coming back, that they might have released him. I just lashed out. It was stupid, I know. I'm so sorry. I hope I didn't injure you. I would never want to hurt the police. The police have been so good to me, through all the ... all the troubles with John... You've protected me from him. I'd be dead now if it wasn't for the police. He's such a violent man... I'm so sorry. It was a terrible mistake...' She was trembling as she spoke. 'I don't know what else to say...'

'Someone else will interview you about all that later,' Karen said. 'For now I'd like you to tell me about Rebecca Farrar. That's more important.'

'Poor Becky...' She actually interrupted Karen, shaking her head as if she couldn't believe what had happened. 'Poor, poor Becky.'

'What about Becky?'

Mary shook her head again, eyes down. She screwed up her face and muttered something.

'You'll have to speak loud enough to be heard on the tape, Mary.'

'I can't believe it ... poor Becky.'

She started to cry quietly, the tears running down her nose and dripping onto her arm. Karen waited, but it just got worse. After a few minutes Lane suggested a break. There didn't seem to be much else they could do.

They stopped the tapes. Custody staff took Mary back to her cell with Lane, to recover. Marcus and Karen paced around just outside the custody area, waiting, Karen feeling impatient and annoyed.

When they resumed Mary was dry-eyed. She started apologizing for the tears, but Karen silenced her by asking her to listen to something that she had to read to her.

'It's from my notebook,' she explained. 'Someone else will deal with the rest of what happened this afternoon, but I have to cover this. I have to read it out to you and offer it to you to sign, as a true account of words you've said. That's the law. It's a pure formality. Your solicitor will confirm that.' She didn't wait for him to do so. Instead she went straight into reading out Mary's 'reply' to caution, three pages of the twenty-minute rant she had sat through in Gary Swales's kitchen, unedited. When she had finished she looked up and saw that Mary was staring at her, an expression of pure astonishment on her face. Her mouth was hanging open. Karen passed the book across to her, along with the pen.

'Assuming you agree that's a true account then could you just sign here, please?' She pointed to the spot.

Mary closed her mouth, shook her head slightly. As if it were a kind of dream and she needed to wake up from it. She looked at her solicitor, still speechless.

'Do you realize what this officer is asking you to do?' Lane asked her.

Mary shook her head. 'But I didn't say any of that,' she said. She almost whispered the words. She glanced at Karen, confusion in her eyes. 'I don't understand,' she said. 'Is there a mistake? You're not saying I said those things?'

'I am, Mary. Those things are exactly what you said. There were two other police officers to witness it all.'

A sob escaped from Mary's throat. She turned back to the solicitor. 'I don't understand. I didn't say any of that.'

'That's OK,' he said. 'If you didn't say those things then don't sign the book.' He looked at Karen. 'I think that's clear, Officer?'

'But why would she say I said those things?' Mary asked. She was looking at Marcus now. 'I don't understand.'

Marcus stared back at her, face impassive.

Karen pulled the notebook back.

'I can't see the relevance anyway,' Lane said. 'What has any of that to do with the reason we are here? Can't we get on to the main allegations? My client is primary carer for two small children. They will be suffering needless distress for as long as she is stuck here.'

The mention of the children was enough to start Mary crying again. Karen sighed and moved her hands beneath the table, where the camera wouldn't be able to see the impatient drumming of her fingers. She waited to see if the tears were going to stop or get worse. They got worse. After a while Swales was sobbing so loudly it was uncomfortable on the ears. Marcus passed her a box of tissues, he gave her a cup of water, he offered tea and coffee, but nothing could stop her. It was a consummate performance and there was nothing they could do to prevent it. To show that they knew Mary was acting would play right into her hands on camera. Her defence team would have a guaranteed argument for excluding the interview from evidence because Mary had been 'oppressed'. After another ten minutes of it Lane again suggested they take another break.

The third try began better. Karen managed to get her talking about life with Rebecca, before Rebecca 'walked out' on them. The account sounded much the same as John's first account of this period, except Mary manoeuvred it so that there was a little woman's alliance – between Rebecca and herself – against the male threat.

'So John didn't get on with Rebecca?' Karen asked her.

'John has no patience. He's a hard man to live with.'

'No patience? What does that mean?'

'Rebecca – God love her – she was a difficult girl. Not what John was used to. That's my fault.' She shivered a little, no doubt thinking about it. 'I've always given John what he wants in life. Or tried to. I learned by hard means that that was the only way to get on with him. I learned it early. He didn't seem like the man he is – not when we first met, when we married. But I've felt his fist since then...' The words trailed off. 'Too many times...' The tears were starting again. 'I'm sorry. I'm so sorry...' She was sniffling, her hands over her mouth.

'You have to take your hands away from your face,' Marcus said. 'If you don't the microphones won't pick up what you're saying.'

'It's all my fault,' she continued, letting her hands fall. 'I could have stopped it happening. If I'd been stronger. If I'd fought back, or left him. But it's hard … it's so hard...' Her head sank down. 'You know what he was like. You have the records. I called you twice when it got too bad to bear. I tried to bear it for the children, to keep us together as a family. I tried as best I could. But he used to … he used to...' She broke off, unable to continue. It was a tragic picture.

'So John didn't get on with Rebecca? Is that what you're saying?' Karen asked again, keeping her voice flat, monotone.

'He hated her. He really hated her. The poor

girl was so confused, so messed up. I don't know what had happened to her to make her that way, but she was like that when we first met her. I knew she needed help, but John just couldn't stand it. He caught her slashing herself one day. It made him feel ill. He was disgusted with her. He was like that. That's the kind of man he is.'

'She needed help, you say. Did you try to get her any help?'

'I tried to help her myself. I tried to talk to her, to find out why she did the things she did. I did my best. But John didn't like me talking to her. He didn't even like to see us together. He didn't want her living with us but she was married to our child – to Martin – so what could he do? She should have left earlier. The poor kid. She should have got out, away from him. All the time she was with us she was just rubbing John up the wrong way. She didn't seem to care what he was like. She had no fear. She used to shout at him, goad him. I would never have dared do the things she did.'

'Do you think that's what happened the day she died?' There was no option but to run with the story a little, to see what its limits were.

'I don't know.'

'My client has already made it clear she wasn't present when–'

'Has she? To you, maybe. Not to us. Not in this interview. Where were you, Mary, on the day Rebecca came back to pick up some of her possessions? Maybe you should tell us that bit of the story now?'

'That's not the way to put these things, Officer.

284

You know that. Can we keep this professional, please?'

'Mary? Tell us where you were on that day, please. Saturday the eighth. That's nine days ago.'

'I was with Martin, Simon and the kids. We were all at Mavis Rimmer's house. She's Gary's aunt, his mother's sister. She will tell you I was there.' Mavis Rimmer was the relative Social Services had eventually decided to place the kids with while Mary and Martin were in custody.

'You went out of the house when you knew Rebecca was coming back?'

'Yes. To keep the kids away from her.'

'Her own children?'

'She had already walked out on her own children. She had already made her choices...' A slightly harder tone, but she caught herself quickly. 'The poor little thing. Maybe she didn't know what choices she was making. Maybe she was too ill.'

'And you still left her to go back to the house alone, with John.'

'I did what John told me to do.'

'He said you had to leave?'

'He told us to get out. He didn't want her to start an argument.'

'Who? Rebecca?'

'Yes.'

'An argument with whom?'

'With any of us. That's what she did. She liked to argue.'

'With you as well?'

A pause, Swales seeing where it was going. 'Not so much with me. She trusted me more than the others. Because I tried to talk to her.'

285

'But you did argue with her?'

'Not really. John argued with her mainly.'

'But you said he sent you all out because he didn't want any arguments.'

'And Martin.'

'Martin? He argued with her, too?'

She looked momentarily uncomfortable. Her answers had gone beyond the preparation, Karen could see. She was in danger of incriminating Martin now.

'They argued like married couples argue, I mean,' she added quickly. 'That's all I meant. Nothing big. But John used to hate it. It was one of the things that used to goad him. That and her cheek. That's what he called it. She used to answer him back.'

'Even after he had hit her?'

'I never saw him hit her. I never said that. It was me John hit. Just me. As far as I know...'

'Do you think he hit her on that day?'

'I wasn't there. I told you.'

'You sound like you want to protect John.'

'He's my husband.'

'Despite everything he's done to you?'

'I can't help it. I try to be loyal. Maybe I deserved everything. Maybe it should be me that got beaten to death...' Her shoulders started to shake. Her head was in her hands again now, right over the table, so Karen could no longer see her face.

'You think Rebecca was beaten to death by John?'

'I don't know... I don't know ... I wasn't there. I saw the blood when we came back. I asked him.

But he wouldn't tell me anything. I couldn't push it. I knew what would happen if I pushed it. He'd kill me. You understand?' She looked up suddenly, her face imploring Karen to understand. The mask of mental pain was so convincing Karen couldn't bear to look at her. She broke eye contact and looked at her feet, disgusted.

'He's threatened to kill me before. You know that. I daren't even look at him when he gets like that. There was blood on the stairs. That's all I saw. I knew he'd done *something*. Obviously he'd done *something*. But I didn't know what and he wouldn't tell me. What has he told you? Has he told you what he did?'

That was it, then. That was going to be the story. Karen sighed and opened the legal pad on the desk. She wasn't going to pierce the act. The best she could do would be to dig in and ask detailed questions. If she forced enough detail then she might prise the collusion open a little, find out where they hadn't put their heads together and agreed it all. She looked up at Mary. She was sobbing and choking now, all over again. Karen wondered where she got the strength to keep it up. It was exhausting just watching her.

'I think we should break again,' Lane said.

Tuesday

28

Simon Bradley surfaced early that morning. Mary Swales had refused to give any information that might help locate her elder son. Martin was similarly reticent. They wouldn't even help with information on the precise nature of his 'disability'. Since they were both in custody at the time, Marcus found that unsurprising. It didn't mean, for him, that either Mary or Martin didn't get on with Simon. Maybe they were just trying to protect him from police attention.

That was Karen's take on it, though – if they were going to prise apart the Swales' defence then Simon was the one to work on. Unloved, maybe even despised, on account of his disability, he would feel less of a bond to his parents. Mary had her story 'off pat' (that was Karen's view) – she had given almost exactly the same account as Martin, in the end – so Karen wanted everyone out trying to locate Simon. At one point she even mooted the idea that he might have been 'silenced' by the Bradleys. When the suggestion failed to draw additional resources from Alan White they were left going about it in the usual ways, all five of them. In the end they got nowhere throughout the rest of Monday, but Simon turned up overnight anyway, in the cells at Milgarth.

He had been arrested as a vagrant in Leeds city centre. It seemed he had spent the last couple of days sleeping rough, in the open air. The actual reason for his arrest was that he was seen defecating in the middle of the Headrow at four-thirty in the morning.

Marcus picked him up directly from Milgarth, at just after 11.30 am. It took the information systems that long to work out who he was and to connect him to the murder enquiry. When Marcus got there he found Simon seated on a bench in the booking-in area. The custody sergeant told him they had moved him from his cell during the early hours of the morning when the noise got too bad. Simon had a problem with enclosed spaces, it seemed, a form of claustrophobia. Marcus asked how that had manifested itself.

'Put him in a cell and the poor kid starts screaming at the top of his voice.'

Marcus could recall many an evening of custody duty ruined by the howls of panicking or mentally ill detainees. Usually, he recalled, the custody staff would go through the motions, call the doctor, write it all up carefully, wait for the morning's court appearance to decide what to do. There had never been much empathy for the prisoner as a human being. Yet here the custody sergeant was almost sympathetic.

'*Is* he a kid?' Marcus had asked. 'I thought he was twenty-eight years old, and he's nearly seven feet tall.'

'He acts like a kid.' A shrug. 'He's a brick short. You'll see.'

Maybe it was the arm that made the difference. It was easier to feel sorry for the physically dis-abled.

As Marcus stood in front of him, quietly explaining the situation, Simon looked tired more than anything. He was dressed in a pair of nondescript dark-blue trousers – provided by the custody sergeant to replace the jeans he had soiled in the Headrow – a dirty brown T-shirt bearing a Radiohead logo and a denim jacket. He was so skinny and tall he looked fragile rather than large. The face, too, was skull-thin and hollow, with sunken eyes. He held the deformed left arm carefully across his body, as if protecting it. The arm looked well formed to Marcus – from what he could see of it, trying to be discreet – just too small: it looked like the arm of a child. Simon stared dreamily at the floor as Marcus spoke and looked on the point of sliding off the bench. Too exhausted to be nervous, perhaps, he had the sluggish movements of someone drugged with sedatives.

Marcus was to take him to a hostel they had arranged for him, unless, of course, he wished to return to Lower Wyke Manor. He didn't (communicated by a slow shake of the head), which was a relief, because all Karen's plans hinged on being able to get him placed in the hostel. Thereafter she intended to seek authorizations to get probes inserted to record what was said to him when either Mary or Martin visited him to find out what was happening. Ricky Spencer had already told her he wouldn't agree to that, but she wasn't giving up. The hostel belonged to a specialist charity they had worked with before on this kind of thing; the probes would have to be planted with their permission, too.

They had made a tactical decision to treat

Simon as a witness, not a suspect, so he would have to go voluntarily. Mary and Martin would be permitted back to their home (or to Gary's home), though only if Karen couldn't get Mary charged. She was still hopeful about that, though Marcus couldn't see it happening. He wasn't sure of the point to the probes either, since it was highly unlikely anything recorded could ever be used as evidence in court.

Simon responded to Marcus's little chat by telling him he was hungry. It wasn't quite the sort of flat non-sequitur he was used to from Oscar, but it was near enough.

'OK. I'll take you to eat on the way,' he said. 'Is there anything you like eating?'

'Curry. I only like curry.'

They ended up in the Balaka, on Leeds Road. Marcus ate there often and was known to the staff. Consequently, it was easy enough to get a table in the corner, away from everyone else. They got there just after midday and the place was already half-full. Simon walked through it with his head down, heavily stooped, almost shuffling. Marcus thought he looked like someone on day release from an institution. Yet the first thing he said when they sat down was, 'You think I'm stupid, right?'

Marcus frowned. 'No. Why do you say that?'

'Because everyone does. Because of this...' He raised the tiny arm over the table. The jacket sleeve looked almost empty. 'Because I'm so tall and thin. Because I don't like to say much.'

'None of those things makes you stupid.'

'No. So remember that.'

A little warning, then. He had said nothing at all in the car on the way over and Marcus hadn't tried too hard get him talking. A comment about the Radiohead T-shirt (one of Marcus's favourite bands, at an earlier stage in his life) had fallen flat, Simon clearly not being aware of what was written on the T-shirt. (The custody staff had warned Marcus he was near illiterate.) The T-shirt belonged to his brother, Martin.

That was what he was meant to do, of course – establish some kind of bond, get him talking. Karen had picked him specially because of some perceived skill he was meant to have in mixing with the 'disabled' due to the experience of growing up with Oscar. He'd tried in vain to explain to her that Oscar's disability was very different from Simon's. But she could be very persuasive when she wanted to. The conversation about getting probes placed had taken place in Ricky Spencer's empty office and Karen had gone out of her way, it seemed, to flirt with him, standing much closer than she usually did, suggesting more than once that they have a 'good night out' together. Eventually he agreed to meet her the following night, for dinner, which wasn't unusual – they had eaten out together many times – but it felt as if she were suggesting a date. He'd no idea what was going on with her. The behaviour was very different to the cold shoulder she'd given him over the weekend.

A waiter appeared with the menus. Marcus waved him away – he knew what was on offer by heart – then Simon did the same. 'I always have chicken korma,' he said. 'Onion bahji and chicken korma.' But he said it in a petulant way which was definitely suggestive of a child. Did he stick his lip out, too? As if the production of menus meant there was a threat he wouldn't be permitted to have his usual dish. Something incomprehensible and childish like that. The random switching between the two personas – adult and child – was something Marcus was used to from Oscar, but there seemed to be few other similarities. Oscar had problems in his brain. Portions of it had died during childbirth and that was that. Simon Bradley – as far as Marcus could determine – had only a withered arm. That shouldn't have led – as far as he knew – to any mental issues at all. Unless his carers had created them. Or maybe there was something else wrong with Simon, too – something he didn't know about.

'I don't think you're stupid, Simon,' he said, as they were waiting for their starters. 'You've got an arm that's a bit different. So what? That doesn't affect your brain and it doesn't mean anything to me. There are ways in which I'm different, too. Everyone is different in some way.'

Simon looked away from him, but said nothing. The lip was still pouting a little.

'It doesn't mean you have to sleep rough in Leeds city centre, for example. Or shit in the middle of the street.'

'That was an accident.'

'Of course. I was just giving an example. How was it an accident?'

'I needed a poo-poo. There was no toilet.'

Marcus kept his reaction minimal. The man in front of him – he *was* clearly a man – was twenty-eight years old.

'Why were you out on the streets at all?'

Simon shrugged. 'I didn't want to be alone.'

'At your mum's place?'

'Yes.'

'Why was that?'

'I get frightened when I'm alone. I shiver.'

'Did your mother and brother leave you alone, then?'

'Yes. I already answered these questions.'

'I'm not asking you as a policeman, Simon. I'm asking you because I'm interested. You've been released. Nothing is going to happen now about last night.'

'I told you I wasn't stupid.'

Marcus put a puzzled look on his face. 'Meaning?'

'You work on the murder enquiry. They told me that. That's why you're asking about me. That's why we're here.'

The adult again. Perfectly lucid reasoning. He was getting more like Oscar by the minute. 'That's right. I'm investigating Rebecca's death. But you haven't been arrested. No one suspects you of anything.'

'I didn't do anything.'

'No one says you did.'

'No. That's the point. I didn't do anything.' His face creased up suddenly, tears welling in his eyes. The change was abrupt, without warning.

'You mean you could have done something to stop it?'

'She was nice. She was the loveliest person I've ever met.' His voice was low now, almost too quiet to hear.

297

Marcus leaned forward a little. 'You got on OK with Rebecca, then?'

He nodded dumbly. A tear spilled out of his left eye and ran unchecked to his chin.

'Was she very friendly with you?'

Mute silence.

'Did she speak to you a lot?'

He didn't move, didn't reply. His body had stiffened. He was holding himself rigidly in the same position. Another tear ran down his cheek, from the same eye. He was looking at the table-cloth, perfectly still.

'It was terrible what happened to Rebecca,' Marcus tried. 'She must have suffered...'

A sob broke from Simon's lips, stopping him. Then he began to shake his head vigorously, screwing his eyes closed. Marcus looked around him. No one seemed to have noticed, yet. But if Simon was going to get any worse then this wasn't the place to be doing this.

'She was my friend,' Simon said suddenly, almost a whimper. 'I think about her all the time.'

Marcus waited to see if he'd go on. He didn't, but he did manage to look up. Marcus nodded understanding. 'I didn't know her,' he said. 'I'd like you to tell me about her. Can you do that?'

'She was my friend.'

Silence.

'Yes. Did you spend a lot of time with her?'

'I can't get her out of my head...'

'I can understand. It's terrible to lose a friend.'

'I haven't lost her. She's here.' He raised the good arm and tapped his temple. 'Sometimes she speaks to me. She tells me what she's doing and where she is. She makes me laugh.' He smiled unexpectedly, his open mouth so large in the thin face it looked incongruous, slightly grotesque.

'Did she make you laugh when she was living with you?'

A nod, then the stunted arm came up and drew the sleeve across his eyes, wiping them. 'She didn't mind my arm. She didn't shout at me. She didn't call me a shit.'

'Do other people do that?'

No response.

'What about your mum? She must be nice to you, also?'

The smile vanished, but he didn't say anything.

'And your dad – John?'

The eyes flicked up, met Marcus's own, then slipped down again.

'You want me to talk about them?'

'No. Not really. But–'

'I know what you're doing. I know my rights.'

'Of course.'

'I won't say anything. I can't.' He was getting agitated now, just thinking about it.

'But you will tell me about Becky?'

'Nothing. I won't say anything. I'm hungry.' He glanced up, looking for the food. His mood had changed in a matter of seconds.

'The starters won't be long. Do you want a drink of water while we're waiting?'

'No. I want my curry.'

'It won't be long, Simon. Will you talk to me about Rebecca after we've eaten?'

'Shut up.'

'Sorry?'

'*Shut up.*' He raised his voice, then shifted nervously in the seat. 'You're upsetting me. You're talking too much about ... about *them* ... about *things*... I don't want to think. I don't want to talk about it. I'm hungry. I want to eat.' He took a deep breath, then looked directly at Marcus. '*I want to fucking eat.*'

Marcus sat back. The words had been hissed at him through gritted teeth. The body language was tense, disturbed.

'That's OK,' Marcus said quietly. 'We'll just eat.'

Karen had picked him for this because she thought he would develop an empathy for the man, but already he was hating him the same way he hated Oscar, if he were honest about it. The man was difficult, unpredictable and rude. There was something wrong with him other than the arm – that was clear now – because he couldn't bring himself to behave in a simple adult way for more than a few seconds. He couldn't relate at the same level as Marcus. Maybe he couldn't relate to adults at all – at least not in a normal way. Or only to Rebecca, who had been nice to him.

How had that happened, that he could have developed something like warmth for her? Aside from crying over her death there didn't seem to be the possibility of normal adult responses. Marcus didn't have a clue how he would get past that problem. By being nice to him maybe, like Rebecca had. It would be worth it, because Karen was right – he was certainly the weak link. But could he bring himself to do it? He felt sick just thinking about it. It was bad enough that he'd been forced to exude false sympathy towards Oscar his entire childhood.

Besides, now that it came to sitting a few feet away from him, he could smell Simon Bradley. An underlying smell of faeces and piss, mixed with stale sweat. The man was scruffy, a health hazard. Oscar had been the same. Never able to look after himself, never even able to wipe himself after he'd been to the toilet. At least, not for a long time. Marcus had done it for him until he was nearly fourteen years old. Being sent to Oxford early had at least got him out of that.

29

By midday Tuesday most of the decisions had been made. John Bradley was charged with manslaughter just after 11 am.; Mary and Martin were released an hour later. If they were to be released at all Karen had wanted them both on bail, but Ricky Spencer and Alan White wouldn't go that far. They had been forced to agree her plan to put Simon under surveillance – because that was a little fait accompli she had pulled on them courtesy of Francis Doyle – but they were insistent on taking a statement from Mary, determined to convert her into a victim and a crown witness. As Karen had expected, the duty lawyer wouldn't authorize assault police charges against Mary, because there was the possibility that Karen had entered Gary Swales's house illegally. Through Lane, Gary had made it clear he would be taking that further.

Karen wouldn't lose sleep over a complaint, but in the circumstances she had no chance of keeping the kids out of Mary's grasp. She called Toby Hughes at Social Services, but could only raise Shola Clarke, the last person she wanted to speak to. In the last few hours she had managed to find out why Clarke had been so worked up at their last meeting. She was the daughter of a man called Vernon Clarke-Butler, a company director Karen had charged with fraud during a long spell investigating thefts and frauds about five years ago. The case had failed, in the end, but not before Vernon'd been detained, accused and had his life ruined. It was always the way. Karen had sympathy for him, but it was no use explaining that to his daughter.

She tried in vain to get Clarke to consider options other than returning Katy and Andrew to their father and grandmother, but it was a waste of time. It would have been a waste of time even without the personal factor to muddy the waters. If Mary and Martin were released without bail and without charge they were innocent. That simple. What excuse could there be for taking the children from them?

Authorizations for surveillance on the hostel came in only half an hour before Martin and Mary were due for release. That surprised Ricky so much he had to call Alan White to check. As he put the phone down Karen could tell that he was thinking along the right lines, but didn't dare suggest anything. For authorizations to have been given in such hopeless circumstances Karen had to have pulled some strings.

Karen skipped the inevitable celebrations and drove out to a pub in Calderdale, up in the middle of nowhere above a former milltown on the borders of Lancashire and Yorkshire. Todmorden sat in a deep cleft where three valleys met, but the pub was high above it on a back road leading up to the moors. The Shepherd's Rest (what else?) was one of three places Francis Doyle had been using to meet her for almost two years now. She wished he would make do with more centrally located pubs, but was grateful for small mercies – the other two venues were both motorway service areas, neither even in West Yorkshire.

It was grey and raining hard as she pulled into the car park, with low cloud that threatened to sink even lower and turn into a fog. Back in Dudley Hill it had been another clear, hot late-summer day, so she wasn't dressed for the squall that greeted her as she opened the car door. She'd had the same experience last time she met Doyle here. Whatever the weather elsewhere, it always seemed to be shitty in the Pennines.

She greeted Doyle with a handshake and sat down opposite him at a table in a deserted lounge area with windows opening – weather permitting – on to panoramic views across the valley. She could see as far as a field containing two dirty tufts of sheep.

'Nice to see you, Francis,' she said.

'And you, Karen.'

She was being honest. Her ill-defined dealings with the security services had often been ruined (sometimes with serious consequences) by incompetent or petty handlers. Prior to Francis

Doyle taking over in West Yorkshire she had suffered many years of a military type called Sutherland. He had never liked her or taken much care to ensure her safety. But Sutherland had been deemed incompetent just over a year ago, as part of the fall-out from having the London bombers originate on his patch undetected. Doyle had replaced him and things had been better almost at once. It was nearly always pleasant to meet Doyle, even if, as now, he was going to ask her for something in return for ensuring that authorizations were given for the probes on Simon Bradley.

'Did it work out OK?' he asked.

'Yes. Thanks. They were a bit pissed off, I think, because they don't know who has jerked their chain, but they're guessing it must be something to do with me.'

'Because you're the only one looking at Mary Swales.'

'So it seems.' She frowned. 'You know anything about her?'

'This and that. Mainly about her brother, of course.' He smiled. 'Not as much as you know, I'm sure. What would you like to drink?'

'An orange juice.'

He walked over to the bar to order. He was an unimpressive figure, she thought, for someone in his position. None of the swagger and dash of Sutherland. Doyle was about four inches shorter than her, of completely average build (for a man she guessed to be in his early fifties) with a slight paunch and thinning hair. He was dressed in cords and an open-necked, blue checked shirt. He left a nondescript green anorak lying on the chair. The shoes were ordinary black brogues. His face was normal enough, with inquisitive blue eyes and thin lips. He walked normally, without the unmistakeable military bearing Sutherland paraded. He looked slightly out of shape, in fact. He spoke with a southern accent, but nothing more placeable than that. Standing at the bar chatting to the barman, you would guess him to be a salesman, the hard briefcase he kept in the car containing samples of pharmaceuticals or paints. Yet on more than one occasion he had been quite open to Karen about his background. Despite appearances he was as military as Sutherland, with ten years in Special Services preceding his change to this type of work. It didn't show. She assumed the four-year-old Golf in the car park was his. There hadn't been any other cars.

He came back with an orange juice and a glass of water. She had never seen him drink anything but water.

'They must love you here,' she remarked. 'You probably keep the place afloat.'

He looked around the pub. 'No doubt,' he said, as if there were some secret involved.

'How did you pull the authorizations?' she asked.

'I said we were interested.'

'Are you?'

'No. Not really. Not in volume crime.' He managed to say it without implying a sneer. 'I'm more interested in how you and Mr Surani are doing.'

She summarized it, telling him almost everything, so he would know exactly what she was getting them into. The core of it was that Surani was beginning to trust her, certainly liked her and wanted more of her (let him guess the detail from that), but thus far hadn't mentioned his brother. She was sure it would come in time, and that the best way would be to let him get there off his own bat, if time wasn't of the essence.

'You're enjoying it, then?' he asked, when she was finished.

'I like him. He's hard not to like, once you get to know him.'

He nodded, but didn't comment.

'No sermon?'

'I know what you do best. Just be careful.'

She wondered what he thought that was – what she did best. Sutherland would have thought it something akin to prostitution, but Doyle had never given that impression. He responded always – and this wasn't the first time she'd taken on this kind of task for him – as if she were engaging in some kind of purely professional activity. Of course, she spared him the details that would make it crystal clear. She never told him she was sleeping with Surani, or how much she actually liked him. But did she know that herself? Would she fall for Michael Surani if there was no danger involved, if it wasn't some kind of elaborate game? Every time she met him she became someone else, subtly but significantly.

'You're worried about me losing perspective?' she asked.

He took a sip from his water, apparently considering that. '*Is* there that danger?' There'd been in the past, on other jobs. He knew that too well.

'There's always that danger. If there wasn't it

306

wouldn't work.'

'Well, you would need to reassure me that we aren't going to have the kinds of complications we had seven years ago.'

On New Year's Eve 1999 it had been Doyle's job to extract her from an experience she would never forget. That was when she had first met him, first learned to trust him.

'I'm sure we're not,' she said.

'Are you *really* sure?'

Her turn to shrug. 'I think so. Nothing's guaranteed. But you didn't call me here to chat about Surani. It's not that long since our last little chat.'

He leaned his elbows on the table and moved closer, shifting his glass so as to be able to talk in a slightly lowered voice. 'I did come to talk about Surani, actually,' he said. 'Do you know where he is now?'

'Pakistan.'

'That's what he told you?'

'Yes. Did he lie?'

'I imagine so. He's in London, and he's about to get his fingers burned, we think.'

She kept silent, listening, trying to ignore the information about Michael lying. Why shouldn't Michael lie to her? What was she to him? A mistress? He had a wife, of course – a Bollywood producer – but he barely mentioned her and Karen knew he hardly saw her these days. But she was still his wife, the mother of his mysterious absent son. Maybe he had obligations there. She could be deceiving herself very badly. Maybe he thought of her as nothing but an easy fuck.

'Do you know what kind of businesses he's

307

involved in?' Doyle asked.

'You mean do I know if he's dirty?'

'Dirty? That's a strange word in this business – our business, I mean. I don't think we need to focus on that. I meant generally. I meant legitimately.'

'I've told you what I know before. As far as I know, he has controlling interests in several haulage companies, one of which he started himself. That's the main thing, I believe. There are other little sidelines, but it's haulage that brought the cash in.'

'That's right. And our friends in Customs are always interested in the movement of goods between Pakistan and the UK. Because of that I'm told some sections of the Customs hierarchy have become keenly interested in Surani.'

'I'm sure he's guessed that already.'

'Of course. But he might not he able to guess the extent of their investment in him.'

'Are we talking about an interest in import duty, that kind of thing? Whether he pays what he should pay? If so he has lawyers to deal with all that, I'm sure.'

'After tonight he might have to swap them for trial lawyers.'

She raised her eyebrows, only just realizing what was going on. 'This isn't about tax, then?'

'I don't know. It might be about duty owed, or even about evasion of prohibitions – as you say, if it is then I'm sure he can handle it – but it may be that other fish are frying.'

'Like what?'

'The kind that might cause Customs to make a

deeper investment.'

She thought about that. 'A more penetrating investment?'

'Perhaps.'

She looked around her. The room was empty, the barman not in sight. 'Can't we just say what we mean, Francis?'

He smiled. 'Of course. If you prefer that. That's why we're here, in this place. They may have someone inside his network. That's what I mean.'

She took a breath. She could barely believe what he had said. In all her dealings with Doyle she had always thought him honourable, in a rough, practical way. Everything about him said that, every way he had ever dealt with her. But he was crossing a line now. 'And you're telling me this?' she asked him. 'Why?'

'I thought you ought to know.'

She sipped her drink carefully. The reply was ridiculous, but Doyle's eyes hadn't changed expression. She made a mental note: if he was capable of burning a Customs agent then he could do the same to her.

'Are you being serious, Francis? Are you telling me the truth?'

'Of course.'

Again the eyes looked transparent, honest, fixed on her own. And why would he invent something like that?

'It doesn't sound like the sort of thing you should be telling me,' she said. 'Or anyone.'

'I'll have to be the judge of that. That's my role, my job. You know that.' As it would be to turn his back on her, if it ever came to it. 'I'm not inviting you to burn anyone,' he added, reading her thoughts. 'You need to be very, very careful how you handle the information. But if things are as Customs think they are then my information is that you won't have any chance of getting close to Surani after tonight. That's a serious situation for us.'

'I see.' Not as serious as it was for the Customs agent, though. She had been in that position. She had even been tossed out to rot – burned, as they so eloquently put it. Was he forgetting that?

'Today, I mean, might be your last chance to find out about his brother,' he said.

'Which obviously won't work. What could there be to find out? I assume we know all about him already. Or you do. I assumed the point was to get a way in, not to recover information we already have.'

'Exactly. And all that may run aground tonight. We've tried reasoning with them, obviously. But you know how these things are. We have to be careful they don't put two and two together. So there's little we can say that's effective. We don't compromise our own. Not ever.'

She had to smirk at that. Maybe he *had* forgotten her file

'I mean it,' he said, his voice harder, reading her again. 'The way things were done in the past is in the past. It won't happen again. It's because we need to protect your position that it comes to this.'

'A Customs agent or me?'

'I think that's the sum of it. They're doing their best, of course. They might even have something relatively serious going down. But it's chicken-shit compared to getting a lever on Surani's brother. Our latest information puts him very close to the top slice out there. In personal contact with top targets.'

He'd said as much to her before. 'Out there' meant the Pakistani/Afghan border, where the Surani family held considerable tracts of land. The 'targets' were the Al-Qaeda hierarchy, she assumed.

'So you want me to tip off Surani?' she asked.

He looked embarrassed, now that it was stated so directly. 'That's not the language I'd use,' he said. 'You need to be very careful, like I said. You need to find a way round the dangers. You don't have to tell him there's a Customs officer deeply embedded into the lower management structure of Global Trade Ltd. There must be more subtle ways to get him to avoid a personal involvement in his business.'

'What kind of involvement?'

'Travelling to a meeting in the early hours of to-morrow morning where the precise nature of a specific shipment will be discussed in front of others. Not sensible for a manager at his level, surely?'

'What kind of shipment is it?'

'I don't know. There are rumours, but that's not evidence. Maybe it's nothing extraordinary after all.'

'Is it drugs?'

'It could be. But I'm being truthful when I say I don't know. Would it affect things for you if it were drugs?'

'Not at all. I'm doing a job.' It took an effort to

keep her face blank. 'But I might not like the idea of burning an agent who was fighting that kind of thing.'

'Don't muck around, Karen. You know we don't want you to burn him.'

Didn't they? He was even giving her the gender of the officer. With a few additional enquiries she already had enough information to identify him herself.

'We don't want anyone burned,' he repeated. 'We want Surani to be more cautious. That's all. Anyway, what do you mean "that kind of thing"? You know full well what Surani does. You know exactly who you're getting into bed with.' He sat back in the chair.

She let the metaphor slip by. It wasn't intended as a metaphor. She knew that. It was intended as some kind of insult, which was uncharacteristic of him, to say the least. But she would take it as a metaphor. Let it go.

'Do I?' she asked him. 'Do I know? Really? I'm not sure I do.'

She didn't have evidence either, just rumours and information. That was enough for her in other circumstances. She was turning a blind eye to it, of course, every minute she was with Michael. She felt a little shiver of dread run through her body. Not because she might be enjoying intimate relations with a major heroin importer, but because she wasn't sure whether she cared.

Doyle shrugged. 'Anyway. There it is. I think you have enough material to make a decision.'

'But not long to make it.'

'Until about midnight tomorrow.'

Wednesday

30

The evening with Marcus started as a vague plan to teach him some kind of lesson, she thought, but within a few hours things weren't so clear. They ate at a restaurant in central Leeds, then went back to his flat. Throughout the meal she was preoccupied with the Surani/Doyle problem and conscious of the clock ticking away on her options.

She had been out with Marcus before, of course – many times. But she had never set it up like this, with the more or less overt implication that she was interested in him. In the past she had been careful to give the reverse impression. Maybe that made a difference. He was certainly more fascinating to talk to when he was anticipating something. His personality went into a different gear. Or maybe it wasn't a game that was so easy to play without really feeling the things she was meant to be faking.

Either way, for one reason or another something new was there almost from the outset. She found herself trying to examine why that should surprise her. She had always liked Marcus, always got on well with him. What they were doing wasn't unusual or sneaky in itself. He was a friend. They had done things like this – gone out together, ate, drank wine chatted – since long before Mairead arrived back home to complicate matters. Her intention had been to repeat that and bluff the rest. Lead him on, then drop him cold. Not purely for Mairead, she saw now – who wouldn't even get to know about this – but also for herself, because his failure to tell her he was sleeping with her daughter was a kind of insult to *her*, too.

But maybe she had been deceiving herself about what she *could* feel for a man over ten years her junior. If she kept him firmly in that mental box – as if he were no more threatening than a child to whom she had to teach a silly little lesson – then the idea that something else might be going on between them didn't even arise. But she'd let the genie out. And now it suddenly seemed very easy to see Marcus as something different, something grown-up, attractive, dangerous. That confused her. She drank quite a bit, too, and wasn't used to that. She didn't enjoy the loss of control.

Before long she had forgotten all the cutting remarks she had wanted to deliver as she turned and walked out (when he was least expecting it, she had loosely imagined, when he was just at the point of thinking something really was starting between them). Even before they got back to his she knew that something *really was* going on between them and she wasn't sure she wanted to stop it. That brought on a powerful sensation of guilt. This was the man Mairead was sitting at home moping about. She had no right to, per-haps – Mairead herself was meant to be with another man. (Karen assumed Marcus didn't even know about Julian.) Nevertheless, part of her knew that to continue like this was to transfer the blow she had been planning from Marcus to her daughter. It was a betrayal of Mairead, even though Mairead would never realize that. She was left not knowing what she should do, or even what she wanted to do.

Meanwhile time passed fairly effortlessly. She found herself relaxing into his company, accepting the mild intoxication, enjoying the attention, the subtle flattery, the intensity of interest in her life, her past, her thoughts. She couldn't believe that it was already well after eleven by the time they got back to his place. That meant he had managed to get her mind off Michael as well. She immediately made excuses and stepped out onto his balcony to make the call, pulling the glass doors shut behind her.

There was a view of the 'regenerated' canal area below – which meant a thin stretch of water crowded by buildings much like the one Marcus had bought into – warehouses and wharfs converted into mixed residential and office space, the ground floors stocked with expensive little restaurants, tapas bars and shops selling the sort of over-designed assorted junk that might look apt in a loft conversion. All quiet now, close on midnight, midweek, though it could be loud and lively into the early hours during the weekend. The evening was cooling so she buttoned up the cardigan she was wearing.

She didn't know what she was going to do until some moments after Michael answered the phone. She expected him to sound hassled, maybe to make excuses for not speaking to her. That would have clinched it for her, perhaps. But he sounded pleased to hear from her.

'You're not in a rush? It's not a bad time to talk?' she asked.

'Of course not. I'm delighted to hear from you. It's quite late, though. What are you doing?'

She glanced back through the double-glazed doors at Marcus, standing by his hi-fi system, back to her. Absurdly, she felt a twinge of something like remorse. But on account of whom? She owed neither man any kind of loyalty.

'I had a problem earlier,' she said.

'What kind of problem?'

'I tried to call you on the other phone – the cheap mobile – but couldn't get through.' Doyle had told her Customs had intercepts on three mobiles Surani was known to use, giving her the precise details. She imagined Surani was more careful than to talk carelessly. During the murder enquiry they suspected he had a pay-as-you-go phone, but had never recovered it. When asked about it, he had said he had in the past bought a 'cheap mobile' due to accidentally travelling once without his normal phones. He claimed he had thrown it away long since, which she was sure was true. She hoped he had bought another, though – not one of the phones on the Customs list.

'My cheap mobile?'

She didn't repeat anything. She let him think about it.

'I don't have that any more,' he said, eventually. 'I'll tell you which numbers I do have.'

Had he caught on? She took the slip of paper that Doyle had given her from her pocket and read it as he gave her the exact three phone numbers Doyle had said were insecure.

'Yes. I think I tried those, too,' she said. 'You should check they're all right. Text me about next week, OK?'

'No problem.' He cut the line at once. She still wasn't sure he'd cottoned on.

She waited only a few moments before an anonymous text came through. Nothing in the message except a new number. He'd sussed it. She rang the number.

'Can we talk?' he asked, at once.

'I think so. If my info is correct.' If Doyle had given her the right information then they were safe to speak, provided Michael destroyed whatever phone he was using afterwards. If it was seized then traffic to and from it could be retrospectively tracked. She was sure he would get rid of it, but still, she felt unsure. She was taking a risk.

'Shoot,' he said.

'London can be an interesting place. But you shouldn't really be going out in the early hours of the morning. Not today, anyway. It's too cold.'

She listened carefully to the long silence that greeted this.

'Are you sure?' he asked finally.

'I'm certain.'

'Why?'

'It will be nice to see you in person again. We can talk properly then. Meanwhile just a little friendly advice.'

'I'll take it. Of course. Thank you.'

He didn't sound as if he had just been caught out. He sounded normal, perfectly calm. She assumed he understood perfectly. She hoped she had given nothing dangerous to him. Best to make that clear, though. 'There cannot be any consequences,' she said. 'It will come back to me if there are.' Not necessarily true, if the line was secure.

'I won't be using this phone again,' he said.

'Yes. But you'll think about things and work it out. When that happens you must remember that there could be a trail back to me, which would damage us both.' She felt physically uncomfortable saying the words, despite Doyle's reassurances about secure contact. Everything was too unguarded. But she couldn't say it any other way and get him to understand. 'So no consequences. OK?'

'Surely you know me better than that, Karen? You have nothing to fear. No one has anything to fear. You should know that. I'm surprised. These things do not need to be stated.' He sounded mildly hurt, reproving.

'I know that,' she said, lying. In reality, she had no idea what he was capable of. Could he arrange the murder of a Customs agent? 'But I had to be sure.'

'I understand that. And I'm grateful to you for this. I have something you should know, too.' He didn't say 'in return'. 'It's about Gary Swales.'

That surprised her. 'What about him?'

'I told you I knew him. We have business interests that overlap, so sometimes I hear things. Specifically, he's not reacting rationally to the arrest of his family. He's made a few phone calls that I've got to know about.'

'What kind of things? What phone calls?' She

could hear her voice rising.

'He's talking about trying something similar to the thing you said he tried in the past.'

She stood for a moment in silence, gripping the mobile so hard her knuckles began to ache. She stared at the view, thoughts rushing into her head. Where was Mairead right now?

'Has he done anything?' she asked. 'Has he done anything already?'

'No. Not yet. For a variety of reasons I would think he would find such a thing difficult at the moment. He has problems in the business world. It may be he couldn't find anyone to oblige even if he wanted to, which is not certain...'

'Were you going to tell me this anyway? If I hadn't called you?' Or was it a favour in return? A dirty little favour in return. Her welcome to the world of organized crime. She had been there long before meeting Michael Surani, done much worse, but that was her past – she wanted to keep it that way.

'I was thinking about it,' he said. 'I didn't want to worry you unnecessarily. I was going to deal with it myself.'

'Is this your idea of payment? A favour in return?'

'Payment?' He sounded shocked. 'Please don't think such things, Karen. That's not the way things are between us. Like I said, I was going to deal with it myself.'

She took a breath, tried to relax her muscles, think clearly about it. 'Is there any immediate danger?'

'No. He hasn't done anything yet. And to be

'honest it sounded like bluster to me.'

'Bluster?' The word sounded old-fashioned, out of place next to the threat.

'Yes. He's angry and a little cornered. It may not mean anything. Just like the last time.'

'The last time? What do you mean?'

'It all came to nothing, right? It was a rumour only, I heard. Didn't you tell me that?'

'Not me. It was real last time. That's what I told you.' That wasn't what the enquiry had found, of course. The enquiry had more or less stated that the threat was in her head. 'That was my information,' she said. 'So it could be real again. He's a fucking idiot. He's capable of it.'

'So you say. But I'm not sure. At any rate, you're right to be cautious. You should always be careful. You know that.'

'Can you give me anything more specific?'

'Face to face. Yes.' So he was being cautious, too.

'Well, maybe that should happen soon.'

'As soon as I can. Meanwhile, as I said, there are ways I can deal with this. So don't worry too much. I'll call you if I get to know more. It's possible I'll get something later tonight. I'm working on it. For now I have to go. Once again, thank you for the assistance.'

She waited for him to say something else. Some kind of goodbye, but he didn't. Instead the line was cut. Maybe someone had walked in on him.

She leaned against the balcony railing and tried to take in what he had told her. How was he going to deal with it? she wondered. Put out the word that she was in his pocket, not to be touched? That made her shiver with more than cold. She pulled the cardigan tighter and tried to regulate her breathing. Behind her she heard the balcony doors slide open.

'You OK there?'

Marcus. She tried to smile at him. But in her head all she could think about was calling Mairead and warning her. She had to resist that. It was only a couple of days since they had arrested Mary Swales. She had already been released and was going to end up as a crown witness if Ricky Spencer got his way. Mary had even been told that. It was absurd to think that in those circumstances Gary Swales would put a contract on her. There was nothing to be that angry about. And Michael had clearly said that nothing had been done just yet. So no need to start panicking Mairead.

'Not really,' she said, turning towards Marcus. Then again, Swales was mad. She had always thought that about him – that he had a screw loose, literally, that he should have been in an institution. Not because, as they knew for certain, he had ordered the killing of Ben Smalley, but because he had put a contract on a serving police officer. To do that he had to be unbalanced. Which meant he *could* be trying to do it again. It was possible.

'What's up?'

He came out and stood beside her on the narrow ledge. She could feel her head beginning to churn with the problem. Was it all going to start again?

'I don't know whether I can tell you,' she said. After all, this was what she had wanted. To provoke Swales again, to settle the scores. She had to deal with it alone.

She was as insane as Swales. Risking Mairead, not just herself. Another example of how atrocious a mother she was. She edged closer to Marcus, feeling suddenly unsure of herself. He was a good friend, she thought. Or good enough. *Should* she tell him what was happening? She put her arm round his waist and leaned her head against his shoulder. It could have been something a friend would do, so why not? It felt natural enough. Comfortable. He moved to accommodate her and put an arm round her shoulders. Nothing else.

They stood there for a long time, not saying anything. She thought it looked like they might be standing on the balcony staring out at the night view. Young lovers? Or an old, worn couple, but still with that bond of affection. From a distance it could look like that. But he was at least ten years younger than her. More like a mother and son. Would she ever get the real thing? It was getting to be too late now. Michael wasn't the real thing. He was another game, one of the endless games with her own personality. It made her feel sick to think about it. Why couldn't she just relax, be who she was? Why had it always been this way?

'Is it a work thing?' he asked quietly.

'I don't want to think about it,' she said. Should she call Mairead? The thought kept coming back, obsessively. She was being silly. She had to control it. She should wait to see what Michael came up with. Maybe ask Doyle about it. It could wait until tomorrow. Nothing was going to happen now. She kept telling herself that.

'Shall we go inside, then?' he asked. 'It's a bit cold.'

'Let's go inside and go to bed,' she said. The words came out without prior thought. She realized it was what she wanted only as she spoke. Warmth, comfort, affection. Something to stop her brain going into overdrive. So why not do it? She was old enough to he his mother. Not quite, but as a metaphor. It wasn't going to harm anybody. In a week Mairead would be back at university, back with Julian. Marcus would be forgotten. And Mairead shouldn't have started with him anyway. He was her mother's friend. Worse – someone her mother worked with and had a responsibility for. She knew that, but had gone ahead and done it anyway, behind Karen's back. Wasn't that what was really offensive about the episode? Not Marcus's actions. If she thought about it clearly then she didn't care enough about Marcus to be truly hurt by him. But Mairead had probably slept with him deliberately to betray her. Mairead could be a bitch. And she had a lifetime of scores to settle with her mother. Not just the real issues, but all the silly, innumerable teenage conflicts.

Marcus didn't reply.

'Did you hear me?' she asked after a while.

'Yes,' he said. His voice sounded strained.

'Shouldn't I have said that?' She had a moment of doubt. 'We don't have to do anything,' she added. 'Just lie there. Be nice to each other.'

'Is that what you meant? Is that all you want?'

She felt his hand stroking her hair, gently, with real affection. He liked her too much. But it was all right, for now. It was what she needed. She kept telling herself that. He would get hurt. But he was young enough for that not to matter. He had all his life to recover. And wasn't that what she had intended anyway? Wasn't that Plan A? Lead him on, then drop him. This was just leading him on a fraction further to drop him from higher. She could tell herself that.

'Let's take it one step at a time,' she said, 'and see what happens.'

31

They got into bed carefully, with clothes on, then lay against each other for a while, pretending they were there to sleep. Like some farce from her teenage years. But she was determined not to make the moves. She wasn't that clear about what she wanted. The guilt was still bothering her. In any case, in her experience the sexual act hadn't usually been a good way to get or convey affection. And she was telling herself that affection was why she was here. Not sex. So let him make the decisions. If this was as far as it went she would be happy. Maybe. She put an arm round him, let his head rest on her shoulders.

It took him a long time to get past that. He was interested in her sexually – that was physically obvious – but less than he was interested in talking to her, it seemed. Or hugging her. Or telling her things about herself. So instead of going

326

straight for it – as she might have imagined of someone his age – he started talking.

He wanted to know her better, he said. He had many questions, mainly about her past – 'the past is what makes you as you are...' Little did he know. She told him nothing of consequence, but it didn't put him off. He lay beside her for a long time, holding her close to him, one hand stroking her hair, the other gradually progressing to more provocative movements. She went along with it. Why not?

There were many reasons why not. She tried to keep them in focus, but then there was the alcohol, blurring the moral lines, the pure emotional need, the sense of rising panic about Swales that she wanted to control – and the excitement, of course. Increasingly, what he was doing to her had a physical effect, and as the effect kicked in, her brain began to zone out, her thoughts sliding into the background, taking her conscience with them.

She let it happen.

The talking continued throughout. She thought it would be off-putting, but he was more intelligent than that. Everything was part of the seduction – words and movements working together to gradually lull her closer to him. He told her about the first time he saw her, what he thought about the way she walked, the way she dressed, the way she handled the guys in the office and so on. He almost whispered the sentences into her ear. And all the time his hands caressed her, moving slowly and precisely over her body, taking off her clothing along the way.

It was a litany of adoration, and it took her

completely by surprise. It wasn't at all what she had expected of him. She was surprised that he had noticed so much about her, so many tiny details, surprised that he had learned so young how to use his fingers so effectively. He managed to break it up with humour, too. So that she found herself laughing with him as he went through an argument she'd had with Ricky Spencer, for instance, the first day he had joined her team. And he was self-deprecating enough for it not to sink into the merely embarrassing, gently poking fun at himself for being so 'hung up' on her. That was how he described it. But not as if that were a bad thing.

Behind the words she could hear the voice of someone who had watched her carefully, with eyes terribly clouded by attraction. Why hadn't she realized this was going on? He made her sound like someone in a film, it wasn't reality. But if she stopped herself thinking about it then he could almost make her feel good about herself, as if some of his admiration actually rubbed off and stuck, as if she were like that. After all, he wasn't quite young enough for her to be able to write it off as a childish infatuation. And it was flattering, of course: she was old and he was young; young and fit, with the kind of physique she might have dreamed about twenty years ago. And she knew already how bright he was. It wasn't someone stupid who was lying here telling her all these things about herself, so slowly bringing his hands closer to where she wanted them.

Afterwards she felt disgusted with herself.

The act changed nothing for him, it seemed. He lay close to her and continued as before – whispering how fantastic she was, moving his hands over her, concentrating the same level of attention on her. Probably he wanted to start again.

But she felt too ashamed. He seemed like a child. It was too simplistic, what he felt – only a child could experience it like that. Probably Mairead, who had less to learn of life, was more mature than he was. Mairead was no doubt lying awake now, longing for him.

She wasn't missing anything, Karen thought, but she still felt dirty when she thought about that. Her daughter had also done what she had just done. Probably he had gone through exactly the same script with her. Men were like that, boys especially. And Marcus was a boy. It had been nice at the time, but now it felt like a species of child abuse.

'That meant something to me,' he said, whispering in her ear. He didn't have a clue.

She moved away from him. He'd been a friend, but she'd torn that up. She told him he didn't even know her. 'What's the worst you think you know?' she asked. 'Tell me the worst thing you think I've done.'

He was breathing rapidly, but she felt him tensing slightly. He had picked up the change in her tone.

'I know you've killed people,' he said, eventually.

'Is that bad?'

'Not necessarily ... I suppose. Depends on the circumstances...'

329

'And how you do it.'

'Maybe.'

He believed all the things they wanted you to believe about killing, of course – all the things you saw in films, or read of in fiction. And that despite his having seen the consequences for real. But it was different if you hadn't *done* it. Totally different.

'Why did you laugh?' he asked.

'I didn't.'

'You made a noise like you laughed.'

'I should have laughed. But it's not that funny. You don't know the half of it.'

'I haven't killed anyone. If that's what you–'

'Killing is easy. That's what you don't know. It can be done without regret, without emotion, without even pausing to think too much about it afterwards. I used to think I was some kind of psychopath. But everyone is like that. When people ask me about it I have to pretend I care about them. In reality I don't give a shit.' The words came out in a rush, surprising her.

'Care about them? Who do you mean?'

'The people I killed.'

'I see.' Alarm in his tone.

'I doubt you do.' She took a breath. 'It can be *normal* for people to burn children to death, or brutalize them.' She heard her voice crack as she said the words. 'Those things can be normal. There are parts of the world – not too far from where we are now – where they are normal. We spend our lives trying to obscure that. You do. I do. That's the game.'

That left them both silent. She regretted open-

330

ing her mouth. She hadn't thought it through. Still, better he should learn *something* from this.

'I read about you shooting three men who had kidnapped and abused a kid,' he said eventually. 'Ten years ago, was it? And then the case where you killed the guy in Rochdale five years ago. Is that what you're talking about?'

'Not really,' she said. 'There was worse than all that. From further back, when I was young. That's what made me like this. In my head I have the mentality of a terrorist. That's what you're in bed with. Best you should know. Would you lie here with me and tell me all those things if you thought I'd planted a bomb that had blown a kid to ribbons?'

'You're talking about Northern Ireland?' He sounded very uncertain now.

'That was where I grew up. Yes.' How did he know that, though?

'Mairead said something about Northern Ireland. About her dad.'

So Mairead had spoken to him about Jim. In bed? Like this? She rolled away from him, so that she was on her back, eyes on the ceiling. The reality of how she had ended up here came back to her again. It was a complete betrayal of her daughter. No two ways about it. She could still taste him, she realized. It felt filthy. She resisted the urge to spit. 'Mairead shouldn't have told you anything,' she said. 'She should know better.'

He said nothing. She hoped he could feel the frost now. She was setting herself against him. She *wanted* him to feel it.

'I was born in Northern Ireland,' she said. 'And

I worked there a long time ago. I worked for a covert military unit that they now deny even existed. It was a different world. But it was reality. I'll say that.'

'I don't think that's true, Karen.' He said the words very gently. 'I don't know what you've done. I hope you haven't planted bombs that have killed kids, or had anything to do with that. I'm sure you've done traumatic things, things that have caused you to suffer.'

'That's the point I'm making,' she said. 'I didn't suffer at all. Not for those things. Those aren't even the worst of it. Not for me.'

'So what is?'

'For the first eight years of Mairead's life she was with her father, not me. Maybe she told you that. I don't know. Did she tell you her father was a convicted terrorist, a killer?'

'She didn't tell me anything.'

'I loved him. That was love. The real thing. He was meant to be my target, but I loved him.' She held her breath. She could feel the emotion starting. 'I knew what he did. But that didn't make a difference. We were two of a kind. But I didn't want a baby by him. I had to have it – her, Mairead, my daughter because they wouldn't let me walk out on him. *They*, the British, the people I was working for. He was meant to be a target; it was meant to be a game. But Mairead fucked that up. So you know what I did?'

He didn't reply.

'I walked out on her. Left her with him. She was three months old. I didn't see her again for over eight years. She didn't fit the plan, so I left her...'

In fact she had been so ill she couldn't remember leaving them. And she still couldn't talk about it without this happening – without her heart thumping and her skin beginning to burn. If she gave in to it she would break down, start crying. He would think she was human then, confused. She didn't want that. As it was he was just lying there staring at her. In bed with the beast.

From the pile of clothes alongside the bed, she heard her mobile ringing. She rolled quickly to get it, with tremendous relief. He didn't try to stop her. The number was withheld. She pressed to answer anyway and heard Surani's quiet, assured voice. Surani was a man who already knew all this about her, who understood. She would have been safer in bed with him. To have come here, like this, was stupid pure weakness. She had to keep it from Mairead at all costs. 'Wait a moment,' she said into the phone. She stood quickly and pulled on her T-shirt. 'I'll take this in the other room,' she said to Marcus, not bothering to mute the phone. She saw something like fear in his eyes.

In his living room she listened as Surani quickly passed on information. Gary Swales had a store room, he said, a lock-up garage. He gave her the address. She memorized it. There would be things there that might be useful to her, he said. She was puzzled. She had been expecting something about Swales trying to damage her, something urgent. It was nearly two in the morning.

'Why tell me this?'

'It's best to have insurance,' Surani said. 'You might find it there. I'm told the dead woman kept a diary.'

'And it's in Swales's lock-up?' That was interesting. It might have brought a smile to her face, had Surani's knowledge of it not felt like a punch. How well did he really know Gary Swales, to be able to get information like that? For some reason she had assumed some looser connection between them. But it had to be something much closer, she knew now. Either Swales trusted Surani implicitly (and how could that come about?) or Surani had somebody very close to Swales on the payroll (and why would that be?). There was no explanation that didn't taint Surani badly.

'You won't be able to prove it's Swales's lock-up,' Surani said. 'I know that for sure. That's why he has it. It's secure.'

'So how would finding the diary there be insurance?'

'If it was found somewhere else it might be,' he said, then cut the line as suddenly as the last time.

Marcus was right behind her as she came off the line, a worried look on his face. Had he heard anything? He didn't say anything.

'I have to go,' she said.

He nodded, not looking at her.

She washed and dressed in silence, thinking hard. He remained in the living room. When she came through – ten minutes later – he stood up from the sofa and made an effort to smile. He looked as if he wanted to say something to her, something personal. But instead he held his hand out towards her, offering her a small package, like it was a present. She frowned, taking it. It was a brown-paper packet containing a small heavy object.

'What's this?' she asked him. 'A goodbye gift?'

'A mail-order Asp.'

She had forgotten that. She suppressed a smile and almost felt sorry for him, but not sorry enough to tell him what she was going to do with it. That part of her plan she could stick to.

'Good boy,' she said. Back into work mode. She looked inside the packet and checked the Asp, enough to see that it had a serial number, but being careful not to touch it. 'You can tell me all about it later.'

Did he feel triumphant? she wondered. He had bedded them both now – mother and child. She felt a wave of nausea looking at him. But she knew it was for herself mainly, because what he had done to her had been beautiful. The first part, anyway. He wasn't to blame, but she was going to blame him anyway. The things she felt were complicated. They would take time to think through. But she was in a hurry now.

'I have to go somewhere,' she said. 'And I need you to come with me.'

Thursday

32

For the very first time in a very long time, Marcus felt vulnerable and confused because of a woman. He dressed quickly in the bedroom, trying to work out what had just happened. The change had been so quick it had taken him unawares; there had been no time to think how best to control it. They had spent over two hours in bed and he had been completely lost in the act. It seemed that Karen had been, too. Everything had gone well – better than well, he thought. They had fitted together perfectly. Everything had happened as it should have, when it should have. There had been no dishonesty, no sexual lies. It was a technical and emotional success, and you couldn't ask much more of sex. In his experience, that didn't happen often.

When Karen had started telling him about killing people in Northern Ireland he had at first thought she was joking. But as she had continued he had realized quite quickly that she was not. She became emotional about it before he could think how to react then pulled away from him. He had felt an unmistakeable resentment flowing out of her. She had deliberately tried to break the spell binding them together, he thought. There had been a unique bond between them – he had felt it so strongly he could not be mistaken but she wanted to destroy it. And now she was playing the back-to-work-as-normal game. As if nothing had happened. It left him reeling. He had given something special to her, something he didn't give away lightly. But she had taken it as if it meant nothing.

'Can you tell me what's going on, please?' he asked her, as he stepped back into his living room. She was pulling on his jacket (without asking). She had showered very quickly, but told him he didn't have time.

'I had a call from an informant,' she started. 'He gave me the address of–'

'Not that.' He reached over and took her hand. It was very warm – hot, in fact, as if she might have a fever. 'What's happening between us? You know what I mean.'

She frowned at him – as if she really didn't know what he meant – then gently removed her hand from his. 'Let's get things back to normal,' she said quietly. 'We have to work together.'

'That's how you want this to be?'

'Of course.' She paused, looking at him. 'You know how to do this, Marcus. You know all too well. So if you're ready we can leave.'

They took his car. She directed him to Wakefield. He drove carefully through near-deserted streets. They had both drunk too much to drive, if it came to it. He asked her where they were going, and why, but she was playing another game now – the it's-a-surprise game. He had overheard a part of her conversation with the informant, but that hadn't given much away. She seemed relaxed on the surface, but there was a forced quality to

340

it, betrayed every now and then by her speaking faster than normal with a slight breathlessness.

He decided to try again. 'I think we should talk about tonight. I feel as if–'

'I don't want to talk about it.'

She was facing away from him, looking out of the window. He drove up the long, empty slip leading to the M1. The motorway lights striped the side of her face in yellow and white, but he couldn't see her expression.

'Watch where you're going,' she said, aware that he was looking at her.

'I don't understand why you've–'

'I don't want to talk about it.' A firmer note now, as if she were in boss mode, instructing him what to do. He sighed long and hard, feeling very confused.

As they neared the city she consulted the Tom-Tom, but wherever they were going wasn't covered in enough detail, so she had to resort to a normal map. They left the motorway and she took him into the countryside to the north-east of Wakefield, following a series of back roads that led into open fields and higher land. To his right he could see the lights of Wakefield city centre. They drove for over ten minutes in absolute silence – the tension unbearable for him – then turned down a lane with a poor surface and pulled up outside a row of three or four cottages at a minor cross-roads. The curtains were all drawn, the lights off. It was almost three in the morning. She pointed beyond the cottages to another narrow lane. He could see a line of low buildings at the end of it, but the only street lamp was at the entrance to the lane, so he couldn't see what they were. He drove the car to the end of the lane. She got out without speaking to him. He felt heavy with disappointment.

She had transferred a toolbox from her own car to his. She opened it now and extracted a pair of heavy-duty bolt-clippers and a torch. She gave him the torch. For the first time he began to worry about what they were doing, rather than what they had just done. He realized he no longer wanted to be there with her – whatever it was she was going to do; he wanted to be at home sleeping. Or thinking about it all. He had to think calmly about the night, work out what was going on. That was his way of approaching these things, to think them through in isolation. But she wasn't giving him the chance.

'A little night-time commercial burglary,' she said, then set off towards the lane, beckoning him to follow. Was she joking?

The buildings were lock-up garages, a row of eight. She read the numbers on the doors and stopped outside number six. It was a simple affair. No windows, built of brick and corrugated sheet, a conventional double door held shut with a padlock.

'You haven't got another padlock in the car, have you?' she asked.

'No. Obviously. Why?'

'Because after we've cut it we'll need to replace it.'

The cutters were large and the lock small, so it didn't take her long. She took the sheared lock off and put it in the pocket of the suede jacket she was wearing. *His* suede jacket. He began to wonder about the legality of what she was up to.

She pulled the doors open and looked in. He could see a car, rear end facing them. He switched on the torch, illuminating the registration plate. She read the numbers and letters. The car was a grey Nissan SUV.

'You recognize the plate?' she asked.

'No.' He was trying to remember his PACE course, to think of a way they might have a legal right of entry. He couldn't come up with one. 'Do you have information I don't have?' he asked her. 'Information that would give us grounds to do this?'

She laughed. 'Getting worried about it?'

'Yes. I can't see a way we would be authorized to do this. A legal way.'

'No? You want to leave?' She turned and looked at him.

'Maybe,' he said. 'You'll have to tell me more.'

'The garage belongs to Gary Swales,' she said. 'This car – if I'm not mistaken – features in two places in the enquiry. Firstly, it's on the CCTV footage from the scene. Secondly, it's registered to Mary Swales.'

'Mary Bradley.'

'Yes.'

'You remember the plate?'

'Of course.'

'You remember also, then, that Mary was asked about it when we pulled in John. She said it was John's car, despite being registered to her, and that she thought he'd sold it years ago.'

'So she said.'

343

'And anyway, that still doesn't give us the right to be here.'

'No. That's why we'll need to replace the lock. Before we get the warrant and come back.'

'Jesus Christ, Karen.' He frowned at her. He felt angry now. 'Why? Why do this? What's the point? Why didn't we knock up a magistrate and get the fucking warrant before coming here?'

She shrugged. 'It hardly matters. Let's take a look, now that we're here.' She winked at him. 'Let's see what else there is.'

She took the torch off him and stepped in. There wasn't much room to get round the car. After a while he heard her moving things at the far end; then an electric light came on above the car, blinding him. He shielded his eyes and watched, feet firmly placed beyond the doors.

'You're not coming in?' she called out to him. Through the car windows he could see her searching through some boxes stacked in front of the vehicle.

'No,' he called back. He looked around him, nervously. They were out of sight of the cottages, screened by a slope in the land and a high hawthorn hedge. He could see no sign of life anywhere. No CCTV cameras. Probably she could get away with it. But why? Why do it at all? He began to think about the things she had said to him, about killing people. For the first time it occurred to him that she really was different from anyone else he'd ever met in his life. Even if he only took into account the killings he knew about – the legal killings – she had snapped someone's neck, for Christ's sake. What kind of person did you have to be to be capable of that? And where had she learned it? In the military unit she had spoken of, presumably. But even that was just the tip of it. She had suggested much more. What had her comment about planting bombs meant? In the dark, in the middle of nowhere, tricked by her into acting as a lookout while she made an illegal entry and search, he realized he really didn't know her at all. She was right; he had no idea what she was capable of. Her behaviour had been inexplicable, weird, her mood volatile. Maybe she *was* a kind of psychopath.

He heard her squeezing back along the side of the car. She reappeared, smiling. The naked bulb cast a hard light over her features.

'Look at this,' she said. She held something towards him. It looked like a book.

'I don't want to touch it,' he said. 'I'm annoyed with you for bringing me here.'

'It's a diary,' she said, ignoring him. 'A diary kept by Rebecca Farrar. I just read the last pages. They're loose leaf, stuffed in here, dated a couple of weeks before she died. She was at Gary Swales's place. A prisoner there.'

He was torn between wanting to look at it – to check she wasn't inventing it – and the absurdity of their position. If it was evidence – if it really was as important as she was suggesting – then why had she taken so much trouble to seize it illegally? Evidentially, it was useless to them now.

'You want to look?' she asked, holding it towards him again.

'No. What do you do now? Put it back and get a warrant?'

'Yes.' She started flicking through the pages, reading it.

'You're fucking up possible forensics, Karen. You know that.'

She closed it. 'You're right. I'll put it back.'

She walked back past the car. He took a deep breath and looked around again. He couldn't work out what was going on. More than he thought – he was sure of that. But what? He didn't know what to say to her, how to react. She was his boss, but this was all wrong. She had never done anything like this before. Not with him, anyway.

The light went out and she came back.

'Learn anything?' she asked him.

'Like what?'

'About me, I mean.'

'I don't know, Karen. I don't know why you've done this. What was the point?'

'I couldn't wait. It was better than lying in your bed and worrying about my past. There's no harm done.' She pulled the garage doors closed and hooped the broken padlock through the rings.

'There is if anyone finds out we've done this,' he said. He was only just beginning to realize the complexity of it.

'But there's only me and you here,' she said. 'I can replace this lock later today, set up the warrant. No one will have a clue.' She sounded blithe about it. He felt like panicking.

'I don't like it,' he said. 'You're expecting me not to say anything. You tricked me into this.'

'Tricked you? The man who did pure maths at fourteen? How did I trick you?' She winked again. 'Trust me, Marcus. There's no harm done. Nobody got hurt; no evidence was corrupted. And I won't say anything if you don't.'

33

Andrew wanted his mum so badly it was like a shooting pain in his tummy. He felt so ill he could barely cry. He lay on the little bed, covered in sweat, shivering uncontrollably, trying to remember to reach for the bowl beside the bed when the sick started to come up his throat, because if he forgot that and was sick on the floor, or the bed itself, then Mary might shake him again, and that made everything worse.

All he could think about was his mum. When his mum had been with him, and he had got sick, she had wrapped him up warmly, in soft blankets, and laid him in bed and looked after him. She had stroked his head and read him stories and given him little sips of water to drink. His mouth was so dry now he could hardly speak, but no one was giving him water. No one was there to look after him at all. His mum had told him how much she loved him, that he would be OK, that the horrible dizziness would go away. She had given him medicine as well. Sometimes, when he was a little better, she had let him sit up in bed and watch TV. But there was nothing in this room except the bed. Nothing to do but lie here wanting to cry, his eyes dry and stinging because he had cried so much already.

He felt bad about Katy, because he was meant to look after her, but since the shivering and the aches had started he hadn't seen Katy. He didn't know where she was. Sometimes it seemed as if he might be the only one in the house. If he could have stood up he would have gone to the door and tried to get out, but to go where? To ask someone for water, or something to eat. But he couldn't eat. As soon as he ate something he started to retch again. He had been sick so much his throat was burning.

Sometimes he could tell – without opening his eyes – that there was someone else in the room with him, without knowing who. He tried to curl up into a ball, so they wouldn't touch him. He was so hot his clothes were soaking wet. He had pains in his tummy that made him pull his knees into his chest and shout out. He hoped he wouldn't have to go to the toilet again, because that had been horrible. When his mum had been there she had gone to the toilet with him and wiped him, because it was hard to wipe yourself when you were feeling dizzy. But Mary just kicked him in the room and shouted at him. So he tried his best to wipe himself, but when he was being sick all the time, and falling over, it was too hard. Once he had just sat on the floor in the bathroom, unable to move, unable to do anything. Mary had come in then and shook him so hard his head had felt like that time he fell off his bike and hit his face on the door. She had been screaming and shouting at him, but he couldn't understand the words.

They had told him his mum wasn't coming back, but he didn't believe them. His mum would come back. She wouldn't leave him like this. He had seen her in the bathtub. He had seen her lying there, blood running out of her head. Mary and Martin had been standing beside her, Mary holding something in her hand, a stick, or a piece of wood. Martin had been holding Mary, trying to stop her doing something. He had seen it all through the crack in the door. He remembered. So he knew his mum hadn't gone away. He knew they were keeping her somewhere, no matter what they said about it, no matter what anyone said.

If he could stand up he could try to look for her, but his legs were too weak. He had tried to stand before, to get over to the door, but he had just fallen to the floor instead. His legs were like jelly. His mum had been very still in the bathtub, like she was asleep. Lying in the bathtub. The thought made him shiver even more. He knew there was something wrong with his mum. He had seen the blood running across her face. Her eyes had been open, but she was still, so she must have been asleep. He couldn't think too long about it because it made him so frightened.

They were talking about him now, in the room. He couldn't see them, because he was facing the wall, back to them, but he knew who they were from the voices. It was Mary and her brother, Gary. He tried to roll over, so he could see them and ask them for a drink. He was panting and panting, something bumping really hard in his chest. Gary was whispering something to him, whispering it into his ear: '*This is what happens if you tell me lies. This is what happens. Nobody likes you, Andrew. Nobody will help you. You will lie shivering like this until you die. Do you know what that means? Do you know what happens when you die?*'

He didn't want to listen, but it was like the voice was *inside* his head. He pushed himself over and opened his eyes. He couldn't see Gary, only Mary. She was standing over him, arms folded, staring at him. He must have been having a dream.

'*It will kill him.*' He heard the words but couldn't see her lips moving. Did she say the words? Who was she speaking to? Maybe someone else had spoken. He couldn't tell who was speaking. '*You've given him too much. We can't even speak to him now. It's meant to relax him, not kill him. What use is it if we can't ask him what he saw?*'

Then another voice. '*Maybe the guy gave you snide stuff. Maybe it's just rat poison. Did he know what he was talking about?*'

'*He's a fucking pharmacist. Of course he knows.*'

'*But where did he get the stuff?*'

'*It's prescription stuff. They give it to depressives, psychotics. If he's shafted me I'll kill him.*'

He tried to see who else was in the room but everything was blurred and shimmering, like when he tried to see through his tears when he was crying.

'*Let the little fucker die, then. That would solve it.*'

'*They would know, though. They would know from his body, you idiot. They can find traces and stuff. We can't do it like this. We need to get him well, so they can't find any of the stuff in his body. We need to do that first. You should have listened to me…'*

The words went away for a while and all he could hear was his own breathing. When they had lived in the other place his mum had let him have the teddy bear when he was poorly. He wished he had the teddy bear now, something to hold on to, something to cuddle. He wished he had his mum. His mum would make all this go away; she would make him better.

'I'm not heping him. I can't bear to touch him. The little Paki fucker. It makes me feel sick to look at him.'

The voices were back. He tried to move his hands to cover his ears, but his arms were too heavy.

'Get Martin to do it. If we don't get him back from this then you've had it. I mean it. I know how they do these things.'

'We could say he took it by accident. He found it and ate it.'

'So why didn't we get a doctor in?'

'We didn't know. We thought it was a stomach bug.'

'I don't like it. Get Martin in and get him well. He'll tell us the truth after this…'

'I know the truth already. He'll tell them the first chance he gets. You know that. He's evil. He's an evil little fucker. He's like his mother was.'

'We should get him away. Take him to Blackpool. Say you were doing it to cheer him up. You can use the house there. Carter's place. They don't know about that…'

'I'm not touching him. He stinks. He's covered in shit…'

'Get Martin to do it, then. If we can pretend it's all happy families, then do something in Blackpool. It

351

has to be an accident.'

'Drop him off the pier. Say he fell, or jumped.'

Someone started to laugh. It went on and on, echoing in his head. It sounded like a witch he had seen on the TV.

'Maybe. I need to think. You need to get him better, though. Give him something to drink.'

He thought it might have been a television he was hearing. It didn't even sound like Mary. It sounded like the witch on that programme. And he couldn't see Mary now. His eyes had closed again. He was dreaming, or having a nightmare. It wasn't real. He had to tell himself that, over and over again – like his mum had told him to. He had to tell himself it wasn't real. It was make-believe. It wouldn't hurt him. It was something on TV, or a nightmare. He would wake up and his mum would be there. She would switch the TV off. Everything would be OK.

34

Why had he never noticed that before? The way, as she was arguing with him, she reached her hand across to Ricky Spencer, every now and then – just at the right time to defuse things, in fact – and touched him – a fleeting, momentary contact, the fingers just brushing his sleeve, or his arm. Just to keep it somewhere in his subconscious that she was a woman, no doubt, to keep him off-guard at some deep level. It was flirtatious. Did she do that with everyone, and he hadn't noticed? Spencer didn't seem to notice it, either. It can't have been something new. Just something he had only started noticing. Since last night.

'Let's read it through, then,' Spencer said. There were six of them round the table, in Spencer's office at HMET West. Karen's whole team, plus Spencer. The entire Exile squad, in fact. Not for long, though, if she got her way. And it looked like she would, one way or another. There were two or three sheets of transcript summaries in front of each chair when they came in. Karen and Spencer had huge, fat piles of papers before them – the full transcript. Everyone else had summaries. Someone had obviously worked that morning to get it all prepared.

'We can summarize it quite quickly,' Karen said, as if she were in charge. 'No need to read it all through.' Ricky didn't demur.

Marcus couldn't keep his eyes off her. He felt he was going mad. She was wearing a man's checked shirt with a button-down collar, open to just the start of her cleavage. (Not that she had much of a cleavage, but that didn't matter, because that part of her body was still – as an art historian had described it on some BBC 2 arts programme he had seen about classical sculpture – the focal point of female beauty, or something like that. From her bare throat down to her sternum, with just the enticement of what would be below, nothing more, and the lure of the throat, where he had certainly fixed his mouth with a real hunger. She had leaned her whole body into him, stretching her head back to let him get his teeth round her windpipe. The urge to kiss and suck had been overwhelming. He had resisted, but he was still surprised there were no marks there.) Below the shirt, a pair of black cords, quite loose-fitting, so that they were pleated too much where the belt pulled them in round her waist. She had a very thin waist. He had only first noticed that last night. That and the scars. She had scars all over her body. You wouldn't know that if you hadn't been in bed with her, if you hadn't carefully explored every available inch of her body. He had wanted to ask her about them, but had been too afraid of spoiling the mood. Then she had started telling him about her past. The scars would be from her past and he still wasn't sure what he wanted to make of all that. Those on her back were definitely burns. He felt slightly ashamed, thinking about the detail. It brought colour to his face. He could feel it. Could she be noticing? He turned his head down to the sheets of paper, tried to concentrate.

'We had a probe in place – in Simon's room – for nearly thirty-six hours,' she said. 'Unfortunately, he doesn't seem deranged enough to have talked to himself, or even talked in his sleep. He had one visit from his brother, midday yesterday. Mary Swales didn't show. Martin and he started off OK, but quickly ended up arguing about why Simon was there. Clearly, from what was said – it's summarized halfway down page two – Mary was keen to have Simon back home, under her control. But Simon wasn't having it. Why? Because he thinks they're killers. That's what he says at the top of page three. It couldn't be clearer. I'll read you the passage verbatim...' She turned slowly through the huge wad of A4 transcription until she found the page. 'Here it is. It's recorded verbatim in your summaries, too.'

Marcus looked down at his summary and read as she spoke:

MARTIN: That's not what you mean...
SIMON: You did nothing to stop her...
MARTIN: She's our mother, for God's sake. She brought you up. How can you...
SIMON: She killed her. You both did.
MARTIN: Shut up. Don't speak so loud. Don't fucking say that. I'll fucking slap you, Simon. I'll slap you if I have to...
SIMON: (incomprehensible)
MARTIN: We have to stick together now. It's important...
SIMON: I don't want anything to do with you. You're filthy. You fucking killed her. You couldn't just leave her. She was your wife. But you still did it...
MARTIN: Shut the fuck up, Simon. Shut the fuck ... (incomprehensible)
SIMON: (shouting – incomprehensible ... perhaps 'the stick thing'. Scuffling noises. A loud bang.)
MARTIN: You want me to? You want me to?
SIMON: (crying?) Please no. Please don't...
MARTIN: You fucking want me to. You do!
SIMON: No. No. NO. Poor ... poor... She was ... (incomprehensible)
MARTIN: She's dead. Get over it. She's gone.

She didn't give a shit about you or anyone...
SIMON: (crying)

'And so on,' Karen said, looking up. 'After that Simon just cries. Finally one of the volunteers comes in and Martin leaves.'

'That's it,' Spencer said. 'That's what we got from thirty-six hours of covert surveillance. It seems to me that it's–'

'Enough to make clear that John Bradley has been lying,' Karen interrupted, then touched him again, smiling slightly.

Spencer shrugged. 'Yes. It might suggest that,' he said. 'Certainly we've been through this material with Chris Gregg and he wants some further enquiries. That's where we're at. We always knew, of course, that the charge against John alone was a provisional conclusion, because the mass of injuries on the body cannot be explained by John Bradley's account of how Becky died. That's why he's on for murder, not manslaughter. That's why we never believed his story entirely. Now we have a little something to play with.'

'Not something we can use in evidence, though,' Gerry Owen said, from next to Karen.

'No,' she agreed. 'Probably not. We might be able to get the tapes in, but Martin himself makes no admissions. Simon's accusations against him – and against Mary – would likely be hearsay. That's why we need to turn Simon. We need him to give us a statement about all this. That's what we've got to concentrate on now.

'Do we get more manpower for that?' Owen asked.

Spencer shook his head. 'Let's not get too excited about it,' he said. 'Apart from working on Simon there's nothing much more we can do to take this forward.'

'We will re-arrest Martin and Mary, of course,' Karen chipped in.

'Not yet. As it stands, this is evidentially useless, Karen.' Spencer tapped a finger on the pile of papers. 'You know how a lawyer would treat it if we got it to court. It's open to too many differing interpretations. And anyway, we can't get it into court, because, as you say, it's all total hearsay. Plus it's a covert probe, and getting covert evidence in is never certain. If you can get a decent statement from Simon then things might change. Maybe. Because there are still questions over his mental condition and competence to give evidence. It may be he has a mental age of three. Who the fuck knows? So as it is—'

'It's enough information to make sure the kids are removed from Martin and Mary's custody. Social Services can be told about this. They don't need it in evidential form.'

'So we show them this,' Spencer replied. 'I agree. And I'm doing that this afternoon. We have an inter-agency meeting this afternoon to discuss this. If they think it's enough then proceedings could be started to ensure the safety of the children, but that's got nothing to do with arresting anyone else.'

'The eldest – the boy, Andrew – could give a video statement. He might know things. He might himself be a witness.'

'I'll consult Social Services about that, too. You

know procedure, Karen. We don't just go at these things single-handed. Inter-agency partnership is the buzzword when it comes to kids.'

Buzzwords, Marcus thought. Plural. He could see Karen wasn't going to win.

'We'll turn Simon,' she said. 'Marcus has already softened him up.'

Everyone looked at him.

'Meanwhile, you better get on with the search of this lock-up,' Spencer said. He pushed his chair back, meeting over. 'De-brief at five-thirty.'

The way she had sold it to them, she had received information late yesterday that John Bradley rented a lock-up garage near Wakefield. She had then sent a uniform from Wakefield Division to guard the place while she checked out the rental details with the owner of the garage, supposedly because the information wasn't from a top-grade source. It turned out that John Bradley did indeed rent the place, so she sent Gerry Owen to get a warrant. Now they were going to execute the warrant – Karen, Marcus, Owen and Sanderson.

They took a Focus from the car pool and sat in it together. Owen driving, Karen in the front beside him. Marcus watched from the back as she went through a convincing act of looking up the location on a map. If he hadn't been feeling so uneasy about it all, he might have found it funny.

When they got there – at just after 3p.m. – they found a marked car with a bored PC behind the wheel parked at the corner of the lane. The day was overcast, threatening rain for the first time in a few weeks. The garages looked even shabbier by daylight, particularly with the sky so grey. The cottages on the main road were half dilapidated; one had boarded-up windows. The fields to the rear, running down to the garages, were overgrown with some kind of thistle.

The PC got out to greet them. He reported that no one had been anywhere near the garage.

They walked up to it, Sanderson wielding the bolt-cutters, Karen whistling, which Marcus thought was overdoing it. He tried not to look nervous. She caught his eye and smiled. 'You know that tune, Marcus?'

He swallowed. 'The one you're whistling? It's "Night and Day". Cole Porter.' He tried to sound normal, but she was playing a game with him, yet again. He felt on edge, irritable.

She nudged Sanderson. 'Marcus likes jazz,' she said.

'That right?' he replied. 'I like silence, myself.'

The padlock was slightly larger than the one Karen had cut. Marcus wondered when she had got round to replacing it. He could feel his stomach fluttering just thinking about it. What was about to happen? She had been back and replaced the lock, without him. So why had she wanted him there at all, the first time?

In the end Gerry Owen had to use his superior bulk to get the metal to shear. Sanderson hauled the doors open and the place looked the same as when he had last seen it. The car, the naked lightbulb, the boxes at the far end. He almost felt relieved.

'Can you call in that plate, Marcus?' Karen asked him. She passed him the only radio they'd booked out. He stood outside the garage again while they went in and looked around. He used the radio to call a check on the Nissan's registration plate.

'Registered to Mary Bradley,' the operator told him, after a while. By then they were all at the back, rummaging. He stepped into the doorway and tried frantically to gauge how excited he should sound, passing on the result. 'Bingo!' he called out. 'It comes back to Mary Bradley.'

He heard Karen laugh. Sanderson appeared, eyebrows raised, looking impressed. 'Was it on the list from the CCTV?' Sanderson said. 'That would be a coup.'

Marcus shrugged. 'I don't know. Ask the boss. She's the one with the memory.' He had to look away from Sanderson because it felt obvious that he was lying. Surely Sanderson could see that in his eyes. If he didn't look away he would start to blush. Then they really would know.

'There's fuck all here,' Gerry Owen was saying from beyond the car. 'Old car parts, old magazines. It's all junk.'

'Shall we take a peek in the car?' Sanderson asked, looking to where Karen was searching through a small plastic toolbox.

'Leave it,' she shouted back. 'Call it through to get SOCO out. It's probably the car she was dumped from.'

'Fucking good information after all,' Sanderson said.

'Look at this,' Karen called out. She stood up holding the box. 'You got an exhibit bag, Gerry? You're exhibits officer for this. As of now.' She was frowning, looking serious.

Gerry Owen passed her a clear ziplock bag. She took a pair of latex roll-ons from her pocket and pulled one onto her left hand. Was she left-handed? Marcus hadn't noticed that before.

She moved into the light, past the car and nearer to Marcus, still carrying the box. Using her finger and thumb, she carefully extracted a slim black object. The others gathered round to watch. Marcus felt his pulse trip, then begin to race. He was expecting it to be the diary, but it wasn't. It was an Asp. She was holding up an Asp. It looked brand-new. It looked, in fact, like the one he had bought online and given to her. She looked up at Marcus and grinned. 'What do you think, Marcus? Could be the murder weapon, if we're lucky.' He could feel the blood draining from his face.

'Is that it, then?' Sanderson asked.

Karen was still looking at him, still smiling. 'That's it,' she said. 'Let's get SOCO in.'

No diary, then. The diary wasn't there. He had to say it to himself, in his head, over and over again. The diary wasn't there and she had found an Asp. She was watching him, a slight, ironic smile at the corners of her mouth. He turned away from her, catching his breath. He didn't understand her at all.

35

That evening – once SOCO had finished at the lock-up – Karen had an early dinner in town with Mairead and Pete Bains. Pete was an acting DI, working on intelligence co-ordination at HQ in Wakefield. Mairead still saw Pete frequently. She even visited his parents every now and then, and they regarded Mairead as a granddaughter. Prem, Mairead's close friend on the gap year in Australia, was Pete's niece.

Karen found it hard sitting with them, trying to pretend that she and Pete still got on, but she did it because Mairead was keen. They ate, on this occasion, at a restaurant not very far from Marcus's place, in the canal area. Karen sat mostly in silence as Mairead told Pete about uni and Julian. She seemed upbeat and happy. Was Marcus already forgotten? That was what kids were like. They moved on quickly. Easier anyway, if you already had a steady boyfriend. That didn't stop Karen flushing with shame when she thought about Marcus and herself, less than twenty-four hours ago, doing it. She tried not to think.

Every now and then Karen would catch Pete's eye and see the resentment and hurt still there beneath the surface. Pete wasn't too good at letting bygones be bygones. She had walked out on him twice and each time he had welcomed her back, before finally getting so sick of it that he found the strength to say a final no. That didn't stop him acting as if it had been Karen who had done the dumping. But he was good to Mairead, at least. There was no doubt about that.

Afterwards, they walked the short distance back to Karen's car, parked in a multi-storey in town. Pete chatted to Mairead all the way. Karen tagged along, worrying about Andrew Farrar, or thinking about Swales (who had managed to set up the owner of the lock-up garage to say John Bradley rented it at very short notice, assuming Michael Surani had given correct information – but then Surani was clearly passing information both ways), or pondering the dead girl's diary (which she had read and re-read very carefully now, every single page), or fretting about whether Swales really was mad enough to try to harm her (surely unlikely, she thought, in the clarity of daylight – but she had asked Francis Doyle to look into it anyway), or thinking about Mairead and Marcus or herself and Marcus, all sweating under Marcus's duvet. Through all these worries life had to go on, she thought – you had to meet people and eat with them. What was happening to Andrew Farrar while she was off-duty? Was he locked in a room again, shivering, alone? She kept a vague smile on her face and linked her arm through Mairead's. At the other side Mairead was linking Pete's arm. They must have looked like a proper little happy family.

Pete was still chatting to Mairead, standing at the rear of Karen's car, saying goodbye and so on, and Karen was already getting into the driver's seat when she heard the engine. High revs, from the direction of the floor above. Kids sometimes drove cars into multi-storeys and messed around but still...

She stepped back out and looked for it. It was driving along the floor a split level higher than them, turning onto the down ramp. When it came out it would be at their level. At the speed it was going it was seconds away. Mairead and Pete – if they had heard it – were still chatting, not reacting. Mairead was standing about two yards away from their car, hands in pockets, Pete in front of her. Karen called out to her at once, telling her to move out of the open. But Mairead didn't respond, didn't even appear to hear. Karen saw her look for the noise only as the car exited the ramp and turned towards her.

Karen started to move back towards her, shouting at her at the same time, but with more urgency. She had got as far as the rear of her own car before Mairead began to move. The car was accelerating fast – a black Audi, was it? A very old model. Karen had it in the corner of her eye, could see the single occupant, see his face, but knew at once that she was too far from Mairead to do anything.

'*Move!*' she yelled. '*Move!*'

She saw Mairead's face freeze with momentary fear, saw the car swerve slightly – towards her? But it was travelling too fast to stop before it reached the end of the level. The driver must have realized that at the exact time she did. The brakes squealed. She saw the car lurch on its shocks – still out of the corner of her eye – then Mairead really did jump, desperate to get out of its path.

364

Too slow. The car spun slightly as it passed her, some part of it clipping some part of her, without any noise of impact, but sending her reeling towards Pete. She hit him so hard he went to the ground with her. By then Karen was right beside them and the car was already past, still braking fiercely, skidding towards the next down ramp. The rear end went wide, sliding across the concrete and smashing into a parked Saab with a crunch of metal and shattered glass, very loud in the enclosed space. Then the driver slipped the gears, recovered it and was onto the ramp.

Mairead was screaming at the top of her voice, sprawled across Pete. Pete was trying to get out from underneath her. Mairead's face was twisted with pain. Karen had a moment to decide – check her, or go after it? She hadn't even had time to note the plate. She wanted desperately to go after it. If she cut through the pedestrian exit she could head it off at the floor below. She would come out behind it, but at least she could get the plate.

She couldn't, though. Mairead was the priority. She was sure Mairead could be no more than bruised, because the blow had been a glancing blow, from the side of the vehicle, into Mairead's back. She was sure Mairead was screaming more with shock than pain. But she couldn't take chances. She hesitated for a fraction of a second, then knelt beside them and helped Pete up. Mairead rolled into a sitting position, hands on her back. She was swearing at the top of her voice.

'Where did it hit you?' Karen asked her. 'Where did it hit you?' Her voice was charged with fear. She tried to control her breathing. Pete was running towards the pedestrian doors. He'd be too late, though. 'Where did it hit you?' she repeated.

'The fucker rammed my back! The fucker rammed into me...' Mairead was still clutching at her lower back.

Karen helped her stand. She could just about do it. But her back was too painful for her to remain upright. Karen got her into the rear of the car, then pulled her shirt up and looked. Her lower back was red already, the skin not broken, but heating up. She could feel the swelling starting, beneath her fingertips. Contact had been across the base of the pelvis and lower spine. 'I'll take you to A&E,' she said. 'They can check it out.' She tried to put an arm around her, to hug her, but Mairead didn't want that. She was too angry. Karen looked back for Pete instead, but couldn't see him. She would probably pass him on the way down. Mairead was still swearing. She was definitely more angry than hurt. More angry than frightened, even. That was because she thought it had been an accident.

'Did you see the little fucker?' she was asking. 'Did you see his face? Did you get the registration number?'

Maybe it had been blacked out, Karen thought. If it was a real professional the plate would have been obscured. 'We'll get you to hospital,' she said to Mairead. 'Just in case. You should try to relax. You've had a shock.'

'He came right into my fucking back. If I hadn't jumped I'd have gone straight over. For fuck's sake...'

She was getting indignant, but she still wasn't

366

thinking about it. If she thought about it she would register the swerve, the deliberate turn towards her. Then she would start to get frightened. Then Karen would have to tell her what had happened. She would have to tell her anyway now. First things first, though.

'Let's get to an A&E,' Karen said. 'Just try to relax. Don't tense the muscles.'

Drive her to hospital, get some painkillers inside her. It would be a bruise, nothing else. Fingers crossed. No crack in the pelvis. Poor Mairead. She would be in pain. Lucky he hadn't snapped her spine, or hit her head-on. Karen exhaled in a rush. If he had hit her head-on she would be gone. Dead. The thought brought a sudden flood of rage and panic. It was so intense her vision actually blurred. She shook her head physically to banish it, to concentrate. Mairead could move. She would be OK. They would X-ray her, check for hairline fractures and internal damage. But it was unlikely. The force of the contact hadn't been enough.

How long would it take? She could be delayed by an hour in A&E. Maybe more. But she could let it build inside her, while she was waiting. Let it build and simmer so that when she finally stood in front of him she could just let it all uncoil. Let it lash right into his face. She knew what had happened. The muscles in her chest were locking up, the anger boiling. She clenched her teeth. Gary Swales would have to pay now. Now was the time. She would find him as soon as she was out of the hospital. He had tried to kill her daughter. Kill or injure her, it didn't matter. She would break his skull this time.

36

Marcus was just starting a ready meal – described on the box as 'Chicken Provençale', but tasting terribly like the chemical orange sauce he remembered from tins of baked beans during his youth – when the door buzzer went. He left the meal and went over to look at the tiny CCTV screen. Karen, looking straight up at him. He opened his mouth to speak, but didn't get the chance.

'I need you down here, Marcus. Quickly. Can you get out right now?' She was shifting impatiently from side to side, moving out of the camera view. She sounded panicked.

'Of course,' he said.

He took his jacket and went straight down. When he got to the street he saw she was double-parked right outside, the car engine already running, passenger door open and waiting for him. He hardly had the door closed before she was pulling away from the kerb. He looked over at her. She was concentrating on the road, but she looked furious.

"What's up?' he asked.

'Mairead was knocked over tonight.' She leaned on the horn to warn off a slow-moving white van threatening to hold her at the turn, then slipped around it and accelerated away so fast Marcus was snapped back into his seat.

'Is she hurt?'

'Not really. Bruises. A bit shocked. She's over at Pete's place now. She was lucky.'

'Pete?'

'Pete Bains. Didn't she tell you about him? I thought you two were close.'

'The DI?'

'Yes. He's like a father to her. At least that's how she thinks of it.'

He felt mildly shocked. Mairead hadn't said anything about Pete Bains. Nor had he known anything about Karen and Bains – yet if Mairead thought Bains was 'like a father' presumably Karen was seeing him, or had been, for some time.

'I used to see Pete,' she said, frowning hard. 'A few years back. We used to live with him, in fact.'

'Are we going to see Mairead now?' he asked.

'Are we fuck. She's safe. We're going to find the fucker who did it to her.'

That set alarm bells ringing. 'What happened?'

'We were in a multi-storey, about to go. She was standing talking to Pete. We'd just had dinner. A black Audi came from the level above and tried to drive over her. She moved in time. The mirror clipped her, I think. She was lucky.'

'You got the plate?'

'No. Pete has got them looking for it now. On the CCTV.'

'You saw the driver?'

'A glimpse...' She paused, overtaking a long line of stationary cars at the next lights. She was driving very fast, but concentrating, not looking at him as she spoke. 'Might be able to recognize him again.'

'So where are we going now?'

369

'To find Swales.'

'Swales?' He was lost. 'What's he got to do with it?'

'I got information yesterday that he was looking to put a hit on me again. On me and Mairead.'

'Jesus Christ. Why would he do that?'

She shrugged. 'I don't know. But he's got a screw loose. He got away with it last time. Why shouldn't he try again?'

He thought about it. Quickly. He knew what most people knew about the last contract Swales was meant to have put on her. The enquiry had found no evidence of it. A full enquiry. 'You sure?' he asked hesitantly. 'You sure about the information?'

'Of course. And he's already shown he's capable.'

He opened his mouth to mention the enquiry, then shut it. 'What are we going to do when we find him?'

She said nothing. On the wheel her knuckles were white.

'What are you planning to do, Karen? Have you evidence linking him—'

'Let's find him first.'

He took a breath. 'I don't like it,' he said. 'You seem angry, Karen. Very angry. I can understand that. You should be. But if you have no evidence you can use then there's nothing we can do to Swales.'

'We'll see.'

'I don't want to see. I'm in enough trouble already because of you.'

'Trouble?' She glanced over to him for the first

time. 'Like what?' She looked confused.

'Illegal entries and searches. You know what I mean.'

She scowled. 'Don't be dim, Marcus. No harm came of that.'

'I didn't like it.'

She shrugged. 'Part of your education.'

'The Asp you recovered,' he started. 'Did it have a serial number?' He had wanted desperately to check for one himself, but hadn't been confident of looking normal, calm and innocent and getting close enough to it before SOCO took it away. The one he had bought had a serial number, traceable to him, if enquiries were made. It was a totally and utterly absurd thought that she would actually have planted that Asp – that very Asp – in the garage. He didn't want to just ask her about it outright – *did you plant an Asp in there?* – because the very idea was insulting. But he was still plagued by the idea. He needed to ask her about the diary, too. He assumed she had left it in the garage for SOCO to recover, but he hadn't as yet heard confirmation of that.

'I'm not worried about that now,' she said. 'Nor should you be. You should trust me more.'

'Not like this. I don't know what you will do if we find Swales.'

'When we find him.'

'Well, whatever it is I don't want to be there. Why pick me up? I don't get it.'

'I need a witness,' she said, looking at him again. 'And someone to control me. You're doing a good job so far.'

She drove to Lower Wyke Manor first. By the time they got there it was after nine. There were no street lights along the track to the gloomy stone block where Rebecca Farrar had suffered so much. The place was dark, the curtains drawn. There were no cars in sight. She went up to the door and rapped hard. He sat in the car while she ran round the place, trying to make sure there was nobody there. She looked frantic. He wondered who he could phone to speak to her, to try to calm her down.

'They must be at his place,' she said when she got back.

It took another half-hour to get to Thornton. By then he could see she was settling down. He knew Swales's place had security gates and a high wall, so couldn't see how she was going to get in without a warrant. She would have to speak to Swales, try to persuade him to let them in. The thought of that might put her off.

'Shall I call Bains and ask about the CCTV?' he said.

'No need. He'll call if he gets something. Anyway, the guy I saw was just a kid, an amateur. If he'd been a pro Mairead would be dead by now.'

Wrong train of thought. He could see she was working herself up all over again now.

As they drove up the hill to Swales's complex his heart sank. The gates were wide open.

She drove straight through and stopped the car in a kind of courtyard, alongside a red Renault, which he guessed was rented, from the sticker in the back windscreen. They had seized John Bradley's van and Martin's car when they had first searched Lower Wyke. As far as he knew, neither Mary nor Martin had another vehicle, now that they also had her Nissan. Swales, on the other hand, wouldn't be driving a hired Clio. When Gary was arrested he had come to the station in an SLK.

'Not Swales's car,' he said. 'He drives a Merc.'

'I know what he drives.' She was already out, door left open, marching up to the front entrance. He got out quickly, following her.

There was a bell, which she pressed continuously with one hand, hammering the door with the other. Marcus stood back, worried, scanning the windows for life. There were lights on in one of the smaller buildings to the side, but nothing in the main block. If someone looked out before answering, he thought, they would see it was her and just ignore it. Or maybe not. Maybe they'd think she was here legitimately, with a warrant.

The door started to open. He stepped closer to Karen, putting out a hand to restrain her, then holding off, arm still extended towards her as the door opened. He didn't know what she was going to do. If it were Swales she might just hit him. She had already done it once, broken his arm. He saw her take a breath, step forward, then stop, pulled up short. It was Mary Swales in the doorway, but in her arms was the smaller of Rebecca's kids, Katy. She was asleep.

'What the fuck do you want?' Mary asked. She almost whispered it, but not quite. It was more a hiss.

For a moment Karen was silent. The presence of the child had stopped her in her tracks. He could see her hands clenching and unclenching by her sides.

'Is your brother in?' she asked finally. She managed to keep her voice low. 'I want your fucking brother.'

'He's out. You fucking slut. Get off our property.' Spoken louder. The child stirred, pressed against Mary's ample chest. Karen stepped forward, closer to her. Marcus put an arm out and touched her sleeve. She shook him off immediately.

'You listen to me...' Karen started. But the child was turning now, turning to look at her. She stopped speaking.

'You've woken Katy, you little bitch.'

Marcus put a hand out again. This time he held her arm, just below the elbow. 'Let's go, Karen,' he said quietly. 'We don't want to frighten the kid. And he's not here.'

Mary was backing up already, pulling the door shut. Karen shook his arm away again. He thought she was going to step forward, put her foot in the door. Or kick it.

'He's not here,' he said again. 'His car's not here.' The door slammed shut, the noise surely sufficient to alarm the child, certainly to wake her. There was a pause; then, sure enough, from behind it he heard her beginning to cry.

'She's got that kid locked up,' Karen said. 'Not the girl. Andrew. The other one. She's doing something to him. Fucking with him. I know it.' For a moment she looked crushed. Her shoulders sagged, her chin dropped. He couldn't understand it. She turned to him, eyes filling with tears, he thought. He put his hand out again. This time she let him hold her upper arm. Was she going to cry? It was weird. He had no idea how to read her. Above them the sky was black now, but there were lights all over the courtyard.

'She's got him in there,' she said. 'Suffering. And there's nothing we can do.'

'It's not true,' he said. 'Social Services have–'

'Fucking wankers. They don't care. Or Ricky. No one fucking cares. I can *see* it. I know what's going on.' She looked back at the door. 'I should just go in. Pull him out.'

'We can't do that, Karen. You know we can't.' He sounded desperate. 'We have to trust the system. We've done everything we should have done.' He was pleading with her.

She twitched her arm, releasing his grip, then pulled her sleeve across her eyes. 'I'll walk round,' she said. 'I'll check.'

'We can't even do that.'

'I'm doing it.'

He sat in the car waiting for her, windows down, listening. He didn't want to walk round with her, because they had been told to leave. There were cameras all over, so there could be no lying about it. Even sitting in the car on the property was too much, but what could he do? Walk back to the gates and leave her to it? What if Mary Swales came out again? There might be a fight. He needed to stay to control Karen. She was right. So he sat in the car with the windows down, waiting for screams, or blows, or whatever. In the darkness by the smaller buildings he could see her pacing around, trying to peer through windows. Once she even pulled at a door handle.

When she came back she looked terrifying. He had never seen her so emotional, so filled with suppressed rage. Her face was quivering. 'It's fucking mad,' she said, under her breath. She started the engine. 'They're in there damaging him, but I can't get in.'

'You don't know that,' he said. 'We don't know that at all.'

'Shut the fuck up, Marcus. I know it. I know it *here*.' She drummed her fist against her chest, roughly where her heart was.

'Did you see something, hear anything?'

She ignored him, pulling slowly through the rear gates.

'If you didn't then I think you need to think clearly about it, Karen. What you suspect is understandable, but there's no evidence. Social Services are involved. If something was going on then the kids wouldn't be in there. They'd get them out.'

'Is that what happens in the real world, Marcus? Is that what happens?'

He opened his mouth to answer.

'You would know, of course,' she said. 'You're the one with the experience.' She slowed the car and turned suddenly towards him. 'Listen to me! Listen to me, you stupid fucker. I *know*. I fucking know. I've been doing these cases for years. Listen and fucking learn!'

She slammed a fist off the door, so hard he jumped. He stared at her, jaw hanging open, but didn't say anything.

They turned onto the back lane that ran from

the rear of Swales's place. It was deserted, but she drove slowly. He should offer her a drink somewhere. That would be better than letting her just go home in this condition. But the truth was he didn't want to be with her when she was like this. He started to ask her to take him back to Leeds, but then saw her eyes narrow. She was staring through the windscreen, focusing in the distance. They were going slowly downhill, back towards Bradford, and the lane was almost single carriageway, poorly lit. He could see a car coming fast towards them, from the opposite direction.

'That's him,' she said.

The car was too far away. He couldn't make out any details. It was travelling too fast as well.

'That's fucking him.'

'Even if it is, there's nothing–'

She hit the brakes suddenly, throwing him against the seatbelt. Then she was turning the car in the road.

'What ... what the fuck are you...'

He thought she was trying to spin it, to be ready to drive back in the other direction. As it slowed he realized she was instead turning it across the road, making a road block. He couldn't believe it.

'For Christ's sake, Karen! He'll drive straight into us...'

He saw the other car's headlights dip sharply as it braked. They were stationary already, right across the road. He could see the car clearly now. It was a blue Merc. She was right. Probably an SLK. Maybe it *was* him. The wheels on an SLK couldn't lock – they had ABS – but it slewed from side to side as the driver decelerated rapidly.

377

When it was no more than a few feet away it turned as if to go round the back of them. But she was ready for that. She already had their car in reverse. She pulled it back and the SLK stopped suddenly, at a slight angle to them, realizing she was meaning to stop him, that there was no way round.

'It is him,' she said. 'I've found the fucker.' She was getting out.

Marcus leaned over and reached for her, to stop her, or to try to. But he was too slow. He saw the driver's door of the Merc open and a man step out. Gary Swales. She was right. He was shouting at them even as he stepped out.

It was happening too fast. Marcus pushed himself out of the car and raised his hands in the air, trying to warn the man to calm down, shouting at him to calm down, but he was trying to slow Karen, too, hoping she would hear and react. He could see the man clearly now – short, stocky, in a suit and tie. He was moving towards Karen, aggressively, shouting at the top of his voice, stripping off his jacket as if he were about to fight her, it was ridiculous! Marcus shouted warnings again, then moved to get round the car. But Karen was also moving, closing on Swales so fast it looked like they would hit each other full on. Marcus came round the front of the car at a run, still shouting.

Then Swales was on the ground. One minute he was rushing at Karen, the next he was down. Just like that. On the ground, doubled up, writhing, gasping for air, both hands clutching at his throat.

Marcus thought he had his eyes on them the whole time, but he had seen no movement from Karen, no sudden change of stance. He didn't see what she did, couldn't work it out. He paused as he realized she was out of danger. She was standing over Swales, screaming at him, her face a livid colour, both fists clenched. She was so angry the words didn't make sense. He walked towards them, watching Swales, thinking it was over, that she might calm down now. But immediately she stepped forward and leaned back. He saw her raise her left foot and stamp on Swales's head, twice in quick succession. He saw the heel of her shoe connect both times, heard the blow, witnessed the head recoil, hit the tarmac, bounce. He felt his heart jump, the blood emptying from his face, his stomach twisting. Swales rolled over onto his back, his hands moving to his head. He was making a rasping sound, as if he couldn't breathe. But Karen was still there, foot pulled back for another go. This time she was going to kick him. She was going to kick him in the head and she was going to put all her strength into it.

Marcus came behind her, locked his arms round her waist, tried to pull her away. She struggled against him, throwing him off with an ease that surprised him, then turned to yell in his face. He started shouting back, 'You'll kill him. You'll kill him like that. He can't breathe.'

He stepped around her and bent down, putting his body between her and Swales, shielding him. Swales's face was blue, the forehead cut and bleeding profusely across his hair. He was pushing himself into a kneeling position. Marcus ran a hand over him, checking for obvious weapons, then put a hand on his back and started talking to him, trying to calm him, trying to get him to breathe regularly. He spoke slowly and clearly, face close to Swales's ear. Swales was clutching at his throat with one hand, the other on his head. There was blood all over the road. Marcus felt sick. She was like some kind of thug. It was barbaric. He looked up to find her. She was over by Swales's car, opening the doors, shouting back the standard PACE warnings, telling him she was going to search his vehicle for weapons, as if this were a standard stop and search and she had done nothing. Swales couldn't hear a thing. He was getting his breath back, but he was in pain. It was taking all his concentration just to get the air past his throat. Had she hit him in the throat? She must have.

In the periphery of his vision he saw her walk back to their own car. Was she going for the first-aid kit? He shouted back to her to bring it but she didn't reply. So he continued talking to Swales, continued trying to reassure him. As soon as he knew Swales wasn't going to pass out he would call an ambulance. He told Swales all this, carefully, gently, told him not to stand yet, just to try to get the air into his lungs. The scalp wound was from the road, Marcus thought, from where the head had bounced off it. It *was* superficial, probably, but the blood was pouring all over his clothing now. Scalp wounds always bled heavily. He told Swales this as well, told him not to be alarmed by it, that it was worse than it looked. Swales took a long deep breath, then raised his head and looked at him. 'Get your fucking hands off me, you fucking faggot. Get your hands off me or I'll break your fucking back.'

It felt like a slap in the face. Marcus stood up and took a step back. He heard Karen laughing, from inside Swales's car. She emerged again and looked over to him. 'You playing Florence Nightingale?' she asked. 'Because he's no cripple. The man's a killer, Marcus. He doesn't need your kind words. He needs the shit kicking out of him.'

Marcus said nothing. He looked from one to the other. They were staring at each other like two jungle apes. They were the same, the same kind of person, with the same automatic, feral responses to situations. Karen dipped back inside the car and rummaged in the door pockets.

'Get out of my fucking car!' Swales shouted. He tried to stand.

'Stay down on your knees, please,' Marcus said. 'Do not get up.' He was afraid he would have to take on the man himself. Swales was shorter than him, but undoubtedly heavier and stronger. Whatever Karen had done, Marcus couldn't. He didn't have a clue about fighting. The training they gave you was useless, defensive stuff. 'Stay on your knees, Mr Swales.'

He heard Karen laughing again, from behind the car door. 'Kick his knees from under him,' she called back. 'Don't try to talk to him. He's an animal, not a person. Would you speak to a wild dog like that?' She stepped back from the door holding something in her hand. 'What have we got here, Gary? You been keeping a diary? Didn't think you had it in you. You don't seem the literary type, if you don't mind me saying so.'

Marcus watched with a mounting sense of horror as she walked over to them, holding the object between finger and thumb. He could see it was a book, but still didn't believe what he was hearing. She stood next to Swales in the middle of the road and leafed through it. 'Oh, no,' he could hear her saying. 'It's not your diary at all...' His eyes felt huge. He wanted to control his reactions, but couldn't. He could see the book clearly now. It was the diary they had found in the garage the first time. 'Looks like you've got Rebecca Farrar's diary in your car,' she said. She looked up at Marcus and smiled. 'Can you get an exhibit bag, DC Roth?' she asked. 'This could be important.'

Swales was spluttering, almost foaming at the mouth. He looked like he was about to have some kind of seizure.

'You hear me, DC Roth?'

Marcus was rooted to the spot. He didn't know what to do.

'You're under arrest, Gary Swales. You know all the formulas. You know your rights. I won't bother repeating them. You're nicked for the murder of Rebecca Farrar.' She switched her gaze to Marcus again. He was still standing there, speechless. 'That means we'll have to do a Section Eighteen search of your house,' she said, speaking to Swales, but still looking at Marcus. She held the diary out towards him for the second time that day. 'Bag this, Marcus,' she said. 'Make yourself useful.'

37

One way to have done it would have been to take Swales back to his house, find and check Andrew Farrar, let Marcus search the place with uniformed help, sit down somewhere and pretend to read the diary for the first time. Then – armed with everything it said about Martin, Mary and Gary – arrest them all and see how it fell out. That would get the message through to Gary. It would also get Andrew to safety. But probably not for long.

It would certainly irritate her own management. She was sure Ricky Spencer didn't mind her hounding Mary and Gary Swales provided the predicted court result was favourable. But it wasn't. She knew enough about the law of evidence to realize that. And the more she kicked at Martin and Mary, the dirtier she made them as victims and witnesses against John. That was Ricky's concern, and it was legitimate. In addition, she didn't want to irritate Ricky too much because what she was doing was already leaving her exposed. She didn't need to attract more attention to herself.

So in the end she did what she was meant to do – she called Ricky, told him about the arrest and the seizure of the diary, but said she hadn't had a chance to look at it yet. She then tried to persuade him to let her handle it her own way. Not surprisingly, he wouldn't have that. He told her to get John Sanderson out to do the search with Marcus. He didn't want her anywhere near Mary. There were two complaints against her already, from Mary and Gary both. 'Back off, Karen,' he said. 'That's an instruction. You understand? Get others in to do the house, make no more arrests until I've had a chance to review what you have so far. Get yourself over to Dudley Hill with the diary immediately.'

'I'll have to wait until DC Sanderson comes before I can get away.' She was standing by her car as she spoke, itching to get up to Swales's place. Swales was already in a van she'd called up, with a uniformed crew. He'd refused medical help, of course. Marcus was standing in darkness by the edge of the road, brooding about it all.

'Leave it to Marcus,' Ricky said. 'I do not want you in contact with Mary, Martin or Gary. We have a court case to think about, for Christ's sake. Think about it, Karen. Use your fucking head.'

She took a breath. 'Marcus isn't experienced enough.'

'He is. I say he is. Let him do it. I am on my way out of my house now. I'm going straight to Dudley Hill. I'm calling the lawyer on the way. I want you there with the diary when I arrive. I expect no more complications. I hope this is really clear.' He cut the line. She hadn't told him about having already seen Mary, or about the little matter of Gary's injuries.

She took Swales's keys and repositioned his SLK, carelessly dropping the nearside wheels into the ditch at the side of the road so as to let other traffic past. Then she sat with Marcus in her own car and spoke to him. Marcus was having a hard time. She could see that quite clearly. He'd been having a hard time since she dragged him along to the lock-up garage, and each little incident since then had made things worse. Now he was so confused he didn't know what to do.

'Listen to me,' she said to him. 'In a moment I'm going to go and meet Ricky, to show him the diary. You're going to take Swales back up the road and do the Section Eighteen search. I'll get John Sanderson out to help you. Ricky won't let me go back there. I'll come back to that in a moment. For now you have to listen to what I'm going to tell you. Are you listening?'

He nodded. He looked fragile. Maybe he'd already reached his limit and had decided to report her. But that seemed unlikely. 'I'll tell you what I'm going to write in my notebook,' she said.

She told him.

In essence they had gone to Swales's place to check the children, if possible with Mary's consent, not to look for Gary. On the way back Gary had tried to ram them in his car. They didn't know why. They had stopped him and he had come at them with a metal bar, since discovered to be the wheel brace from the SLK. 'It's lying over by the SLK now,' she said. 'He had it in his hand when he came towards me.' She stopped. Marcus was shaking his head slowly, eyes on the floor. 'Didn't you see it?' she asked him. He snorted. She couldn't work out which way he was leaning, so she just went on and told him the rest. She had taken Swales to the ground; they had arrested

385

him, then found the diary. 'Simple,' she said, finishing.

'It's a pack of lies,' he said.

'Some of it is slightly different to the reality. Yes. But there's a lot at stake.'

He shook his head again. He looked disappointed. 'I didn't think you were like this,' he said. 'Not you.'

She leaned over the gear stick and grabbed his sleeve at the shoulder, pulling him towards her. 'Forget yourself, Marcus,' she hissed. She was gritting her teeth. 'Forget your fucking integrity. This is about Andrew Farrar.'

'Is it? You sure it's not about you and Gary Swales? About you thinking he set someone up to hurt your daughter?' He spoke softly, but didn't look frightened. He pulled his arm away.

'That as well,' she said. 'You don't think it's worth the effort?'

'Stealing and planting evidence?' He looked shocked just speaking about it. 'Let alone the' – he waved out of the window, roughly in Swales's direction – 'the brutality...'

'Don't be lame. He was coming for me, jacket off.'

'So you took him down, then kicked him in the head, twice, while he was down–'

'It's not a fucking boxing match, Marcus. It's not Marquis of Queensbury rules. I have to be sure he can't get up. He's a man. I'm a woman. He's strong. Undoubtedly stronger than either of us. You don't take risks. You should have learned that as a probationer.'

He looked away from her. Disgusted or unsure?

Probably disgusted, she thought. Could she trust him?

'You will have to write up your notebook,' she said. 'Not right now, but later. Can I trust you to say roughly what I've just said?'

He laughed, a bitter little noise in his throat. 'Decision time,' he said. 'Drop you or support you.'

OK, she thought. If that's the way it is. 'Not only me,' she said carefully. 'You were there when I first found the diary.'

His head snapped round, eyes wide with anger. 'I fucking know that, Karen. I'm not fucking stupid. There's no neeed to make threats. I realize exactly the position I'm in. Through my own stupidity I've got myself here. Or through your guile...'

'Both,' she offered, and gave him a half-hearted smile. She really did feel sorry for him.

'Both. Yes.' He looked like he wanted to spit at her. 'And because of what I felt for you.'

'Is that past tense, then? So easy to get rid of?'

He took a long, deep breath, looked into her eyes, then looked away. 'You used me,' he said.

'You're an adult. You knew what was happening.' And it's not over yet, she thought. He had a bigger surprise still to come. Through the window she saw the serial sergeant walking from the van, coming towards them. 'Time's up,' she said. 'You can think about it for a while. You'll do the right thing. I know you. Meanwhile I have to go. She wound the window down and shouted to the sergeant, telling him she would only be a minute longer. He backed off. 'Now I have to tell

387

you what to do up at Swales's house,' she said.

'Is that going to be bent, too?' he asked. He sounded petulant. 'You want me to plant something for you?'

'Don't be pathetic, Marcus. Grow up. I have to tell you the procedure, that's all. You're a *trainee* detective. Remember?'

She drove to Dudley Hill feeling sure of him, not overly worried about second-guessing whether he would have lied for her without being implicated. Given what was at stake it hardly mattered. The consequences were what mattered. Besides, this way it was going to be easier to disentangle their personal lives.

She was surprised to find both Ricky Spencer and the CPS lawyer in the case waiting for her at Dudley Hill. The lawyer was a woman called Andrea Rees, a little older than her, about five feet six inches tall, thin, smartly dressed and looking alert, despite the short-notice call-out. Karen had come across her before and had found her generally sound. She wasn't as cautious as some of them, and she knew the law. Moreover, she was happy to pass the file to counsel quite early on. Generally the CPS lawyers tended to be careful about taking risks. Counsel – who had to take the cases before the judge – were, on the other hand, more cavalier. If you could get a file as far as counsel you were usually OK. It didn't mean you would win in court, but at least it would get to court.

They sat in Ricky's office and Karen told them about Swales's arrest, then carefully took the diary from the exhibit bag into which Marcus had dropped it (as if he were touching something radioactive). They gathered around the corner of Ricky's table and skipped very quickly through the initial entries, turning the pages with extreme care and using a pair of tweezers Ricky produced. Rebecca had made entries intermittently for nearly five years, all in the same volume, except for the last loose-leaf pages. There wasn't much of use in the first fifteen pages. There were only about four entries from the time they were interested in. The last sheet, folded and inserted into the back of the diary, was dated a couple of weeks before she died, and was made while staying in Gary Swales's place. Someone – maybe Rebecca, maybe not – had clearly added it to the diary later.

'It certainly incriminates Mary,' Karen said.

'And John, obviously,' the lawyer put in.

'It's possible some of the injuries on the body were caused by Mary,' Karen said. 'During the attack Becky speaks of at the end, before they go to Gary Swales's house–'

Ricky shrugged as if not convinced. 'Can we prove it's actually her diary?'

'Her name is in the front,' Karen said.

'We would be put to strict proof,' the lawyer said. 'We would need it tested for her prints and DNA. We would have to ask Martin about it, I think. Maybe he knew about it and could give evidence it was hers.'

'He's as bad as the rest,' Karen said. 'He helped them. That's clear from what she says.'

'He didn't attack her,' Ricky said. 'He was weak, maybe. But he didn't attack her.'

'You accept it's clear that Mary attacked her?' Karen asked. 'You accept that it provides a–'

'Anyway,' the lawyer interrupted. 'I'm not too worried about what it says. Our problem is that I can see no way a judge would allow it in as evidence, whatever it says. It's hearsay, and I can't think of an exception that a judge would go for. It's so one-sided. There's no way to argue with the contents, Rebecca being dead. She can't be cross-examined. It will be construed as unfair to put it in, I think. That's if we could actually find a formal way of putting it in. I'll have to think about it.'

That silenced Karen for a moment.

'I agree,' Ricky said. 'The best this does is muck up Mary as a witness for us.'

'Will you ask counsel's opinion?' Karen asked. Ricky shot her a look – annoyed that she was suggesting this? 'Maybe counsel will want to have a go with it.'

'Certainly,' the lawyer said. 'I could get it to Robert Smith tomorrow, if we delay the forensics on it. Or copy the relevant entries.'

There was a chink of hope, then.

'Better to summarize it, I think,' Ricky said. 'That way we don't delay anything.'

'It could all be invented, of course,' the lawyer added. 'I'm just thinking aloud. If Rebecca really did self-harm and try to kill herself then this might be just her ravings. Mary would say that, I'm sure.'

'We've no evidence she self-harmed,' Karen said. 'John Bradley was lying. I've no doubt about that.'

Ricky glanced up at her, frowning. He wanted to say something sharp, no doubt, something about her doubts counting for nothing, but he kept his mouth shut in front of the lawyer. 'Has Marcus arrested Mary already?' he asked, instead.

'I told him to wait for your say-so. So, no, I expect not.'

'That's good, at any rate. At least we can have a little time to ponder what to do.'

'There are two vulnerable children involved,' Karen interjected. 'We have no time at all.'

'Yes,' Ricky said, as if only just recalling that angle. 'The children. Katy obviously isn't in any danger. If this is to be believed Katy provides the best shot we've had at a motive for the attack. Mary's love for her, that is.'

He sounded like he was coming round to at least believing Mary might have played a part. Not fast enough, though. 'Precisely,' Karen said. 'She loves her so much she killed her mother. She's not safe to be with any children if that's the case. And Andrew is clearly in danger. We should get him out of there regardless of whether we arrest Mary.'

Ricky shook his head. 'We will ask Social Services,' he said. 'No need for us to take that decision alone.'

Why was he so fucking cautious? 'We show them the diary?' Karen asked.

Ricky looked at the lawyer. She shrugged. 'I can't see why not,' she said.

'I'll interview Gary Swales,' Ricky said. 'I suppose there's a faint chance he will say it's Rebecca's diary and he was hiding it. More likely he will say you planted it.' He looked at Karen and raised his eyebrows. 'He might even say you

391

fabricated it, wrote out the entries yourself.' A brief smile, without humour or warmth. 'I hope you were very careful about continuity evidence.' He turned to the lawyer.

'Karen has had a few run-ins with the Swales family. There's a bit of bad blood between them.'

'That's totally untrue,' Karen said, fighting the urge to shout it. 'I do my job. They're targets. Gary Swales is a high-level nominal. What's the matter with you, Ricky? There's nothing personal about this. I object to you suggesting that. I'm thinking of Andrew Farrar. Everything I'm doing here is focused on saving a vulnerable child.'

'Of course.' He smirked. 'Just try to stay calm when you speak about Swales.'

'There's nothing to incriminate Gary Swales,' the lawyer said, not listening to them. 'That much is at least clear. If anything he comes out of it looking clean.'

'Not quite,' Karen said. 'He knew Rebecca was in danger and did nothing.'

'That's not enough, though,' the lawyer said. 'You know that, Officer. Even if he admits he knew of it in interview I doubt you're going to be able to do anything but release him. Tonight. At the end of the day this diary doesn't say anything about her actual death.'

'Obviously.'

'I mean it appears to stop weeks before she "disappeared". It doesn't help with the events leading directly to her death.'

'She didn't disappear. That's their story.'

'I thought even the children said she disappeared?'

'Yes. She was taken from the children, locked up somewhere and tortured. She didn't run away.'

'We don't know any of that,' Ricky said. 'It's still all guesswork. The only thing we have that's certain is John Bradley's confession.'

'Some of the injuries are four weeks old,' Karen persisted. 'Where did John do it? Where did he torture her for four weeks without the family knowing it was going on?'

'Some of the injuries *could* be up to four weeks old,' Ricky corrected her. 'Not definite. Two weeks, more likely. That's what the PM says.'

'Two weeks, four weeks. The whole family must have known about it if it happened in their house over that period of time.'

'But did it? Probably the last act took place there, when they were all out. We know that from the blood-staining. But we have no idea where she was held prior to that. *If* she was held. We don't really know for certain that she didn't self-inflict some of the damage.'

Karen closed her mouth. It was a waste of time. The confession from John Bradley was infecting all their thinking about it. They should have just ignored it, built a scenario from scratch. 'Anyway, it's too late to interview Swales now,' she said. 'He'll have to stay in overnight at least.'

'I'll ask *him* about that,' Ricky said. 'He might want to get it over with now.'

'I'll come in with you,' Karen said, knowing it was hopeless, but trying anyway.

'I don't think so. He's complained already about you. You can knock off now and get some sleep.'

Friday

38

The opinion from Robert Smith QC was expected that afternoon. Marcus found himself in the terrible position of secretly hoping the silk would say the diary was evidentially useless, a hope that in turn filled him with guilt, because if it were useless Mary Bradley was likely to get off scot-free. But if they could use it he would face the ordeal of having to lie in court, on oath, about its provender. He wanted Mary caught and the children made safe, but not in that way. Perjury didn't tally with his ideas of justice. And the personal risk was considerable.

Karen would argue – had argued, over and over again – that this was the *only* way she could nail Mary. But that wasn't true, it was her desperation to get Gary Swales that had brought things to this pass. If she had left the diary where she had found it then the evidence would be just as strong against Mary. The diary made clear that Gary was probably implicated as well, but he wasn't the one threatening the children. Because of that – and much to Karen's disgust – Gary had been bailed late last night, pending the lawyers deciding whether to charge him with anything.

Ricky Spencer had summarized the contents of the diary that morning at briefing. Marcus had no doubt it was an authentic document and that Rebecca had told the truth. They had been given a window on to her last terrifying days – as the build-up to her incarceration began – and it had shown quite clearly that Mary Bradley was a ruthless, brutal, violent and probably psychotic woman. Karen had been right on all counts. Mary's brother was possibly no better, though there was nothing directly against him except his possession of the document.

Marcus had already burned his bridges on that score. There had been no option. In interview, late last night, Swales had denied ever having seen the diary. He hadn't accused Karen of planting it – overt accusations like that always set the jury against the defendant – instead, intelligently, he had left it to be deduced. Ricky Spencer had immediately wanted to see both Karen and Marcus's notebook entries before they were allowed off duty. So Marcus had sat down with her and concocted a pure fabrication, backing up everything she asserted.

There was no other way. He wasn't stupid. He knew exactly how carefully she had set things up. The option of turning against her was closed off by the personal relationship between them (if it ever came down to it he was quite sure an investigator would be able to find CCTV footage of them entering his apartment before the first search of the garage) combined with his presence at the first, illegal search of the garage and subsequent silence about that. There was no way an enquiry into any allegations he might make could do anything but find him equally culpable.

Not that it would ever have come to that. In a way it was a relief that she had planned things so carefully, so as to leave – and he had seen this at once – no possibility of choice. He didn't want to be the one to mess up the entire enquiry by making allegations against his DS. He didn't want to do that anyway, despite the heavy sense of betrayal he suffered every time he looked at her. Human trust cut across all intelligence and class boundaries. He had trusted her as a friend and as a boss, as a mentor, even. She had known that and used it. It was totally unforgivable.

He should have hated her with a passion. But things were more confusing than that. What he felt for her made it impossible to react clearly to what she was doing. She had excited and disgusted him by turn. But the horror of the one didn't seem to be cancelling out the other. More than anything the sequence of events just left him feeling confused and disorientated. Nothing like this had ever happened to him before. He had no idea how to navigate his way through it safely.

He had sat down with her last night and told her of the events at Swales's place, and she had actually held his hand at one point. He had returned with John Sanderson to the house as soon as Karen had departed to meet Ricky Spencer. At the house they had executed a fruitless Section Eighteen search. That had taken nearly three hours to complete. They had found Andrew asleep in a normal enough bedroom, washed and clean, a quilt over him, the room heated to a normal temperature. There were even toys in there. A far cry from the situation Karen had described after her previous visit to the place. It had taken three uniformed constables to keep

Mary Swales out of the way while Marcus sat Andrew up and tried to talk to him. Andrew was groggy, confused, pale. There was an odour of vomit in the room. He was reluctant to say anything, but when he did speak his voice was feeble. Andrew had decided he was ill.

Mary Swales had readily confirmed this. He had, she claimed, a stomach bug. Social Services, when they arrived, on Marcus's insistence, had called out a doctor. But he had quickly confirmed Mary's diagnosis: a normal, infant bug. So they had left him there, with Mary, in the house. That had been a joint decision by Ricky Spencer and Social Services, pending the silk's analysis of the diary and a meeting scheduled for two o'clock that afternoon to decide whether to charge Mary. But when Marcus told Karen this she had almost started to cry. She had been trembling visibly. She had reached across and held on to his hand, as if she needed him for support. 'I wish none of this was happening,' she had whispered. 'I don't know whether I can take it.' She had leaned her head against his shoulder and for a moment all the old feelings had surfaced to overwhelm his doubts. It was complicated, and she was doing her best to keep it that way.

Had she been acting? This morning it was back to business as usual. He had driven out to the hostel and brought Simon Bradley back to Trafalgar House with him. They had sat him in one of the large meeting rooms, alone, then went off and planned how to deal with him. She seemed as convinced as he that Simon was an innocent party, and was equally concerned with legitimately trying to persuade him to give a statement. Their only dispute had been about where to speak to him. Marcus had warned that any enclosed space would pressurize Simon, but she had refused to delay matters while they transferred him to Dudley Hill, which had more spacious interview rooms for witnesses. They couldn't use the meeting room he was waiting in because it was needed by the division. 'You must be able to get them to delay their meeting,' Marcus had suggested.

'I don't think we need to,' she had said. 'Let's just see how he handles things first. If it's too bad we'll move.'

It crossed his mind, of course, after everything she had done in the last seventy-two hours, that this could be another deliberate ploy.

Simon had looked nervous all morning, reluctant to come in at all. When they walked with him into the little windowless room he didn't seem to change demeanour appreciably, but he was already twitchy, so it was hard to tell whether the confined space affected him.

'I'm really pleased you could come in, Simon,' Karen started. Marcus sat at a slight angle, so he could watch her. Simon sat opposite her, a table between them. She waited for Simon to look up at her, held his eyes and gave him a big, cheerful smile. 'I'm Karen,' she said. 'Marcus tells me you feel a little nervous in small spaces, so we should try to be quick. Is there anything you want before we start?'

Simon shook his head. He was wearing the

same Radiohead T-shirt that Marcus had first seen him in, but different trousers.

'You sure you wouldn't like a drink, or something to eat?' Karen asked. Her voice was soft, carefully modulated. She kept a smile on her face, a concerned, sympathetic look in her eyes and looked directly at Simon the whole time. Marcus wasn't sure if Simon was comfortable with it or not.

'We found a diary,' she said to him. 'A diary kept by Rebecca.' That got his attention. He looked up, frowning. 'There are some things she's written in there that I want to ask you about.'

'About me?' A suspicious tone, as if he were about to be accused. 'Did she write about me?'

'Some things about you, yes. But nothing bad. She really liked you, Simon. It's very clear that she regarded you as a friend, maybe her only friend. Did you know that?'

A look of distress set in his eyes. He shifted from side to side, glanced around him as if noticing the room for the first time. He started to breathe audibly, through his mouth.

'That's good,' Karen said, speaking very gently. 'It's good that she had a friend. It's good you were so nice to her. She thought you were nice to her. She wrote that. She thought you were gentle and kind.'

He shook his head quickly, as if a fly were pestering him. He even moved up a hand as if to swat it.

'So you have nothing at all to be worried about.' She paused, watching him. What she had said hadn't made him feel good, just guilty. Did she realize that? Marcus had briefed her very thoroughly on everything Simon had said to him. 'You should feel happy she liked you,' Karen continued. 'She was a lovely girl, wasn't she?' Her eyes and her expression radiated empathy and warmth, but Simon wasn't looking at her.

'I should have...' he started. 'I should have...'

'You should have done more?' Karen asked. 'You mustn't blame yourself, Simon. You were her only friend. You did what you could.'

'No.'

'I'm *sure* you did. I'm certain.'

'No. No. No. I should have done more.'

'But what could you do? You were probably frightened yourself.'

He shook his head again, more vigorously. Then looked up at the ceiling. 'I don't like it in here. It's too tight.'

'You'll be OK. I'll make sure you're OK. Did you really like Rebecca?'

'I don't want to talk about her.'

'But I need you to talk about her. I need you to tell me what happened to her.'

'I won't. I don't want to.' He sat back, lower lip sticking out. Karen took a breath, then leaned forward across the table dividing them. 'You'll feel much better if you talk about her,' she said, her voice confidential, persuasive. 'I know what you're going through, Simon. I know how hard it is. But you can make things easier by sharing them. That's why I'm here. I want to be your friend, as you were Rebecca's. I want you to think you can tell me anything. Nothing will happen to you if you do. I will protect you.'

He stared at her, trying to work her out, maybe. It was hard to tell.

She kept her eyes on his. 'I liked Rebecca, too,' she said. 'I didn't know her like you did. But I've read her diary–'

'You shouldn't have. It's private.'

'Somebody killed her, Simon. We couldn't ask her if she wanted us to read it, because somebody killed her. Before they killed her they really hurt her. You know that, don't you?'

He began to look agitated.

'You feel bad about it. I know you do.'

Something like a sob came from his lips. There were no tears, so maybe it wasn't a sob, just a burst of pent-up sound.

'But you shouldn't feel bad. And if you tell me about Becky, tell me about how nice she was to you, then you *will* feel better. I promise you will.' She reached a hand across the table. 'You can hold my hand if you want. If it helps you can hold my hand.'

'I don't want to. You're trying to trick me. You're a fucking pig, like him.' He grunted in Marcus's direction. 'You are trying to get me to say things. But I won't.'

Karen sat back, brought her hand away. She was still smiling. Marcus saw her eyes flick to the clock on the wall. She sighed. Marcus flashed her a 'told you so' look. It was worth a try, of course, but he had predicted that Simon wouldn't help. Simon was in the grip of a guilt that was stronger than his need to disclose. And he probably had years of parental pressure locked up in his head, confirming all his suspicions.

404

'Talk to Marcus for a bit,' Karen said. 'I'll be back in a moment.'

She stood up, squeezed past Marcus, without explaining anything, then left the room, leaving the door slightly open.

Marcus didn't know what to say to him. He had tried a similar tack to Karen on the way in with him, and met with similar resistance. Simon was weak and vulnerable, he had juvenile characteristics, but he was clearly intelligent, too. He knew what was going on.

'I might need a solicitor,' he said to Marcus, after a while.

'You can have one if you want,' Marcus said. 'Of course you can. We'll ask Karen when she comes back.'

'I don't like her.'

'No?'

'She's trying to trick me, just like you did.'

'No one is trying to trick you. We're trying to help you, Simon.'

'I don't want to be in here. It's too tight. I feel bad. I feel like I'll be sick.'

'Just breathe normally. You're breathing too quickly. It's OK in here. We won't be in here for much longer anyway.'

'What's she going to do?'

'Just talk to you some more. We want you to feel better, Simon. We want to help you.'

'You're liars. Both of you.' He sniffled a little.

Karen returned, pushing the door shut behind her with a bang that made Simon start. She had a large brown exhibit bag in her hands. She sat down again.

'Simon says he might want a solicitor,' Marcus told her. 'And he's uncomfortable in the room.'

'You don't need a solicitor,' she said, voice still gentle. 'We aren't accusing you of anything.'

'I don't... I don't...'

'You're not uncomfortable because of the room. You're uncomfortable because you feel guilty. But there's no need for that. That's what I keep telling you. You've done nothing wrong. Nothing to be afraid of.' She smiled at him again, placing the brown bag on the table in front of her. Marcus couldn't see what it contained. Nor could Simon, but he was interested, trying to look.

'No one is going to hurt you here,' Karen said. 'All we want you to do is tell us a little bit about Rebecca.'

'What about her?'

'Anything. Just start talking about her. Anything will do. What was she like? Did she laugh a lot?'

'Why do you want to know that?'

'We never met her, Simon. You met her. You were her only friend. The person she relied upon to help her.'

'I couldn't help her.'

'I know you couldn't. But she didn't know that. I know exactly what happened, Simon. I know why you feel so bad.'

'You can't. You weren't there...'

'I can see it in your eyes. You think you should have done more to save her.'

'I'm not talking about that...'

'You *want* to talk about it. You know you do.'

'I don't.'

'Shall I leave you for a while to think about it? Would that help?'

'I want a solicitor, now.'

Karen sighed again, then rubbed a hand across her forehead. 'Did she scream a lot?' she asked harshly. The change of tone came out of the blue. 'When they were hurting her – did she scream and cry out, begging you to help her...?'

'*Shut up!*' Simon drove his chair backwards, away from the table. His face was twisted into a grimace.

'You must have heard her screaming. We know what they did to her.'

'*Shut up! Shut up!*' He slammed his hands over his ears.

'They burned her with an iron,' Karen said, raising her voice. 'Did you know that?'

He started to shake his head again, but so vigorously he looked as if he would damage himself. Marcus looked at Karen in alarm.

'And beat her with sticks...' Her hand went to the exhibit bag. 'I have photos of her injuries, to show you. Photos of her dead body...'

'*No! I won't listen! I won't look. No! Get her away from me!* He stared at Marcus, appealing to him, then pulled his head towards his knees until he was almost bent double, hands still over his ears.

'She was a lovely girl, but they tied her up and burned her, ground cigarettes into her skin. Did you see that? Were you there when that happened?'

Simon began to groan. He was rocking back and forth on the chair, banging it off the wall

407

behind him.

'Tell me if you heard her scream,' Karen said. 'You will feel better if you tell me. It wasn't your fault. How could it be? But you have to tell me about it–'

'*SHUT UP! SHUT THE FUCK UP!*' He raised his head, dropped his hands and yelled it at her, at the top of his voice.

Marcus flinched; Karen didn't move. But the smile was gone now. Her face was set.

'I want a solicitor,' Simon said, breathless. 'I need to get out of here. I NEED to–'

'You took part in it,' Karen said. 'You hit her, too. That's why you won't speak to me.'

'I want out of here. I haven't done anything...' There were tears in his eyes now. She had gone far enough. Marcus wanted it to stop. Did she really have the post-mortem photos? Did she really intend to show him them?

'Maybe you held the iron against her and watched her scream,' she said. 'I can show you the photo of that burn, show you what you did to poor Becky–'

'I didn't do anything... I didn't do anything...' The words came out in bubbles of saliva. He was shaking from head to toe, crying. Marcus felt panicked about it. Surely they must stop and get help for him?

But Karen wasn't even considering that. 'So tell us about it,' she said quietly. 'If you did nothing then tell us what *did* happen.'

It had gone too far. Marcus shifted towards her, to say something, but she held up a hand to stop him.

'Will you tell us, Simon?' she asked again. 'Last chance to do this the nice way.'

Simon couldn't reply. He was too far gone. He was crying too much, the snot running out of his nose.

'We need to stop and get him help,' Marcus said. His voice wavered.

'OK,' she said. He thought she had heard, that she agreed with him, but then she went on, 'Let me tell you what we know about you, Simon. You don't like enclosed spaces. But if you sit there snivelling about it and don't speak to us you are going to end up spending the rest of your life in a space no bigger than this room. You're going to fucking prison, Simon. Do you understand that?'

Her voice had changed timbre completely. Simon brought his head up, looked at her. Marcus cleared his throat to speak. She held up a hand again. She was staring fixedly at Simon. A look of fear started to come into his eyes.

'I'll make sure of it,' she said. 'I'll make sure you are shut up in a space so small you'll wish you were dead. Have you heard of DNA?'

He gave a slight shake of the head. She had all his attention now.

'It works like this,' she said. 'If you touch something we can find out about it, through DNA. If you've touched this table, for example, we can send it off to the scientists and they will tell us if you've touched it. You leave little bits of you on things, whenever you touch things, little bits of skin. That's DNA.' She opened the bag in front of her and brought out a smaller bag. Simon's eyes followed it closely. It was a sealed evidence pouch. Not the photos after all. She tore the seal and put her hand in, took out an object. 'Have you seen this before?' she asked. She held it up for him to see, then stood, slowly. It was an Asp. Marcus assumed it was the Asp found in the garage. Suddenly she flicked her wrist, rapped it against the side of the table and extended it. Simon jumped back, away from it.

'Karen...' Marcus started.

'Shut up, Marcus,' she said. 'Wait.'

'I don't like this...' He saw Simon's eyes flick to him as he spoke, then back to the baton. He was transfixed by the baton.

'You've seen this before, haven't you?' Karen asked.

He shook his head. 'No. I've never... I've never...' He was starting to stutter.

'This was used to kill Rebecca,' she said. 'She was struck with it, many times.'

Did they *know* that? It surely hadn't been analyzed yet. If it had nobody had told him about the result.

'I think you used it on Rebecca.' She walked around the table, coming behind Marcus, moving towards Simon. Marcus felt his panic increase. He had seen her stamp on Gary Swales's head. Was she going to hit Simon now, attack him with an Asp? From the start of the interview to now she had flipped completely. She looked like a different person.

'We will know if you've touched it,' she said, 'because your DNA will be all over it. We will send it to the scientists and they will tell us. That will be enough to charge you. Then the jury will convict you; then you will go to prison. Is that what you want?'

'I haven't touched it. I haven't seen it before. I swear I haven't even–'

Suddenly she was lunging at him. Marcus rose at once, toppling his chair. He thought she was going to lash out. She had her arm back. Simon let out a frightened yell, then stood quickly against the wall, backed into the corner, arms up over his face, trying to protect himself. She stepped towards him and kicked his chair aside. Marcus put a hand to her arm, grabbing the hand with the baton. But in a swift movement she had her other hand at Simon's throat. She pulled him forward, fingers round his windpipe, then slammed him back against the wall.

'Jesus Christ, Karen...' Marcus struggled to get between them, but they were right in the corner.

'You little runt,' she was saying. She wasn't shouting. She was hissing the words between her teeth. Her face was right up against Simon's. 'You fucking little runt. You killed her, didn't you?'

Simon was whimpering without control, flinching every time she moved, trying to keep his hands over his face. She kept knocking his hands away, then pushing him back against the wall.

'I know what you did,' she said. 'I know what a dirty little bastard you are.'

'I didn't ... I didn't... Please don't hurt me ... please...'

'*Shut the fuck up. Shut up!*' She had her hand on his jaw, forcing his mouth open. She was leaning into him, forcing his mouth open by squeezing the sides of his jaw. Marcus tried to drag at her

411

shoulder, to spin her away from him, but couldn't move her. Her feet were widely spaced leaning into Simon, pressing him up against the wall.

Marcus didn't know what to do. He started to speak quickly in her ear, telling her to calm down, asking her did she realize what she was doing, did she realize they would hear her before long, in the custody suite. His heart was hammering in his chest. He didn't know how to stop her, didn't know what she was going to do. He moved to the other side of her, still talking, letting go of the arm with the baton. But immediately she brought it up and pushed at Simon's face with the metal butt.

'*Open your mouth,*' she hissed. '*Open your fucking mouth, you bastard*' She shook his face with her free hand. He was sobbing and crying, terrified, pinned against the wall. She prised his jaw open easily and started to push the end of the baton into his mouth.

Marcus got a shoulder between her and the wall. He was trying to get past her, in between her and Simon. '*Leave him, Karen. For God's sake leave him,*' he cried out. He knew he was heavy enough to move her, but only if he really put his back into it, if he was violent with her.

Simon began to choke and wriggle. The withered arm was flailing around. The Asp was so far into his mouth he was retching onto it. Marcus stepped back. He had to stop it. 'I'm going for the custody sergeant,' he said. 'I can't handle this.' He stepped towards the door. Simon was gagging now. Marcus put his hand on the door handle. 'I'm going now,' he said, very loudly. He could hear footsteps in the corridor beyond. Someone was coming anyway.

Karen stepped back. In a smooth movement she collapsed the baton and slipped around the table. Simon was up against the wall still, taking huge breaths, hyperventilating, face soaked with tears. There was a knock at the door. Marcus opened it. A uniformed sergeant was outside, one he didn't know. 'Do you need help?' he asked. 'We heard shouting...' There was someone behind him as well.

'Its OK,' Marcus heard Karen say. 'He's claustrophobic, that's all. He's panicking.'

Marcus stepped back, away from the door. Simon sank towards the chair, but it was overturned. He tripped on it instead, and fell to the floor.

'We'll need a doctor, I think,' Karen said. She sounded calm. She was walking towards Simon. 'Help me, Marcus,' she said. 'We have to get him out of here...' Her eyes fixed on his own and he couldn't read the expression in them. 'Will you help me?' Louder this time, with more urgency. 'If we don't get him out of here he could choke.'

Marcus nodded, stepping forward. The sergeant was right behind him. On the floor Simon was thrashing around like he was having a fit.

39

Marcus was so angry she had to take him out to her car. She was afraid he would actually shout at her right by the custody suite, within earshot of the custody staff.

In the car he was breathing so hard he could hardly speak.

'Listen, Marcus–' she started, intending to apologize, more or less.

'Enough! Shut up! Shut the fuck up!' He smashed a fist against the door panel. 'Enough! That's fucking enough. Your turn to listen! Your fucking turn!' He almost gasped the words. He was staring at the dashboard, not looking at her. 'I can't fucking believe it!' He struck the door again. 'I can't do it, Karen. I can't do it... I can't work with you... I can't tolerate this... It's too much...'

She sat back in the seat and waited. Was he going to cry about it?

'This is serious, Karen, really serious...'

He would be OK if he could stop running it over in his mind, she thought. She could see him doing that, flinching every time he saw her ramming the Asp into Simon Bradley's mouth, unable to believe it.

'I don't know what to do... Fuck! Fuck!' He looked like he wanted to smash a window. Instead he stuffed his fist into his mouth. 'I can't believe it! I cannot fucking believe what you just did in there!' He risked looking at her. His face was suffused with blood, his eyes gleaming, the muscles around his mouth quivering.

He looked frightening when he was really gone, she thought – the change was remarkable. He was more like her than he realized. She had to stop herself smiling. Was he frightening, or attractive? More male, perhaps. That thought made her want to smile, too. She looked away from him, keeping her face straight.

'You don't get it,' he said. 'You just don't fucking get it. You think I'm like some kind of little lapdog. You think you can just drag me into whatever the fuck you want and I will go along with it. But we've reached a limit here, Karen. Do you understand that? We have already reached and passed a limit. Do you get that?'

She didn't react.

'Are you fucking listening to *me?'* He raised his voice again.

'Be hard not to, in this space,' she said.

'You're not listening. You're not taking it in. Do you understand what I'm saying to you? We are already, right now, past the point where I can support you. It has gone too far. Too fucking far...'

She looked at him, frowning carefully. 'If that were true I hardy think you would be sitting here telling me about it,' she said. 'Surely you have people to talk to.'

'That's right! That's fucking right!' He jabbed a finger at her, stopping an inch from her shoulder. 'I *do* have people to talk to. I have to talk right now to the custody sergeant and after that to

415

Professional Standards. I *have* to, Karen. Don't you see that?' The look in his eyes changed. He was distressed, genuinely distressed and pleading with her, yet without knowing what it was he wanted from her. Some kind of excuse? Something to release him from his obligation to report her? Or her blessing to do it? She realized he really had passed the point of no return.

'That's what you're going to do, then?' she asked.

'I *have* to. I *have* to. I cannot let what happened in there... I cannot let you...'

'You're going to throw away your entire career for that? That's it?'

'For *that*? You say it as if it were nothing. You're like some kind of moral monster, Karen. I can't believe it. I would not have believed it of you... You assaulted a vulnerable, innocent witness. You deliberately bullied and terrified him. *What the fuck were you doing? WHAT THE FUCK DID YOU THINK YOU WERE DOING?*' He was shouting again now, very loud. Her ears rang with it. She checked the car park, to see if anyone was watching or listening, then turned back to him.

'You're very young, Marcus. If you think what went on in there is worth throwing away everything you've achieved so far–'

'I don't care! I don't care! You don't get it, do you? I don't care about the risk. I don't care about you roping me in because I was stupid enough to be dragged into an illegal search with you. You can say that to them, if that's what you mean. I don't care. I'll tell the truth. I don't even care if they find out we were shagging each other.

Because it's like I said – I've reached my limit with you. You've gone a step too far... I have to do what I have to do...'

'I realize you *wish* that were the case,' she said, still speaking calmly. 'But I'm sure it's not. You're just angry at the moment. You need to calm down and think about it.'

'*I do not need you to tell me what I need to do.*' He hissed the words through gritted teeth, moving towards her. Was he thinking of hitting her? He was blinking very rapidly, as if it were a tic.

'I think you do,' she said. 'And I think you need to be fully aware of the risks.'

'*I am already fully aware of the risks of working with you! I know what you are capable of!*'

'Stop shouting, Marcus.' She raised her voice slightly, looking directly into his eyes. 'Stop shouting at me. I've had enough of it.'

He opened his mouth, closed it, then moved back in the seat, realizing how out of control he was. 'My God! You fucking cunt!' He spat the words out violently, but under his breath. 'My God! I cannot believe you!' He stared out of the window. He looked desperate.

'You can get out now and do what you wish,' she said. 'No one is keeping you in the car.' She paused momentarily, to see if he would make a move. He didn't. 'But before you do I think you should listen to me, so you really do know the whole risk.'

Something in her voice snapped his head round. 'Meaning what?'

'What I did in there was deliberate.'

'Give me a fucking break! You totally lost it. You

417

lost it! You cannot mean to tell me that...'

'I didn't lose a thing. You're the one who lost it, Marcus. I set out to try to get Simon Bradley to help us. I tried the easy way. I tried being nice and persuasive. He wasn't moving. You think the real risk here is to yourself, or to Simon, maybe, but it isn't. The real risk, if we don't find out what really happened to Rebecca Farrar, is to her children.' He started to shake his head rapidly, but she ignored it. 'I believe her children are in real danger. That's enough for me. My aim was to turn Simon gently, if it could be done. If it couldn't – and it clearly couldn't, exactly as you predicted – then my aim was to turn him anyway. By whatever means necessary and available.'

'So you *deliberately* tried to terrify him? Is that what you're saying?' He sounded incredulous. 'It was a *decision* to behave like that?'

'Of course. And it worked. He's frightened now. Not frightened enough, because he's a lot harder than you seem to realize. But frightened enough for us to move on to the next step.'

'The next step? *Us.* Are you fucking kidding me?'

'There was no point in doing what I've just done unless we follow through. I will do that with or without you.'

'They won't let you anywhere near him once I've told them what happened in there.'

'Don't be so naïve, Marcus. You think the custody sergeant really gives a fuck what happens to Simon Bradley? You think he's going to believe you, over me?'

'We'll see. I'll take it to him. That's all I can do.'

418

'What I want you to do is support me.'

'You're mad. Totally mad. You haven't listened to a word I've said.' He put his hands on top of his head and hunched forward. He began to rock slightly, exactly as Simon Bradley had done. She felt so sorry for him she wanted to reach over and touch him, but he wasn't going to be reassured by that.

'With or without you, I am going to go back in there,' she said. 'I'm going to present the facts to Simon. The facts – as he will see them – are that his DNA is now all over a murder weapon.'

'What? His DNA? What?' He was frowning. He hadn't got it.'

'The Asp,' she said. 'It's been in his mouth now. His saliva will be all over it.'

'Jesus Christ! Jesus Christ in heaven. You mean...' He stared at her, horrified. 'You mean ... you actually intend...? No... I don't believe it.'

'Do I intend to frame Simon Bradley? Of course not. The whole point is to get a statement from him. He will do that now. I know it for sure. He will do it not because I will tell him his DNA is on the Asp and that he's therefore going to spend the next twenty years in claustrophobic hell, but because he is so guilty about what he did to Rebecca that the DNA will give him the excuse he needs to spit it all out. He's done something. He's played some part. I know it. I'm just going to give him a little help in overriding the patterns his mother has forced upon him. He *wants* to tell us about Becky. He wants *desperately* to tell us what happened. But he can't. Because he grew up with that bitch. Because she's conditioned him. I'm going to help him get over it. That's all.'

He was looking at her with his mouth agape. He shook his head once, as if to clear it. 'You really think that will work.' He said it like he was only just realizing how stupid she was. 'You really think that there's a chance you can bully a statement out of him and he will actually give evidence! You really believe it!'

'Don't be silly.'

'He will tell the lawyers what you have done. It will never get anywhere near a court.'

'Will he? I'm not sure he will. You have to remember how guilty he feels. But anyway, I don't need it to get anywhere near a court. I just need him to tell us about it – to tell us what really happened. That will be enough to crack the family front. It's always the same with these anal, super-controlling families. Once one of them goes they just can't wait to stitch each other up. Deep down, they hate each other – that's what you're forgetting. Simon will crack; then we'll tell Martin what he's said. Martin will crack to extricate himself. He'll stitch up his mother. Then she'll crack and give us Gary. By the time they're finished stabbing each other we won't need Simon to give evidence.'

'But you have no idea whether Simon has anything to say. You have no idea who killed Rebecca. You have no idea whatsoever whether Simon or Martin or Mary or Gary was involved.'

'I could be wrong. But I don't think so. At any rate, we'll find out when Simon starts talking.'

'And in pursuit of that you ruined a legitimate exhibit?'

'Ruined it?'

'There will have been traces on that Asp. Maybe traces from the real killer. But you stuffed the fucking thing into Simon's mouth.'

'The Asp isn't the murder weapon. The Asp didn't have anything to do with Becky's death.'

'What?'

'That's the other thing you need to know. The Asp is the Asp you bought for me. The one with the serial number, traceable to you. There's no evidence that an Asp was used to strike Becky. They thought there was, for a while, but a London expert scotched the idea. We have no idea what weapon was used. I just told you it was an Asp to get you to obtain one.'

She gave him a long time to think that through. As it started to sink in he began to shake.

'I don't understand,' he said quietly. 'You asked me to get that on Sunday...' She let him get there in his own time. 'That means... That means you planned it ... you planned it nearly a week ago...'

She nodded, then shrugged. He looked as if he were sinking into a mental hell.

'You decided *that* long ago that you would do this? That you would get Simon in and ram it into his mouth?'

'No. Obviously not. I decided that I might have to do something to crack this thing apart. I just didn't know what. Whatever it was, though, I knew I would need help, a witness. And I wanted you to help me and be that witness. The person who would say we did everything by the book. I needed someone innocent for that.' She shrugged again. 'But I also knew you would turn out like

421

this. So I needed insurance.'

'Insurance?'

'Yes.'

'Against me?'

'Yes.'

Tears came into his eyes. 'Why, Karen? Why?' He spoke almost inaudibly, eyes on hers, face stricken. 'Why do this to me? What have I done to you? Why me?'

She sighed a long, hard sigh. 'I feel shitty about it now,' she said. 'I think I probably went too far. Sorry. But that's what I'm like.'

'But why?' He was still staring at her, imploring. 'Why pick on me?'

She looked away. 'You'll know why, if you think about it.'

It didn't take him long. 'Because I ... slept with Mairead? Is that what this is about?' He sounded unsure.

'Not because of that. No.' She looked over to him and met his eyes this time, held them. 'But you deceived me. Kept it from me. You are a friend, Marcus. I don't have many friends. I don't let many people in. I let you in and you deceived me. It was a betrayal.'

He looked at the floor, not denying it. 'And sleeping with me? Was that also part of the lesson?'

She shook her head. 'No. That was weakness. You got to me. Just like you got to Mairead, I imagine.' She sounded cold, but didn't feel it. He was still trembling. 'I'm not a very nice person,' she said. 'You knew that already, I expect.'

He couldn't speak.

'Like I said,' she added, after a while, 'I'm sorry.'

'Sorry?' He looked up at her. 'I trusted you...'

'And I you.'

'Mairead is an adult...'

'That's not the issue. She's the most important thing on this planet to me. Full stop. You shagged her and dumped her as if she were nothing. That's a little lesson you've taught her, no doubt. But while you were doing it you were meant to be my friend. That's not what friends do, Marcus.'

'So the whole thing was an act? You pretended to feel all those things for me ... what we did together was ... was...'

'Was genuine. At the time, anyway.' She risked reaching a hand over. She barely touched his sleeve, but he shook her off with force, as if she were contaminated. He looked physically disgusted.

'Don't touch me. I don't want you to ever touch me again.' She saw his expression change, his eyes cloud. He was thinking furiously, working out exactly how implicated he was. Looking for a way out, perhaps.

'Don't bother working it out,' she said. 'It's happened and that's that. The best thing would be if we were both to go back in and listen to what really happened to Becky. You don't have to say a thing. I'll do the talking. All you have to do is write it all down.'

'Or you'll say I planted the Asp at the garage?' That was his conclusion.

'Of course not. You can walk away now, if you want. I'll continue alone. It's only if you start

423

making complaints that life might get a little complicated for you. As I said, that Asp is traceable to you.'

He looked grim, white, shocked. 'And if I help you – if I go back in with you – how do you deal with some defence lawyer later asking us to prove where the Asp came from and finding out I bought it?'

'If we get a statement from Simon that won't happen.'

'Later, when it comes to court it might.'

He had already decided, she thought. He was devastated, stunned, anxious, but he wasn't stupid. He had no real choice and knew it. He would store the hurt, of course, bury the resentment for later. But she could deal with that. He wasn't the kind to harbour grudges once the anger was gone. Not yet.

'We'll cross that bridge when we come to it,' she said. 'For now I just want to see if Simon will talk to us.'

40

Three hours later they had a signed CJA statement. Marcus said nothing. Throughout the time it took to reduce Simon Bradley to tears once more, under the threat of his DNA being found on a murder weapon, Marcus sat in silence, a set, miserable look on his face. No doubt, she imagined, feeling helpless, trapped, cornered. He said nothing throughout the chaotic flood of words that followed, or during the laborious process of organizing them into something resembling a calm, jury-friendly narrative. Karen did all the talking, exactly as she had promised. But Marcus took the notes, did all the writing. It was Marcus's name that appeared as the witness on each page of the statement, not Karen's. Inevitably, as with any statement, but especially with a statement taken from someone with communication difficulties, that meant the result was very much Marcus's work. Marcus had to interpret and re-draft entire sentences, make sense of the incoherent rush of memory, impose his own cold, clear courtroom language on the whole. The way he did it was a little too precise for Karen's tastes. She would have left in more of Simon's uncertainty and disorder, for the sake of realism, at least, but since she didn't expect it ever to be used in court, that didn't much matter. She read it back to Simon, at the end, for him to agree and sign, but the truth was that Simon was not, by himself, even capable of clearly understanding things the way Marcus had written them. But that didn't matter, either. She had what she wanted. Simon had spoken to them. He had told them what had happened.

My name is Simon Bradley and I live at the address shown overleaf. I am twenty-eight years old, single and unemployed. I receive a disability allowance on account of a birth deformity. Up until a few days ago I lived with my parents at Lower Wyke Manor in Wyke, West Yorkshire. They are John Bradley and

Mary Bradley. My younger brother, Martin, also lived with us, plus his two children, Andrew, aged six, and Katy, two years old. Katy is Martin's child by Rebecca Farrar. Andrew is, in fact, Rebecca's child by another man, but Martin has always acted as his father during the time I have known Rebecca and her children.

I am making this statement of my own free will and I understand the declaration I have signed. I want to tell the truth about what has happened because I can no longer bear to live with the burden of knowing what they did to Rebecca. Rebecca – Becky, as she was known to me – was a kind, gentle woman who I never saw hurt anyone. I never even heard her raise her voice to her kids, or to Martin, or anyone else in the family. Mostly, when she was living with us, she was quiet and kept herself to herself. She tried not to get into arguments and tried hard to be everything for her children. She was a clean, neat and organized mother, loving to her children, warm and generous with me. I never saw her showing signs of self-harm, never heard of such things. Before they started hurting her I would not have thought she was depressed or sad. She always had a smile for me. She took time to talk to me and we became friends, I think. I consider myself to have known her a little bit, and liked her. I would not do anything to harm her. We spoke together like this when she first lived with us, and before that, when she used to visit. I cannot remember dates very well, but I think she moved into Lower Wyke for the first time in 2005. Nothing much happened during that period that I can recall, except that it became clear my mother, Mary, did not like Becky and would deliberately set out to argue with her, or turn her husband against her. During that period I do not recall Martin ever saying anything bad about Becky, but he didn't argue with my mother, either.

This was when Becky was pregnant with Katy. Martin tried his best to look after her. They slept in separate rooms, though. Becky was given a room on the top floor and my mother used to watch her closely. My room was on the top floor also, which is how Becky and I used to talk. I have been asked if she kept a diary. If she did, I never saw one and she never told me about it.

My mother didn't like Martin and Becky spending too much time together. She said this was because Becky was pregnant and had to be careful. I don't know what that meant. I think Becky didn't like being in the room by herself. Martin didn't like it, either, but they both did as they were told because that's the way things are at Lower Wyke – you do what you're told. By that I mean you do what Mary and John tell you to do.

Both Mary and John can be violent people. By that I mean that they can argue and if it gets bad they can hit each other, or hit me. I have never seen my mother hit Martin but I have seen Martin fighting with my father, a few years ago. I would say my mother is worse than my father. My father has a vicious temper, but it doesn't show often. My mother is unpredictable, though. She can become very angry quite quickly. She has hit me with her hands, her fists and with objects such as pans or bottles. She has thrown things at me and kicked me also. She has grabbed me by the hair and pulled me to the ground. She is a small woman, but she is strong.

I cannot fight anyone because I have a disability, in the form of an arm that has not developed properly.

My mother doesn't like this. She has told me she finds my arm disgusting to look at. The last time she hit me was only a few weeks ago. I cannot remember why. Sometimes I have bruises after she hits me, mostly not, though. On the other hand, if my father has ever hit me I have always been hurt quite badly. Twice I had to go to hospital because he kicked me in the head. On both occasions we told the doctors that youths had picked on me because of my arm. The police were never called.

I would say that I have not been happy living with my parents like this, but they are still my parents. I am saying these things because I have been asked about them, but I do not want to take any action against them. I am making this statement not because of what happened to me, but because of Becky.

My mother was happy when Becky became pregnant with Katy. Katy is my mother's choice of name for her, in fact. Becky wanted to call her Alison. She told me that, as a secret. I think for a while my mother wanted Becky to be a real part of our family when she was pregnant. But it didn't work out like that. Before the baby was born Martin and Becky had to go into hospital because there were some problems. They never came back to live with us after that, not until Becky was forced back a few weeks ago. For a while my mother didn't even know where they were living. That made her very angry. The period when they moved out was hard for me because my mother was so angry about it. Sometimes I have seen her sitting by herself crying. I know she was crying about it because she was whispering Katy's name over and over again. I don't think my father was bothered that they had moved out, though he did go with my mother to bring them back.

428

That is what I am going to talk about now. I have been asked how many times I saw Becky and Martin, or their children, between Katy being born and a few weeks ago. I cannot remember. It may be that I did not see Becky or the kids at all. But Martin used to still come round almost every week. Not in the beginning, when they first moved out, but shortly after that. I did hear my mother and Martin talking about Katy, but I can't recall exactly what was said. I know my mother wanted to see more of Katy. I don't know whether she ever visited Becky, Martin and Katy where they lived. I don't even know where they lived.

About two months ago, late at night, I think, my father came back to the house and told me to go to my room. I did as he said. I heard then a lot of screaming and shouting from downstairs. I though they must be having an argument. After a while I realized I could hear Becky's voice also, though I didn't recognize it at first because it was so long since I'd seen her. She sounded upset and crying. I could hear one of her children crying, too – I think Katy. I didn't hear Martin until I crept down the stairs.

I went as far as the first-floor landing and listened. I couldn't see anything. From the noises I could hear I am certain they were fighting with someone. I mean fighting physically, with blows. I thought it must be Becky because of the way she was crying and asking for help. I didn't know what to do. I went into my parents' bedroom, where there is a phone, and I thought about calling the police. I wanted to, because I was frightened that something very bad was happening to Becky, but I was too frightened of what would happen to me if I did. I also thought that since Martin was there he would help. Martin was arguing with John,

429

mostly, but also with our mother.

The fight didn't last long. After about ten minutes everything went silent and Katy and Andrew were brought upstairs to go to bed. I heard this. I didn't see them. I don't know what happened to Becky.

In the morning they were all gone – Becky, Martin, Andrew and Katy. I was woken by my father, asking if I had heard or seen anything. He looked drunk and annoyed. He had scratches down his face. But I had slept straight through. I am a very deep sleeper. My father and mother said they had all 'done a runner'. They were angry and nervous, and my mother smashed a window in the kitchen by throwing a pan at it. Then, about halfway through the day, they drove off in my father's van. They didn't tell me where they were going.

They came back many hours later, in the middle of the night. I know from what they said later that they had been to my uncle Gary's place. Gary is my mother's brother. I didn't see Gary that night, but I heard him. When they first got back I heard him say that Becky was 'fucked' already because there was something wrong with her head. He said if they left her like that she would die. He also said they should 'finish her off' because it would be too dangerous to get her to a doctor. He asked them if they knew anyone who could 'do it'. I was listening from the first-floor landing when he said these things. I heard him very clearly. I am certain it was my uncle Gary Swales. I know him well. I have known him all my life. I didn't think he could be serious when he said Becky might die. I didn't expect my parents would do what he said, either. I still thought that they wouldn't do something so terrible. Gary stayed for a few hours, I think, but I didn't hear *anything else he said because I had to go back to my room, so I wouldn't get caught listening to them.*

I don't know what vehicle they came back in, but they brought Martin, Becky, Katy and Andrew with them. I don't know whether Gary came with them or in his own car. Becky was very ill. I don't know what had happened to her. She couldn't walk up the stairs without Martin helping her. If she stood by herself she just fell over. She looked very white and was sweating a lot. She looked dirty. There was blood on her face and down the front of her shirt. Her face looked puffy. One of her eyes was closed up. She was breathing very heavily. They put her in the room next to mine and locked the door, but I was worried about her. I went in and tried to speak to her, but she just pulled away from me and put her hands to her face, like she was terrified of me. I don't think she knew it was me. The room they put her in is one of the store rooms in the loft, and has no windows. There was nothing in there except the radiator on the wall.

She was in that room for four to five weeks. I can't be sure of the exact time. She did come out sometimes, once to have a bath in the bathroom next door. Later on, when she was feeling better, I saw her downstairs, in the kitchen, sitting on the floor. I don't know what was happening. She was sitting on the floor and my mother was bent over shouting at her. Becky was just sitting there. She could have been crying. I didn't see properly because my mother closed the door when she saw me. They told me she was feeling better so had come down to eat.

During the first week my mother would come up and go in to see her. I could hear her shouting at her from my room. I have been asked if my mother

431

wanted Becky to do anything, but I didn't ever hear her say that. She just used to shout at her, call her names. She called her a slut, a tart, a little bitch. That sort of thing. She was hitting her as well. I didn't see that in the first week, but I could hear the noises and I could hear Becky sobbing and asking her to stop.

Once Becky's door was open when I went past and I looked in. She was lying on a bed they had put in there, hunched up, with her knees pulled up to her chin. Her mouth was gagged with a black towel or rag and her eyes were closed. I could see she was breathing, though. Another time I didn't hear anything from her and I went to the door and turned the key. Inside she was lying on the floor and her arms were tied to the radiator with some chain. I think it was a bicycle lock. Again, she didn't open her eyes and wasn't moving. I was worried about her, but I did nothing. I just shut the door. I feel very bad about that, very guilty. I couldn't sleep for thinking about her, lying there alone. But I was too frightened to do anything. I should have done something. If I had done something she might still be alive today.

After a few weeks my father and mother started going to see Becky together. This happened at night usually, when the kids were asleep. I could hear Becky asking to be allowed to see her children, begging with them, but they just laughed at her or hit her. Once again, I did not actually see them hitting her, but I did hear the noises. Once I heard Becky screaming really loud for a long time. I don't know what they were doing. I have been asked if they burned her with anything, but I didn't see that. The only time I actually saw them hitting her was near the end when Becky had tried to get out and fell down the stairs. I was downstairs and I ran to see. Martin was there, too. He didn't go to Becky, though. He just took the kids away so they wouldn't see her. The kids were told about that time that Becky had run away, but they must have been able to hear their mother shouting and crying for them. When she fell down the stairs my father went to take her back, but my mother pulled him away and started hitting Becky with a piece of wood. They kept pieces of wood to hit her with in the cupboard under the stairs. They gave the pieces of wood names. One was called Mr Woody; the other was called Sticky. They had a metal bar as well. They called the metal bar Mr Hard Knock. They used to sit there when we were eating, laughing about it. They didn't laugh in front of Katy or Andrew, but when Martin was there they used to try to get him to laugh, too. Martin knew what was going on. They used to say things like 'Time to get out Mr Sticky,' or 'Time to take Mr Woody for a walk.' Or 'About time for another visit to the school of Hard Knock...' I don't know why they started hitting her like this, but they did it every day, or nearly every day. I have seen them take the sticks out – my mother and father – and take them upstairs, then heard the noise of them hitting Becky. At first Becky used to shout a lot, but then they must have stopped her somehow. At the end, in the last week, she didn't shout at all.

In the last week Martin started going up there with them. They never asked me to go up. Martin started talking about Becky as if she were not his wife. He started calling her the same names they did. Once, I know Andrew managed to get out of his room and creep up there. I know because I heard them talking about it afterwards. They think he saw them doing something, but when they asked him about it he denied it. I was there when they questioned him. My mother took his trousers down and slapped him between his legs until he couldn't do anything but sob and cry and shout for his mummy, but still he wouldn't tell them what he had seen. By 'between his legs', I mean she slapped him on his willy. My mother also used to do that to me when I was little. I can remember. I heard them talking about it several times afterwards – Mary, Martin and John. They were sure he had seen something. They were worried about it.

I have been asked if my uncle Gary took part in any of this. I didn't ever see him take part. He didn't visit much. I don't recall him visiting while Becky was shut in the top room. After he brought her back they called him on the last night, but that was all.

On the night she died my father came to me and told me I had to help him. This was very late and the children were all in bed, I think. I went down and found my mother, Martin and my father all in the front room. They were very agitated. Becky was in the kitchen, lying on the floor. There was a lot of blood lying around her. My mother told me she had 'given the bitch what she deserved'. Those were her exact words. My father was arguing with her, angry with her. He said she had gone too far. Martin looked very sick. He was just sitting there, not saying anything. They called my uncle Gary and told him that Becky had died. That was what they said. I don't know what he said to them.

I didn't dare go through to the kitchen to look more closely at her. I just stood there, frightened now, wondering what they wanted me to do. I don't know what Gary said, but afterwards my mother decided that they had to put Becky in her car and take her somewhere.

Her car was a big grey car. I don't know what kind. Gary bought her it. My mother told my father to move her and said I would have to help. She couldn't touch 'the bitch' she said. It made her feel sick to think about it. I didn't want to help. I tried to get them to use Martin instead. I cried about it. But Martin got annoyed and slapped me until I stopped. My father twisted my arm behind my back – my good arm – and told me he would break it if I didn't help him. So I helped him.

I am not very good at lifting. I have only one arm I can use and I am not very strong. I dropped Becky three times while we were moving her outside. I dropped my end of her, her legs. I have been asked what she felt like. When I touched her she felt warm but stiff. I thought she was dead when I moved her, because that's what they told me. Her head was just rolling about. When I dropped her she didn't respond in any way. Her eyes were open, like you see on dead people on the TV. She had no clothes on and she smelled very bad. She smelled like she had done a poo all over herself. There was blood on her body and bruises. I was terrified throughout the time I was touching her, really frightened. I believed they had killed her, by hitting her with the sticks. I believe they all took part in that, including Martin, who was meant to be her husband.

We put her in the boot of the car and started to drive. I don't know where we were going. My father was cursing my mother all the way. He said she had gone too far. He said it over and over again. We had been driving about five minutes when I thought I heard a noise from the boot. I thought it sounded like a shout, or someone crying. I told my father what I heard and he just laughed at me. But the sound got worse. I could hear her knocking on the boot. I am sure she was alive and calling out for me to help her. I think I even heard her shout my name. I couldn't stand it. I told my father to stop and let me out, but he wouldn't. I was so desperate I punched him in the face. I punched him so hard his nose began to bleed and he had to stop the car. He stopped the car to beat me, but when he stopped I jumped out and ran. He couldn't follow because he had to do something with Becky. I made my own way back home by stopping and asking people for help. I even asked a policeman where I was, at one point. It took me a long time and I felt very cold.

That is the only time I have ever punched my father. I thought he would kill me when I got back, but he didn't touch me. He was already in the house when I got back. They were all sitting in the kitchen talking in whispers. Katy and Andrew were playing in the front room. I went straight up to my room. This was sometime in the morning. I noticed then that there were blood stains on the stairs and in the room they had kept Becky in, but that the kitchen was clean. My father came up to see me and told he would deal with me later. But that hasn't happened yet and now he has been arrested by the police. A little later they made me help wash the blood off the stairs and take the carpet out of Becky's room. They took the carpet away somewhere in the car, I think.

I don't know what he did with her. I was told she was found on the edge of the motorway, but I don't know exactly where the motorway is. When I jumped out we were on a little road, with houses around. I jumped out and ran away from her. I have been told, just now, that it is unlikely that Becky was still alive then, but I believe she was. I believe she was alive and I left her. If I had done something more she might have lived. I cannot sleep because of that. I feel sick every time I think about it. I could have done something. I could have done more. All the time it was happening I could have done more. She was a beautiful person who was only nice to me. But I did nothing to help her.

I have been asked if I knew why all of this happened, why my parents and brother were so horrible to Becky. I think it was because they didn't like her.

41

It was all happening now. Karen sat in her car in the fading evening light and tried to stay calm. Robert Smith QC had faxed an opinion on the diary about five minutes before she and Marcus were finished with Simon Bradley. She came out of the interview and found Ricky Spencer standing in the corridor, waiting to give her it. He looked like someone who had to pass on bad news, but wasn't too sad about that. She took the fax off him and gave him Simon's statement in return.

'What's this?' he asked, as if it might be some new irritation.

'A statement from Simon Bradley. Read it.'

She kept half an eye on him as he turned the pages. His face was expressionless, but growing fractionally redder by the minute. At the same time she quickly read Smith's advice. There wasn't much to it. The gist of it was that he would attempt to use the diary in evidence against John Bradley and anyone else charged with Rebecca's murder, but was requesting more paperwork, information and time before deciding whether Mary, Martin or Gary should also be charged. Hedging his bets. Not surprising, considering Ricky had only given him the diary to work with.

When Ricky was done he looked up, took a breath and smiled at her. 'Good work,' he said quietly. To his credit, he got on the phone to Alan White at once.

They held an emergency meeting. Chris Gregg came over and chaired it. The squad was immediately increased to six teams, the other five all pulled from murders on HMET East. There was an air of desperation, she thought. In the meeting, people kept looking at her, as if they wanted her to comment, say something like, 'Too little, too late.' She kept her mouth shut.

The priority was clear: Mary, Martin and Gary had to be found and re-arrested and the children removed from their care. Both children – but especially Andrew – were in imminent danger. If they could not be located at either of the Swaleses' addresses then the threat would be sufficient for Gregg to invoke the procedures the Force had only recently established to locate kidnapped minors – there would be national alerts at ports, harbours and airports, priority media interviews and the rapid distribution of images of the kids to key public areas within the county, then the country.

They went from a mop-up enquiry involving a

handful of detectives to a priority major enquiry of thirty-five in less than an hour.

Within half an hour they had tracked down Martin (driving away from his workplace) and had him back in custody. But there the success stalled. Neither Mary nor Gary were at their addresses. Raids on the addresses of known associates and family achieved nothing. By 3.30 p.m. they were facing up to it: Mary and Gary had disappeared overnight, and they had taken Andrew and Katy with them.

Chris Gregg applied the emergency provisions and the entire Force went into alert mode. Martin was interviewed urgently, solely to glean information as to his children's whereabouts. But Geoffrey Lane was already on hand. Martin had a lengthy consultation with him, then invoked his right to silence. The interviewers broke off and disclosed the contents of Simon's statement to Martin, in Lane's absence. Within fifteen minutes Lane was sacked and Martin was giving an interview without representation, tearfully regurgitating the same account his brother had given, but minimizing his own culpability. On the down side, he had no idea where his mother, uncle or children were.

Alan White had turned down Karen's request to conduct the interview (they had dedicated interviewers now the squad was back to normal size), so she heard of Martin's change of heart from Marcus, while she was still occupied in searching Swales's home for clues as to where he might have fled.

'You were right, of course,' Marcus said, still

sounding bitter.

'So what?' she replied, letting her frustration slip out. 'We're too fucking late.'

As the afternoon progressed without result she grew frantic. At 5 p.m. she called Michael Surani, desperate to use any connection that might help locate Andrew Farrar quickly. He hinted he might know something, but wouldn't disclose it over a public network. He was at Heathrow, about to fly back to Leeds/Bradford. He agreed to meet her as soon as he was back in the county. They decided on a small back road within minutes of the airport.

She knew it because just over seven years ago she had witnessed a murder nearby, following which both herself and Mairead had been kidnapped at gunpoint. It had been the start of a harrowing twenty-four-hour ordeal that she did not like to remember. The kidnapper had picked his spot well, though – the road was screened from vision by high dry-stone walls and a thick pine wood on a slight incline, so that in the distance the valley leading south to Leeds was visible (twinkling harmlessly in the dusk), but there were no houses close enough to observe. The road was minor, poorly surfaced, and served only a collection of farms at the other side of the hill leading to the Otley Chevin. You could hear traffic approaching from quite far away. There was no street lighting.

Surani arrived in a new Jag, an S-type she hadn't seen him drive before. He parked at the widest point of the road, about twenty yards from where her own car was tucked into a passing point, wheels on the overgrown verge. She realized as the rear door of the Jag opened and Surani emerged that he had not come alone; someone had driven him. She was in the rear seat of her own car. She leaned over and opened the door for him. He paused beside the open door, took off a light overcoat and got in beside her. Outside the evening was cooling fast.

'Hello, Karen,' he said, arranging the coat over his knees. He was wearing a suit and tie, a pale shirt. As if he had just been to a board meeting. Maybe he had. 'This is all a bit cloak and dagger,' he said.

She smiled at him. 'You're the one who wouldn't speak on the phone.'

'No. I'm having to review all my communications since your call a few nights ago.'

She nodded, but didn't ask more. Things were at a different level between them now. She had saved his neck, shown her colours. He owed her for that. She assumed he had extricated himself from his difficulty without compromising her or harming anyone from HM Customs. If it were otherwise she would have heard about it already from Doyle.

'I'll need to change all my numbers,' he said, 'just to be sure. But I can't do everything at once. That might look a little suspicious.'

She frowned at him. 'I don't need the detail.'

'No.' He smiled, for the first time since getting into the car. 'Of course not. I was just–'

'Who brought you?' She nodded towards his car.

'David,' he said. 'Why?'

'David Ostler?'

'Yes.'

For some reason it made her pulse pick up a little. She had a good view of his car, through the front windscreen, but that wouldn't be much use if Ostler had been told to do something. She had no weapon and wasn't in the driving seat. If she had guessed he would come with Ostler she would have remained at the wheel.

'He's back with me. There's no need to worry about him,' Surani said, as if that were all that needed to be said on the matter, as if Ostler were nothing but a chauffeur.

'What can you tell me?' she asked.

'It's that urgent? No pleasantries. No polite conversation?'

'Why do you think we're meeting here? I have to get back in immediately. We've got a major manhunt underway.'

'Looking for Gary Swales?'

'And his sister.'

Surani only raised his eyebrows a little. 'Gary is having a lot of difficulties lately,' he said thoughtfully. 'Why do you want him?'

He had implied that other people were also looking for Swales. 'We're after the children his sister has with her,' she replied. 'She means to harm one of them. We have to get to her first. Gary is a secondary concern, but he's implicated. He will be arrested for murder when we find him. Do you know where he is?'

He shrugged. 'He was in Blackpool earlier this afternoon. He had his sister with him. I didn't know anything about the children. Are they the

442

children of the dead girl?'

'Yes.' She tried to remember the details they had unearthed on Swales. She could think of nothing relating to Blackpool. 'Why Blackpool?' she asked.

'I don't know. But he's probably no longer there. He told me you had a relative in custody and had tricked him into saying things about him and his sister. Things he assured me were false. Those were *his* words, you understand. He is sufficiently worried to be planning to leave the country, I think.'

'You should have told me all this immediately.'

'I didn't know about the manhunt,' he said reasonably, then added, 'And I'm not your staff.'

'No. Sorry.' She reached over and took hold of his hand. 'I'm very nervous and uptight,' she said. She tried to look him in the eye, pick it up from where they'd left off, before she'd slept with Marcus. 'I'm really worried about the dead woman's children. I don't want them to be killed as well.'

'I can see you're very tense,' he said. He didn't respond to the pressure on his hand.

'I'm sorry,' she said again. 'It's just my brain is having difficulty focusing on anything other than finding Swales. Did he tell you he was in Black-pool?'

'No. But he called from a normal residential number. Silly man.'

'Can you give me it? I'll get it traced.'

'I've already done that for you.' He took a leatherbound notebook from the pocket of his jacket, extracted a slip of paper from it and passed

443

it to her. She let go of his hand and took it. 'Well, actually, David did it for you,' he clarified.

She looked at it. It was an address in Blackpool. 'Do you know what it is?' she asked.

'I think it's a house belonging to a business associate of Swales. A Mr Christopher Carter.'

That name seemed vaguely familiar.

'But I doubt Swales is still there,' Surani added. 'He rang me later from his mobile and he was possibly at an airport then. I could hear them announcing flights, I think. I assumed his sister was with him still. I could be wrong, but, as I said, his plan was to leave the country. That might have already happened.'

'There are alerts out at the airports,' she said. It didn't mean they wouldn't get through.

'Well, perhaps you will catch them, then.' He didn't seem concerned whether they did or didn't.

'Let me call someone,' she said.

She called Marcus first, and gave him the Blackpool address. She told him she had received information that Swales and his sister had been there earlier in the day. 'Probably they've moved on,' she said. 'But I need you to check it.'

'Call it through to Lancashire?' he asked.

She thought about that for a moment. 'No. Go yourself, if you can. Just in case she's still there. We don't want a bunch of uniformed pro- bationers fucking things up. Can you go?'

'You're the boss,' he said. 'I do what you tell me. You know that.'

She ignored him. 'The place is probably empty,' she said. 'But don't assume that. Just check it out.

If she's there then back off and call me. I'll organize help from this end. OK?'

Next she called Ricky and told him she had information that Swales might be going through a regional airport, most likely either Liverpool or Manchester. Could they increase awareness at all airports? Ricky said he would deal with it. She got off the line before he could pry.

'What about the other matter?' she asked Surani immediately.

'The contract? It was a bluff, as I told you.'

'I don't think it was.'

'I *know* it was. At this point in time Gary Swales has neither the money nor the clout to arrange a hit on a police officer. Any type of hit.'

'Hits are cheap.'

He frowned at her. 'Your market information is erroneous, I fear. Hits on serving police officers are, on the contrary, very expensive indeed.'

'Someone ran a car into Mairead last night. They were trying to kill her.'

Sympathy softened his eyes immediately. 'Is she OK?'

'She's fine. We were lucky.'

'How frightening for you. I'm sorry I told you about the rumour. It can only have made you more fearful. And it was nothing but that. A rumour.'

'A coincidence? You tell me Swales wants to harm me or my daughter, then someone tries to harm her. I don't think it sounds like a coincidence.'

He sighed, then reached over and took her hand. There was concern in his voice when he spoke. 'Some things I know with a high degree of accuracy,' he said. Some things less so. I know for certain that Gary Swales could not at this precise time place a contract on you or your daughter, however much he might wish to. Gary Swales is suffering quite critical liquidity problems at the moment. And an almost total loss of respect in the circle he largely inhabits. No one would believe him capable of paying.'

It was good to know. 'Maybe he paid a cheap amateur.'

'Maybe. But that would be very stupid. Amateurs are not discreet. I know you think him stupid, but I haven't noticed that. Not to that extent, at least. And besides, he has his hands very full of other issues at the moment. So maybe it was a coincidence.'

'You know a lot about him.'

He didn't reply to that.

'You two seem much closer than I thought.'

'Business,' he said. 'We have certain business interests in common.' He let go of her hand. He seemed mildly irritated by her tone.

'Like what?'

'Nothing improper, I assure you.' He looked away from her, out of the window. 'You mentioned that Swales was involved in drugs. But that's not my involvement with him, if it's true...'

'You know it's true. You just referred to a loss of respect in the circles he inhabits. Did you mean the stock exchange?'

He turned his head and smiled at her. 'You're very prickly tonight, Karen. Perhaps you should get back to your manhunt. It's making you a little rude. We can talk about my connection to Gary Swales when you're calmer.'

'I'm a police officer in a car with a man who I have recently tipped off about the attentions of HM Customs, a man who consequently sees the need to change all his phone numbers–'

'If you thought for a moment that I was involved in drugs you would not have "tipped me off", as you call it.'

He was wrong about that, but she couldn't point out the nature of the error – to do that she would have to say, *I would still tip you off because my bosses told me to, because we need your help with something bigger.* She looked away from him instead.

'Look,' he said, 'I am extremely grateful for your information. But that does not mean that I was about to seal a drugs deal or that I have ever had anything to do with drugs. For God's sake, Karen, you know that. Someone in Customs doesn't, though. So I have to take precautions, clean things up a little. In this country you don't have to be guilty to be targeted. And you don't have to be guilty to be convicted. You just have to be a Paki running a freight company that does business with heroin-exporting countries. That's what I'm having to guard against.'

He had a point. Did she believe him, though? Not for a minute. But that hardly mattered. 'And Swales?' she asked.

'Gary Swales owned approximately thirty per cent of a property company I control. Until this afternoon, when I bought him out. As I told you, Gary has major liquidity problems.'

'But not any more. You bought him out. So he

has cash now. Now he can pay whoever–'

'He can pay his creditors. That's all Gary Swales will be trying to do. Believe me.'

'His creditors?'

'Yes. And I don't mean banks. Gary has been borrowing from people who are a little less forgiving than your average bank.'

42

Andrew felt better, but still too sick to move around for very long. He had tried this afternoon to enjoy himself – because everything had been different this afternoon – but had quickly felt dizzy as he ran around on the pier, chasing Katy, trying to make her scream like she was really frightened of him. Then he had just sat down and breathed deeply. He had thought he was going to be sick and that Mary would smack him for that. But Mary had instead crouched down beside him and spoken nicely to him. It had been so strange, so different, it had made him cry. He had thought that would make her angry, too. But she had just smiled at him, then given him a hug, just like she would have with Katy. He couldn't believe it. It had made him cry more, but not because he was sad.

She had been nice to him since the doctor had come and said he was sick with a poorly stomach. He wanted the dizziness and the sickness to go away, because when his head spun like that he felt awful, like he would just have to fall over and lie on the ground, but a part of him wanted it to go on a little bit now as well. Mary was only being nice to him because he was poorly, and he didn't want that to stop. So now, when he had a little pain in his tummy – which he would never have told her about before – he pulled a face and told her. And she came over and stroked his head and told him it wouldn't be long now before everything was better. Once today she had even kissed him, on the top of his head.

They had come here – the place was called Blackpool, she said – so that he could get better quicker. It was a holiday, she said. They had come here with Gary, in one of his cars. Gary hadn't been so nice to him, and he was still frightened of him, but at least he hadn't shouted at him, or squeezed his throat. They were staying in a big, tall house with furniture that Mary said was very expensive. She had told him to be careful with it, but hadn't slapped him for climbing on it, or put sheets down on top of things so as he wouldn't make them dirty. This afternoon she had made them a picnic and they had gone out to the beach, after Gary had gone away again. Gary had been on the telephone and had got very angry about something; then Mary and he had gone into the kitchen and whispered a lot. Andrew thought everything might change then. But when Gary had gone things had been the same. Mary had made his favourite sandwich – strawberry jam – and had taken them to the beach.

It wasn't very hot – he had to wear a coat to stop himself shivering – but there were still lots of

449

people. They had to queue to get a ride on a donkey, and then he had almost fallen off because he had felt so sick with the wobbly movement. So they had gone up to the pier instead and walked along it. Mary had bought them chips at a stall and they had sat on the benches eating them. There were lots of people there, sitting in chairs, reading, or lying on towels on the wooden boards. He had played with Katy until she started to cry because she missed her daddy. But Mary had said they would see Martin soon. He didn't care about seeing Martin.

When he was eating his chips he had held Mary's hand and had almost forgotten about Martin and Gary and the horrible house where they used to live. And his mum. He couldn't think about his mum. If he thought about her he would start getting really upset. So he squeezed Mary's hand tighter and tried to pretend she was his mum. The chips tasted nice, salty and soft.

He had only eaten five or six of them before he started being sick. He felt bad about it. He didn't want to spoil things. But Mary had just wiped it off him and told him not to worry. Then she had let him walk along the benches by the edge of the pier, so that he could see through the railings where the waves were, far below. The waves looked big and scary and very loud. She even held him up to the railings, with his head over the edge, looking down at them, until some horrible man came up and told her it was dangerous.

She had brought them all back then, and they had eaten the jam sandwiches for tea instead, sitting in the kitchen in the tall house. She had promised they could go back to the pier later, when the horrible man had gone. But he could see out of the window that it was dark already, so maybe they wouldn't be able to.

'Where will I sleep tonight?' he asked Mary, in between mouthfuls of sandwich and sips of lemonade. 'Will I be able to sleep in with Katy?'

'You can sleep where you want,' she said, not turning to him. She was at the sink, washing dishes. Katy was in a high chair, eating a pot of yoghurt. 'But we're going out again first. As soon as you're finished eating we're going out again. The tide will be in now. It will be nicer to look at.'

He didn't know what the tide was.

'Will I get a ride on a donkey again?' he asked, just to talk to her, not because he wanted a ride on a donkey. Normally she told him to shut up when he spoke.

'It will be too late for the donkeys,' she said. She turned round and looked at him, wiping her hands on her jeans. 'But we can go on the pier again. We can go right to the end and you can walk along the railings if you want. Like a real daredevil.'

He didn't know what a daredevil was either. 'That sounds scary,' he said, unsure.

'If it's scary you needn't do it,' she said. She smiled at him. 'Hurry up and eat your tea. It will be time for your sister to sleep soon. We need to get out before that. Go for our walk.' He watched her take a deep breath, then look away from him. Where her hand was hanging at her side he could see it was shaking.

'Are you OK, Aunt Mary?' he asked her.

'I'm fine,' she said. 'I just need to get you out...'
She stopped, then looked at him again. 'The fresh
air is good for you. That's what the doctor said.'

The doctor hadn't said that to him. He had told
him to stay in and keep warm and drink lots of
water.

'You feeling better?' she asked.

He nodded.

'See. That's the sea air. It's good for you.' She
looked at her watch, then looked at the plate in
front of him. 'Come on,' she said. 'We haven't got
all night.' She sounded a bit like before. Enough
to make him shiver a little. She had pulled sticky
tape across his mouth, kicked him. He remembered that. She had burned him once as well,
held a match to his arm until he screamed out
with pain.

'Did you hear me?' she asked.

He picked up the sandwich and stuffed it into
his mouth, but almost immediately he felt the
sick coming up his throat.

43

Blackpool. The salt air coming through the open
car windows smelled of rotting vegetable matter.
There were seagulls wheeling and screaming to
his right, dipping and diving towards an attraction Marcus couldn't see for houses, but they
were a long way from the water, so he guessed
maybe a rubbish tip. Up ahead the early evening

452

sky glowed with an aura of neon, criss-crossed by search lights from another attraction he couldn't see, presumably down at the seafront. A club, a casino, a big dipper? At the outskirts Blackpool looked like any other working-class northern town – estates of red-brick semis punctuated by low-rise blocks and concentrations of back-to-back terraces, bored kids hanging around suped-up old cars with rap beats blaring from the open boot, everything looking decayed and in need of regeneration.

Marcus had never been here before. When he was in junior school – before the experiment – he could recall that other children had gone for weekends to Blackpool, and come back with riotous stories of fairground fun, the illuminations, the beach, fish and chips, donkey rides and the Tower. Cheap mass entertainment, but clean enough. More recently the resort had become associated in his mind with something slightly sordid – drunken nightlife, incontinent stag and hen parties, outrageous binge-drinking – the whole malaise summed up by an image (from some state-of-the-nation documentary) of an inebriated young woman in bridal wear squatting in a main street in full public view, dress hitched, urinating.

Whatever the pull, the Roths had been above it all. His dad wouldn't have considered stooping so low just to give the kids some fun. Blackpool was too tacky, too working class. He wasn't even sure if his parents had ever been here.

He drove down Talbot Road through stretches of Poundsavers and equally cut-price pie and sandwich shops, following the directions given him by the TomTom. At the far end he could see the North Pier and the Tower, lit up by garish Las Vegas animations featuring, amongst other things, flashing dollar symbols. He was curious enough to want to see more, but the address Karen had given him was buried in darker, residential streets a little south of the North Pier, about two blocks back from the seafront. He was in a hurry to get there.

Karen had been right, of course. She was the only one on the entire squad who had guessed it correctly. She had said John Bradley was being set up to protect Mary. She had said the children were in danger. They now had two statements to prove this. She had even been right about Gary Swales's involvement. It made him wonder what else she could be guessing accurately. He had thought it absurd that Gary Swales might have sent someone to drive a car into Mairead, but wasn't so sure now.

The fretting about her methods had stopped as soon as Simon words had sunk in, replaced by a physical, nauseous horror at the details. A woman beaten and locked up, systematically tortured and starved, and all of it so casual, so utterly without a reason he could comprehend. It *was* horrific, truly horrific, yet it was the sheer banality that gripped and shook him. It was exactly as Karen had said. The Bradleys had acted as if they were doing something *normal*, as if that was simply the way they lived and thought. Rebecca Farrar and her suffering had served only to amuse them. Their cruelties to her were on a par with those he had seen visited upon dumb animals when as a

454

probationer he had been asked to enter filthy tower-block slums in order to rescue whimpering dogs. She had been dehumanized for them – or was never human in the first place – just something to be ritually treated to a dose of Mr Woody or Mr Hard Knock.

The naming of the blunt instruments opened a sickening vista on to their psychological landscape. It was their idea of a light-hearted joke. He imagined them sitting round the table after dinner, clearing the plates away, picking the food from their teeth, then Mary turning to John and winking. 'Time to take Mr Woody for a walk, eh?' Just a little evening entertainment. Upstairs the girl shivered and vomited, her own children kept away from her, tied up so she couldn't even defend herself when they came to have their fun. Marcus's brain boiled with the images. He could not get rid of them. Becky chained in an unlit room, slowly dying of a brain haemorrhage – and knowing that, perhaps – desperate to see her children before it happened. What could that have felt like for a young mother? Could they not see that in her eyes, as they were holding a burning iron to her buttocks. The effect on him was like a psychic shock. It blotted out all other considerations. What Karen had done, how she had set him up and deliberately used him to get this result – right now all that seemed trivial, vague, inconsequential. The only and absolute priority was to find Mary Swales before she did something to the boy.

He found the address easily enough. It was a tall, white-fronted, Victorian townhouse in an area full of similar buildings, most of them convened into guesthouses. He parked almost opposite. Ten minutes staring at the blank windows convinced him they were too late, as Karen had suggested they would be. As far as he could see – and assuming he had the address correct – the curtains were all drawn and there were no lights on. The house looked large – both tall and deep – so it was possible there were occupants at the rear of the building. He got out of the car and walked to the end of the block, trying to find an angle from which he could get a view of the rear, but without success. The evening was cold, brisk with the sea air, and he had left without a jacket. He went back to the car to think about his options.

There weren't many. The only quick way he could see to check whether there was anyone in would be to walk up to the door and listen. But Karen had wanted this to be discreet, and had specifically asked him not to confront Mary, if he found her. He supposed that was because he wasn't meant to be here at all without informing Lancashire Constabulary. So maybe he should just wait in the car for a few hours, watching the place. He considered calling Karen, to ask her what she wanted, but that seemed too dependent. He had to be able to show some initiative.

He got out and walked over to the front door. There were steps leading up and a view to a basement beneath them. Again, no lights, no sign of life. He opened the letter box, squatted down and peered through. A hallway, carpeted, then stairs up, all in darkness. Unclear shapes of pictures on the walls, a grandfather clock in a corner. The place was a cut or two above Mary Swales's natural habitat, he thought, then remembered the designer furniture in Lower Wyke, where they had killed Becky. It was all too bizarre.

He went back to the car and switched on the radio, flicking through the local channels without interest. He slotted in a Kaiser Chiefs CD that Mairead had given him. Given her capacity for independent thought, she was remarkably un-adventurous musically. She liked all the bands that everyone else her age went for and – like everyone else – seemed to believe the carefully designed industry myths; the bands were driven by tre-mendously talented, angst-ridden teenagers who were fiercely original and on the edge of culture – so much so they were usually drug-dependent to cope with it all. To Marcus they sounded like a mix of all the bands he had listened to ten years ago, with a little extra punk thrown in for flavour. The music was derivative, which didn't mean it was trash, just very familiar. The posturing was boring because he had seen it all before.

He listened for about fifteen minutes, keeping half an eye on the building. When there was no change he switched the CD off, got out again and walked over to the steps. He was almost sure the place was empty, but he would ring the bell any-way to see if there was a response. If there was, he would retreat to the car (no other option since Mary knew who he was); if not, he'd call Karen and get out of here.

He was almost at the door when a light came on behind it. There was no window, but it was dark enough now to see the change in the tiny gap at the bottom of the door. He paused, almost panicking he was so surprised. He could hear a child's voice. Turn and run, or bluff it out? Too late – the door was opening. He decided quickly, raised a hand, as if he had been about to knock, then composed his features into a polite smile. The door swung open on Mary Swales, Katy in arms, Andrew at her side, standing on the floor.

She almost jumped two paces back.

'Jesus Christ!' she exclaimed. 'What the fuck are you doing? You almost killed me with shock.'

Marcus swallowed hard, barely able to believe it. He had found them. They were looking for them across the entire country, and he had found them. His heart began to race. What should he do? He moved back, down a step, so that his face was more or less on a level with hers. 'DC Roth, Mary,' he said. 'We've met before. Remember?'

'Of course I fucking remember.'

She didn't look dangerous. She wasn't with Gary. She was dressed in a thick black coat, wearing a muffler hat. Both Andrew and Katy had on winter coats. They looked like they were all about to go out for a walk. Happy families. What to do? Arrest her now? She might explode. Bluff it until he could get help?

'Can I come in?' he asked.

'We were just going out...' Something in her eyes was different from the last time he had seen her. She was breathing very heavily, rapidly, as if she were frightened, or panicking and trying to conceal it. Was that because he had surprised her? The woman who had killed Becky. He was face to face with her and knew what she had done. He was looking into her eyes.

'I won't be long...' he started. She looked desperate. Could she see that he knew? A voice whispered to him, deep within his head, *Be careful. Don't assume.*

'How did you find me here?' she demanded. She was holding Andrew by the hand. He was looking up at Marcus, eyes glazed, swaying slightly. There was something wrong with him.

'I need to ask you some questions,' Marcus said. He stepped up, then moved to go round her and into the building. She inched sideways, frowning at him, still looking like a startled animal. She put Katy on the floor next to Andrew.

He walked past Andrew, trying to take control, to radiate control from his body language. Andrew turned to watch him, but looked as if he couldn't see properly. He was squinting, his face layered with perspiration.

'Is there somewhere we can go?' Marcus asked. He tried to keep his voice calm, authoritative. Mary was starting to close the door to the street. He couldn't see any weapons on her. There was a table right behind her, with a lamp. That was the light that had come on. Surely he could handle her? Should he just arrest her now? He looked behind him, wanting to be sure Gary wasn't around. There was a door off to a room, slightly open. 'Do you know where Gary is?' he asked, then stepped towards the door, intending to push it further open, to have a quick look, to check. If Gary was right there it would be dangerous. If he was upstairs there would be more time to think. He placed his hand on the door and pushed. As it was opening he realized she was moving towards him, fast. He started to turn towards her, speaking again.

The blow hit him across the back of the head. He felt a massive jolt, then a blinding pain as he tumbled forward. He heard something break and immediately felt blood across his neck. His knees hit the floor and he collapsed sideways. He tried to twist to see her, but she hit him again at once, smashing something hard off the side of his face. He had time to think it must have been the lamp – a short, squat, decorative metal thing – then everything was black and spinning. He could hear the kids crying, frantic movement, Mary shouting unintelligibly. He tried to move his arms, struggled to sit, but it was as if she had pulled the plug on him. Nothing was connecting; nothing would move. He was totally incapacitated. He felt himself being sick where he was lying, then coughing. He wondered if he would choke to death, or if she would hit him again. Silly probationer error – underestimating her level of desperation. He tried to suck the air in deep breaths, to clear his head, but the pain threw a thick miasma of pulsating pressure across his sight. The world became muffled, then vanished completely.

44

'This is an emergency alarm,' Karen said, speaking slowly and clearly. She pointed it out to Simon Bradley. It was on the wall, next to the front doorway. It was a large red button. It *looked* like an emergency alarm, but she still wasn't sure he was taking it in. 'It rings directly in the police station,' she said. 'If you press it you won't hear anything, but we will hear you. We will come immediately. Do you understand?'

He nodded.

'OK. Well, I'll go now, then. Is there anything else you need?'

He shook his head. He was standing where he had stood since they had entered the flat, in the middle of the floor, head down. He looked disturbed, unsafe, dishevelled and drained. He had spent most of the afternoon in tears, coming to terms with the consequences of his decisions.

'You're no more alone now than you were this morning,' she said. 'Your mother didn't want you then and she doesn't now.' It sounded harsh – cruel, even – but she was trying to pick words that might penetrate the fog of fear he was living in. It didn't work. He remained motionless, expressionless, as if he were in shock. 'What you've done is the right thing,' she continued. 'You can't help Becky now, but what you've done might save her children. That's what Becky would have wanted.

She would have thanked you for it.' It was maybe the fifteenth time she had said these things.

She sighed. 'There's food in the cupboards,' she added. She had already showed him the delicious mix of ready meals. He had assured her with monosyllabic grunts that he was capable of using the microwave and feeding himself. The place was so small he hadn't had to move to see the cupboards. There was a counter dividing off one half of the room, making the end into a kitchenette. The food cupboards were beneath the counter. The bed was a sofa-bed at the opposite end of the room. The only other room was a tiny toilet and shower, coming off the kitchen.

She walked to the windows and checked the street outside. She could see nothing suspicious. She had been very wary of being followed on the way over and had taken several deviations to be sure of flushing out anyone following her. There had been no one. She was pretty certain of that. 'Best to keep the curtains drawn,' she said, turning back to him. He didn't reply. She walked to the door and opened it.

There was nothing more she could do. He was an adult, the doctors had said. He was not high risk, contrary to appearances. He was not a suicide threat. He could look after himself. All the same, she thought she would leave him only an hour or so, then call in to check. 'Will you be going out?' she asked again.

'No,' he said. 'Where would I go?'

'Best you stay in tonight,' she said. 'Stay in, eat, watch some TV, get some sleep. Tomorrow things will be clearer. We have an interview with witness protection at nine. I will take you to it.'

He looked up, fixing his eyes on hers only for a moment. But it was enough for her to see the hatred.

'You tricked me,' he said. 'You did this to me.'

She wondered what 'this' was exactly, in his mind. Being without a family who had hated him? Being in a police safe house? Being confused and frightened?

'I helped you,' she said, tired of repeating the line. He had accused her all the way over in the car, the same thing over and over again – 'You tricked me.' He was like a stuck record. She considered reminding him what had happened – that a young girl had been bludgeoned to death in a room next door to him while he had sat back and done nothing – but she'd had enough of him. She needed to get out.

'You didn't help me,' he said, briefly defiant.

'No. Maybe I didn't,' she said. 'But I'm the only person helping you now. Remember that.'

She shut the door behind her and stood in the small hallway for a moment, listening. She heard nothing. No objects breaking, no floods of tears, no screaming. He was probably still standing there, wondering what to do. She took the lift, let herself out and walked back to her car, parked on the same street.

On the way she phoned Mairead but got no reply, so she tried Pete Bains instead. Mairead had decided without any prompting to stay with Pete until Karen's work pattern settled into something regular, which meant until they had found and processed Mary and Gary Swales.

Karen was secretly relieved. Pete was on rests for the next five days, so would he around to watch out for her.

'It's Karen,' she said, when he answered. He said a polite hello. 'Is she still in?' she asked.

'You want to talk to her?'

'No. Just to know she's safe and OK.'

'She's fine. She says she might go out tonight.'

'Don't let her.'

She heard him groan. There was a half-hearted investigation into the 'accident' – that was what they were calling it at Milgarth, where a numpty DI called Prosser was doing his best to do nothing quickly – and so far they had managed to secure three video images of the car and occupant. Nobody had been able to identify the occupant, but he was a youth in his twenties. The car he had driven was stolen from the same multi-storey that was the scene of the incident, from two floors above where Karen's car had been. Prosser thought it was a silly joyriding incident and since Mairead's injury was nothing more than a bruise over her pelvis wasn't giving much time to finding the youth. Pete clearly agreed with Prosser. Karen would have liked to have disabused them both, but couldn't without starting a train of enquiries that would result in the exposure of her relationship with Surani.

'She's an adult, Karen,' Pete said. 'I have no control over her. If she wants to go out she will.'

'Try to persuade her.'

'Why?'

'Because this wasn't a joyriding incident.' She got into her car and pulled the door shut. The car was positioned near the safe house, in a row of parked cars. She had a good line of sight. It would do. 'I need her to be careful,' she said. 'At least until we have Swales in custody.'

'Maybe you should speak to her if you think that.'

'I already have.' She was the last person to be able to influence Mairead.

She listened to the silence while Pete thought it over.

'I'll try,' he said at last.

'Thanks, Pete.' She cut the line.

Was she the only person who thought Gary Swales was dangerous, despite everything they knew about him, despite his clear involvement in Rebecca's murder? She pushed the seat right back and leaned her head against the window. She thought about it, half an eye on the flat, and watched the seconds tick by on the car clock.

The afternoon's events had been frustrating. It had taken her the better part of an hour to persuade Alan White that Simon Bradley needed protection, but even then he had refused to prioritize it. Instead he had categorized the threat as 'real, but not immediate' – which meant witness protection would have forty-eight hours to assess and place Simon.

Meanwhile he had to get through a night without a home. Karen had been able to set up the placement in this safe house only because she had spent so long in the Child Protection and Domestic Violence Unit. The flat looked inconspicuous – taking up a single floor of a modern block comprising four similar flats, all owned by a housing trust. It was unlikely the other occupants even knew that the neighbouring flat was a domestic-violence refuge. The street was a normal, middle-class residential avenue at the north end of Allerton, on the edge of Bradford, with mature chestnut trees lining both pavements. That meant it was relatively dark because the tops of the street lights were lost in foliage, but there was a strong light at the common entry to the block and she could see clearly enough. There was a gentle curve to the road, allowing her a good, uninterrupted view for almost its entire length. She checked her watch. Nearly eight. Only a few minutes since she had dropped him off. Was she really going to stay here all night?

That was what she had told Alan White she would do. She had said it in a fit of temper, mainly to get him to think about the threat. It hadn't worked so well. He certainly hadn't seen the need for a uniformed presence. It was tempting to give in to the majority view and go home. Simon wasn't her personal responsibility, after all. She had brought him to this – he was right about that – but only because he had made sickening choices. The choice to ignore Becky's cries for help, for example. That didn't make him legally guilty of murder, but he was far from completely innocent, morally speaking. He had a deformity, was a little challenged, mentally, but he had known what he was doing. He had turned his back on Becky and let her die. Not in the car with his father, as he thought, but long before that, when his parents were systematically thrashing the life out of her and he knew what was going on. For her that was enough. So why not leave him to it?

But she couldn't. As she had repeatedly warned them all afternoon, Gary Swales was a killer. They knew that for certain because they had rock-solid intelligence about the killing he had been acquitted of. The victim – a courier named Ben Smalley who had screwed up a run because his need for substance had been stronger than his fear of his boss – had been shot in the head, execution style. He had been made to kneel on the floor of his cramped, filthy Holbeck flat, with a pillowcase pulled over his head; then someone had put a bullet into the back of his head. Clean, neat, professional. Those were, at any rate, the words most often used to describe such killings. But the victim had looked far from clean and neat the morning they took the pillowcase off his head. Karen knew. She had been one of the first detectives at the scene.

They hadn't even come close to finding out who had carried out the hit, and given that, the evidence against Swales had been predictably weak. But they had known for certain that Swales had paid the money and ordered it. Michael Surani had tried to convince her Swales was legitimate, but she knew better. He had legitimate fronts, had businesses to wash the proceeds white, but the better part of his income came from the same place it had always come from – the sale of heroin and marijuana. That alone made him dangerous. He was outside the normal structure of society. He couldn't simply call the police when he had a problem. But add to that the fact that he had killed and got away with it. That made him a different category of beast altogether. She knew because she had been there. Once you had killed someone – deliberately – you moved into a different moral sphere. It didn't matter whether you pulled the trigger or just handed over the money and the photo. She knew precisely how much the psychological and social boundaries shifted.

Would Swales send someone for Simon Bradley? That depended on many factors, not least of which was whether he could find out where Simon was. That should have been impossible, but Karen knew from bitter experience that police stations were leaky environments and money bought you everything. It was possible Swales was connected and liquid enough to get someone to check the computer systems for him. The flat was a refuge, but it was far from secure. It was no substitute for the full witness protection scheme. To ensure a rapid response to the panic alarm the details of the flat had to be entered on the Force computer systems. That made it vulnerable. And Swales was at least capable of thinking within those parameters – capable of countenancing the idea that a solution might be to kill someone. Most people were not.

It wouldn't do Swales much good to kill Simon, of course, because they still had the statement from Martin. But Swales wouldn't be aware of that. Martin was still in custody and would probably be charged. They could control the information about his status. But Simon's status was out in the open – Geoffrey Lane had seen to that. That was his purpose.

She moved in the seat, trying to get comfortable. Was she being crazy again? Was she blowing everything out of proportion? It was difficult to keep perspective when you were convinced a threat was so real, but she was pretty certain her hunches were sound. She was in a minority of one, it seemed, but that *was* nothing new. It wasn't a good reason to fall into line.

She watched a car drive slowly past, then checked her watch again. Time was dragging. She was impatient, but if he was going to come it wouldn't be now; it would be later, in the night. So now might be a good chance to rest. Could she risk sleeping a little? The day had been non-stop and her sleep had been disrupted for several nights now. She was tired enough to sleep.

She set the alarm on her mobile to wake her in two hours, just in case. She could get out then and go back to the flat. Check Simon was handling it OK, then consider the position again.

45

How long had he been down? He rolled onto his back and looked at the ceiling. It seemed very far away. The details of the architrave emerged, then a painting on the wall, lower down. His eyes tracked down to a door; then he picked up the cold night air on his face. He sat up. Too quickly. His head reeled, his eyes blurred. 'Shit,' he said, out loud. He heard the word clearly. It sounded normal, not slurred or fuzzy. There was a pain slicing through the back of his head, though. He reached up a hand and touched the source. Warmth, wetness. He brought his hand round and looked, needlessly. Blood. His own. And quite a lot of it. No need to panic. Scalp wounds bled profusely, as he had so carefully explained to Gary Swales. It meant nothing. He probed again, wincing. The wound was a lump like an egg with a pulsating hole in the middle. He looked around him and found the lamp, overturned beside him. Plenty of sharp protrusions in the design. He was lucky – assuming his skull wasn't cracked.

He stood up. His skull didn't feel cracked, but what did a cracked skull feel like? He could stand without falling, though it felt far from certain he could keep it up for long. Outside, through the open doorway, the night looked the same as when she had hit him. How long ago could it have been? If you were out too long it led to brain damage. *Fuck*. The realization of what it meant – him being there, alone, the floor soaked with his blood – sank in like a punch to his gut. He had to lean on the wall to take it. He'd screwed it up. He'd had them and lost them.

What could he do now? Time to call it in and ask for help. Mary Swales could be anywhere by now.

He took out his mobile and looked at the time. Just after eight. What time had he come in? He felt a switch trip in his head, then the immediate rush of adrenalin. *He had come in only minutes ago.* It felt like he had been out cold for an hour, but it was minutes, maybe not even a minute. That meant…

He stepped quickly out into the street and looked down the length of it. Christ! There they were. He could see them. She was at the end of the street, running, carrying them both.

He stepped out quickly, intending to run down the steps, two at a time, but something happened to his legs and he fell down them instead, only just stopping himself from going headfirst by hanging on to the railings. He bent over double and tried to get his breath. His head was spinning again, his breathing constricted. He tried to take a step but pitched over immediately. He started to be sick again, physically sick, there in the street. Shit. Shit. Shit. What could it be? A concussion? Too soon. Just the shock of it. Bile dribbled from his mouth. He had eaten nothing since breakfast. He pulled himself up and looked along the street again. They had reached the end, vanished.

He started to walk after them. It worked. He didn't tumble. He sped up, gaining confidence, and tried getting his mobile to work at the same time, but that was too much for his brain to handle. He put it in his pocket. He didn't even know the number for Lancashire Police. Call Karen? Call 999? Not an option. He would have to stop to do it. Better to chase them. They weren't that far ahead. He could do it. He could salvage this.

He started to run a little. How fast could she go carrying two kids? She was as incapacitated as he was, in a different way. He would catch her. He couldn't let her get away. The foul bitch. He had to get his hands on her. What had she done to the boy, so that he was sweating like that?

His legs started to get the rhythm. He concentrated on his breathing. The headache was a distraction. He tried to see it that way, but it was so savage he felt as if his face would split apart every time his feet hit the ground. He could feel the pulse of blood increasing. Irrelevant. Get to her. Stop her. Then worry about the little injuries.

He started to sprint. It was too much, though. His balance was precarious. He was going fast but he must have looked drunk, veering all over the pavement. He slowed for fear of falling again. He was coming to the end of the street. Could he remember where it led – from the map on the TomTom? To the Promenade, was it?

Suddenly he was there. He turned left and he could see it – the lights stabbing into his eyes. So many of them, So much it was like daylight, but more blinding. He squinted and stopped. There was a building like a tacky Disney castle, dripping with multi-coloured neon, a huge illuminated skull mounted high on its wall – some kind of pirate thing? Children milling all around it. 'Coral Island', it said. Blackpool Tower was right behind it, massive, too bright to stare at. He turned from them and started looking for her, shielding his eyes from the glare.

He could see the sea. He ran towards it and came suddenly into a wide open space. A long, broad road, streams of cars and buses, trams. There was noise all over now. Crowds of people to his right, a wide stretch of grass, kiosks, more lights, lights all over, burning his eyes. Where was the pier? He turned and found it, half a kilometre away, no more. Which pier was it? Blackpool had three, he had been told as a child. People were stopping now, staring at him. He came down some steps, or was it just the edge of the pavement? He was on a seafront boulevard, the air in his face freezing and fresh, the Tower to the right of him. Life was going on at a fast pace, as if nothing had happened. People queuing, eating, laughing, talking, running. Too much movement all at the same time. His vision felt narrowed, unreal. He scanned faces carelessly, not paying any attention to what they were saying, looking only for her. There was a crowd around him. He could hear himself saying he was a police officer, call for assistance, then... There she was! Moving along the very far pavement, alongside the railings, past the grass area, about a hundred feet away, hurrying, still carrying both of them. He could see her looking back, then running. She was moving towards the pier.

He sprinted across the road, hands high in the air to stop the cars. How many lanes? It seemed like a football pitch, thick with slow-moving cars and trams. But nothing hit him. He heard a few horns, a remote noise. He was focused only on where she was. He could hear the sea now, see it beyond the embankment. A drop of how much – twenty feet? Onto the beach with the donkeys. None there now. The water was right up against the stone banks. That meant high tide. He kept going, fixing his eyes on her, pushing it. He was gaining. She was staggering with the weight of them. She couldn't go on. He started to shout at her, yelling at her to stop. Heads turned, people stared. A crowd of Japanese tourists parted suddenly in front of him. He glimpsed the fear in their eyes; then he was past.

He stopped abruptly. She had disappeared. One minute there, the next gone. He checked the road. Had she crossed over? No. The pier? Still too far away. That only left one option. The embankment railing was split every five hundred paces with steps leading down to the sea. She must have turned down one. What the fuck was she doing?

He started to panic. He ran to the first gap in the railings and looked down. Two large flights of steps, converging on a blank space filled with heaving water. How deep was it? *Don't focus on it. Don't focus on the water.* There was nobody there. She must be at the next one. He pushed through people to get to it, staggering now, desperate. What was she capable of? He heard shouts of alarm, saw sudden movement up ahead, next to the nearest set of steps down. People were running towards the embankment wall. He took a breath and ran full speed, ignoring the dizziness, the panting, the disorientation. Only one thing mattered now. She was going to try to drown the boy. He had to get to her before she could push him in.

46

Karen didn't have time to fall asleep. Within minutes the door to the block opened and a figure emerged. From the height alone she would guess it was Simon, but he had the stoop, too. He paused right under the entrance light and brought his head up. He looked quickly up and down the street. It was him. Definitely. What was he doing? He started quickly in the other direction, away from her.

What were her options? Follow him on foot or by car. She started the engine. He was free to come and go. She couldn't stop him. But it was just possible that either Mary or Gary had contacted him – or he had called them. Was he that stupid? He had a mobile that had been seized in the original search of Lower Wyke, a fortnight ago. They had returned it to him today, though, along with the rest of his property. He was a witness now, no longer a suspect. She had told him not to answer the phone if they called him, but to ring her instead. He knew the risk, so why would he take chances? Almost the first thing he had said when they had read his statement back to him was, 'Gary will kill me for this.' He wouldn't talk to Gary, then. But maybe to Mary? She was his mother, after all. She cursed, thinking about it. She should have covered it more thoroughly. If she had thought about it earlier she might have been able to persuade Alan White to set up something with the mobile provider, to get a fix on Mary if she did call.

No need now, though. If Mary had called and Simon was now on his way to her then all Karen had to do was follow him. She watched him cross to the other side of the road, pulling a hooded top over his head and slouching, like a robber. It was possible, of course, that he was simply going to get something to eat. Or even...

475

Her thoughts froze. He had stopped by a car, was leaning over by the passenger door, speaking to someone inside. She pulled the binoculars from the dashboard and focused them on his head, her pulse picking up, her hands fumbling. There was someone in the car, but it was too dark to make out the detail. She tried to make sense of what was happening.

Had the car always been there, or had it arrived when she was in the flat? She should have paid closer attention. She saw Simon straighten up and look down the street. Could it be someone asking directions? Something as innocuous as that, a coincidence?

Her brain clicked into gear. She was being stupid. There was no coincidence here. Something was going on. She saw the passenger door open and Simon get in. She took a deep breath.

Now what should she do?

Check it out. Check it out quickly. She indicated and pulled out into the road. There were no other cars in sight. She drove slowly towards them, saw the rear lights come on, a puff of smoke from the exhaust. Then it moved, rocked a little on its suspension, as if someone heavy had shifted weight inside it. It was a small car, a blue Golf, with an old plate – maybe ten years old. She put her hand out to her mobile to call in the registration number, then paused as the car bounced on its shocks again. She was close enough to see movement inside now. Something *was* happening. She had a feeling in her gut, a wrenching, nauseating lurch of fear. Her brain interpreted the blur of shapes. What she could see was arms flailing, desperate movement, violence. She could hear shouting, too. Simon's voice, muffled but loud, screaming something. They were fighting, struggling.

She had already started to floor the accelerator when there was a sadden flash from within the car. The entire interior seemed to flare white and yellow, like the flash of a camera. Bright, then black, in an instant, She was so surprised it took her a second to register the sound – the dull, familiar crack that had accompanied the burst of light. Someone had fired a gun.

47

In the time it took to barge full speed through the first rank of onlookers and stand on the edge of the flight of steps, Marcus's brain registered a chaotic, ghastly tableau of fear. It snapped into his brain like an image caught in an explosion of artificial light: the steps down to the water crowded with shouting men; the larger crowd above on the promenade itself; women carrying balloons, candy-floss, ice cream; children looking confused, uncertain of the adult drama, some crying, others still smiling and looking at the Tower; more men running across the road, their voices strained and cracked with the adrenalin-pitches of danger, shouting to others to call the police, to call the coastguard, the emergency services. And below them all the sea, pulling away from the steps with an elemental force, dropping six feet in a split second with a terrible, powerful sucking roar, then the swell coming back, mounting like a tidal wave, rolling forward, lashing into the stone with a great slapping bass boom of sound that sent spray flying through the air, drenching them all.

Katy was on the bottom step, pinned against the back wall, cringing from it, a man with his arm over her, crouching beside her, her grand-mother screaming and lashing out at another man standing between Katy and herself, her fists landing on his face. Someone else – two people – were dragging her back, one shouting, *'She pushed him, I saw it,'* the words echoed and dis-torted by a woman with bleached-blonde hair screaming down from the promenade in a broad Liverpool accent, *I saw it. I saw it. She threw him into the water. She threw him in.'* Then the gasps and cries of distress, all faces turned outwards, as if they were at the cinema watching a horror film, riveted to the nylon line snaking away from the red-and-white circular float, tossed useless on the cap of a wave. The men were shouting, again and again – *'Swim! Swim for it!* – shouting at a tiny blur of arms and legs, lost in the immense black of the water. Andrew Farrar, thrashing for dear life, nowhere near the float they had cast out to him, already twenty feet away from the embank-ment wall and disappearing fast, the force of the tide washing him out to sea like a cork, a piece of wood, his head going under, coming up again, mouth spluttering, eyes wide with terror...

'Swim for it! Swim for it!'

But he didn't stand a chance.

Those were the words that ripped through

478

Marcus's brain. He didn't stand a chance.

The tide's going out. The current's too strong.

The men were shouting for help.

'It's too strong... Someone get help!'

But nobody was jumping in.

He kicked his shoes off on the top step, shouting that he was a police officer, that they were to hold her – pointing at Mary, face turned up to him, a grimace of hatred twisting her features – then tore his trousers off as he stumbled down the steps, almost falling. He heard shouts of warning, telling him to wait, it was too dangerous, the swell was too great. Another float arched off into the air from somewhere above him, landing with a splash some distance from Andrew.

Cold wind on his chest as his shirt came off. His head pounding with the injury, his eyes amazingly clear, though, his heart strong, his whole body inundated with adrenalin, so that it was like an electric buzz behind his eyeballs, thrilling through his veins. He was still ten steps from the bottom, clearing people from his path. There was a drop of fifteen feet into the black, heaving mass. He took a breath, timing it for when the water started to rush away from the edge.

Then dived.

He dived like he had at school, not thinking about it, just letting his body slip into the motions, as if it were natural. Between his feet leaving the cold stone and the initial stunning shock of the icy water smashing into his face, immersing him, swallowing him, his brain was racing with thoughts. His body was poised between the flood and the stone, but inside everything was slow, precise, deliberate. In a fraction of a second he had time to think about everything.

Memories of the last time, mostly. The metal gangplank twisting, the drop into the arctic water, the moving boat.

The last time didn't matter, though. He had to be rational. A child would die if he stood around waiting for the fear to pass, worrying about his own life. And there was no need. He told himself that again and again. He was a strong swimmer, a prize swimmer at university. He used to do one hundred lengths of the full Olympic pool three days a week, to relax. And what seas had he plunged into? The North Sea, the Barents Sea – for Christ's sake! – the Barents Sea, with chunks of ice like miniature icebergs all around him. The Baltic in winter, through a hole in the ice. These were all far more freezing and treacherous than this. Stormy waters too: the Mediterranean off Malaga in a storm when his pleasure boat had capsized, the English Channel, a mile out and back on a choppy day in just over half an hour, so that he felt bruised when he reached Deal sands again. He had handled it all because he was fit and strong and young and his heart could take it. He knew how to swim. He knew how to swim well. He even knew how to deal with cramp. But that wasn't going to happen. He could handle worse than this and he had. Forget the last time, forget the irrational fear of water. Water was his element, what he was born from, swimming around for nine months in his mother's womb...

But the panic ran deeper than thought. It scissored through him the moment he was submerged, urging him with every fibre of his body to pull to the surface, take in air, scream for help. He screwed his eyes shut and pulled against it, hauling himself into it and down. He felt the current plucking at him, trying to spin him. He dug in and pulled again. One stroke, two, three. All long and careful, all deep below the surface. All around him the tremendous rushing and roaring of the waves.

Then he rolled and opened his eyes.

There was light, but it was murky and green, full of sand and sediment – and sewage, most probably. He pulled up to the surface at an angle, his brain still working, still calculating. If he had got it right he should be right where Andrew had been.

A riot of noise assailed his ears as he broke through. He forced himself to hold his breath while he looked and assessed, then filled his lungs again, as calmly as he could. He told himself the panic was working *for* him, animating everything with a frenetic energy. There was so much adrenalin in his system he had to worry fleetingly whether that alone could provoke a shock response, everything too dilated, his heart unable to cope with the volume of blood needed to keep him going.

He had to tread water with all his might to push himself high enough above the surge to be able to scan his immediate vicinity. He could see the floats – the nearest an arm's length away – he could hear the shouts and directions from the shore, but he couldn't see Andrew anywhere.

'He's gone under. Right there.'

That's what they were screaming at him.

'Dive for him! He's gone under!'

He sucked another lungful and dived again, arms spread out. His fingers brushed something at once. He looked but could see nothing but disturbance and muck. The water was freezing his blood. He pushed forward and knocked into something. He was trying desperately to hold his position against the tug of the tide, the ceaseless in and out motion. He brought his other hand up, got his fingers into some fabric, then felt the body beneath it.

It was Andrew. It had to be.

He closed his fingers and dragged up and backwards, then got a whole arm round some part of him, maybe his legs. In seconds they were both at the surface. He could hear cheering from the shore, but what he had brought up was a dead weight. He had to get it back to land quickly.

He started to swim at once, kicking backwards, on his back, transferring the flaccid body onto his chest. He managed to get an arm beneath the neck, supporting the head, keeping it out of the water. He could see him clearly now. It was Andrew, eyes closed, mouth hanging open. No reactions. Not even any reflex twitches. He was a limp, sodden weight.

Marcus's head banged into a float and he seized it with his free hand and hauled them against it. It began to move at once, reeling him in. He strained his head back and could see three or four men, tugging at the rope. He would make it.

A twinge of relief sent an uncontrollable shudder through his limbs. For the first time he really noticed the cold, noticed how tight it was around his chest, how heavy in his muscles. There was no space to relax. If he relaxed even a little he would slip off the float and freeze to death. He gritted his teeth and kicked his legs harder, straining his body so high in the water that Andrew was almost out of it completely, wedged against his chest.

He looked back again. They were nearly there. He had done it. He had jumped in and survived, brought back the child. A crude, animal elation wanted to leap up in him, make him scream and cry with an instinctive joy. He felt the float bang against the stone, then sink with the water. The wave came over his head, pushing him under. He held his breath, his legs sinking now, but his arm still tight round Andrew. His feet kicked out and struck the stone of the embankment with a numb pain. He felt a slippery surface against his toes and knees and let go of the float at once, striking off towards the hands reaching out towards him from above. He could see everything through a confused smear of spray. One hand caught him by the fingers, another took his arm, below the elbow. Then they were dragging him up. Someone was shouting for him to let go of the boy, that they already had him. But he couldn't do that. He couldn't see what was happening clearly enough, couldn't trust them. He didn't want the next wave to take the child out once more, to have to do it all over again.

He got his chest onto the stone. He could hear cheering from the pavement above. He had Andrew out with him. He let go of him reluctantly and they took him away, further towards the

483

wall. Other hands had him round his chest. He thought there must be ten men crowded on the level platform and the steps back up. They were shouting with the effort of lifting him. He kicked at the water again and with a gasp he was landed, a dripping, shivering mass of tired muscle.

He crawled away from the edge immediately, still being helped. People were patting him on the back, congratulating him. Andrew was already out of sight, up the steps onto the promenade. There was relief in the voices now, but still an edge of fear. He could see blue flashing emergency lights up there. He let his head sink a little, let the knowledge of what he had done penetrate.

There was nothing to cheer about. He had jumped in the water and brought out a body.

He asked unclearly if there was an ambulance. Someone was close to his ear, listening, telling him there was, that the boy was alive, that they were with him now. A woman's voice. He wondered if they had kept hold of Mary, taken Katy from her. He had to check, but not at once. Get his breath first.

Andrew hadn't moved in all the time he had held him. Not one breath. Yet it was possible they would revive him, he thought. If they were good they would get him back. They had done it to him, three years ago.

A man in a black and yellow uniform wrapped a blanket round him and held something to his mouth, telling him to drink. Someone else was asking him about the blood. He had forgotten about his head.

He was still only feet from the water. Every

second wave rocketed up the stonework and soaked him again. He wanted to laugh, or cry. He didn't know which.

48

She had automatically slipped her foot from the accelerator to the brake. She was so shocked she allowed the car to stop, in the middle of the street. Then it sank in – it wouldn't have been Simon Bradley who was firing a gun inside the car, and he wasn't getting out – so the fight was over.

She hit the horn. It was her second impulse. She didn't know what else to do. Her first had been to floor the gas pedal and ram the car – stop it dead. But someone in there was armed, and she was not. That was a lesson she had learned the hard way. Don't take on armed men unless you have a weapon. So she let the car sit there, in full view and leaned on the horn instead. She leaned on the horn with her left hand and keyed 999 on the mobile with her right.

As the operator came on the line the driver's door of the Golf opened and she saw a face, peering back through the gap, looking towards her. The light was too poor to make out details clearly, but she could see the shape of the head filling the space. It *could* have been the youth who had driven the car into Mairead. It was possible. Then the door banged shut. A second later – as she was talking to the control room, giving them the plate, beginning to explain who she was – the Golf pulled out of the line of parked cars.

It accelerated very quickly. She followed slowly at first, still talking on the mobile, still telling them what was going on, requesting urgent assistance and an armed response team. As it reached the end of the road she had to drop the phone to concentrate. She didn't want a chase. She didn't want the driver to feel any threat at all. But she didn't want to lose sight of it, either. Simon Bradley was in there with a gunshot wound. That was the only reasonable assumption to make, because the car was moving and the driver was unharmed. Simon was a key witness. If she didn't get to him quickly he was going to be a dead witness.

She floored the pedal and closed the distance. The Golf was at the end of the road, turning towards Stony Lane. The route would take it down to the Sandy Lane crossroads. From there it could go straight on to Cottingley and Bingley, uphill to Bradford, via Toller Lane, or back towards Haworth and the moors, depending what it did at the crossroads. There were traffic lights at the crossroads. She hoped they would be on green.

She started to shout, assuming the operator was still listening at the other end of the line. She shouted out where she was, where she thought the car was going. She prayed it wasn't going to turn towards Toller Lane. That would mean an increased likelihood of speedy assistance – maybe even the armed response team – but also the complication of being forced to stop the Golf in a built-up residential area. She didn't want to be in a shoot-out in Bradford town centre, especially not with a jumpy little kid. If the driver was the youth who had gone for Mairead then he hadn't looked old enough to control himself. On the other hand, if the Golf headed out west, into the countryside she was unlikely to get help until it neared the next big town. For now all she could do was follow it. Whatever Simon's condition, she wasn't going to attempt to tackle someone with a gun on her own.

The car skidded onto Stony Lane without slowing, then took off with a cloud of black smoke belching from the exhaust, headed for the crossroads. She slowed at the junction and had time to pick up the phone. 'You still there?' she demanded. She heard the woman start to say something, then put the phone on the seat next to her and took the corner with both hands. As the road straightened she could see that already the Golf was approaching the next bend. Past that it would be out of sight. 'I'm going to start a commentary,' she yelled. 'Make sure its recorded.' It was standard practice in a marked car, using the radio, preferably with the passenger giving the blow-by-blow account. 'He's taking the bend in Stony Lane,' she said. 'He must be doing well over a hundred. He's out of sight already, dropping down to Sandy Lane.'

She slipped down a gear and pressed the accelerator hard. She was driving a year-old Volvo, her own car. A diesel model, it shared with all Volvos the solid safety features she had chosen it for, but 'solid' came at a price. The car was heavy and burning a low-octane fuel: it wasn't cut out for chases. The Golf was old, maybe even clapped-out, but it was light and fast by comparison.

She came through the bend and just caught sight of its rear lights, hurtling round the corner just before the crossroads. 'Wait before detailing a response,' she shouted. 'Don't task anyone until he's gone through Sandy Lane and we know where he's heading. But get something on...' She broke off, concentrating, both hands on the wheel as she slung the car round the corner. She had closed the distance by reaching a speed of 120 miles per hour on the straight stretch. 'Get some-one on stand-by,' she finished as the junction loomed in front of her, bright with a concen-tration of street lighting. But the Golf was already at the traffic lights. It was braking hard, skidding slightly. The lights were red. She shouted this out and began to brake herself. The Golf swung straight into the junction, passing inches in front of a bus. The bus swerved and braked sharply. The Golf pulled right, then turned onto Haworth Road. 'He's going for Haworth Road,' she yelled. The bus started to move again and she held her hand on the horn. She saw the driver notice her. 'Christ! she hissed. 'Get out of the fucking way!' The anti-lock kicked in, bringing her to a juddering stop inches from the front of the bus. She wrenched the gear stick into reverse, backed up, spun, then knocked it into first and listened to the engine screaming as she went round the bus.

The road ahead of her led sharply uphill towards the water works at the crest of Daisy Hill. It was completely empty. 'He's heading up to Daisy Hill on Haworth Road,' she called out.

She was assuming it was a man, but it might just as easily have been Mary Swales. Was Mary that stupid? Was she capable of using a gun on her own son? The Volvo seemed painfully slow on the hill. Finally it was straining so much she had to slip it into second. She rounded the turn at the crest and saw the long, well-lit stretch of Haworth Road opening out ahead of her. He was still there, not as far ahead as she had guessed – just passing the Stony Ridge Avenue turn-off. Other cars were travelling in both directions.

She kept the Volvo in second until the rev counter was in the red, then shifted to third until the speedo showed nearly seventy. As she switched into fourth she saw his lights swerve around a single vehicle travelling ahead of him. The manoeuvre was so sudden a car in the opposite carriageway had to execute an emergency stop to avoid hitting him. She forgot the commentary. 'Toller Lane,' she shouted. 'Try to get something out at Toller Lane.' It ought to be possible, she thought. Where he was headed was only minutes from Lawcroft House Police Station.

She was going downhill now, the Volvo's weight an advantage. She was gaining on him rapidly. He came into the wider part of the road, shops on the left. There was a wide central reservation here, created by cross-hatching down the middle of the road. It was a clear run downhill all the way to the next lights, about two miles away. She could catch him.

But there was no need to pressurize him, she realized. From where she was she could see the traffic lights at the Toller Lane junction. She was already doing over a hundred. She took her foot off the pedal. He was coming up to a line of slower-moving cars, two or three of them. She indicated and went carefully wide – into the opposite lane – to get round the car he had already passed. She began to relax a little. No need to drive like a lunatic. He wasn't going to be able to lose her now.

As she came back over the cross-hatching she saw him shoot out at the last moment, when he was almost into the rear end of the first of the slower-moving cars. He slewed a little, then straightened out in the opposite carriageway. She saw the car approaching flash him and the bonnet dip as it braked to avoid a head-on. That should have been on the commentary. She opened her mouth to say it. At the same moment she saw powerful headlights in a street to the left – a truck pulling into the main road. She thought it was going to turn left, towards Toller Lane. That would put it in front of the Golf, but only just. The Golf would be able to turn round it. She caught her breath as she saw the truck instead drive into the opposite lane, intending to come back up the hill, towards her. She started braking immediately. Not because there was any danger she would hit it – there were at least two other cars and the Golf in between – but because she knew at once what was going to happen.

She saw the Golf wobble, unsure, then a cloud of smoke from the back tyres, a squeal of burning rubber. He was going too fast to brake so hard, but had no choice. Everything must have locked. She saw the truck jerk to a stop as the driver realized what was happening. It stalled just short of the central reservation and the Golf tried to get round it. Not a chance.

The collision was massive. A deafening clash of metal on metal, an explosion of shattered glass. The Golf must have been travelling at over seventy miles per hour as the driver's side of the boot struck the front nearside of the truck. The Golf flicked sideways like a toy, the tail end flying into the air. The entire car lifted off the road, spinning past the front of the truck. She saw the cars on the opposite side of the road swerving in all directions to avoid it. It landed at least twenty feet further down the road with a hideous shrieking noise, sparks flying off the concrete as it slid along on its roof, then turned and rolled again. It came to a sudden halt upside-down on the pavement, rammed into a low garden wall.

'He's had it,' she shouted into the phone. 'He's hit a truck and gone over. Repeat. He's hit a truck on Haworth Road and gone over.'

She straightened her own car and squeezed the brake, gently slowing as she came up to the two cars in front of the truck. The phone had fallen into the passenger seat well. She stooped and picked it up. 'You hear that?' she asked.

'Collision on Haworth Road. Affirmative.'

'Major RTA,' she said. Her voice was high-pitched with excitement. Ahead of her the other cars had stopped and drivers were getting out already. 'We'll need everything, and quick.'

She pulled the car round them, winding her window down. 'Keep back! Police!' she yelled at them. They were starting to walk towards the truck. 'This is an armed-response situation! Keep back for your own safety!' She waved frantically at them through the window, cut the engine and jumped out.

The cab of the truck was caved in over the front wheel, the windscreen shattered, but the wheel had taken the brunt of it. It was driven into the engine space, deflated. There was glass, water and oil all over the road surface. She shouted again at the men. *'I am police. Remain in your cars! There may be a weapon!'* She could see the truck driver up in the cab. He was moving, trying to get the passenger door open. She ran past him. If he was moving he could wait.

On the other side of the road she could see people getting out of cars also, past the wreck of the Golf. She screamed at them, yelling the same message over and over. It seemed unlikely anyone was going to start shooting civilians, but she couldn't take a chance. She ran to the Golf with her arms in the air. There was someone coming out of the nearest house as well. But they were pausing, uncertain what to do. She hoped they were getting the idea.

The Golf was lying mangled in a pool of glistening water and oil, fragments of broken glass all over the place. There was a low hissing noise coming from the engine, but apart from that the silence was unreal, startling. She squatted down in the road about ten feet from it, trying to see in through the crushed windows. The car was on its roof with the rear end crushed flat to the level of the body. The front end still had its door frames intact. The doors themselves were lying in the middle of the road.

To the far side she could see someone sprawled with their head and chest on the pavement, legs still trapped in the passenger space. That would be Simon Bradley. He was stock-still, twisted, blood pooling rapidly around his head, eyes wide open. She knew he was dead without going anywhere near him.

She couldn't see the driver. There was a streetlight nearby, but the driver's side was in its shadow.

She crept forward in a crouch, noticing again the silence. No one was screaming, no one was shouting, there were no horns blaring. Just the faint hiss from the engine. When she got within reach of the driver's side she shouted out a warning again, just to be sure, then looked down the road. A queue of cars had stopped and the doors were all open, people walking closer. But no one was coming past the first car.

She flattened herself against the road and looked in. The driver was still inside, head covered with something – a balaclava? He was upside-down, crushed double, the steering wheel and part of the engine block driven into his chest. The head was twisted sharply, resting against the roof. But she didn't have the same certainty about his condition. What was it about the dead that communicated their lifelessness so clearly? Whatever it was, Simon's body had it and this one didn't.

She backed off a bit, then smelled the air. There was an odour of petrol. She inched forward and spoke into the dark space: 'Can you hear me, sir?' No response. 'I am a police officer. I am going to come closer and examine you. Please don't try to move. You may be seriously hurt.' That was the understatement of the year.

She reached a hand in and felt cautiously around the back of the neck. She was frightened the whole body would drop down, trapping her hand. The driver was compressed into a space no bigger than the average large suitcase, but most of his weight was still above his head, resting on it. There was a balaclava over the face. She couldn't find a pulse because of it. She held it gently at one side and tried to ease it off. It wouldn't come, so she rolled it the other way, from the chin upwards, folding it roughly around the top of the head. She watched the features as they emerged, then let out a long, stunned breath. She was looking at Gary Swales.

Behind her she could hear sirens in the distance. She got to her knees and looked around. One of the men was relaying her instructions to stay back, holding his arms wide to stop people getting too close. There was a crowd now, but they wouldn't be able to see too much from where they were. The street lighting was good, but not that good. She looked the other way. The truck driver was out of his cab, seated on the pavement, two men bending over him, another crouched at his side.

She went down onto her belly again and dragged herself over the broken glass until her head was almost inside the driver's space. As far as she could determine, there was no one else in the car. She reached a hand in and found Swales's neck. His eyes were closed, his features still, the head resting on one side of the face, at a bad angle. The nose had come into contact with something and was broken and flattened, covered in blood. But there was a pulse at his neck – weak and slow, but there all the same. She held her fingers over the open mouth. He wouldn't be getting any air through his nose. She felt the breath on her skin, very faint. He was alive.

She pushed back, stood up and walked on trembling legs to look at Simon Bradley. He was certainly dead. She bent down and checked, though. No pulse, no signs of life. She pulled his T-shirt up and found a messy exit wound in the lower back. He was face down and she didn't want to turn him over to see where the entry point was. But she guessed in the stomach some-where, which meant he was possibly alive before the crash. Probably it meant Swales had not intended to kill him. He was family, after all. Deformed, unloved and shunned, but still blood. If Swales had wanted him dead he would have put a second in the head, or even the first. It was the only sure way. In fact, not even head wounds were sure these days, but Swales probably didn't know that. Something had clearly gone wrong. Simon had panicked when he saw the gun, tried to fight him? It was all guesswork. It always would be now. Even if Swales lived, he wasn't going to give them the truth.

She went back to him. The sirens were getting closer. She lay down again and looked around. The men by the truck driver were watching her. 'Stay over there,' she called out. 'There's petrol all over. The driver is injured. I'm going to try to help him.' She pushed her hand in, then her head. She managed to get so close to him she could smell him. It was absurd, but he was wearing some kind of aftershave or fragrance. She could hear his breathing now. Laboured and faltering. She had no torch so couldn't see too well, but it was clear there was nothing she could do. They would need cutting gear to get him out. She was sure he would have severe internal injuries from the position of the steering wheel. It must have crushed his rib cage. The likelihood was that he would die before they could get him out.

But that wasn't certain. She closed her eyes and thought about it. The paramedics were good. The Fire Service also. There was a chance they would save him. She heard him groan and opened her eyes. Blood was coming out of his mouth now – bright, frothy blood. He began to cough. Short, constricted splutters. Some of his blood spattered her face.

If they got him out and he wasn't reduced to a vegetable then he would go down for the murder of Simon. Surely that was certain?

She thought about that, too. He could claim some kind of self-defence. He could say he had the gun to frighten Simon, Simon tried to get it off him and it went off accidentally. He panicked when he heard her sounding the horn and drove off. There were no witnesses. It was a *possible* defence. Stranger things had happened.

She reached over and placed both hands under his jaw, pulling the mouth shut. There was no reaction, but after about ten seconds the body started to convulse, jumping and jerking in the cramped space, pushing against itself and the car.

She twisted her head and saw that the men were still watching her. But her body was in the way. They wouldn't be able to see where her hands were. She pulled back, tightening her hold, then watched Swales's face in the half-light.

She realized she didn't actually know him at all. She had spent so long worrying about him, about what he might do to Mairead or to herself, about trying to find enough evidence to get him convicted of a murder he had ordered, that she had imagined to herself that he was as familiar as people she worked with. He had been in her thoughts every day for the better part of a year. She had interviewed him, as well. But that had given nothing away. In reality it was the same with every target she went for, every arrest, every criminal. She didn't know them at all. She couldn't get inside their heads, see what made them tick, what made them do these things. They were like objects to her. If you spoke to them they only lied to you, so there was never a chance of getting under their skin. They were closed off from her. Would that end if you lived with them? If you found out how they liked their eggs in the morning, or what paper they read, if any? She tried to imagine Swales getting up alone in his huge house. What did he do? Did he stand in front of his wardrobe for minutes deciding what clothes to wear, or did he just grab the first thing to hand? Did he shit regularly? Clean his teeth twice a day? How did he like his coffee? She tried hard to see him, a normal man, sitting down at a breakfast table and eating some cereal. If he heard on the radio that there had been a flood in

Bangladesh did he care about it? Or soldiers dying in Iraq? He must have some thoughts, just like everyone else. But she didn't know what they were. He was like a caricature for her, a cardboard cut-out. All she could see him doing was dealing drugs, frightening people, killing them.

The convulsions stopped. She held on, though, to be sure. She counted to sixty, slowly, closing her eyes, concentrating. It was quite hard to keep her hands in place, to keep up the necessary pressure in such an awkward space. The muscles in her forearms were shaking.

Behind her the sirens were very close now. They were so loud she couldn't hear anything else. As she finished counting she could see, out of the corner of her eye, people running towards her across the glass-spangled road. The fifth cavalry.

She took her hands away. His mouth fell open, slack-jawed. The eyes were still closed. She pressed her fingers to his neck again. There was no pulse.

Four Days Later

49

It was 9.25 am, by the time Ricky Spencer and Karen could agree on how to present it to the lawyer. That meant they were half an hour late for her. She had been waiting in Spencer's office since 8.55 a.m. They had both got in at six-thirty that morning, precisely so that they had plenty of time to go through it. They got coffees from the machine and spread out the paperwork on the large desks in the main conference room, while the place was still a dead zone. The only noise was from a cleaner with a hoover doing the corridor, but Spencer sent her to the floor below. Then they sat down and tried desperately to fit together a case against Mary Bradley that would be acceptable to a legal mind.

Alan White was there for five minutes, just after eight-thirty, but he wasn't interested in the detail. 'It doesn't work by evidence,' he said. 'Forget all that legal shite. All women are the same. You need to go in there and make her feel like she's gorgeous.' He winked at Karen, who looked away. 'You can do it, Ricky,' White said. 'I know Andrea Rees. She's a single woman in need of a man. You could make her day.'

'I'm married,' Spencer said, face straight.

White shrugged. 'So what? So am I.'

Marcus was standing in the corridor as they came out.

'Morning, Clark,' Spencer said, his face showing no trace of humour. Marcus looked irritated. The jokes had started the moment they had found out the chief was after him, keen to give him some kind of commendation – 'for swimming off a beach where thousands swim every summer', as Spencer had put it. Karen hadn't joined in. Marcus had told her months ago about nearly drowning, before joining the police. Yet he had saved a sick child from that horror. He had dived into a treacherous and exceptionally high tide in darkness, despite a profound fear of water, despite a head injury, despite freezing conditions. And he had done what an entire Force on alert had failed to do – he had arrested Mary Swales. Marcus was a hero. Full stop. She had nothing but admiration for him.

'I'll catch you up, Ricky,' she said. 'I don't want to cramp your style.'

Spencer scowled at her and walked on. She waited until he had gone into his office and closed the door.

'You doing OK?' she asked Marcus. He still had a bandage wrapped round the top of his head.

'Fine,' he muttered. He looked away from her, colouring. He was finding it hard to know how to deal with her, she thought. He didn't know whether he needed to bear a grudge or not. Everything had worked out so well. The bad guys were either dead or behind bars. That's how he would see it, she guessed. In certain respects his mind was still relatively simplistic.

'Just ignore Ricky,' she said. 'He's jealous. He knows how proud I am of you.' She put her hand to the side of his face and stroked it momentarily. She imagined it was something his mother would do, an affectionate gesture, but he flicked his head away and looked anxiously up and down the corridor. 'Christ, Karen...' he said, but he didn't go on.

'There's no one here,' she said. She was looking at him, waiting for him to meet her eyes, but he wouldn't.

'That doesn't matter,' he said. 'I'd rather you were more careful.'

'I'm very careful,' she said. 'You want me to pretend I don't know you?'

He looked uncomfortable. 'I just want to work with you,' he said. 'Without complications.'

She smiled. 'No problem. Were you waiting to speak to me?'

He shifted stance and looked uncomfortable. 'I don't mean...' He paused. He was looking at the floor. 'I don't mean to say that...'

'Were you wanting to speak to me?' she asked again.

He sighed. 'Yes. Just to ask how Mairead is.' Finally he looked up at her.

'Mairead's fine,' she said. 'Nothing wrong with her. A bruise. You should give her a ring before she goes north again. Meet up. She's more your age than I am.' She stepped round him and went into Spencer's office without looking back. But she could feel his puzzled stare all the way in. It wasn't even true, after all.

The same lawyer as before – Andrea Rees. If she was put out by having been made to wait she didn't look it. When Karen got in she was laughing at some joke Spencer had made. Spencer was at her side of the desk, leaning over her, ostensibly pointing something out in the local newspaper. Maybe he was taking Alan White seriously. He was red-faced when he looked up at Karen. They both were.

Introductions and pleasantries over, they settled in and took their time with it, Spencer behind the desk, Karen on a chair next to the lawyer. They presented the whole case carefully, all the evidence they wanted her to know about, all the information. If material didn't help – and there was plenty of that – they kept it back. If Rees asked to see statements or exhibits they gave them to her and waited while she read them. Of course, if she wasn't aware of the existence of something, she couldn't ask for it.

It went well, Karen thought – exactly to plan. It seemed as if Rees was with them the whole way. At they end they sat back and waited for her verdict. They had until midday to make a decision as to whether to charge Mary Swales with the murder of Rebecca Farrar. Once the custody clock ran out they could get longer by taking it in front of a magistrate – as they already had for Martin – but there wouldn't be much point in that if the lawyer was against them. The case wasn't going to get stronger than it already was. Or weaker.

'So this boy who ran into your daughter...' Rees started.

'Peter Moore' Karen said. 'John Bradley's nephew. He's eighteen years old, but has a wealth of convictions for petty stuff, including TWOC.' Taking a motor vehicle without consent. They had discovered Moore's identity while Mary was still being moved from Blackpool to West Yorkshire. DI Prosser's men had finally produced still images from the CCTV in the multi-storey and passed them round. A PC in Wakefield had recognized the face, who turned out to be John Bradley's sister's youngest son.

'And that makes you think Mary might have asked him to hurt your daughter?' Rees asked.

'It's possible,' Spencer answered for her. 'We're still looking at that angle. The kid has refused to say anything in interview.'

Gary Swales had asked Moore to frighten her, not Mary. It was only a hunch Karen had, but it felt right. Michael Surani had told her Swales was in trouble, with no cash. So it worked that he would get a remote relative to do something stupid like that for free. Especially a relative from John Bradley's side of the family. Mary was vicious, but it wouldn't have occurred to her to ask a nephew to try to frighten a police officer. She would have gone to her brother instead.

'I think it's likely she set him up to do it,' Karen said, lying. '*Someone* told him to do it. And it won't have been Gary. He didn't have that kind of relationship with the kid.' He had *some* kind of relationship with him because they had already established a series of mobile-phone calls between Gary Swales and Moore. But the point was to milk the connection for all it was worth against Mary. They didn't need to establish a case against Gary. It was accepted all round that he

505

had made contact with Simon by mobile phone on the day he died (they could prove that), had persuaded his nephew to meet him and then shot and killed him with the weapon recovered from the crashed car. He had then died at the scene of the accident, choked on his own blood, while Karen desperately tried to keep his airways clear. The chief was thinking of commending her for that. Mary had immediately decided that Karen had killed her brother, of course, but no one was listening to Mary.

'And Mary also?' the lawyer asked. 'She has said nothing through...' She looked at the paperwork. 'How many interviews is it?'

'We've interviewed her six times so far,' Spencer said. 'We've put everything to her. She won't say a thing. Not about Becky.'

'She answered questions about Andrew only?'

'That's right. And you've already seen those answers.'

Mary had insisted that Andrew had fallen into the sea, terrified and off-balance because a 'strange man' was chasing them, trying to separate the children from their grandmother. Five witnesses saw her push Andrew, however, so that was that.

'There's enough for the attempted murder of Andrew,' Rees said. 'No doubt about that.'

Spencer smiled. 'Great stuff,' he said. 'That takes the pressure off. At least we know she's not going anywhere.'

'And we get an inference from her silence apropos of Rebecca, of course,' the lawyer said, moving straight on. An inference of guilt, she meant. The fact that Mary refused to account for so much could be mentioned to the jury, by the prosecution barrister, if they ever got the case that far.

'But our problem is not getting it that far, I fear,' the lawyer added, voicing the precise issue. 'I think a judge might look at it and decide there's insufficient evidence to let it go before a jury. Basically, the only evidence against Mary is the account given by Andrew, a six-year-old. Am I right?'

Spencer started to shake his head, but Karen chipped in before he could answer. 'That's more or less it,' she said. 'Andrew says she killed his mother. He says he saw it.' Andrew had been hospitalized and out of bounds until yesterday. After that he had gone into care with Katy and they had managed to get him on video that morning. He had seemed dazed to Karen, not able to comprehend what was happening, or what had happened to him. But he had given a clear enough account of his mother's last hours.

What had happened to him, the doctors had decided, was that someone – presumably Mary – had given him an overdose of anti-depressants at some point during the last week. They didn't know why, and Mary was denying it point blank. Karen suspected pushing him into the sea was the second desperate attempt to kill him, the first being a botched attempt to stage an accidental drug overdose. But Andrew was recovering well, physically. How he and Katy did in the long term depended upon how long they had to stay in care. The prognosis there was uncertain. Becky's mother had come forward and offered to take the children, but there were problems with that, clearly detailed in Becky's diary. Marcus had spoken to the mother a few times and was of the opinion she had genuinely changed. She had screwed up her own child, but the grandchildren offered redemption. She would love them, he thought. Karen was less sure. But it wasn't their call now. Social Services would make that decision.

'Well, Andrew doesn't quite say he saw them kill her, does he?' Rees pulled a supercilious face, halfway between a grimace and a smile. 'What he says is...' She leafed through the pile of interview transcripts in front of her, looking for it.

'He says he saw his dad and Mary standing over his mother,' Spencer said. 'Mary was holding a stick. His mother had blood on her face and was very still.'

'Exactly. It's hardly evidence that she killed Rebecca.'

'We just need it to be enough to charge her,' Spencer said. 'Then we rely on–'

'And he's only six,' Rees said, still worrying about it. 'I'm not sure the judge will let his evidence in. Six-year-olds are notoriously unreliable witnesses.'

'It's not going to be the main evidence,' Spencer protested. 'The deal with Martin and John is definite.'

'The deal?' She looked worried about that.

'There's no deal, as such,' Karen said quickly. 'DI Spencer means that colloquially.' These days a kind of plea-bargaining deal was sometimes permitted, but it wasn't for the police to arrange it. It happened in court. Which would be a little late for their purposes. 'The lawyers for both John and Martin have approached us,' she clarified. 'They have said they would give prosecution statements against Mary if they are permitted to plead guilty to manslaughter only.'

'Yes,' Rees said. 'You told me that already. But we can't possibly do that for John, can we?' She looked up and stared at them. 'John has admitted killing her.'

It was like an after-dinner conversation for her, Karen realized. An interesting puzzle and a kind of entertainment, a glimpse into a world of filth and rot. But it didn't touch her personally. It was unlikely she would ever have to meet or speak to any of the victims.

'Accidentally,' Spencer said. 'John has admitted accidentally killing Becky.'

'But the diary says he took as great a part as his wife,' Rees said. Robert Smith QC himself had decided the diary was evidentially useful, so Rees couldn't argue with that. Karen wondered if she went to dinner parties at Smith's house, where they laughed about the trivial details of cases like this. Probably not. She was a state employee. He was in a different league. But they were both moving in a different world from the one she inhabited. Or the one Becky had slipped into.

'I agree,' Karen said. 'John should be charged with murder. But Martin is in a slightly different position. I think we should charge him with manslaughter from the outset. We could get a quick plea and use him against his mother. Then we would be able to charge her with Becky's murder also.'

Rees nodded, sagely. 'Yes, that sounds right,' she said.

Karen was as surprised as Spencer. They glanced at each other, uncertain, waiting for the inevitable proviso. But there wasn't one. Rees just looked up at them and smiled.

'Good,' Karen said. 'It's what the bitch deserves.'

This Large Print Book for the partially sighted, who cannot read normal print, is published under the auspices of

THE ULVERSCROFT FOUNDATION